Lake Chapala Serenade II:
Max and Carlotta
Go to Mexico

John Hoopes

Published by Bellamagic Books
www.bellamagicbooks.com

Copyright 2011
All rights reserved under International and
Pan-American Copyright Conventions.
Published in the United States by Bellamagic Books,
Sacramento, California

Distributed by Amazon.com

ISBN-13: 978-1463612108

*This book is for Elena
and for Lupe and the
boys of the barrio.*

CONTENTS

PROLOGUE   11

PART ONE

1   CARLOTTA AND THE BOYS   15
2   BELLACASA IS BORN   27
3   LUPE, MAESTRO DE LA OBRA   37
4   LUPE'S WELCOME HOME PARTY   43
5   MAX AND EL DIABLO   57
6   MAX AND CARLOTTA SHARE PROFIT   67
7   MAX LETS HIM GO   79
8   LUPE'S RESCUE   83
9   LUPE'S BARRIO VIGILANTES   89
10 TACHO CALLS ON ABUELO   97

PART TWO

11 CONSTANCE FINDS A STUDENT   105
12 LA MADRE ENFLAMED   115
13 CARLOTTA AND THE SPARROWS   125
14 MAX AND CARLOTTA GO TO WAR   133
15 LUPE PRAYS TO THE VIRGIN   143
16 LUPE AND COMPANIA SURROUNDED   157
17 LUPE'S MIDNIGHT VISIT   167

PART THREE

18 LA MADRE VISITS MUNICIPIO   175
19 CONSTANCE'S NEW ROOM   187
20 BELLACASA & THE SPITZENBURGENS   199
21 CARLOTTA'S SUNDAY DRIVE   211
22 CARLOTTA IN PURIFICACION   227
23 CARLOTTA'S ESCAPE   245
24 LUPE AND THE WARRIOR'S BOAT   257
25 MAX GOES DOWN   291
26 CARLOTTA'S BEAUTIFUL BOAT   305

PROLOGUE

One September night in the middle years of his life he awoke suddenly, frightened by a dream. On a vast, dark sea he'd drifted, naked and alone on a flimsy raft, beneath an immense canopy of stars he'd never seen. Not a sound he'd ever heard; nor could there be any shore to this desolate ocean.

Awakened in a cold sweat, he lay in bed beside her, staring into the bedroom's warmer darkness, waiting for the stark, sinister images to fade away. But they did not; and soon he saw that it had been not a dream, but his own weary life come to plead with him.

Before the Sun rose, he conceived that his only escape must be a blind leap into the void. Within a week he sold the business and took the money and flew away, his purpose hidden, to a fishing village in Jalisco, Mexico, on the shores of Lake Chapala. He bought a vacant lot in a residential neighborhood; simultaneously he met an honest maestro from the village, who built houses. Ajijic was faraway and picturesque; he might even write his book there, about Maximilian and Carlotta.

He returned home a week later to Mill Valley, California, to Carol's cottage in Blithedale Canyon. He told her everything he'd done in Mexico. She was dismayed and depressed.

Days before he'd returned from Mexico, he had prepared his apologies and persuasions, but as he stood before Carol, who was six feet, and taller than him by an inch and a half, she was formidable; and even moreso because she also had an indisputable grievance.

She shook her long auburn hair and would not give him anything. "This is hard, that you didn't include me in this. It's just shows me that *your* life can suddenly go a new direction, and I'm left standing here. You know I can't accept that."

A year ago he had gradually moved in his books and clothes, and then had finally given up his own apartment in Sausalito. He was surprised to hear her speak of abandoning. "Oh no! I *want* you to go with me. Whenever I've thought of this, it was *us,* doing it together."

This somewhat appeased her; she surrendered to him half her resistance. Yet she was still angry. "But you should have *told* me. Something. Hell, it's your business and your money, but we are at least sharing lives. Or so we say we are. But if *you* don't see it that way, how *can* I trust you? Lake Chapala is a long ways away. And I *can* imagine you just running off again, after God only knows what, leaving me stranded there."

He tried to smile her doubts away, but she didn't accept that. He was a vagabond, and she knew he would always be. Even so, he was full of an energy she admired that moment, even while he complained. "I'm sick of all the crap I've been doing all these years, to keep from having an eight to five job. The crap that made me good money was too dangerous, and the crap that was respectable didn't make any money. If I can't see *some* way out of this, I think it *would* be the end for me."

Still, it astonished her. "But you don't know *anything* about building a house, Max. You didn't even do that much carpentry with Ben."

Even in the late California autumn Max wore tee shirts and levis and Y-thong sandals. His hair was thoroughly gray and grew abundantly curly over his ears. He said, "There *is* no carpentry in Mexico. It's all bricks and cement and iron rebar and stones and tile. They don't even use power tools. The only thing plugged in that I saw was a ghetto blaster. Look-we'll watch them build our house. We'll live in it. Then maybe we'll sell it. And then who knows what."

It was a pretty picture. But she had always lived in beautiful Marin County, a woman of the woods and hills and creeks, and this was much to leave. She had cats. And deer and raccoons. She pretended to weigh his proposal.

He gave her little time. "Carol, you have *nothing* here either. Twenty-two years you've lived in this little place, next door to old, needy, tyrannical Isabel the invalid. It's a nice cozy little living, but gee, Carol-twenty-two years?"

She knew it. Though that argument was irrelevant, since she loved him and she would go with him no matter. Even so, she continued staring at him intently, no doubt trying to uncover something more in that face and those eyes, something he himself couldn't help her with.

12

Although his eyes looked deeply into her eyes too, and he could see everything hidden in her heart. So he spoke the clearest truth he could perceive in the muddy waters inside him. "I want you to go with me. I need you. *Please* trust me. You know how much I care about you."

"Alright," she said, finally dropping her eyes away from him. "I guess that'll have to do. But I will insist on one thing. If you're taking me to Mexico, I want to be there for All Souls' Day. I want to be there for one of those celebrations in the cemetery. I've shown you pictures."

"You have. And that's November first, isn't it? We'll have to hurry."

And so they came down out of the north only on the first day of November, four years till millenium's end, hoping to cross the border sometime before midnight, hoping to find this celebration of the dead and with it to warm their hearts and to bring the life back into them, and dispel their California melancholia.

Carol for the first stretch drove the heavily freighted white Dodge Caravan as they raced ahead beneath the gray smothering sky. They brought with them twelve or fifteen boxes, a slim inventory of their lives. Three cats who were her children and family huddled unhappily in a cage in the back of the van, where she could watch them in the rearview mirror.

They crossed the border as night fell, with hardly a wave from the Mexican customs. He thereafter drove, and he drove ahead with great caution, watching the tall weeds at the roadside for cattle and burros and dogs, calculating that Hermosillo was probably three hours ahead, if he had the energy to push it that far.

Soon the road narrowed, and they began to see battered eaten carcasses of coyotes at the road's edge, and signs that bid them beware of stray cattle. He strained to see into the darkness beyond headlights. By the time they came into Santa Ana, a mere seventy miles from the border, both he and Carol were tense and tired. He gratefully accepted her suggestion they stop there at that desolate waystation.

The clerk at Motel Elba would accept the cats, so he looked ten seconds into the room. It seemed pleasant enough. He paid the clerk. He and Carol brought in the cats one at a time, then a few bags and boxes. She looked carefully into the bathroom, the dresser drawers, under the bed and into the corners, and said with deflated energy, "It's a dump." Which of course by then he was realizing too, as he looked more closely: peeling wallpaint, broken drawer handles, old stained bedding, two little light bulbs keeping it all in merciful obscurity.

Worry not: he could see Carol already overcoming the squalor, going through boxes and removing her little treasures from their newspaper wraps and arranging them on the TV, on the lamp stand, over the Aztec calendar, wherever there was space. Finally she created a shrine on the dresser with three of her votive candles set in front of their bronze of three angels, which represented Larry and John for her and Ben for him, their great losses of the last two years. She placed paper flowers out of her box around them and lit the sad votives and that was it: not remotely the gay cemetery celebration she had been planning these last few weeks, but they *had* made it to Mexico, *and* on All Souls Day, and they were indeed saying their prayers to the dead with the rest of the pagans.

PART ONE

1 CARLOTTA AND THE BOYS

From the day Carol met Alfred and Ramon they had treated her like a princess; though by then she had already come to believe it would all be like this, the great adventure of Mexico, which she had embarked on with her own Prince Max, after he had rescued her from twenty years of servitude to the crippled tyrant Isabel.

Carol had also been treated like royalty by the Mexican workers who had built their house, maestros and peons alike. She had cooked for them each Friday ever more elegant meals, bringing that first time pots and trays of scalloped potatoes, green beans almondine, Tuscany pot roast, hot biscuits. On subsequent Fridays she never brought the same meal twice, serving out the generous portions herself from the back of the van while Max assisted. She called them her boys. They called her Carlotta, though her name was Carol; and she kept the new name.

The boys had worked with great care and the house they'd built was beautiful and finished with dozens of artistic flourishes that both she and Max the artist had designed. On the last day of construction maestro Lupe had gone to the bedroom where Carlotta was crying for the end of it, and he'd begged her to come join them for the official photo Max was taking, for she was an essential part of the team.

So she'd dried her eyes and come out and joined them. In the framed photograph she foreverafter displayed over her bed they all stand proudly in front of the house, she in the middle of all, taller than any. The double domed cupola they'd built especially for her on the housetop seemed in the photograph like a crown settled upon her head, as she smiled her happiness to all the world.

That same month Alfred and Ramon had entered their lives, on the prowl for new listings. They had gushed for the house and that had won her and Max both, and they'd given them the listing. The following week Alfred and Ramon had assessed Carlotta's sociable personality further and convinced her to train and join their sales team, despite a snide reception and frequent sniping by Polly Allen. But that happened in fairy tales too.

Even so, though visitors had gawked and praised it, weeks then months passed and the house they'd built didn't sell. This to Carlotta had been a petite disappointment, the kind princesses are prone to. But she had borne it.

Meanwhile, she had learned the lakeside real estate business. Ninety-five percent of its traffic was Americans and Canadians, all retiring, many buying houses. Most had cashed out their lifetime equities up north and migrated to this idyllic climate, which was rarely much above or below seventy and eighty degrees. Tempering the summer heat, rains fell throughout the summer months, all so conveniently at night, accompanied by spectacular electric violence in the skies over the lake and the village. The lakeside community of gringos was more or less eight thousand. Satisfied. Taking it easy. Conservative. Old.

They were a realtor's dream: they came, bought houses, died soon, and the houses resold. Over and over, to a continuing flow of short-lived retirees dazzled by press releases and brochures that glorified this quiet little lakeside village, where twenty thousand dark-skinned Mexicans have also lived five centuries and more.

Thus, time serenely passed for these two expatriates. Carlotta sold a few houses and brought home a few commission checks. Askance, she and Max watched Alfred and Ramon struggle to begin their own colossal project, MexicoLimpio, for as suspicioned, acquiring water permits did indeed become a problem as the lake receded further and further from the shore. Max and Carlotta would never be so ambitious. They would be happy building their one, perhaps two houses a year.

While they waited for their house to sell and while Carlotta worked for Alfred and Ramon, life was idyllic for Max in this new house they both loved so much. He searched out new exotic plants for the ever-expanding garden. He built himself a latticed pentagon gazebo flanked by royal palms with an oval, brick-lined, raised garden in front of it, full of roses. He read novels and histories and took notes on Maxmilian and Carlotta. His own Carlotta loved their new life. It was almost like being married.

And then the house sold, and everything changed. For better, for worse.

Three weeks after the sale Carlotta came home from the office one Friday afternoon, thrilled because she'd spotted a view lot on the day's new listings. Nobody could have seen it yet. Five hundred meters, a perfect size and a perfect price, too good to be true. It could be their next project, and the fairy tale could resume its happy course.

They drove to the lot immediately. It was on a slope that might require a large foundation, who knew. But the view of the lake was spectacular and the neighborhood was upscale. And her boys could go back to work again.

Monday 9AM Max and Carlotta gave Ramon a check for ten percent down. Two weeks later the deal closed with Lionel Quemado and his aunt, the shy widow dressed all in black, who had recently been bequeathed this property. They all signed documents. Max handed over a check for full price, and everyone shook hands. Max and Carlotta were ecstatic.

The following day Max was there on the property with Lupe and three peons clearing brush, marking boundaries and deciding where the living room would be, the master bedroom, the garage. Carlotta, who'd taken the morning off to share this special moment, was happier than she could ever remember being as she watched them all so busy, making a lot of people's dreams come true.

She also watched a black Chevy Blazer come up the hill. It parked beside her white Dodge Caravan and a large man emerged. He seemed in his fifties, his face round, friendly, fair-skinned, more European than mestizo, wearing round wire glasses like a teacher might. However, he dressed as if he would go tromping through the African veldt, in khaki shorts, khaki jacket, and a tan safari helmet on his head. He carried a folder of papers. He smiled cordially as he walked to join them.

Mysteriously, momentously, Carlotta sensed a sudden intensifying of the air they all now breathed.

Max shook the hand this affable stranger offered, and Max greeted him in Spanish. The man introduced himself. "I am Alejandro Frances. You seem to be preparing to build, senor." Carlotta saw in this stranger's eyes that this was not a casual question; it seemed somehow ominous. Even so soon, she sensed grief coming. She sighed.

Oblivious to such sensitive perceptions, Max was still a proud, new landowner, smiling, eager to show off his property. "Yes we are, Senor Frances. The view is fabulous here–don't you think so?"

17

Carlotta watched this gentle Mexican shift his feet nervously. "Oh, yes," he said, "I have always thought so. But you see–this is not *your* property. It belongs to my family. It has been in our family for a hundred years. More than a hundred."

Carlotta's Spanish was not so good as Max's, but still she knew enough to understand the essence of what this man said, and all the rest it grievously implied. She sobbed once loudly.

This startled Senor Frances. He looked at her, and must have seen the tide of loss already sweeping over her. Max stepped back, for this declaration was of course a shocking blow, and for the moment he could think of nothing to say.

He saw in Alejandro's eyes compassion for Carlotta's sudden sorrow, though Max also saw that this man dared not give that sentiment undue attention, lest he lose his own determination. Senor Frances turned his eyes away from Carlotta to hear Max's response.

Max knew the words he spoke in Spanish lacked conviction, because suddenly he, as well as Carlotta, now felt the fetid breath of doom in the air all around them. "But...I have a deed, Senor Frances."

Senor Frances nodded yes, as if he'd expected Max to say just that, and went on. "But I have the *true* deed, senor." Senor Frances held up to Max the folder thick with papers. Carlotta saw Max had no heart to ask him to open it, to go ahead and prove it all to him, for he knew, as she knew, that it would all be there. But, surely, something could be done. Something. So they could still have *this*.

Utterly bewildered, Max barely managed to control it. He said, "Could you come with me, Senor Frances, and bring your papers? We need to talk to the broker that took this listing, that sold us this property. And to the two who say they are the former owners."

Carlotta blanched as she recalled the forgotten players in this drama; and then she saw it all. Of course–Ramon and Alfred, Lionel, the frail, dark widow...ah yes, too good to be true.

Senor Frances bowed his head graciously, saluting them with his old world dignity, and said most patiently, "I am at your service, senor. I follow you."

Fifteen minutes later Carlotta stomped into the Lakeside Realty office and yelled at Ramon. He insisted he was wholly sympathetic and on her side. Nonetheless, he sent them all away, prolonging their anxiety, saying that they could only meet in two days' time, when he would bring Lionel Quemado back to the office for the meeting. Ramon seemed unruffled by all of it. "I'm sure there's a proper explanation," he said with his exceptional smile, most of it for Senor Frances. "I have had other dealings with Senor Quemado and the widow his aunt, whom he represents. I'm sure they will make this all right."

Senor Frances thanked them all and carried his folder away with him. Ramon attempted to detain Carlotta with what he thought to her would be good news, something to lighten her burden. "Carlotta, you'll be happy to know that, thanks to Polly Allen's mystery ally, not only have we been granted thirty water permits, but we have also sent to Ed Bustamante a copy of our new deed from Senor Cuevas. We just today received a very substantial check from him, and we're starting work at MexicoLimpio in two weeks, three at the most. Isn't that wonderful?"

But he had radically misjudged her. She was fired by great anger; he had never seen her like this. "I don't want to hear another *word* from you until you make good that property, Ramon! *Goddamnit!* You told me you'd checked the title twice! *Twice!*" Not waiting for Ramon to answer or Max to join her, she hurried out the door and down the front steps; she wouldn't let them see her unraveling.

Two days later, accompanied by Max, she went to the meeting without hope. Lionel Quemado the first time she had met him, when he had signed the sales agreement and taken their check, had seemed like a creepy little man preying on his frail, far too trusting aunt. The widow had set silently at his side, unwilling to look at documents, unwilling to look at any of the other participants. She so thoroughly trusted her thin, well dressed, sharp faced young nephew. Her check and his had been separate; perhaps and to all appearances probably a mystery to her how it had all been divided. In the end Carlotta had decided they deserved each other.

However, when Lionel sat down at the table beside Ramon, broker of the fraud, across from Senor Frances, Carlotta looked in Lionel's shifty eyes and she wanted to strangle the little bastard where he sat. She already knew this confrontation between Lionel and Senor Frances would be no contest. She stared at Lionel, daring him to look her in the eye, surprised that he'd had the nerve even to appear. The aunt was absent of course, and probably didn't know anything about this. And maybe never would.

Senor Frances was polite but devastating. He opened his folder and produced his documents. The first was a large map that had to be unfolded section by section until it covered the entire table. The extent of it encompassed hundreds of acres of Rancho del Oro, from the careterra to the hillcrests. Certain large areas were blocked out in blue pencil, and these he said had belonged to the family Frances for four generations. His father had recently died and bequeathed all of it to his widow, who in turn was now parceling it out among her three sons and her daughter. On top of this map, he placed a second smaller one, on which had been inscribed in thick black lines the boundaries of the property in question, which he called Section C. He traced with his finger the five sides of this Section C and said that this comprised 1480 square meters. It had never been further subdivided.

He asked permission of Lionel, who followed all this with the look of a doomed man, and Senor Frances took Lionel's small, sad lot map and he placed this fraud upon his own great display of maps and territories. He showed them all that this little map of Lionel's was not a true map at all, that it was only an arbitrary slice described upon a terrain to which it didn't belong. He then produced a deed dated forty years ago in which Section C had been subdivided out of a property twelve times larger. He read for them all the metric measurements of each of the boundaries and showed that those corresponded to his map of them. He showed them the municipal seals and the signatures of notarios and registry officials for decades. His last document was yellow with age and frayed with usage and he showed them dates that were nearly a hundred years old. He pointed especially to a paragraph wherein a Jalisco governor long dead had agreed to the sale of so many hundreds of acres in Rancho del Oro to the family Frances. This deed adduced that all this property had been in its origin a quitclaim from an even more ancient deed deriving from the King of Spain nearly two centuries ago.

As Senor Frances finished and looked up at the others, he nervously wiped little traces of sweat from his brow, then sat back in his chair, waiting for someone to say that what he'd said could not be true. But no one did.

Max turned to Lionel, whose squinting eyes were still creeping from map to map and deed to deed. Lionel shifted uneasily in his chair when Max said to him in Spanish, "What do you say, amigo? What does your aunt say, the widow?"

Speechless, Lionel at last looked into Max's eyes, since it was the least of payments he could make. However, he could not bear the confrontation long, and his eyes slid away, dipping and floating helplessly. Carlotta could see that someone else might pity those desperate eyes, but not she: who watched him rigid with anger.

Finally Lionel spoke in genteel Spanish, but meekly. "Yes, there is a possibility I have somehow mistaken. My engineer took measurements from a certain reference marker that may not have been the correct marker. I suppose that is possible. My property is part of an inheritance my aunt received this year, from her husband. She meant only to sell it. Her deed comes originally from her father-in-law. Though I see there is no doubt that the documents of Senor Frances are in good order."

Max then turned to Ramon. Before Max spoke, however, Ramon was ready with an answer, trying to smile through his own obvious bewilderment. "I *did* check it, I *swear*, but I checked the deed only, not the map. And not the location. I never imagined, if the deed was correct–and the records showed it *was* correct–that the location would not be what the map shows."

Hearing this, Carlotta slumped, drained of all hope. She said bleakly, "What do we do now, Ramon?" Who in her opinion deserved the shotgun, along with his rascal confederate, Lionel.

But Ramon was already having ideas. Suddenly he perked. His smile blossomed like a merry poppy at a wake. "*Let me offer this!* The lot in question *does* exist–I'm *sure* of that. If Lionel has mislocated it, he can make another survey with greater care, with a *new* engineer. He may use the man we use, Senor Guacho, and establish the true location. It should not be a problem." And to Lionel he said, "You could do this–yes?"

Lionel, sensing a miraculous reprieve, struggled to look optimistic, struggled to make a strong affirmation, desperate for any solution which would allow him to walk away unfettered from this meeting. However he could only mutter a twist of words that no one comprehended, though all believed he was probably trying to say something affirmative.

At the boiling point, Max spoke to Lionel, who tried to wipe the sweat from his forehead with a gesture that would keep its purpose hidden. "And what if I don't like this other lot? Wherever it turns out to be. What if I want my money back?"

Carlotta had already forsaken any hope of that.

Lionel attempted to smile sympathetically but his mouth quivered and could form no such smile. He could only say, "That's not possible I'm afraid. The money's gone."

Max, not surprised, pressed further. "What about your aunt's money?"

"Gone also. But please, no need to talk of money given back. I'm sure the lot in question *must* be close to the other on that hillside, and *all* the properties there have beautiful views."

Max strained to keep it simple and direct. "But you're not hearing me. What if I don't *like* this new location? What if I *don't?*"

Ramon raised his open hand off the table in a gesture that asked for their attention. He said, "Let me make a suggestion. We should hold off any discussion of money being given back until we know where the *actual property* is located. Who knows?–there is even the possibility– considering it's in Rancho del Oro-that the property will be-*Finer!*-than the one you thought you'd purchased." He glowed with optimism.

"Or it could be *way* worse," Carlotta said, for she had seen plenty of that kind too, even in Rancho del Oro. Her hand covered her eyes, drowning in dejection.

"We shouldn't be thinking negatively," said Ramon, refusing to look at her. "Please, let's take this one step at a time. Let's give Lionel's *new* engineer a chance to locate the *real* property. And *then* we can talk about what we have, or don't have. Isn't that reasonable?"

Max stared hard at Ramon and said, "Reasonable or not is something else. But I'll tell you-I'm damned unhappy about this." Max turned to stare as hard at Lionel, who could barely return his look, and Max said, "And that goes for you too."

Max turned to Alejandro Frances who sat next to him. Senor Frances had during all this kept his eyes respectfully downcast, graciously not wishing to call down by his own witnessing any greater shame on those responsible. The anger but not the agitation passed from Max's face and he said in Spanish to the land baron Frances, "I'm sorry for the trouble we've caused you, Senor Frances. I see the property is yours. My men will stop working there."

Senor Frances smiled at him so large with gratitude that Max was surprised and silenced from saying anything further. Senor Frances answered in the same language, "*You* are very kind, senor. I appreciate your honesty very, *very* much." Then he folded his maps and deeds again to their portable sizes and placed them one by one back in his folder. Ready to leave he said to Max, "I wish you luck finding your property. If I may be of any assistance, please call me. Here is my number, I am at your service." He handed him a card. He looked to the others as well and said, "And if I may be of assistance to any of *you*, please call me as well."

"Oh yes, yes," said Ramon, who was assisting Lionel to rise, who was happy he was out on his own recognizance. Confident Ramon spoke for his crippled accomplice: "And rest assured, all this will be resolved to everyone's satisfaction." He flashed them once more the handsome smile that he had ready for this quick getaway, and he ushered Lionel away.

Senor Frances rose to leave and wished Max and Carlotta well again, and thanked them for resolving the problem so graciously. "It does not always happen so, Senor Max, Senora Carlotta. And for that I thank you. My family thanks you." And he departed.

Carlotta again covered her eyes with her hand and Max could not hear her crying; but he saw the steady rise and fall of her chest and he knew she hid her tears and he knew how complete was her misery.

Nothing really changed for weeks. Lionel and his new engineer passed on week to week to Ramon little maps that they'd told him were each *probable* locations of the disputed lot. Ramon likewise passed these on to Max and Carlotta, with smiles more and more feeble. Finally Max and Carlotta gave all their documents to a Mexican lawyer named Carmelo Delavaca of Chapala, a man thin and sleek, always in the best suits, a little moustache, a charming grin, who accepted their retainer and promised swift and certain justice. He assured them he had what was most important of all, the good connections.

Nonetheless, Max and Carlotta came to accept that the property was lost, though the money *might* be recovered. Max, however, admitted one last desperate strategy. He and Senor Frances met at a little sidewalk coffee shop in downtown Chapala where Max had invited him, prepared to be even extravagant in his offer to buy all of Section C.

As they sipped their coffees, however, Senor Frances told him it was no use, that the family soon would begin developing the property. Brother Federigo was an architect. Then he'd shown Max a surprising smile which Max had thought of as elven, for Alejandro's eyes suddenly sparkled when he said, "My father told me and my brothers, many, many times–never sell, only develop. My father said there is only one thing worse than selling undeveloped property." He winked. "But he never told us what that one thing was."

Then he became again merely sympathetic and laid his arm across Max's shoulders. "I understand how you feel and I truly wish I could help you. If it were only up to me, I might. But this selling land is a thing that always involves the entire family. You understand."

Carlotta sighed and began looking again half-heartedly through each day's new listings. A week more passed. Polly and Alfred were spending more and more afternoons at the big Cuevas property doing MexicoLimpio. Ramon was in Guadalajara again, doing who knew what, and it was left for Carlotta one Friday afternoon to close up the office. She afterward went to meet Max in the plaza for their twice a week lounge on the iron park benches in the village community living room, where they watched the locals come and go and sit and gossip.

Carlotta went up the little steps to the plaza and saw there were only a dozen or more Mexicans strolling the plaza or sitting. She saw Max on an iron bench, sitting beside Alejandro Frances. She sighed again remembering the beautiful property that wouldn't be. Both men were laughing as they watched a little boy playing with an empty coke can. Max saw her and waved. She saw another man, perhaps another of the Frances brothers, on the bench next to Max.

Alejandro rose and made her the smile that already had endeared him to her. At the same time Max also rose, hugged her briefly and turned her toward the new Frances and said, "This is Oskar, Alejandro's brother." He rose to greet her; he too had the generous family smile. But unlike Alejandro's conservative gray slacks and open-collared business shirt, Oskar wore levis and a bright short-sleeve with sunsets and palms waving. He seemed younger than his brother, though not much. They both had the identical bald head, the same long wispy hair sweeping left to right across the dome.

The men reseated, making room for her, but she preferred to stand. Alejandro spoke to her in a slow, calculated English, the first time she'd heard him use her language. "Good to see you again, senora. So pretty you look—*Que bonita*—as we say in our language."

"Yes," said jovial Oskar, in English no more polished than his brother's, "you are ready to go to dinner with the mayor."

She laughed, believing it was the new hair color. "I dress this way to sell more houses. It's what the gringos like." She saw it amused them that she'd used that word.

Alejandro said, "Max is telling me that you have still not discovered your mystery lot."

She laughed again, that he'd found in English such a perfect word to describe it. "Yes—our mystery lot! I laugh, but I'm still angry. A lawyer is helping us. I hope he's helping." She hesitated, then decided to say it.

"Ramon is making us deal with Lionel on our own. Says he can't waste any more time on this because it's not resolving quickly." She stopped talking, took a deep breath, and tried to reassert her smile of a moment ago. She wouldn't look at Max.

"Disgraceful," spoke Alejandro shaking his head. "Unfortunately. I have seen this before in these real estate people. I never use them."

"Fine," Max said, surprising her to hear a lilt of humor in his voice. "We'll sue Ramon too, along with Lionel and the widow."

"Go ahead," she responded with an avenging grin, "I wouldn't care. I'm ready to quit."

Alejandro placed his big hand on Max's shoulder and said, "Let me speak to my brother Federigo. He is very resourceful, perhaps something can be done to help. I will call you in a few days." They spoke a few minutes longer, but nothing that seemed memorable. Then the two brothers wandered away.

However, two days later Alejandro telephoned. Max at five minutes before eight in the morning had to take the call in the bedroom, naked and dripping from the shower as he tried to dry himself one-handed with a towel. Alejandro told him that the brothers had conferred and had agreed to sell them Section C. Brother Oskar in addition possessed a piece even bigger than Section C, though with a lesser view, but still very desirable. He would also sell that, well priced, if they wished it.

Carlotta stood beside him bouncing on her toes as she listened, knowing by some psychic osmosis exactly what was transpiring. When he put down the phone, his face stricken with astonishment, she shrieked for joy and couldn't have stopped herself.

That same day they met Alejandro at brother Oskar's village apartment to sign the sales agreement and to give the brothers the ten percent down. Two hours later they met with an accountant named Jesus Calzon, who explained to them the procedures for incorporation, and they signed the appropriate documents and they paid him his fees. Then Carlotta went four hours late to work and gave Ramon her notice to quit, thinly masking her gloat with a smile that was worthy of Ramon himself.

2 BELLACASA IS BORN

Only after all this momentous work was done did Max and Carlotta make their reservations for that night at the Nueva Posada to celebrate. After a year and a half of Mexico, and especially the anxiety of the last few months, it was suddenly all perfect again, the fairy tale resumed. They had signed their names together so many times that day on so many official documents that she almost felt married to this man she had followed with so much trepidation to this corner of the universe. And what had they done? So little and so much. They'd watched the boys build a house. They'd sold it. Today they'd made themselves a legal corporation. Bellacasa they'd be called. They would build beautiful houses.

Their table that sparkling spring night at the beautiful Posada was at the end of the patio nearest the garden, where the light was dim. They sat with their backs to the four or five other occupied tables. The garden was full of flowers. Two old men with painted guitars wandered from table to table of the dining room inside the hotel, their romantic old songs carrying out through the open doors. The ancient rubber tree spread a dense canopy high above Max and Carlotta. When the guitars paused between songs, she could hear the hush of the waves sliding up the shore far beyond the garden wall. Max poured them red wine. He said all the right things, in just the right tone of voice. He was capable of all of it. Even that one tiny regret, even that might be made right on a night like this.

As they looked into the starry sky above the lake their heads almost touched. He asked, knowing the question would please her, "You know we're almost broke now, don't you?"

She glowed. "Yes. We don't have enough money to build a house on *any* of those seven new lots we own."

He was as happy as she. "They'll give us money to build there. Would you like to go to Paris?"

They looked and smiled into each other's eyes. She could see he would like to make it all true. "If you took me to Paris you'd never have to do another thing in the world for me. Not ever."

"Then we'll go to Paris."

Yes, a perfect night, a perfect moment, fit for a princess. The guitars faraway started up again, a melancholy serenade.

Yet all this was suddenly overcome by a nasal-toned human trumpet blaring Max's and Carlotta's names across the patio. There was only one source for it: Morley, the bad boy patriarch of the Eager family, who had ten years ago built this finest showplace in all Ajijic, a five-star fifteen room hotel, restaurant and bar. Today at seventy years old Morley was only a hobbling parody of the man who had so delighted women of all types and ages for much of the twenty-five years of his residence in the village. Now he was dangerous only by his still piercing wit, his piercing voice and his flagrantly uninhibited use of both. Delighted, Carlotta turned to greet him.

Malcolm was beside him, Morley's only slightly younger sidekick, dressed as always in shorts and white knee-length socks, flaunting a trim waist, gray wispy hair on his head, and the usual grin on his round rosy face that reminded Carlotta of what a hobbit must look like. Morley limped, though elegantly, to their table, only sometimes using his cherrywood cane. Max stood to shake both their hands and offer them a seat, equally delighted, saying, "Yes, come sit with us. This is nothing private. We're just celebrating." She might have slapped him if they'd been alone.

Morley leaned down to kiss Carlotta's cheek as she said, "So good to see you, Morley." Then he stood and leaned sassily on his cane, and with his free hand stroked one end of his long, lascivious moustache. He said, "You'd be surprised, dear, how few women these days let me get that close. I appreciate your confidence in me. Malcolm and I have been hitting all the bars on the plaza. Trying to pick up sailors."

"Speak for yourself, you old goat," said Malcolm laughing. Then he too leaned down to kiss Carlotta. "We're not interrupting anything intimate, are we?" he asked in his hobbitish Boston brogue. "*I* ask, because Morley wouldn't know to ask."

"And wouldn't care," Morley added. "Because if it's intimate, I want to be there. Group intimacy is the best kind."

Malcolm laughed and defied him. "Jesus, Morley, you're not fooling anybody–you only get it up once a year."

A satyr's grin lit Morley's face. He looked first at Max, then Carlotta, before he turned back to Malcolm. "Yeah, but that once a year I take no prisoners." Morley set his hand on Max's shoulder a moment, to acknowledge Max's appreciative laugh, and said, "No, I can't stop and socialize, but Malcolm will–I've got to report in to my wife." He winked. "Got to nip those rumors in the bud, you know." And Morley limped away toward the big doors, looking to either side of him as he prowled among his unsuspecting diner guests.

Malcolm noticed someone he knew at a table two removed from them. "Say there, Kriboom, I thought you'd gone back to Florida." Malcolm walked toward him.

Casually dressed Kriboom eased back an empty chair, inviting him to sit. Malcolm instead stood beside him and said, "Say, do you know Max and Carlotta there? Maybe we could all push our tables together, get to know each other. Max and Carlotta like to build houses."

Kriboom said, "I know." He turned to look at the couple, and nodded respectfully. "I've heard people talk about you."

Carlotta looked closer at this man. He seemed faintly familiar. Where? This Mr. Kriboom had dark, wavy hair, bleached at the temples and on the fringe of the wave that looped his forehead. His face was a ruddy, but not from sun. He wore an expensive, loose white sweater, red stripes around the wrists, and dark denim shorts. His long, hairy legs he extended off the side of the table, one sandaled foot cocked on a knobby knee. A modest pot belly. He was probably six feet three or four. Probably mid-fifties. Rugged. Carlotta thought he looked like a drifter, but one who had enough money to keep himself comfortable. Some women would think him appealing, and she imagined it would be the ones who were willing to let him do most of the talking.

Half to Malcolm, half to Max and Carlotta, Kriboom said, "Didn't go back to Florida. Still looking for the right house. Or the right place to build one. So far no luck." Then he gave all his attention to Max and Carlotta. "So you two have a few lots for sale–huh? I couldn't help overhearing."

At that moment the head waiter Armando, in the same creased black slacks and ruffled shirt and magenta cummerbund that all these waiters wore, came striding across the patio, grinning like the wish-granting genie he was. He bore on his fingertips a silver tray and a bottle of wine upon it, and he set all this on the table before Max and Carlotta, who were visibly surprised.

"This, Senor Max and Senora Carlotta," he said grandly, "is a gift from your amigos at the table over there." He indicated with a flourish of his hand a table near the door. Carlotta looked closely, then took a deep, restorative breath when she saw Ramon's teeth smiling at her, his little delicate hand waving hello. Polly Allen sat next to him, unable to smile, but making a little wave of her chubby hand.

Strangling her spite, Carlotta waved back feebly and mouthed to her benefactor so distinctly the words *Thank You*.

But in that instant she suddenly remembered that forgotten morning in the office a week ago, Ramon showing this Mr. Kriboom the drawings of MexicoLimpio, and she wilted.

"Oh Christ!" she said discretely to Max. "Ramon thinks he's caught me stealing his goddamn client Kriboom!" Then she saw that even the bottle of wine would not be gift enough, for Ramon himself rose effusive from his table and launched himself across the patio toward her like a happy missile.

"Oh the little love birds," he twittered and chirped when he came near. That sentimental speech seemed to brake him sufficiently so that he could glide without actually stopping his motion into the seat that Max had pulled out previously for Malcolm. Ramon settled in adroitly. With a flourish he smoothed the front of his silk heliotrope shirt and poised his elbows onto the table so that he could lean confidentially toward them. His gorgeous smile was for them alone.

Mr. Kriboom in the meantime had drawn back his chair, relinquishing the floor to him who could not be upstaged.

"I hope you like the wine," Ramon enthused, "it's for several reasons. A going away present for you, dear Carlotta, just so you know there are no hard feelings. At least on my part. Secondly, I want to congratulate you on your very impressive acquisitions today-"

Carlotta gulped. "How do you know anything about that, Ramon?"

His smile quickly softened. "Oh I find out things. You should know that by now. But *how* doesn't matter-now does it? It'll be public record in a day or two anyway. So I congratulate you-these Frances brothers are quite the catch! Oh I knew we couldn't hold on to you long, Carlotta. I've always been sure that you and your prince of a husband would do great things."

Then Ramon looked to Mr. Kriboom, who was watching all of this intently, and Ramon extended a generous arm to him as well, saying, "Why Mr. Kriboom, I see you're getting acquainted with my former star salesman Carlotta and her husband Max. They'll soon to be our newest tycoons—I believe that's the American word."

This recalled to Carlotta her embarrassment of the moment before. "Look, Ramon–I've not even said *one word* to Mr. Kriboom–he just introduced himself. We haven't said a word about business–I don't know *anything* about *anything*."

Nothing could have delighted Ramon more. He squealed. "Oh dear, dear Carlotta–*no, no!*– it's *you* who misunderstand. Mr. Kriboom is my *other* gift to you. He's looking to build, but walled-in communities are not for him. I recommended you to him. He and I talked in the office recently, I believe you were there, and he's just not the type for MexicoLimpio. He's another kind of rare bird. Aren't you, Mr. Kriboom?"

Mr. Kriboom seemed flattered by the description and moved his chair once again a little toward them. He spoke now with a clever smile. "The question is, Ramon–*which* rare bird." He probed his shirt pocket for a thin panatella and lit it with a chrome lighter, a USMC shield affixed to its face. He did it all without taking his eyes off his two interesting new friends, the builders. Malcolm had settled in a chair at the far side of Kriboom's table and was allowing them their business talk, though he watched them with obvious interest.

Master of ceremonies Ramon had apparently finished his work. He stood and quickly surveyed them all, a little patchwork family now. He leaned and spoke so only Carlotta could hear. "I expect full commission on Kriboom, my dear." Then he stood clear, and spoke so anyone might hear. "And I do hope you solve the puzzle of your mystery lot. That has been *so much* distressing me. But I'm sure you know that."

Max's smile was a dare. "OK–then show us *how* distressed–give back your commission."

Ramon's explosive laugh blew all of that away.

Carlotta felt Max beneath the table step on her toes. She squirmed her foot loose. Then Max suddenly said something that surprised her–not for the truth of the statement itself, with which she would've agreed; but it surprised her that he would confess the truth to their adversary in this.

"You know, Ramon, if the price we pay for knowing the Frances brothers is to get screwed by Lionel, then so be it, I'll take the trade."

Ramon glowed his brightest, as if nothing in that moment could have pleased him more, and so it might have been. "Oh that is *so* generous of you to say, Max. I *love* that about you, your generosity. And yet, you know, it is *just* what I have been thinking myself recently–a fair trade!" He laughed a little too much in their faces, and he seemed a moment later to sense it, for he then looked toward Polly Allen, who sat still at their table looking at them all with no visible emotion.

Ramon let his gleeful laugh overflow and flood in Polly's direction, no doubt that she might see how he could walk into the lion's den and laugh at the lions, and then turn and walk away. For so he did, feeling no need to say farewell, merely turning as he laughed, and then walking away, the sweetness of his laughter trailing behind him like a matador's cape.

"Good God!" said Carlotta, "I feel like I've just been slobbered on by a fucking Saint Bernard! And *why* did you let him off the hook like that?"

Max smirked. "I feel generous tonight." Then he looked to Kriboom, smiled and said, "Come join us. You too, Malcolm, let's drink this wine, though it might turn out to be vinegar."

Carlotta saw it might be their last private moment and she leaned to Max and said quietly, "What's happening to *our* night out?"

Kriboom would leave them none of it. He stood, bigger even than he seemed stretched out in his chair, and then he resat himself in the chair Ramon had vacated. Malcolm drew his own chair to the table beside Kriboom and accepted the panatella Kriboom offered. He accepted from him as well a light, and said to him between puffs, "Max's writing a book, too. He's a man of multiple talents."

Kriboom said, "Oh?" and might or might not have been genuinely interested.

"How's that coming?" Malcolm prompted the author.

Max poured a glass from Ramon's bottle for each one. "Slowly. Ten pages or so a week."

"He's writing a *novel* about Maximilian and Carlotta–it *is* a novel, isn't it, Max?–you're not doing something factual, are you?"

Max tasted from his own glass and smiled, then put it down. "No, nothing factual. *Based* on fact. But it's actually fantasy. You know, everyone laughs at Maximilian because he's such a mad idealist, but what if he'd really had the full support of the Mexican people, the church and the military? Maybe he'd been able to make a lot of those ideals come true, and then what would Mexico be like now? I think he could've made Mexico healthy, maybe even a strong country, an equal to the United States before he was through. But everything was against him. He came at the wrong time probably. And he was doomed."

Kriboom seemed to follow all this. Carlotta sat back in her chair, enjoying not having to push the business, as if none of it were more important than this little conversation about Max's literary hobby.

"So this will be, like, something that never actually *happened?*" asked Kriboom.

"That's right," said Max, "a what-if. I never really liked the way Maximilian and Carlotta's story ended. It's not even tragic, it's just senseless. It's almost comic. At least that's the way I read it. I had an urge to rewrite it, make it end like it should have ended. So yes, it's a what-if."

"Yeah," interjected Malcolm, again a hobbit, "and *what if* Maximilian and Carlotta hadn't had their heads up their asses and they'd actually *seen* what was going on all around them, right in front of them? All that opposition. That subterfuge. What if *that?*"

Max laughed. "Well, yes, that's true too. But that's another story. Maybe it'll be part of *my* story, who knows." Then he looked at Kriboom, and offered what seemed a more frivolous topic. "So, you're looking to build a house."

Kriboom sat forward, setting one big hand on his knobbed knees and with the other withdrawing the panatella from between his clenched teeth. He said, "Yes I do. The lot doesn't have to be big. I want a nice view. A super view would be better. And I want a builder I can work with, so I can incorporate some of my own ideas."

"You married?" Max asked, like an interviewer with a significant question.

"Not really."

Then Max thought of another. "And did somebody say you're from Florida?"

"Yeah. Key West. I gotta boat."

Malcolm snorted. "You won't need it here!"

Kriboom seemed to miss the joke, or he was thinking about something else. He said, "So–what did *you* do before Mexico, Max? Construction, I suppose." Carlotta sensed that he supposed nothing like that.

Max smiled pleasantly. Carlotta knew Max would not be enjoying this turn to the conversation; though he would be prepared. Max said, "Yeah, construction. Though mostly it was remodeling. And I was a salesman." Only she knew that these were partial truths, that he'd omitted a world of significance. Then Max slipped away from Kriboom's question with one of his own. "And how about you?"

Kriboom seemed happy Max had asked him. "Oh I was in special services in the war. Couldn't ever talk much about it, top secret stuff. Still is. I was leader of an assault team." He looked away, and Carlotta was sure he was enjoying the effect his resume must be making on them.

A moment later Kriboom turned back again and said, like a crafty CEO might look at a sadly under-qualified applicant. "I've already researched your company. There wasn't much. I know you're the new kid in town, that you don't have a lot of experience. But I might be willing to go with you, despite that. I like your enthusiasm, and you seem willing to listen to other ideas." Then he winked, and it might have been for fun, or maybe it was for something else only he knew. Carlotta thought he spoke the next a little too intensely. "I know you'll let me have what I want." It made her shiver.

"OK," said Max, "what say we go look at the property tomorrow?"

They agreed. Carlotta saw a capture. And still a dangerous animal.

Only a few moments later Carlotta convinced Max to say goodbye so she could take him outside. As they paid their bill, Carlotta said to Max, "Frankly, the guy makes me a little nervous. How do you think it'll be working with him?"

He smiled at her and spoke the truth as he knew it. "What do I know? We sign a contract. He gives us a big down. What could go wrong? We'll modify the house plans we used on the Chula Vista house, that was a good one. We'll probably need a little more foundation I guess, but no big deal I suppose. I'm sure Judy Tovar could help us work in the changes Kriboom wants. She'll be doing the final plans anyway."

Carlotta could accept that. Despite all the snags, here they were, dreams coming true, and it still felt to her like the wind was at their backs. They walked away from the Nueva Posada, first on the cobblestoned street, then on sand, where she removed her sandals. No moonlight was on the lake, but even so the foamcrests of waves were bright, rolling across the beach just ahead. Taller than he, she laid her head on his shoulder when they slowed to admire the bright cluster of lights on the faraway shore that was the pueblo rustico of San Luis Soyatlan, and the lesser cluster further east, Tuxcueca. The lake separating them from these lights lay black and still, to dull eyes invisible in the bigger darkness.

But at last the Moon rose, a little past fullness, illuminating for them a huge tide of lirio that in its aggregate passing had settled tonight along this shore. Because of this clog of moonlit lirio no waves or water lapped the sand beach; only bobbing, flowerless water lilies gently pushed forward, then sagged back, to indicate the baffled pulse of the lake.

Carlotta and Max halted where a fishing boat had been staked among all this vegetation, tied by several meters of rope to a tall iron spike anchored in the sand. The boat was of the kind they saw everywhere along the shore west of the village, anchored like this one. Like this also were those rowed slowly in the cool mornings upon the lake by one or two fishermen, who played out long handfuls of net behind them to capture the lake carp or the tiny white charales that swarmed in these shallow waters.

All these boats were made by hand of rough planks nailed to stout branches, chosen for the perfect angle of their branching. Upon these branches, the planks for sides and bottom were nailed and then sealed. Lupe had told them that only a few old artisans on Scorpion Island could make these boats. Rarely were these lakecraft painted or adorned. Each fishing boat, however, had the identical elegant, narrowing prow that curved to a point a meter higher than the water.

She said, "Someday I'd love to own one of these beautiful boats."

He would dream with her. "You deserve one nicer, more elegant. Safer."

"No. This is what I like. This is the one. Aren't the lines beautiful?"

She let go his hand and sat cautiously upon the upswept bow, but it accepted her weight without shifting. She passed her other hand fondly along the gunwales of it. Her eyes followed the caress of her hand. Then she turned to face him and said, "Isn't it amazing how all this is turning out?"

His head was very pleasantly light from the wine. This sudden, new, who they were, Bellacasa, made him feel like he was considering the life of someone else. "It's going a little faster than I expected. Are we ready to build someone a house?"

She beamed. "How about two houses? I was saving it to tell you. Another agent called me today, asking about our lots. She has someone else who wants to build. So you tell me—are we ready?"

He laughed. Yes, this was what dreams were made of. "How can we stop now? I assume we say yes to all of it."

She glowed. "That's what I say too! Lupe will have to hire a lot more men. That thrills me. And it also means I can go back to California and drive down my blue Chevy pickup. It's my baby, you know. I've been thinking about it, missing it. Mexico is what it was born to do."

He loved her like this. "But this is the ultimate question—aren't *you* as happy as you get?"

Perhaps it was an unfortunate question, for Carlotta let slip both the smile and the laugh, and soberly said, "Not quite." But then she laughed. "You know what I want. Even if we don't talk about it. Hey, it's not *my* fault! *You* asked the question. Besides, romantic nights bring up these things."

She saw in his eyes tonight that he would give her anything. He said, "No—talk about whatever you want. I love seeing you happy, seeing that in your face. And knowing I helped put it there."

The princess was again pleased. "Well you did. And I thank you. Yes, you know what else I want. And you know I'll wait. And I won't press you. I was just answering your question–which is no, I'm not as happy as I can get. Though this is all quite wonderful, I will admit."

He pulled her close. He couldn't quite say it, ask it; but he did say, "You'll get everything you want, I promise you. I'm almost there."

So here she was, year and a half in Mexico, sitting beside Lake Chapala with this man she so loved, on the happiest, most romantic night of her life. And again, his words would just have to do.

3 LUPE, MAESTRO OF THE OBRA

Guadalupe Gonzalez, maestro of the obra, stood on the boundary where the diablo Kriboom's property joined the dirt road that was Calle Mina del Oro. His arms crossed upon his chest, he watched his maestros and peons move like an army of ants from the mound of wet cement and the gas-powered mixer on the road behind him. They plodded down their uneven slope of trail to the frames that shaped this foundation, so long abuilding, that it could not be believed. Each man carried on his shoulder a twenty kilo bucket of fresh cement. Two others stood on a platform beside the foundation to receive each bucket and pour it into the massive forms. A column of men trekked back with their empty buckets the way they'd come, passing the approaching others, who were yet unburdened.

Behind Lupe was a plastic tarp that looked like it covered a car, but which in actuality covered nine tons of powder cement still in bags stacked beside the mixer. Beside those was a man-tall mound of gravel. Beside that was an equally massive mountain of river sand.

Also upon this road that went nowhere, four other peons cut and formed several thicknesses of rebar into long armatures that would reinforce the foundation where the engineer's plans so specified. The engineer had personally shown them how to build the iron forms that allowed them to bend the rebar into the shape of each armature. More than a hundred lengths of five meter rebar lay beside these four peons. A dozen formed armatures lay beside them ready for use.

In all his twenty-two years of working construction Lupe had never seen such a foundation. The base of it was a meter and a half thick. The far wall of it downslope was eight meters tall, so that the principle floor of the house would be level with the road. They had been digging and framing and mixing and pouring and making armatures more than a month. The foundation looked like a military fortress, itself bigger already than most of the houses Lupe had built. It would still be another week before they laid their first brick of wall. The finished house would be two tall floors above the street. Every day when the senor came to look at it Lupe saw the misery in his face.

This unprecedented labor caused other problems for maestro Lupe as well. It was customary for all, maestros and peons alike, to share the labor of digging foundation trenches, mixing and pouring cement to fill them. But in all the houses Lupe had worked this initial labor was a thing of a week, hardly ever more. After that the division of labor was well defined. The maestros set stone and laid brick, plastered the walls, built fireplaces, built cupolas, built scalloped and vaulted ceilings, and laid the tiles for the floors, and kitchens and bathrooms. The peons assisted them, performing all the strenuous tasks of preparing cement and mortar, hauling brick and iron, hauling water. As well as that, they also did the tedious jobs of sifting sand and grouting bricks and keeping the jobsite well ordered and clean.

But this foundation and all the mixing and lifting and carrying–there was no end to it. To maestro Lupe it was a measure of the good character of all his maestros that no one complained. They had all worked together many times, many years. Cousins, brothers, nephews, uncles, friends. All from Six Corners. And Lupe knew as well that half the reason no one complained was because it was for the senor. And the senora. They had become a compania. There would be many houses. Continuous work. For many. If this pinche foundation did not bankrupt the senor and shatter his courage.

Lupe's eyes drifted beyond the foundation, down the long slope of hillside toward the carretera, and even beyond that, to the small, frail and mostly adobe structures of his barrio, which had been there hundreds of years, no one knew how many. And just beyond Six Corners, the resplendent lake, one hundred fifty thousand years situate.

In the heart of Six Corners he spotted the cross upon the iglesia of the Virgin, around the corner from his own adobe house. This recalled to him the preparations sister Magdalena was even at that moment making for the party that afternoon. This thought made him wish to smoke a cigarette, though he had none. He knew he would have to buy a pack, or two, before he was home. The last time Tacho had seen him he had smoked. Tacho would not think it unusual to see his father with a cigarette. But these thoughts began to make Lupe's stomach churn again, and he paced away toward the houses at the neighborly end of dirty Mina del Oro, where it abutted Calle Rio Nazas, the long cobblestone street connecting them to the carretera downhill.

Then he saw a thing that stressed him as much as thinking of the party: he saw the senora's old blue Chevy pickup, which the senor usually drove, coming up Rio Nazas, and no more than a car length behind him the new red jeep of Senor Kriboom. That, for Lupe, was the story exacto, the red diablo on the senor's ass.

His instinct was to call out and warn the men that the diablo was coming; but he knew it would serve no good purpose. So he merely watched him pursuing the senor's truck up the hill. Already Lupe had begun to withdraw into the sanctuary of his apparent ignorance of the diablo's language.

The senor parked beside Lupe's battered twenty-two year old Cadillac of all problems, got out and slowly walked toward him without waiting for the diablo. The senor smiled. Perhaps there was some rare bit of good news. Or more likely he had already prepared his own sanctuary, the smile that could not be broken down. There would no doubt be many questions and directions and dissatisfactions that would be announced by the diablo, and there would be for the senor no hiding from these words. He would answer them all from the sanctuary of that smile that could not be broken down.

The senor stopped beside him and studied the work. He wore as usual his levis and a dark green tee shirt, and the naked huaraches with only the Y-strap over the toes. Curly graying hair over his ears, the senor was a half foot taller than the maestro. As Lupe watched two peons pouring buckets of cement into the foundation frames, he glanced to the senor, who smiled truly, and said to Lupe as he always did, "Buenos dias, maestro." His Spanish sounded very nearly like their own. Rafael, Lupe's nephew, half deaf and also impeded in his speech, walked past them carrying two armatures, and the senor spoke his name and greeted him also.

Lupe tried to give the senor courage; he swelled with enthusiasm. "We *will* finish the fortress this next week, senor, then we can begin the walls. Pues, it will go fast, you'll see." Lupe saw Kriboom come out of his car of the true diablo's own red color, and walk slowly toward them, lighting his nasty cigar as he walked.

The senor said, "When will Figueroa come with the bricks?"

None of these details ever escaped the maestro. Lupe spoke with great confidence. "Pues, senor, he will be here this afternoon, without doubt."

Without looking Lupe knew that Kriboom had halted behind them, though for a long ominous moment the ghost said nothing. When the words did come they sounded playful and friendly, though Lupe knew they were not, but merely the sound of the assassin who enjoyed his work.

Lupe's English was a long work in progress. Over years he had accumulated a knowledge of many words, and especially those of construction. He knew no grammar. And odd dialects of English baffled him, as did the slang terms that made no sense until someone like Marcos his nephew explained them. The senor spoke his English slowly and distinctly, so Lupe could understand him most of the time when the senor spoke to other gringos. Though the senor without doubt knew it not. And of course Lupe never spoke English. The pronunciation of this Kriboom, who knew no Spanish, sometimes was clear, though at other times he seemed to slip into his own peculiar American dialect that Lupe could understand none of. But Lupe knew that Kriboom's first words spoke the usual dissatisfaction. The work was going too slow for him.

This seemed not to bother the senor, not this fiftieth time. He answered him what he usually answered, that they were going as fast as possible, that Kriboom could not expect with so much foundation that they could have progressed any further.

Kriboom said, "Hire more men, you've got a deadline."

This word deadline made Lupe grit his teeth. He would not look at the tall, pushing man. Most gringos loved this word deadline. It was more important to them than anything. In honor to it they were rude, barbarous even. Building the house in Chula Vista the senor and the senora had never been guilty of this. That if nothing else made them unusual. But in the house for the diablo the senor had several times been impatient and had used the word deadline; though Lupe excused him, because he knew it was the diablo pushing him, always pushing him.

The senor told the diablo now that if there were any more men on the job they would be bumping over each other constantly. And that was true. For a long moment this Kriboom said nothing. Lupe glanced at him: this gringo smoking and so well pleased. Lupe looked away, then heard him speak. "Last night I was looking at that first set of plans you gave me—remember that? The ones you based your price on? I was comparing them to the foundation plans the engineer in Guadalajara made for you." He snickered. Lupe knew he was saying this only because he enjoyed reminding the senor of his great mistake.

The senor said nothing. And what could he say? Lupe took some of the blame for this—he too should have known. Pues, actually he had

40

suspicioned. But it was very hard to tell sometimes what the angle of a slope was. Lupe had not seen the senor's plans for the foundation until they'd begun work. And it had been Lupe who had finally said, We must stop, we must bring an engineer from Guadalajara to look at this. And he had come to look, and then the engineer had drawn the plans that Lupe had almost cried over when he saw them.

Several huge pages. One page alone with drawings of all the complicated and expensive armatures that would have to be built for reinforcement. A triple thickness of foundation. Several massive pads of concrete and rebar anchored deep in the earth to support such a tall foundation at its critical corners. And no limestone to be added to the concrete. None. The senor had to pay the engineer to come to the job site several times just to help Lupe read these plans, so complex they were.

Lupe heard the diablo walking away. The senor watched him too, as the diablo went to scrutinize the peons making armatures. The senor walked that way himself. Lupe followed them. The diablo wore a bright flowery shirt. He wore khaki shorts and cleated rubber walking shoes. Long dark hair combed forward to obscure the lack of all hair near his forehead. The man grinned; evidently all this strain and stress of contractor and foreman and workmen pleased him much.

Kriboom said to the senor, "No wonder you're so slow. All those men working together there—see them laughing and talking?—that's wasted time. I learned that a long time ago, training my assault team. Keep them isolated. You get a lot more accomplished." The senor made him no response, as if what he'd said mattered nothing, which it didn't. Yes, Carlos and Porfirio were talking and laughing—why not? Then the diablo went on. "Maybe you forgot—you promised me I'd be living here by Christmas, and I'm holding you to that. And I mean it."

This was how he did it, little by little, pushing the senor to the brink. Dead-lines. Lupe saw the senor shake his head, as if to make that annoyance go away. He said, "Hey—we had two months more work than we'd planned— all to your benefit, and at no extra cost to you. You know we can't still be done by Christmas."

The diablo seemed not to hear him. He pointed his cigar at Carlos. "See how slow he works? Better supervision's the answer here. Get him moving. Get them all moving. They're all slow as hell. Take my advice and you'll make up your two months, save a little money and we'll both be happy. The truth is, I could save you a lot of money here, if you had the sense to listen to me."

41

Lupe was happy the senor was not responding to this, for Lupe had come to see that Kriboom liked to be contradicted and argued with. He always had more to say. Such cajones. He must know they all hated him; yet he loved to come here and tell them what to do and laugh at them. And always–hurry, hurry–never forget the Dead-Line. Marcos had only just told him that this evil word described a procession of those who had died. The diablo should think about this.

4 LUPE'S WELCOME HOME PARTY

Three months Lupe had longed for and dreaded this Saturday afternoon in July. He had returned from the jobsite to the barrio with all the men who would fit in his 1979 Cadillac of all problems, and he had parked in front of his house on Calle Obregon. But then, instead of going into his house where so much awaited him, Lupe walked the half block to Six Corners and turned right to walk the further block to the iglesia of the Virgin of Guadalupe, his name saint.

He passed old Arturo the butcher standing in the doorway behind his counter, waving away flies from the cuts of raw beef heaped on the counter. Arturo called to him and winked, for he also knew this was Lupe's big day. Antonia saw him too as she cut limes at the card table set up outside her doorway, for the customers who bought her crisp delectables every day: *Chicharrones y limones ooolala*, she sometimes sang. She waved, then thought to ask if Tacho had yet arrived. Lupe told her yes, yes, yesterday, staying of course with Tia Costanza Romero. Antonia had nursed Tacho when he had been so severely ill with the grippa that winter, many, many years ago. She had been Marlena's closest friend, and she like all the others had advised Marlena to leave him eleven years ago. And look at her now, waving, smiling. Antonia had forgiven him long ago.

Roderigo, half drunk and unsteady in the street, saw him too and stumbled toward him with great urgency. "Lupe, Lupe," he said, "you must help me. My idiot son I think is going out nights with the bad ones again, I'm afraid he's stealing. Help me talk to him."

Today was not the time for it. "Come to my house tomorrow, Roderigo. No, no, come *Monday*, after my work. Then we'll talk about it. Today I have important business of my own."

Roderigo came close, put a hand on Lupe's shoulder, partly for friendship, partly to steady himself. He breathed his contaminated breath into Lupe's face as he said, "Oh I know, maestro-Tacho has come home. I know, yes. Then I'll come Monday. And I'll pray that until then my son is not put in jail."

Lupe hurried on, only greeting and waving to those he could not avoid, and to those only briefly. At the little store in the doorway of Senora Santos, whose son Guillermo worked as a peon at the Kriboom fortress, he bought two packs of Toro Bravo cigarettes; but then had to suffer through the nosey Senora Santos' wishing him well seeing Tacho again that afternoon. Yes, it seemed that everyone knew everything.

He stopped at the open doors of the iglesia, the bright daylight illuminating everything inside, where only four or five alone there prayed. The great painting of the Virgin hung upon the wall behind the altar, perpetually blessing all the humble citizens of the barrio. Lupe hesitated, wanting not to encounter Padre Morelia, who would be friendly but who might also want to make comments about Lupe's very rare visits to the iglesia. Not seeing the padre, just as he had expected not to see him this time of day, Lupe entered. He took a breath to relax himself, to breathe in the holy air, that it might stabilize him, invigorate him, make him worthy.

He walked silently to the nearest row of seats, kneeled and crossed himself, then sat. And waited. With eyes closed. And eyes opened. He stared at the compassionate Virgin, who loved all sinners. Even great sinners. He waited for momentous words to arise in him, that he might express and plead his case eloquently. He had a great desire to express and plead. He waited. But no great words came to him. Until he began to feel himself unworthy even of a good man's prayer.

No, this was not making him feel better. He crossed himself again. He uttered silently a simple prayer that he be forgiven those old crimes against his family, that he be no longer tormented at night by the bad dreams of recent weeks, and that Tacho might forgive him and accept him as a father again. That would have to be prayer enough. He crossed himself. He stood and stepped into the aisle where he kneeled and crossed himself again. Then he walked out and away from the iglesia, feeling no better or worse. Lupe reflected that it must be as the padre had since long ago warned the congregation-the Virgin cannot be used to satisfy personal desires.

Yet when he turned the latch of his own front gate and stepped inside, when he heard the musica and the loud laughing voices, he knew Gloria, who always came to him, and Marcos, who'd been through all of it with him, and sister Magdalena-they would be there for him. As would be his fellow maestros, several of whom were Romeros, but who had stood by him in spite of that. And hopefully the senor and the senora would be there. That might be enough.

Lupe stopped, stealthy as an intruder, and looked into the yard. He saw Old Marcos pass by; he saw Gloria's friend Isabel sitting primly in a chair listening to someone Lupe could not see. The musica was from a radio in the main house, the obnoxious rock and roll that meant the young ones were inside controlling the musica, when he himself had planned for the mariachis. With the musica was probably where Tacho would be, with all the cousins. Lupe realized that the yard then might be for the moment a safe-zone where he could settle a moment with his allies, have a last cigarette, and then...then face whatever would happen.

He peeked his head around the corner. No senor and senora. Que lastima. But Marcos was there, poking in the adobe oven at the birria. His father, Old Marcos beside him, was telling his son that the birria had been in there more than enough time. Two card tables stood near them, with paper plates and plastic cups and double liters of Fanta and Coke. A bowl of guacamole, another of the fried frijoles. Old Jesus sat across the yard in one of a dozen white plastic chairs that had been set out. Jesus saw Lupe and grinned and lifted a plastic cup that Lupe knew would be half tequila, half agua mineral, toasting him. Five others who had lived on his block of Obregon all their lives now occupied five other white chairs, and as each one saw Lupe advance a few steps further into the yard, they called out to him.

Gloria, who had returned to sit beside Isabel, heard this and looked at him and smiled. "Oh Lupe, you're late for your own party. Tacho's inside."

Marcos also looked at him, and grinned to see the terror in his face. He called out. "Have a tequila, hombre. Or a little mota, that's what you need." None of them could see what bad jokes these were. He walked to Gloria, who hugged him well, just what he needed, and she spoke intimately to him. "He's *such* a handsome boy, Lupe." He stood free of her, tried to smile what good news that was as he opened the new pack of Toros and lit one nervously with a lighter Isabel handed him. Gloria leaned close again and said, "Let me take you in the house. It will be worse the longer you wait. He's happy to be here, he'll be happy to see you"

45

He let her lead him forward as he quickly practiced his smile of recognition, but he knew it was a bad smile and only made him feel even worse. Passing through the door he heard young voices. He looked with rapidly rising alarm at the three seated on the sofa-no, not these-he knew these faces. He continued on behind Gloria, smoking, smoking, toward the kitchen, toward the loudest voices, seeing over Gloria's shoulder Antonio, Porfirio, David, Rafael-and then the face that didn't belong with these, indeed a handsome boy, the handsomest of all-such a smile!-making them all laugh at his joke. Lupe stopped walking, but couldn't stop staring. Eventually he saw the ash of his cigarette ready to fall and he looked about him for an ashtray, even as he realized how foolish in everything he seemed now. Gloria mercifully took the cigarette from his fingers and nudged him forward. The young ones stopped talking.

Tacho stood several inches taller than his father, in fine clothes that could not be found in the village stores. His hair he'd combed straight back, and the dark eyes sparkled. The face was just as Lupe remembered it. Yet Tacho was a man. With all the memories of the boy.

Lupe became rigid in the unbearable silence that ensued. It seemed he could not move or speak. Someone said something. Someone laughed. Then as if he were watching from faraway he was aware that Tacho and he somehow stood together, embraced awkwardly, said something to each other, and then stepped apart, both continuing to look at the other, both seeing a great mystery. Then each one laughed self-consciously the same moment, and then each looked away from the other.

Lupe saw them all in his kitchen. The five young men all leaned against the sink counter, three of them drinking Corona cervezas. Seated at the kitchen table was Maria Perez, Porfirio's merry wife. There was the gas stove. The refrigerator. Gloria standing beside him. All as it always was. And yet there was Tacho too.

Tacho said how he was, how he liked the village now. Lupe said how he was, how things were going. Yet after these first words were spoken Lupe remembered nothing they had said, nor could he imagine any new words to speak.

Then he heard the voice of the senora Carlotta outside: joy rose in his throat, for it was as if the Virgin herself had come to save him from this strangulation of manners.

The senora Carlotta and the senor Max entered the kitchen and with great relief Lupe stepped back to allow them all the attention. The senora had dressed for a special occasion, a long floral dress of deep, dark colors, a short sleeved blouse in bright blue, her pretty, long auburn hair, and that fine smile. The senor dressed plainly, in his usual levis, though these were freshly clean, and in a white, loose, cotton summer shirt buttoned down the front. As always he wore his naked Y-thong huaraches, which made his feet look like they had no shoes at all.

The senora briefly embraced Lupe, then turned to the young men, knowing that the only one she didn't recognize must be Tacho. She moved toward him, extending her hand as Lupe spoke in Spanish to both her and his son, "This is my son Tacho. This is the Senora Carlotta. And the Senor Max."

The senora had perceived that Tacho's English was perfect, so as all three shook hands she said in that language, "Your father's told us a lot about you. I hope you decide to stay. How have you liked it in California? That's where Max and I are from." This conversation seemed to put Tacho more at his ease too. Perhaps it was–who knew?–that Tacho in California spoke more English than Spanish; perhaps he had become more comfortable with gringos than with his own people of the village; though he seemed very relaxed and happy with his cousins and old friends. Perhaps it was only the old demon father that made him awkward, uncomfortable. Lupe took another Toro from the pack and lit it, as he did so retreating a little more toward the obscurity and comfort of the doorframe, where he leaned and smoked and watched.

The senora seemed to be asking Tacho about life in California, how he had learned English so well. Tacho said, "I went to American schools. I was two years at a junior college. I have been learning carpentry. But my cousins have been writing me and telling me that I should come back and see what the village is like now; that there are many new opportunities. Oh I like many things about California. The money's good...but life can be hard. For *us*. And America's not for everyone. You know my cousins?" He turned his head to indicate those beside him, two of them Romeros.

"Yes," the senora said, "they work for us. For your father."

Max came to stand next to Lupe, but he spoke privately to his friend. "How goes it, maestro?"

Lupe looked at him. He tried to smile, but it faded quickly. "Mas o menos, senor." But Lupe could speak no more; instead he looked again to his son, who was saying to the senora, "My cousins tell me you're building unusual houses."

"Oh yes!" she laughed, and it gave Lupe a brief happiness that she could laugh about the fortress monstrosity of the diablo Kriboom. "You should come see it. You should come see our other houses too–the first one we built in Chula Vista, and the other one we started two weeks ago down the hill from the fortress. Your father's our chief maestro. We could do nothing without him."

This was very good of the senora to say but it embarrassed Lupe, and he stepped back into the deeper shadow of the doorway; though first he glanced to see his son's reaction, who was even then looking at him, a littlest smile showing. Tacho turned his eyes away when they met his father's.

"Yes," Tacho said, "I'd like to see all your houses before I go back next week."

The senora said, "It must be good to come back home." An innocent comment, yes, but it pained Lupe to hear it. As he saw Tacho's eyes flicker away from the senora he knew it was not an innocent question for Tacho either. His son seemed unable or unwilling to reply. That was well, for both son and father.

No doubt to divert Lupe and relieve him, the senor said to him, "I see you've laid new tile on your sink counter, maestro. Very nice." Magdalena kept it gleaming, a lustrous blue cobalto.

"Yes," Lupe replied, "poco a poco." But now he wished he'd done more, wished he'd retiled the floor too, all the floors. Removed the wall separating the dining room from the living room. Made windows bigger. Repainted everything. Added the room upstairs. That it might be a new house to Tacho. That it might bring back none of the old memories.

Marcos entered the kitchen, carrying a bottle of Corona. He saw Lupe and came to stand beside him and the senor. He winked and grinned. "Just like old times–eh, Lupe?" Another bad joke. But perhaps this would all be nothing but that, many bad jokes. Lupe could smell the beer and the mota as well on Marcos' breath. There would be no stopping any of them.

The senora was saying, "Well if you decided to come back permanently, Tacho, I know we could offer you a job. Your English is perfect. I'm sure you must drive. You could help us *very* much. You could work with your father. We'd pay you well."

Marcos laughed and spoke in Spanish to the Romeros what the senora had said. They laughed too, and Lupe stepped back further into the shadow of the hallway.

No doubt it was a surprise to the senora that Tacho showed not appreciation for her generous offer, but a frown. "That wouldn't be possible, senora, though it's very kind of you to offer. But even if I wanted to, my family would object. Very much. My mother's family."

Marcos said to the senora in English, "An explosive subject, Carlotta."

Carlos Romero grinned slyly and said in Spanish to Tacho, "You could do it and not tell your mother. We would keep a secret."

Unobserved by Lupe, Felipe Romero, brother to Carlos, had also come into the kitchen and he spoke loudly before Lupe had noticed him. He was obviously well loosened with tequila. He'd heard his nephew, and he had laughed like the others and now said, "You would never keep a secret from *our* father though. We told Lupe we would protect him. But we didn't mean we'd protect him from *Abuelo*." They all laughed.

Lupe would like to have strangled all of them. This was supposed to be a party for re-acquainting. Not to stir up all these conflicts and to make bad jokes. Tacho had become somber, he was not enjoying this either.

The senora tried to untangle this, saying to Tacho, "It couldn't be bad if you worked for our company. It might even help your family feel better about your father. He's a good man. He's helped *us* very much. We couldn't have done *anything* without him. He's *so* very good with the men, and supervising the jobs."

But all this praise, even from the senora, was too much. Lupe needed no one to plead for him. He felt all his frustration and anger burst out of him. "These are bad jokes and bad gossip. You all know that. Perhaps even Tacho knows that. I have had nothing to drink for eleven years. I have paid for my mistakes."

But Tacho seemed not moved by these words. He spoke to his father in Spanish, looking intently at him. "Who is to say when mistakes are paid for? It is not just my mother and my grandfather who have bad memories. I have bad memories too. This house has many bad memories for me, even now. And my brothers and sisters, they also remember terrible times, when the fighting made them cry. It would be a great insult to my mother, and to my grandfather, if I were to disobey their wishes and work for you."

Now the anger and determination no longer showed in Lupe's face, only a misery he could not speak of. He turned away and left the room.

If Lupe were not host, but a guest, he would go far away and leave them all to their party. Instead he retreated to the bathroom and sat there with the door locked and smoked two more Toros. But what else had he expected? In the last weeks he had imagined worse than this. Though it hurt Lupe to admit, Tacho had a right to say these things; and worse. Lupe could not be a coward. He would have to take the blows and stand strong and wait. If anything good were ever to come of this it would take time. Poco a poco.

He went out the rear door and walked back around to the yard where Claudio had just laid the great slabs of birria on the table and was unwinding the wire that held the now charred maguey cactus leaves around the joints of veal and goat. As he did so a great bloom of steam rose off the meat he knew would be more juicy and succulent than any. The senor and the senora stood beside Marcos, who was explaining how this birria was so long marinated, and then wrapped so, and then cooked all day in this dome of an adobe oven he and Lupe had constructed eight years ago.

Lupe went to them and lit another cigarette. The senor put a hand on his shoulder, meant no doubt to console him. The senor congratulated him on the fabulous birria, which sin duda it was. However, Lupe moved so that the senor would have to remove his arm, for Lupe would not be consoled. Lupe watched the meat juice running out the tortilla over the senor's hand. The senor should be using both hands to eat this anyway.

The senor leaned to him and whispered in Spanish, the language they always conversed in. "I hope you're not setting a bad example with your cigarettes, maestro." And Lupe looked to him without enjoying the joke and said, "Already they all have enough bad examples. And anyway they don't take examples from old fathers. Some of them don't take anything from their fathers." Immediately he regretted saying that; so he added, "I thank you and the senora for saying all those kind things about me. But no need to worry–all this will settle itself in time. I am sure of it."

The senor nodded that he was sure of that also. Then he said, "When you have an opportunity, maestro, you might say this to Tacho, that the senora and I have decided that when we finish the two houses we're working on, we're going to have a big fiesta, and we're going to have a profit sharing with all the workers."

Lupe did not understand the phrase. The senor explained it. But this puzzled him even more. "Senor, with respect, but I do not think there will be a profit with this Kriboom house. I am even fearing that you will lose much money. What will be to share?"

The senor laughed, such a strange sense of humor. "No doubt you're right, maestro. But we will make something from the second house, even though perhaps I did not charge the new client as much as I should have. But we are also I believe selling another property next week, and signing a contract for another house that we'll build on it. There'll be a down payment. Yes, things are bad with the fortress, but Carlotta and I are confident that they will improve, that there will be profits. Eventually. In any case we have a cash flow."

This needed to be explained as well. Most curious. A river of money. That may or may not belong to him, but from which he could partake. Only the gringos would have such a thing as this. Lupe could not dispute it, for all he knew was the paycheck, and buying things. Until twenty-five years ago, in the village it was all trading; no one *had* money.

The senor continued. "Anyway, maestro, it is our problem to solve. But Carlotta and I both want this very much, for the men to be part of the company, to share in the profits. We have talked about it a long time. So when we finish the Kriboom house and the other–even if there are *no* profits–we will have our fiesta and our profit sharing. Some money. At least two weeks' pay, for all the men. Carlotta and I want this very much. You may tell the men if you wish. And you may tell Tacho."

This was good news indeed. Neither he nor any of the men had ever heard of such a thing, this sharing of profits. And even when there were no profits. Ay caray. It was a mystery he could still in no way comprehend.

The senor and the senora stayed until the twilight. He drank several Dos Equis and she sangria and they ate the birria both veal and goat until they couldn't eat more. Lupe took the radio from the young ones in the kitchen and with a long cord brought it outside and played the mariachis and many danced. Lupe and Gloria, and Lupe and the senora, sister Magdalena with the senor, who flirted shamelessly with her. Then the senor and senora, and maestros Felipe Romero and Lupe's brother Polin each with their wives when the musica was slow. Rafael, half deaf, half intelligible, but always smiling, danced continually with the wives and girlfriends of all their shy husbands and boyfriends.

When the senor and the senora came to say farewell, Lupe asked them if they would come greet his old mother before they left. He led them back into the house and down a hallway to a back bedroom where Lupe eased open the door already ajar. He stood aside for them to pass in ahead of him.

The room was small, a dresser with three drawers and upon it small boxes of carved wood and of pasteboard and a blue opaque bottle of lotion and a picture of the Guadalupe Virgin above the dresser. A dark wooden chair without upholstery rested beside it against the wall.

Lupe passed silently to a single bed beneath a curtained window whereupon lay on her side a curled and perhaps sleeping figure. A pale blue embroidered cotton covered to her chin. Skeletal fingers beside it clutched the cover's shiny blue hemmed border. Her long hair was fine, mixed gray and white. It lay sweeping back across the parchment skin of her dark face and across the white pillow in a way that made her hair seem as if an ethereal wind were blowing through it, and that she herself were in some inconceivable way, eyes closed, in silent flight toward the mysterious source of it.

Lupe knelt to her level and spoke beside her ear what was little more than a whisper. "Mama, it's Lupe. I see you're awake. I would like to present you my friends, Max and Carlotta. They're here beside me." He looked up to them and motioned with his head for them to come nearer. "She's blind," he said softly. "And she has almost ninety years. But she understands well sometimes."

The gaunt lady of so many years with some effort turned her deepset and never opening eyes toward her son, and seemed to smile. She lifted her hand of bones a few inches off the blanket and held it there until Carlotta first reached down to take it and say in Spanish, "So good to meet you, senora. You have a wonderful son. He's been very *very* good to us." This old woman may have smiled again. The young senora let go her hand and stepped back, with difficulty containing her emotion. The senor moved forward and took up the weightless hand and said to her, "Mucho gusto, senora. It is an honor to meet you. Thank you for having us in your home. Your grandson Tacho is a beautiful boy too." She nodded her head, though she hardly moved it where it lay on the pillow. The senor laid her hand back where it had been and indicated to Lupe that they would leave her to rest, and all three departed the room.

A few hours later the party had become only old Jesus drunk and asleep still in his same white chair and the young ones all gone to the plaza. Lupe and Magdalena alone were left to gather all the used paper and plastic into garbage bags, store the remaining birria and beans in the refrigerator, and return the borrowed plastic chairs to the neighbors who owned them. Twilight had settled upon the barrio and the darkening sky over the hills across the lake assured rain.

Lupe had smoked all but four of the Toros, and he decided to leave those in the house. He put on his light jacket and he told Magdalena that he was going for a walk on the beach. But when he stepped outside onto the broken sidewalk of Obregon, he saw Marcos, who had gone away earlier with the young men, walking alone now toward him.

"Hey, where you going, hombre?"

"For a walk. Down to the lake. Where are you going?"

Marcos had the impish look of being high on the mota. "I came back to see you, como no?" He looked above, then said, "You're going to get wet."

Lupe knew it. There might even be comfort in it. "It's no matter." Both stopped walking, facing each other.

Marcos grinned. "No matter to me either. Mind if I go with you?"

"No, I don't mind." Marcos turned beside him and they both walked in silence down Obregon. They walked past the placita of Six Corners, and on between the columns of poplars that grew on either side of Obregon for two more blocks, and then no more, as Calle Obregon was no more. Thereafter they walked only a dirt lane bisecting wire-enclosed pastures for cows, then made a quick descent through an arroyo and up the other side, and suddenly onto the beach that was barren sand and here and there scrawny brushweed, some of them man-tall. Yet no water to be seen, for in recent years the lake had abandoned the beach and now broke in little waves upon a faroff beach a hundred meters distant. In the profound quiet of the evening Lupe and Marcos could hear the faraway waves breaking, though the view of them was obscured by fields of knee-high corn that had been planted on the former beach and lake bed by neighbors and vagrants.

They turned left, toward the pueblo, walking still in silence, past the beachfields of corn. Past those finally, they could see everywhere out there a whitecapped procession of small wavecrests moving toward them, urged on by the still soft winds that were prelude to the nightly rains of summer.

By then, though they had spoken nothing since passing the placita, Marcos knew where Lupe was headed. The two palms and the galeana tree at the old beach crest had been their haunt in the old days, when Lupe was king of the Lobos Solos; though everyone else in the barrio called them the Lobos Borrachos, or the Lobos Locos.

They stopped walking when they arrived at the spot, and before they sat, Lupe stared for a moment at the faraway whitecaps so bright in the shine of the overhead half Moon. "I haven't come here in a long time," he finally said. "I have hated this place. I once vowed I would never go to it again." He leaned his open hand against the rough trunk of the tall fan palm as if feeling it, remembering it. He looked at its twin only three meters distant from it. This was their station, between these two, where the Lobos Solos had made their daily drunk. A hammock could be strung between the palms, and sometimes had been. Eventually they came to see how dangerous this was, since all of them at least one time, sleeping, had fallen out of the hammock in the drunkest of the afternoons.

Twenty meters further up the beach were the adobe ruins that had been the home and sales depot of Tomas Ruiz. It was because of this man's inexhaustible and cheap supply of homemade diablo blanco pulque that the Lobos Solos had chosen this campground between palm trees in the first place. Ruiz' tin roof had long since been dismantled and taken for other uses. The doors and windows had been removed. Many slabs of adobe had fallen from the top of walls. Vagrants sometimes now camped here; though none were there tonight.

"You knew that Ruiz died last February, amigo? Amazing he lived so long."

Lupe stared at the ruins. "No, I didn't hear that. Then it means that only your father and I are still alive, among the Lobos. We counted Ruiz as a Lobo of course."

"Of course."

Lupe could still name all of them, could still see their faces. He shivered.

The great galeana tree seemed to have grown twice its former size, its branches reaching now almost to the highest palm tree. The fiery orange flowers were in full profusion, cupped skyward, and the deepening twilight only slightly obscured their brilliance. Hundreds of fallen petals lay beneath the tree, faded from their perfect bloom of color and forming on the sand beneath it the exact shape of the galeana's great branching: as if a ghost tree, drained of its bright color, were being mirrored there on the sand in a two dimensional world.

Marcos said, "Want to sit down?"

Lupe looked about him. "No. That wouldn't be right. It would be too much. For me. You sit if you wish." But Marcos remained standing. They watched the first lightning show itself in the densest darkness of sky faraway. It would come, steadily, relentlessly.

"I am having bad dreams, Marcos. I am dreaming of this, where we spent all our days, where every day we drank ourselves stupid. Into oblivion."

Marcos laughed. He had been of the younger generation. They had drunk, but not like the Lobos. They had preferred the mota. And during most of the Lobos' wild years Marcos had been living in Los Angeles, learning his electrician's trade. But he had heard all the stories from his father, who still laughed about them even today. He'd heard some stories from Lupe, but there had never been laughing when Lupe told his stories.

"Forgive me, Lupe, I know this is not funny to you."

"No, not funny. And especially the dreams are not funny. I have always remembered most of our stupidities on the beach here. Yes, many of those I might still think of as funny. It is what happened when I went home that I have never remembered well."

"Como no, maestro. You were most often carried home. As all the Lobos were."

"Yes, I admit it. But of course I heard it from everyone the next day—what a barbarian I had been when I woke up late at night. Yes, I have had everyone to remind me. Marlena the foremost. My closest neighbors. In honesty, I thought most of what they told me was exaggeration."

"Oh no-you were The Great Warrior."

Lupe flinched hearing that name again. Hearing it in this place. But he spoke the name again, good to feel the stripes on his back tonight. "Yes, The Great Warrior. The Great Warrior. You know I always said I remembered nothing of those nights when I came to and began yelling and demanding and terrorizing my family. And I swear it was true. I swear, for all these years, I remembered none of that. But these dreams, they are suddenly haunting me now–they are terrible–I see myself waking from my drunkenness, screaming, cursing, frightening my children, frightening Marlena. I see myself breaking things, yelling terrible things. Even striking her. I struck her. May God forgive me."

Though these revelations were new to him, the sorrow of the man was not, and Marcos could only stand by him silently; until he was moved finally to say, "I am sure he has, Lupe."

But Lupe would accept nothing so cheaply won. "No, he has not. I will know when he has."

The darkest density of rain clouds was now passing over the lake and the lightning flashed explosively in multitudinous forks toward the lake. Other long jagged forkings blazed parallel to the lake and lit up the turbulent underbelly of storm clouds and the seething whitecaps and the stark beach these two small figures stood upon. The many fanned fronds of the palms high above waved wildly as if to signal surrender. Every sudden great thundering shook the ground beneath their feet. The same moment they felt the storm winds gusting into them, they felt the first pelts of rain in the face.

"Caray amigo!" yelled Marcos. "Enough of this–let's get going!" And he turned and started trotting away, pulling his own jacket up to cover his head.

But Lupe did not move. He called to him. "No, you go ahead. I'm staying a little longer." But by then Marcos had disappeared running.

Lupe stood there facing the rain, feeling it stream into his face and chest and thighs. In seconds water was running down his face. His shirt and pants were soaked and still he stood there, letting it come, letting it wash over him, letting it cover him, wishing it could be a flood.

5 MAX AND EL DIABLO

Max drove with Lupe to the diablo Kriboom's palace with little hope and none of their usual jokes. A cloud of doom had shadowed Max since he'd woken, but in truth it had been looming larger for months. Lupe knew it too, the danger, not to either of them personally, but to la compania, which was all of them, everyone.

These two warriors arrived in Carlotta's eighty Chevy pickup, both in huaraches, the senor in levis and tee shirt, Lupe in clean pants, clean short-sleeved shirt. These two brothers in arms parked before the tall steelrib gates, which were wrought like a great shield, black and impenetrable, spikes crowning it at the apex. Beyond the gates, on the roof of this tall, sleek white palace were three byzantine cupolas, each a different size, each tiled in glossy black.

More prominently even that these however, beside the wide canopied entrance, rose the tower of glass block eight meters tall: in the daytime flooding the three floors of staircase with sunlight, and in the night the tower's light shining out brighter than a Hollywood theatric upon that rural Mexican hillside, where only one other house further up the hill would see it.

Otherwise the palace seemed stark and stern, ruled by Nordic straight lines and tall ceilings. Even so arches had been designed by Senorita Tovar in all the many windows, and arches shaped the overhang of three tiers of balconies facing the lake from this spectacular vantage. By the master's order the floors and bathrooms were white marble with black marble accents and black marble countertops, even in the kitchen. The Scandanavian furniture and cabinets were also black and white. The stove, refrigerator and other appliances were black. Max knew every square inch of the palace well. Lupe knew it better. And both cursed the diablo. Max pressed the buzzer.

Kriboom came out the front door, warden of his fortress, seen by them through the gate's bars strolling in camouflage military jumpsuit toward his visitors. He sported a Florida Marlins baseball cap for the fun, smoking his cigar, his eyelids only a slit apart, assessing them. He smiled for Lupe alone. "Maestro, buenos dia. Como es?"

This was new with Kriboom, these little words of Spanish. Lupe and Max both knew this was likely the extent of his vocabulary. Lupe, a courteous man, smiled in return, but his smile today was no more geniune that the Kriboom's. Lupe responded to him in rapid Spanish, gradually turning toward Max as he spoke, "So this means the bastard wants to be friends now?" Max enjoyed the joke immensely, though he could not afford, for battle-readiness, to give himself completely to it.

Today there would be no need for the small talk. Max extended to Kriboom through the bars a white envelope. Kriboom took it. He carefully fingered open the seal while he kept his eyes on Max, seeming to smile as he did so. He pulled forth the folded sheet, then held it in one hand as he mashed the envelope into his pants pocket with the other hand. Then with both hands he unfolded the sheet and held it up carefully, like a judge of old, so his sharp eyes could examine it.

There were eleven itemizations to consider, none of them a surprise to Kriboom. He'd seen a couple of shorter versions of the list in the last six months. Both times he'd sent Max away with hope, but certainly also with anxiety, for no money on this bill had he paid his contractor.

Kriboom stopped reading. He lowered the letter so he could squint directly into Max's eyes through the black bars of the gate, and he said, "This is a pretty fancy bottom line, Max. Twenty-three thousand dollars."

"It's all itemized," said Max coldly, who'd expected every possible deflection and confusion. "What could you not agree with? We've been talking about this extras bill for months, all the while we've been doing the work."

"Y siempre pidiendo mas," Lupe added, for the senor to remind the diablo. The senor concurred and felt he should repeat his maestro's observation. "Yes, and you've kept adding on extras constantly."

"Yes," Kriboom said, well prepared for the accusation. "As long as we're doing it, we might as well make it just right. Don't you think?"

Max said, "That depends on whether I get paid or not."

Kriboom smiled. Not because he was having it his way, for he was already assured of the outcome of this skirmish. No, he smiled because he enjoyed the resistance, enjoyed this striking back of his prey, the more fiercely the better. But it was a pathetic resistance, the foolish adversary not yet realizing how it must end.

Kriboom grinned. He raised the unfolded invoice close before his eyes again and seemed to be studying it minutely. Then he turned the sheet toward Max and pointed to the top line. "This I don't agree with. Eight thousand dollars for the glass block tower."

Max was truly surprised. "What? You don't agree with the figure? Eight thousand? Christ—there's nearly two thousand glass blocks in that thing. Those alone are more than half the cost."

"Oh no," said Kriboom in a voice that seemed meant to reassure, though that was hardly its intention, for he continued, "No, it's not the *figure*. I mean I don't agree with *the item*. I mean, I say I don't owe you *anything* for it."

Max was stunned. "How could you possibly not think you owed me for this? You know it's not in the plans."

Kriboom nodded smugly. "That depends on who you ask. You say the plans show a couple of windows in the stairwell tower. I read it that the plans call for glass block to be used for the entire structure. And that *is* how we built it—am I right?"

Max could feel it slipping away. Knowing not what other appeal to make, he said, "The architect will agree with *me*. I can take you to court and the *judge* would agree with me *and* the architect. He'll say you owe me the money."

Kriboom knew well that when the talk resorted to courts and judges, his strangling victim had now seen the inevitability of his fate, and was making a little death rattle imagining lawsuits and judgments. Still, the assassin might be able to prolong the death agonies with a little last taunting.

"We'll certainly come back to that in a moment. But first..." Kriboom turned his attention back to the document. "These extra meters, for the extra balconies, you say one hundred seventy meters...hmmm...nine thousand six hundred. That's way overpriced."

Max began to see his opponent's strategy. "Wait a minute. You gave me your word you'd pay me. You and I have more or less agreed on this a long time ago."

Kriboom laughed, heartily, waving his cigar between them. "Oh that's a good one, Mr. Max. So I guess we have a, *more or less* agreement then, don't we? But wait—there must be something on paper—*isn't there? Something?*" He suspended his laugh to await the further amusement of Max's response.

An ill wind gusted through Max's mind. Paper? *On* paper? What was this jerk talking about? Did he really think it would come down to some stupid thing like that. They had agreed. Had talked about it. Had argued over it. And had, more or less, agreed. Despite that peptalk to himself, Max spoke with less conviction. "You told me every time we've talked about these bills that you would pay me when the last of the extras was done."

"On no, Max!" cried out Kriboom with gusto. "Oh I never said *pay*." *Oh no!* I said I would *settle* the account. I *said* settle. You *imagined* I said pay. No, I said *settle*. Always *settle*. And I'm true to my word, for you and I are standing here now, and for the first time, we are *settling* our account."

"So then why do you ask what I have on paper?"

Kriboom seemed to be amiably helping him to a solution. "Why Mr. Max, for when you go to court against me, as you just said you must. You'll need papers. Signed papers. Between *us*. A contract for extras."

Even as Kriboom knew it would be, at that moment Max felt himself deluged by a mighty and unexpected wave, even though it was in fact the same dark cloud under which he had awoken that morning, now fully come to term, bursting its floodgates.

Max raised a feeble protest against the great force submerging him. "Kriboom, after all this time, after all the work my men have put in, you can't just tell me that you owe me *nothing* for all these extras."

Kriboom moderated a laugh that even he decided would be too cruel. "Oh Mr. Max. It's time to be realistic, and stop playing these games. Your other big extras, the fancy pump house for the pool, that fancy fish design your men so *slowly* laid on the bottom of the pool, and the moonwalk along the side of the house—it looks like they come to something like six, seven thousand. Yes—I contest those too. I claim that these were included in the original price. Believe me, I've talked to lawyers. Law suits? *Please!* We'd be going back and forth in the Mexican courts for *years*."

Then Kriboom seemed to have had enough of the play. "Look, Max, I shouldn't have to tell you this *again*, but you went on my shit list the day you started fucking with our deadlines. Remember that?" Max refused to answer, though he remembered it well. "You were two months late finishing that house, and that pissed me off. I told you it would. And I told you I'd make you pay for it."

Max began half-heartedly to protest again that the unforeseen fortress foundation had made the delay inevitable, but Kriboom stopped him. "No, no, I've heard that excuse before. I don't accept excuses. You gave me your word and you didn't keep it, so you get the consequences. The truth is—and I told you this before too—your men are slow as hell and *you* don't know how to make them haul ass. The other truth is, that I spent a *lotta* time watching over everything, making sure you did it right, trying to hurry this project along. For all the good it did me. I feel like you owe *me* something for *my* supervising."

Kriboom hesitated a moment, and Max felt the surge of anger burn in his face. And though Lupe could decipher few of these words the diablo spoke, he understood well their meaning. Lupe spoke a curse upon the man and his house, and Kriboom comprehended that he'd been cursed, though he knew not the specifics of it. Still it was nothing to him.

And he had more to say. "Now you don't have to go away empty-handed, Mr. Max. I'm not as completely heartless as you think. These last couple of items, the enclosure of the storage room over there, and the installation of the remote control gate opener—I accept those. I'll pay for that. It looks like it comes to seven hundred twenty dollars. Fair enough. I'll send you a check in the mail tomorrow."

Hopelessness and desperation now boiled his blood, made his head giddy with a sudden lack of oxygen, while his rage poisoned every cell of his brain. Max clinched the black bars of the gates with each hand and leaned forward till his hot face nearly touched the cold steel. "I know you think you've beaten me, Kriboom. But I've created something fabulous for you here. Some people believe it's a work of art. A monument even. And this house will still be here long after you've gone, and no one will remember you, but they will remember Bellacasa."

But those harsh and vainglorious words seemed only to amuse him, for Kriboom smiled again. "If that's the consolation you want, you're welcome to it. But hey!—there's a lesson to be learned here too. For you that is. I'm sure you'll figure it out. And when you do, you'll see that I've been a good teacher. You made a lot of mistakes working with me. I bet you're remembering a lot of them now. But hey!—that was to be expected, wasn't it? Only your first or second house? So stop whining, take your medicine. Learn your lessons. You're a smart guy, I bet you already know you won't make most of these mistakes again. Am I right? Sure I am. A little ways down the road you'll look back on all this and thank me. Sure I'm a tough teacher, and my lessons are expensive. But that's true of all the good teachers, isn't it, mister artist?"

Max could only glare at him through the iron bars. Kriboom then looked at Lupe and said clumsily, "Pero buen casa, maestro. Buen traba joe. Mi gusta. Si, buen casa."

Lupe, as angry as his patron, stared back at Kriboom and spoke bitterly in Spanish. "You son-of-a-bitch are the biggest gringo bastard I've ever known." Lupe hesitated and seemed to snarl, wanting to be certain that this diablo understood him perfectly, though he would understand none of his words. "Curses on you! May a watersnake one day soon come out of the lake and drown your house and wash it away."

Max drove Lupe to his house on Obregon. They talked little and had little heart for any of it. All the anger at Kriboom still rumbled turbulently inside Max. He needed a little relief. A little glass of wine with Malcolm, though it was mid-afternoon and the little glass of wine, or two, would demolish the rest of the day and he would thereafter only be good for an early dinner out and then bed. But that was about all the rest of the day would be worth anyway.

Max parked the blue Chevy pickup at the curb in front of Malcolm's apartment. The door at the sidewalk was opened, as most often it was in the daytime. Stepping inside, Max smelled peanut oil and heard Malcolm in the kitchen chopping at the cutting board. He called out, and was called back to in Malcolm's merry voice. Max went through the garage that Malcolm had converted to a weight room, and went into the kitchen. Malcolm looked up from his chopping block and smiled.

"Right on time, compadre. I'm just finished up here and was wondering what kind of excuse I'd have to pour an early glass of wine for myself."

Turning off the pot of rice, Malcolm put the onions and peppers and tomatoes into the wok atop the gas stove, then turned the fire down to its lowest and set the lid on the wok. He took up an already uncorked bottle of red wine from the counter and two water glasses and led the way out onto the patio, where a black wrought iron table supported a round glass top, which had hosted hundreds of such afternoons in the nine years Malcolm had lived in this apartment; until last year, hostessed by a wife, since departed forever to California, leaving Malcolm to host his callers as the village bachelor in residence.

Through the afternoon they sipped their wine, a second bottle opened and brought forth to fuel the lament of Max's conversation and the gentle humor and witty consolation of host Malcolm. Some two or three or who knew how many hours later, Max was not completely consoled, but he was in far better humor than when he'd arrived. He was vaguely aware that Carlotta was probably home by now, not wondering where he would be, but only how long he would be there.

As he came outside he was more inebriated than he had perceived himself when sitting at the table underneath the orange tree. Fortunately it was not a long drive home. He removed the key ring from his pocket as he stood at the sidewalk and looked where he thought he had parked the pickup. He didn't see it there. He blamed his alcohol-glazed brain. He looked around the corner, where he sometimes parked; but saw the truck not there either. He went back to the original spot and of course it was still not there. His confusion compounded. He walked a few steps into the cobbled street and looked down both sides of the street, imagining how he could have parked so contrary to his memory. The blue pickup was nowhere to be seen.

Through the dim alcohol fog fuzzing his brain the truth slowly, painfully began to materialize, like a tree might have, looming suddenly, unexpectedly out of a fog in the middle of a road that he was driving, going straight at it, until he must halt his driving right there and look at the sad, undeniable fact of that tree, the horrible truth of it: the truck had been stolen.

By the time Max arrived in Canacinta in the taxi, he was so depressed about the theft he neither felt any longer the wine nor was he remembering the bad news at Kriboom's. The pickup was her baby. She had owned it eleven years and it was intimately entwined in all the important events of those eleven years. She would not have dispossessed herself of it for husband, family, or anything she possessed or ever would have possessed. A new million dollar pickup with zero miles on the odometer would not compensate her.

When he told her she raged and then she cried, and after his initial apologies and sympathies she refused any further consolation from him. Finally she went into the bedroom and put herself to bed without changing clothes and pulled the blankets tightly up around her and might have seemed to have gone into a deep sleep, although Max knew better. He also knew to leave her alone in her grief and mourning. Nor would she have cared that moment to hear about his disastrous conversation with Kriboom. That catastrophe would have to wait till the next morning.

However, when he awoke with a mild hangover and memories of troubled sleep, she was already up and gone. He knew her first action would have been to go to the police station and file the Stolen Vehicle report; though he had little faith in that.

Max called a taxi and rode it to their new office, recently rented. It had been formerly a little house among other low rent residentials, most lived in by poor Mexicans, three blocks upslope from the carretera. Carlotta was there in the back room, at her desk, looking at him when he entered, as gloomy as Max had expected. He said, "Dear, about the truck—"

But she cut him off fiercely. "No! I don't want to talk anymore about that. What about Kriboom?"

No more happy to broach this subject than the other, he could at least recall his frustration and anger of the day before and generate some force into his voice, which otherwise would have none. She had been waiting for his arrival, anxious and bracing herself for bad news. She saw it in his face, so that all his words were not only anticlimax but unnecessary. Nonetheless, she watched him pace and spew it out.

"I'm a fool, Carlotta. And I don't mean just about the money, which is bad enough. But because I trusted that man. Somehow he convinced me that I could trust him. That we didn't need a contract. I had his word. Lupe and I don't need contracts. Marcos and I don't need contracts. When Senor Frances tells me something, I don't need his signature and witnesses." He hesitated, looking at her as she stared out the window, the misery showing in her eyes, which saw nothing of the blue sky or the world beyond, perhaps not even hearing his words.

He paused and she saw that he was only gathering energy for a further rant, and she snapped at him. "Stop it, Max." She shook her head. "I know all that, and I agree with you. But the bottom line is that we're running out of money."

She stared forlornly at him. "Twenty-three thousand dollars, Max. That's a lot of money we don't have now, that we very badly need. And it's not just Kriboom we're losing money on either. I finally finished tallying up all the expenses on the other four houses, and all that is *way* different than we've been thinking. We are *not* making *lots of money*, like we think we are. There are costs we have that somehow I *never* saw as costs, but they sure as hell are. Like making the work day eight hours instead of nine. Like the holidays we give them extra. Remember the World Cup? And days off for the birthdays? That free standing cupola you insisted on doing for Smokey Stover—because you wanted to see what it would look like—cost us a thousand dollars before it was done. You were right—it's fabulous, but we paid for it, not Smokey. Fonzo himself is a cost I never figure in. Your and my gas. The rent on this office. And now we have to buy another pickup. Hidden costs. And suddenly I don't know what the hell the point of any of this is."

He stopped pacing. Perhaps he had found his way to something, however vague or irrelevant it seemed. He looked at her. "You're the only bright spot I see in all this. Thank God I had the good sense to make you come with me."

Usually that would have made her smile, but not today. She spoke the cold truth. "We are running out of money, Max. How are we going to finish the Mariano house?"

But he too had been thinking about this, for days. "One solution is to use the money we set aside to buy our little knoll from Alejandro, to build our own beautiful house. Or we could cancel the profit sharing. That would give us three thousand dollars. That would be a start. I mean, it's really a joke now isn't it? Planning a profit sharing while you're losing money."

He saw her bite her lip, to hold back these grim possibilities which she had also considered. She said, "Honestly I think I would rather give up the knoll than the profit sharing, no matter how stupid it is under the circumstances. And it is stupid. But we already told Lupe that we're having the fiesta on the tenth. We can always get the knoll, Max. But going back on our word about this fiesta would really hurt me. We've talked about this a lot. You ask me what is the point of it? Well, for me, sharing this company with them is one of the main points. We obviously have no money to build ourselves a house now anyway. Even a little one." Then she relaxed the deep tensions in her face, and said, "We can also use the down payment from Mr. Penton to finish the Mariano house."

He'd thought of that too. "Christ, Carlotta, we haven't even *signed* Penton yet. We've haven't even *met* him yet. And I *really* didn't want to have to do that kind of borrowing from the future to pay for the past. Again."

She kept her eyes on him. "No, of course not. But."

He shook his head wearily. "God what a mess!" For the true horror of this borrowing for Max was the fear that they would be doomed to finish every house this way now, with money from the next. Until suddenly there would be no next. And he said, only to himself, his little mantra of consolation: thank God for the cash flow.

She stood and went to him and took his shoulders in her hands and looked warmly into his eyes. "I have an idea. Let's go to Barra de Navidad for a few days. We both need to shake this out of our systems. Get a new look at things."

He brightened. "Well, that sounds good. I *do* need to let go of all this. Cause right now, I really don't know what to do about all this mess."

She would help him to it. "Then let's go tomorrow. I can already see the good it's going to do you. And we'll make a deal, not to talk about any of this until we've had a good rest and have a little more strength for it. OK?"

"What would I do without you? You're definitely wife material."

"Ooo, watch your talk, Mister Max. I'll get you drunk in Barra and you'll wake up with a ring on your finger."

A moment later Fonzo Suarez arrived on foot, having walked two dusty blocks from the bus stop. Dust was still on his polished burgundy shoes, but nowhere else, for Fonzo had been careful to keep his best gray pressed slacks clean of all blemishes. Neither blemished nor wrinkled was the lemony long-sleeved rayon shirt, with white bone buttons. His hair he now parted in the middle, a pleasant surprise for him to find that in doing so the troublesome cowlicks that he had always been pushing out of his eyes, now flopped harmlessly about his ears. His most recent purchase was the shiny black jacket that zipped up the front and showed off an embossed gold medallion on the left pocket.

He came through the gate and entered the house that was an office, without knocking. Max and Carlotta had not heard him at the gate, and both looked up surprised to see him enter the front door. Both were glad for the change of focus.

Fonzo saw them, saw that nothing seemed amiss, and he said, "Those people at Seguro Social really make it hard for you, I see that. I was there two hours just getting the new men listed. I still have to go back Monday. It looks like you'll owe them more money than you thought."

Carlotta spoke another concern. "I'll give that to you in the morning. Will maestro Felipe's wife be able to see the doctor about her stomach trouble this week?"

Fonzo puzzled a moment to recall the detail. "Maybe—but they won't have a number for him for his clinic till Monday, when I go back there."

Carlotta stood and became again La Senora. "Monday's soon enough, thanks. When will everyone on the Wilson job be covered?"

He considered. "Probably within a week. But IMSS said they had to be paid from the day the job started. Oh I almost forgot. Senor Reynoso, at the IMSS, said they'll be coming by the office here once a month now, to collect, personally. He says it's the new policy."

"Oh boy," said Carlotta, rising from the equipale, as if here was another need to defend her position. "That weasel Reynoso. He's another one. I'll damn sure keep an eye on *him*."

6 MAX AND CARLOTTA SHARE PROFIT

Three days later they returned from Barra de Navidad and they met Jim and Marilyn Penton and signed a contract with them the same day. He was a retired Canadian professor with a jolly laugh who talked to Max about books. His diminutive wife Marilyn obviously still idolized the man she'd married thirty years ago. With the down payment check in her pocket, Carlotta felt rejuvenated and confident that la compania had survived Kriboom's perfidy. They would spend two thousand for an upgrade on the stolen pickup he must still not mention. She drove with Fonzo in her van to Banco Ultimo, giving herself up with great pleasure to the preparations for the profit-sharing fiesta.

Enjoying unprecedented prosperity itself, the bank had recently opened a branch in Ajijic, a massive new construction on a midtown corner, facing the carretera. Polished pillars with gilded capitals sustained ten meter ceilings. Floors were ochre-veined marble; mahogany for all the wainscoting, the counters, partitions and desktops and filing cabinets. Handsome young tellers and secretaries in uniformed yellow jackets smiled graciously everywhere, and spoke both Spanish and English flawlessly. The old local branch in Chapala still operated, but it was cramped and drab by comparison.

Greeting the security guard at the entrance, Carlotta led Fonzo inside, where she halted, seeing two long lines of gringos, a fourth of whom she knew to speak to or by name. None of them were impatient, for this being in the bank was as enjoyable for most of them as what they had come from or what yet awaited them at home. Carlotta saw Carioca Cantadora through the plate glass of her president's office hang up the telephone and settle back in her burgundy velveteen chair. Carlotta went directly there. She leaned her head inside and spoke cheerfully. "Are you busy, Carioca? Do you have a minute for me?" Fonzo hovered closely, eyes roving, enchanted by all this opulence.

Carioca smiled the smile none could resist. She was no more than five feet tall, and red hair curled luxuriously upon the shoulders of her white chiffon blouse. Her face was lovely and sweet as any child's. "Of course, of course," she said, gesturing to the chairs before her desk.

Carlotta motioned Fonzo to sit in one as she sat in the other, but Carioca sat only when her guests had. Carlotta laid Jim Penton's check upon the desk. "I'm here to make a deposit. And I also want to make a large withdrawal."

"It would be my pleasure to help you," Carioca said, leaning forward, picking up the check. "Does this mean you've sold another construction contract?"

Carlotta beamed. "Yes it does."

Carioca sat back and smiled her admiration. "I can't tell you how it pleases me that you and Max are doing so well. And in such a short time. It's very remarkable, you know. Many people say so"

That moment Carlotta felt it again, as so often she had felt it in the beginning, that the wind was at their backs. And she knew that Carioca was one of the rare ones she could confide in, who without envy would truly enjoy and bless their success. "Well, I'm also happy to tell you that we're having a profit-sharing party tomorrow on our little street in Rancho del Oro, Privada Rio Bravo, where we've just finished a house for Mr. and Mrs. Lujack. It's a very big day for Max and me. It's something we've looked forward to for a long time."

"Profit-sharing!" said Carioca with surprise. "In our little village! Whoever heard of such a thing? Oh, you'll make it hard for the other builders, you know. All the maestros and peons will only want to work for Bellacasa."

Carlotta smiled proudly. "Well I'll be happy if we can just keep building and making jobs for the men and their families." Then, remembering Fonzo, she said, "Oh, I should introduce you to our new secretary, Fonzo Suarez. You probably know Fonzo's family, from Tamarindo Tamales. Fonzo's been quite a help to us."

Carioca rose again, respecting him as if he were Uncle Sebastian himself, and offered Fonzo her elegant, small hand. "Oh yes, everyone knows the Suarez family. I've met Senor Suarez, your Uncle Sebastian, at two different meetings with the Governor. Both times when he was here to speak at our Save the Lake fundraising. Mucho gusto, Senor Suarez. It seems like your new employers, Carlotta and Max, are being very progressive. What do you think of this profit-sharing?"

Astonished that his opinion could be of any value or curiosity to this distinguished, graceful woman, Fonzo stammered, letting go of her hand. "Oh, well, then, I really don't know." But then he did know, and it flowed. "No, you're right, they are progressive, and that's why I wanted to work for them. To tell you the truth Tamarindo Tamales is not, that, progressive. With all due respect. I would never speak against the company, or against my fine uncle, or anyone in the family. But I guess I have a little different conscience. I wanted to work for a company, a little, more, progressive. Progresivo. With all due respect."

Carioca still smiled, and seemed to believe and admire everything he said. Carlotta said to Carioca, "Max and I have been thinking about putting Fonzo's name down on our account, so he can make the bank runs for us. What would be involved?"

Carioca sat down again when her clients sat down. The bank president said, "Oh it's very simple. You fill out a card, you all sign it. Then Fonzo would have access, either complete, or to whatever extent you would specify. Would you like me to get you a card?"

Carlotta nodded. "Sure, I could take a card. We're not *quite* ready to do this yet, but I'll probably be ready to sign it sometime next week." Fonzo showed no disappointment, but felt some.

Carioca nodded. "And you also want to make a withdrawal? Oh, I see—for the profit-sharing."

Carlotta from her purse drew a paper, unfolded it, held it in one hand, and read from it. "Thirty-four thousand pesos for the profit-sharing. And twenty-five thousand, five hundred for the regular weekly payroll. I called in the order yesterday. To Valentina."

When Carioca left the room to arrange for the withdrawal, Carlotta looked in leisure now through the plate glass into the lobby and saw the lawyer who had cheated them. She glared, then turned to Fonzo and said, "See that man over there by the door, talking to the security guard? That's Carmelo Delavaca!"

Fonzo shivered to hear it. He turned and recognized the man so named, his uncle, and a mild panic seized him. He was too terrified to say anything, but fortunately Carlotta spoke again, apparently not expecting him to speak.

"I'm trying to sue that cabron. He owes us money. But we can't get the papers served on him because he's never there, he's too tricky. But this gives me an idea. You don't know this man, do you? He's an abogado in Chapala."

Pinned and desperate, Fonzo gulped as he tried to form a sound that could be construed as both yes and no. It sounded to Carlotta only as if he'd moaned, and she asked him the question again. Given the extra few precious seconds of this reprieve, Fonzo saw that he should for personal safety deny it.

"No, I don't know him at all."

"Well, you look at him really well. He dresses really snazzy and sleazy, which is just what he is. Always smiling that way. His hair's never out of place. A little devil's moustache. Watch out for guys like that, Fonzo. Feel lucky you don't know him. But that gives me an idea. I may want you to try and help us nail this guy. I could introduce you to the process server. You could be a little spy for us. You could hang out around this Carmelo's office, then when you see him leave, you follow him, find out where he lives, or where he eats. Or better yet, you could call us when he comes to the office. *Then* we can nab him right there. What do you say?"

Fonzo shrugged as if that would mean yes he would do it. He wanted to show even a little enthusiasm, but the panic that still buzzed in him would not permit it. Fortunately again, Carioca then returned with a small paper that Carlotta signed, and which Carioca passed to a yellow-jacketed latina of twenty years, bright and cheerful, who walked away with it. Carioca and Carlotta talked a moment more. Carlotta resumed her enthusiasm about the celebration, inviting Carioca to attend.

Soon the same pretty yellow jacketed woman returned with an envelope fat with pesos, and she handed it to Carlotta. Carlotta pulled out the stacks of pesos banded and bound, layered in the colors of their denominations. "May I count it here on your desk?" Carlotta asked the president. Carioca answered her. "Of course, no one will bother you." Carioca left the office, shutting the door behind her.

Fonzo watched, trying to hide his enchantment, as Carlotta unbound each bundle, counted it methodically, precisely, and rebound it. She wrote down the figures. She put the stacks back in the envelope, put that in her big purse, and she and Fonzo exited Carioca's office. Carlotta spoke pleasantly to several customers who waved to her, Fonzo at her side, and they passed outside the bank. Fonzo was especially grateful that Uncle Carmelo was nowhere to be seen.

When Fonzo arrived at the Bellacasa office the next morning, Max was already there, sitting on the two-seater equipale, in telephone conversation, one leg crossed over a knee, in the levis and t-shirt he always wore, and the

Y-thong huaraches. Set like a treasure chest upon Fonzo's desk, as if it had been dropped from heaven by the Madonna Herself, Fonzo recognized the wonderful bundle of pesos. He dared not go near it.

Max hung up and turned to Fonzo. "Thanks for being on time, I really need you today. There's a lot of little last minute problems. Lupe's found us a marimba band, and they're going to be at the fiesta by one or so. We're trying to start at one, let everybody have a little food and drinks before the music starts. I've got food coming from three places, plus we need tortillas. The truck from Corona is supposed to set up a tent and fill up the ice chests between twelve and one. I've got very little time for all this. And I've still got to fill up all the pay envelopes."

Then Max remembered the phone conversation. "Oh and something else that's important. I just spoke with the process server. Remember? Carlotta and I are trying to serve papers on that no good lawyer, Carmelo Delavaca. Carlotta said she'd spoken to you about that. Yesterday. You two saw him at the bank."

He looked at Max with a believable cordiality, something he could learn to improve. He said, "I'd be happy to help you that way. If that's what you want. You know I want to help you however I can."

"Great. Delavaca's office is at number forty-three on the avenida into Chapala, six or eight doors before you get to the big intersection. It's an orange building. I'll give you a phone card. You can call his office to see if he's in. Just pretend like you're someone with a problem that wants a lawyer. Tell his secretary you've got money. Find out when he'll be in, or if he *is* in. You can hang out at that little juice stand a block away. You can see him coming or going from there. He drives a fancy yellow car with tail fins."

Max paused. Fonzo saw that the little pause was meant to herald something special, a recompense, the part most worth hearing, and he listened well. "And if you can locate him, so that we can nail him, serve him and get him to court, *I'll give you a thousand pesos.*"

For the moment Fonzo need do nothing but nod that yes, this would be a fair recompense, and he would be their little spy. And snitch.

The phone rang. Max answered. He listened while Fonzo glanced out the window. Max finally said, "OK, OK, it's not that big a deal. I'll get the van, and I'll go get the band. No, Fonzo can't go, he's not insured for the van or the new pickup. It has to be me. I'll be there in thirty minutes. Yes, I know where that is. Yes, goodbye."

To Fonzo he said, "A little emergency. The band is driving up from Guadalajara, in one of their cars. It's blown a radiator. I'm going to have to

71

go get them. That'll still leave me time to pick up the food and be there when they set up the tent."

Max looked at the fat envelope on Fonzo's desk. He sighed. "I'm just not going to have time to do all of this. So I guess, as soon as I leave, you take these two lists I've printed out, here on the table." He rose and went to that treasure-laden desk, where Fonzo customarily worked, and Fonzo followed him.

Max showed him the two lists. "You can see that each list has the names of all the workers, and right next to it, the amount of money that goes to them. So you see we'll need to make up two envelopes for each man. Put each man's name on two envelopes. Count out the exact amount for each envelope, then recount it, and when you're sure it's the right amount, put it in the envelope. There are forty-six envelopes. There's fifty-nine thousand pesos. All counted out exactly. Each of those bundles has in it exactly the amount that's written on the band. If you're careful, and count everything carefully, it will come out exactly. Exactly."

Max looked at Fonzo for a token assurance he was doing the right thing. Fonzo drew his eyes away from the pile of pesos and looked at Max: he radiated confidence, and why would he not. He smiled and said, "Everything will be just fine, senor. Don't worry about anything. I understand exactly what to do." He exuded responsibility and executive potential. Max took up his notebook and his lists and keys and bid his capable secretary *Buena Suerte*, and then Max left the office in peace and drove away.

Three hours later, beneath a glorious sunny sky that so often illuminated and warmed these idyllic January days in Mexico, several tables had been placed upon the front lawn of number seven Privada Rio Bravo. Colorful cloths had been draped over the tables, and plastic Corona tubs of ice filled with Corona beer in bottles had been arranged beside them. From the opened doors of the white van Max carried platters of fried chicken and potato salad and refried beans to the tables. Lupe in a bright long-sleeved shirt assisted him. The immense blue and white Corona canopy kept all this in shade.

The marimba band with no name had set up their instruments in the yard's far corner, but they were each of the five for the moment sitting on the patio steps enjoying a beer. They watched the gradual arrival of peons and maestros, ambling down the cobblestone street toward them, all having walked the little distance from Six Corners. All today were less recognizable in cleaned and pressed shirts and pants, hair combed carefully. Their chatter was fueled by the rumors that senoritas might be attending. These men whiled away their nervous anticipation, dreaming of money to spend, and a little dancing, for those who dared.

As these soldiers of la compania Bellacasa came within the opened gates of their most recently completed construction, the younger went for the beer, as did a few of the older. Most of the more experienced, however, like maestro Felipe Romero, poured tequila in a plastic cup, added a little ice, a luxury, then a little 7up or a splash of water. Each newcomer irresistibly studied the food, still under plastic wrap, but they would let that be, till they all would be summoned. Each one ambled to the wall near the instruments with a drink and sat there on grass, watching as the others slowly arrived and did as these first guests had done.

Only a few minutes tardy, La Senora arrived with *Honk! Honk!* and parked the newly acquired 1991 green Ford pickup behind the van. She climbed out, wearing the billowy long skirt of many colors she'd bought after first watching and screaming with joy at Ballet Folklorico in the Degollado Theater in Guadalajara. She wore the cowgirl boots. She carried only her big purse, filled with pesos and shut tight. Fonzo Suarez stepped down from the other side, dressed unaccountably drab today in gray slacks, gray shirt, gray shoes. As Carlotta looked at him she saw him sullen and downcast. No doubt he was shy before all these men of the barrio that he did not know. She would have to encourage him.

"Fonzo, it looks like all the food's here, and the beer. Do you ever drink, Fonzo?"

He looked at her, making a vain effort to smile, and said, "Oh sometimes. I like a little tequila. Blue agave."

Carlotta smiled. "Well there's no blue agave, I'm pretty sure of that. But there'll be some tequila, that I am sure of. Do you ever like to dance, Fonzo? There may be a young lady or two. I've invited several."

All this came too late to fortify his troubled soul, and Fonzo could only nod his head vaguely, a response that might be read in whatever way La Senora was inclined to take it, committing him to nothing.

But as she entered the gates Carlotta's attention was inevitably drawn to the groups of men sitting leisurely, nodding, waving to her as she looked at them. She saw the marimbas. Lupe busy at the food table with Max. The gorgeous Lujack house all finished, and a stunner. And she knew that this was indeed the wind at their backs. "Eee-HAH!" she cried out to all of them. *"Andale pues!"* And they laughed and some called back, "Andale pues!" They could not hide their admiration of her.

She left Fonzo to himself and went to Max, kissed him, and said, "I'm

73

going to lock all this money in the van, so it'll be safe till it's time to give it out. Are you happy?"

He had been joking with Lupe about Porfirio Corona, who already worried that there would not be enough tequila. Max still smiled as he turned to her and said, "Only if you are. Gee—you look fabulous. Yes, I'm *very* happy. Are you ready to start up the musica?"

Those last words hung in the air and perhaps drifted out to an old Mercedes, faded blue, that was just parking curbside. Carlotta's new friend Corrina, black grandmother and fellow jazz enthusiast, stepped out of her car in a green and blue jumpsuit, flowered sweater over that, and looked toward the fiesta. She saw Carlotta looking her way expectantly, and Corrina shouted, "Hey, how's about we start up the music? Carlotta! Is that you in that fancy dress? My, my."

Carlotta took the van key from Max and waved at Corrina. Carlotta passed through the front gate, still waving, and hugged her friend in the middle of the street, holding the bag of money behind Corrina's back, while all the men watched. Carlotta took her by the arm and led her to the white van, laughing at Corrina's joke. Carlotta opened the door and deposited the full bag, and again locked the van. Then she led her friend inside the gates and they went to Max.

"Corrina, this is my husband, Max, I've told him about you. And this is maestro Lupe, our foreman." Then in Spanish she said to Lupe, "Maestro, this is my friend Corrina."

The three shook hands. Max kissed her on the cheek. He said, "Corrina, I think it's time we had a little music, don't you."

"Hey, I'm ready for a *lotta* music, Max. And say there, Senor Lupe, poco tequila?"

Lupe grinned at her whom he and all the men had often seen and called la negrita. He poured into a clear plastic cup, then added ice. He showed it to her. "Mas? Aqua? Refresco?"

Corrina shook her head decisively once, "Nada, maestro." He handed it to her. She drank, then held up her plastic cup before them all and smiled. "Gee it's good not to have to hide it."

Lupe signaled to the musicians, and they all went to their instruments. They sounded them a moment, then began playing: the melodious vibraphone happy and fast and away, steel drums like electric bells ringing in pursuit, and in moments the energy of the air there came vibrantly alive. Each one instantly felt it. Anything could happen today. The prize to the swift. Rafael the deaf, from where he stood beside the fence, sensing the music somehow, began tapping his foot and he looked around for a partner.

There was only Gloria and Isabel, who were serving, and La Senora, for whom he had not quite the courage to ask.

Louder than the music, Max called out to the men, "Andale!", and he waved his hand. The men all rose and came forward to the food tables like shy children. Yet as they stood in line, the musica infused them again, and they talked and laughed and wished there would be women, younger women, at least to look it and dream about, for those without the courage to dance. Those with filled plastic plates returned to the wall to sit and eat. Some went to sit in folding chairs that had just been arranged by Fonzo and Carlotta.

A motorcycle sputtered and popped coming up the street, and it parked along the far curb. Carlotta and Corrina, each drinking from a plastic cup, walked to the gate to look. Two helmeted riders stood away from the bike and removed their helmets. Both had long hair that shook free, one blond, one black. The dark haired was a young Mexican man in tight leather pants and leather jacket. The blonde was Rebecca Allen, today in levis, black boots and leather jacket, big key chains at her belt, rough and ready.

Seeing Carlotta, Rebecca waved gaily, "Hi, there, Carlotta, it's me, Rebecca. Remember from last week?"

Despite the radical new look, Carlotta saw the same happy girl. "Oh I'm *so* glad you came! And I'm glad you brought a friend," Carlotta held her hand out to the other in leather.

"My name is Amelio," he said, shaking her hand. He was thin and fine-featured, and the long hair made him seem feminine. Yet there was none of that in his voice as he spoke his perfect English. "I just met Rebecca a few days ago. I live in Guadalajara, but a long time ago I lived here in the pueblo. I'm back seeing old friends this weekend. Rebecca invited me to the fiesta."

Carlotta turned back to Rebecca and laughed. "Gee—I thought your mother would *never* let you come here. I'm really surprised she gave you my invitation with the little map."

Lighting a cigarette, Rebecca stopped to laugh and say, "Oh she didn't, believe me! I *never* saw that invitation. Oh no! But I got the last laugh. I met Amelio a couple nights ago, at a little bar I found, and I told him that there was a party I wanted to go to. He asked around the barrio and found out for me where it was. And here we are! Momma's just gonna shit when she finds out!"

Then she grabbed Amelio's hand and jerked him toward the party. "Let's go dance, Amelio!" Laughing he followed her. As Carlotta watched them go she saw Fonzo beckoning to her. She went to him.

75

Fonzo looked like one of the dismally unfavored. He said, "Senora, I was wondering if you might have a little medicine, something for the bad stomach." She paused; it was a strange knot in the beautiful fabric of her day. But she would be gracious regardless.

"I don't have anything in my bag or my van, Fonzo. Just nothing. Probably the nearest store would be the place. Do you think it's that bad? I could send someone to the store."

Fonzo feigned bravery. "Oh no, no. No, not bad enough for anything like that. I'm sure it's just some little thing I ate. It'll pass. I'm sure of it. Sorry I mentioned it. Can I help with something?"

"No, Fonzo, you go sit in one of those chairs and try to relax and maybe drink some water or juice until you feel better. You've already done more than your share today." She patted his head.

She led him to a quieter part of the yard, taking up a folding chair as she walked by. She reset it underneath a flourishing banana tree and guided him to sit. He sagged into it, slumping a little to the side, sadly. She helped right him, and then she patted him again on the head, and took a step as if to leave.

"Are you all right for me to leave you? For a little?" He nodded the littlest possible sadness that he was alright for her to go. She walked away.

She found Max by the gates talking to Tacho and his new girlfriend Dahlia, very bonita. Carlotta greeted them and hugged both of them. She said, "I thought you couldn't get a day off work to come today!"

Tacho looked down embarrassed, then looked back at her smiling. "I wasn't sure, they didn't tell me till the last minute." Dahlia poked him with her elbow. She said, "I don't know why he likes to tease his father like that. He always knew he was coming."

Carlotta glanced at Lupe. She thought how to lead them to each other; then thought otherwise. Though she couldn't help herself saying, "This is a special day for your father. If we didn't have maestro Lupe, we wouldn't have la compania. And la compania needs you, Tacho. I hope you're still remembering my offer."

Tacho resumed the smile that always brightened his face. He said, "Oh I remember, yes, it was very generous of you." And as struggled to express himself the smile again dissolved. "But you see, my grandfather would have to agree to that. I'm not so sure he would do that."

She considered a moment, then said, "I would go with you to ask him, like for support. I could tell you jokes so you wouldn't freeze up with him."

She saw a quiver in the corner of his smile, anticipating this confrontion with his abuelo. She saw how uncomfortable he'd become.

76

Finally he could only say, "Thank you. I'll remember that."

Then Carlotta realized that Fonzo was again hovering just behind her right shoulder. She snapped a look at him. He held his arms folded upon his large stomach, his head drooped, forlorn. He stepped back two paces, then another, to draw her toward him, away from the Tacho and Dahlia.

He spoke in a weak whisper. "It's getting a lot worse, Carlotta. I'm getting the chills. I don't think I can last much longer."

"Oh Fonzo!" she said, "but you'll miss it when Max hands out the envelopes! I wanted you to be there! I have one for you!" When he seemed unmoved by that, she could only be the mother again. "OK, Fonzo, I'll drive you home right now. Is that where you want to go?"

These were the words he'd been praying for. He said, "Yes, home. Just home."

Carlotta helped Fonzo into the van seat, then returned to tell Max that she would be away twenty or so minutes. She drove Fonzo slowly along the careterra, and she spoke to him cheerfully. However, in her pauses she realized he had retreated deep within, ready for a long hibernation, and her words were all spoken in vain.

The rest of this errand she performed in silence, helping him to his front door, passing him on to an aunt who said she would put him directly to bed. He said he was almost too weak to walk. She gave him his profit-sharing envelope and said goodbye.

Carlotta drove the careterra back through Chapala and Ajijic and to the fiesta, where still the musica played, and some danced, and all ate and drank and laughed.

Carlotta for the first time then danced, until she'd danced with everyone, man or woman, who would dance with her. Max danced with all the women, even young Rebecca, until she made him back off with her naughty gyrations.

The next time the marimbas took their break, taking up plates and drinks themselves, Max called for attention and that stopped all the talking and laughing and everyone looked at him.

He wore the same t-shirt and levis, but today both had been newly purchased. He had drunk a few cervezas. Early in the morning he had imagined something eloquent and memorable to speak, but this moment he was not composed enough for all that. He would instead be short and direct.

In Spanish he said, "For Carlotta and me, this is a very proud moment. This will be the first time the workers share with the company. It will happen again, maybe twice a year if we keep building this way." All cheered.

"And eventually the share can be more." Much bigger cheer. "I don't want to draw this out, but I do want to thank maestro Lupe for his great work bringing all of you here to be in la compania. And for his great work as a maestro."

A cascade of hoots, and jibes and jokes poured forth. The maestro smiled as he listened to them, a little embarrassed. "And I also want to thank each man of you personally, as I hand out your envelopes, for your excellent, excellent work. Everyone says our houses are the most beautiful, and that is because of all your fabulous work. I thank you, all of you. Viva la compania!" And they all yelled it back at him, "Viva la compania!"

When Carlotta stepped forward to hand Max the big envelope, she became sentimental and she also spoke to them. "This is a very happy moment for us. And it's just the beginning. Viva la Compania!" And they all yelled it back louder than the last time. Marcos yelled, "Andale pues!"

Max handed out each envelope to each man personally, thanking each one for their good work. Carlotta stood beside him and smiled her happiest and said, "Gracias," to each one of them as well.

And now she felt it more than ever: surely the wind was still at their backs.

7 MAX LETS HIM GO

In the January sunshine of the plaza Fonzo suddenly felt brave enough to walk into Bellacasa, let the shit fly where it may, claim a monumental ignorance and innocence of everything, and see what happened. Nothing could be proven. And perhaps by some miracle nothing had even been revealed. Neither the senor or the senora had called all weekend.

So it was he took the class C bus to Ajijic, and walked the three dusty blocks from the carretera. His courage stayed with him all the way, even when he saw both the senor's new green pickup and la senora's white van parked in front. His firm hand unlatched the front gate, and firmly knocked upon the front door, though it stood partially open. He leaned a happy face inside, but saw no one in the front room where his own desk was unmanned. He heard voices in the back room, Carlotta's domain. He held his breath and stepped one cautious foot inside, then called out, "Hola, it's Fonzo."

All speaking ceased. Max emerged first from the rear room, Carlotta close behind him. To Fonzo this first look on their faces should tell him everything. And yet it did not, for both looked at him for a brief instant as if he were a stranger. Then faint smiles appeared on both their faces; or perhaps they were not smiles but something else, hiding a truth. He couldn't tell. He would have to dare a step inside and await a further revelation.

Carlotta went back into her office, where she spoke a few words of Spanish. Maestro Lupe and maestro Felipe came out looking sullen and walked past Fonzo without looking at him, and went out the front door. Max approached him and seemed to be sincere when he said, "So, how are

79

you feeling now, Fonzo? You're looking well."

Waiting for him to answer, Max sat in one of the chairs at the table. Carlotta reappeared and sat in another beside her partner. Still unsure of them, Fonzo assumed a look of ill health and said, as if he were also trying to force a courageous smile through his misery, "Oh mas o menos. I just came from the doctor. He said I was still not well. Not well at all. But I wanted to come to work tomorrow anyway."

Max indicated that he should sit in the two-seater equipale. "Something's come up, Fonzo, that I wanted to ask you about."

Fonzo knew this was likely the doom he had dreaded, but he could not reasonably do anything except what he'd been asked. He sat down, feeling suddenly lonely by himself on the two-seater. He looked at them with all the innocence he could muster and said weakly, "Yes?"

A hitherto unperceived irritability was suddenly in Carlotta's voice as she spoke to him. "Fonzo, we're missing a lot of money. Almost eight thousand pesos. From the money Max left with you Saturday, to fill up the profit-sharing envelopes for the men. I'm hoping that you miscounted what was to go in each envelope, and that you had money left over, and that you put it away somewhere." A hopeless hope glimmered in her eyes but quickly dimmed.

He swallowed. He'd expected, if they were on to him, that they would creep up on it slowly, like hunters closing on a fox. That would have given him time to call up and set in order the variety of extensively rehearsed excuses and misunderstandings and vows of innocence, and use whichever would be most appropriate to their mode of assault.

But now all of it was a jumble in his head, and he had to force a look of surprise; then let it become shock, as he tried to steady his voice. "Oh that's terrible! No, I didn't put *any* money anywhere. Except in the little envelopes. I *thought* I put in all the right amounts. I *thought* I did." With the words out and hanging in the air, Fonzo gained a small comfort and courage feeling that these words at least sounded plausible, and couldn't be disproved.

Max leaned forward, like he was trying to encourage candor, and spoke. "It's been very hard for me all weekend, Fonzo, having all the men coming to me, and coming to maestro Lupe, and telling us how much is missing from their envelopes. This is their money, Fonzo, not mine. Though of course, if we can't find what's missing, Carlotta and I will have to replace it. Nobody else but you touched that money from the time it was counted until the envelopes were given out to the men. It had to have happened when you filled up the envelopes. Now, Fonzo, look at me."

The request was in order, because Fonzo, despite his supermost efforts, was hardly able to control the panic that began to bubble up inside him, making his eyes feverish to start slipping and drifting in their sockets. As he strained to hold those eyes steady, he seemed to be not quite there. Summoning all his courage, he looked at the senor.

The senor said, "I'm still thinking there's the possibility that, *even accidentally*, you might have taken the missing money home with you, and that you've all along intended to return it."

Yes, Fonzo too would like to believe that. But the prize was too big, and he had already suffered too much for it. He could only give the senor a forlorn look of sorrow and say, "I'm sorry, senor, I guarantee you it's not at my house. I never took any money out of here. I swear it." Then he brightened with a helpful idea. "Wait—I know! It must have been that someone got it at the party, just before you gave it out."

Carlotta glared, restraining her blaze of anger. "That money was either with *me...or* it was locked in the van until I handed it to Max. *You* are the one, Fonzo."

Fonzo fluffed that off, instead embracing the other, the helpful idea. He said, "Then it must have been some thief, a really good one, that picked the lock of the van when nobody was looking and took the money. Then locked it back up. How do you know that didn't happen?"

Carlotta yelled back at him. *"That's ridiculous and you know it! Where's the men's money, Fonzo? You sonuvabitch!"*

He could no way respond to that blast. In any case he had already spent his meager arsenal of energy. To defend himself he could now only reiterate himself in a feeble, faltering voice. "I'm sorry, senor. And senora. But I really don't know what happened to it. Maybe I made mistakes counting it. Maybe."

Max said, "Did you have any money left over, after filling the envelopes? Even ten pesos?"

Sadly, Fonzo nodded no. It had all come out exactly right, even as the senor himself had predicted it would when he left him with all the money.

Max smiled slyly, for all the good it would do him. "Then how could it be that all these amounts were short, and yet you gave out all of it, and yet *nothing* was left over?"

More sad nods. No, he couldn't imagine how.

Carlotta shot it at him. "That isn't all that's missing, Fonzo. This morning I looked up the utility bills that I gave you money last week to go and pay. I called those companies and now I'm finding out that most of those were *not* paid. What happened *there*, Fonzo? Where's *that* money?"

This to Fonzo seemed such a little thing against the other that he could shrug it off. "Oh senora, no, I did pay all those bills, I'm sure of it. I think you must have misplaced those receipts, I'm sure of it."

Carlotta suddenly stood tall and fierce and stomped her boot on the tile and said, "Oh *damn* you, Fonzo!" She swept into her office and slammed the door behind her.

Max then stood but kept his cold eyes fixed on Fonzo. Max set his hands in his pockets and went a few steps to the right, then back to the left, studying his humbled secretary. "What am I going to do with you, Fonzo? What?"

Fonzo looked down. He nodded slowly, he didn't know.

"I certainly can't trust you with money now, can I? I *should* call the sheriff and tell him what I think. But the sheriff's probably your cousin or something, huh, Fonzo?"

There seemed to be nothing more that could be lost, and this might actually shield him, so Fonzo told the truth. "Not *my* cousin, but my *aunt's* cousin. Pablo. My cousin's the judge. Both are in PAN."

"OK then, so what should I do with you Fonzo? You tell me."

Fonzo pondered this. For him it was a puzzle too, how to get out of this mess, to get away. He had never imagined it so emotional. He said, "I think the best thing for me is just to go and not come back."

Max nodded, staring at him. He said, "Yes," like it was a hypnotic suggestion. "Yes, I think that would be best for us too, Fonzo. We'll cut our losses. Someday I'll be thankful it wasn't worse."

Fonzo looked at the senor to be sure he truly had permission to leave. Yes, he might do so. He pulled himself up and walked with eyes appropriately downcast across the tiles to the front door. He stepped outside, then looked back a moment to say...maybe...goodbye. The senor's cold eye was still upon him and that kept him silent. He turned and walked out the gate, and trudged down the road.

8 LUPE'S RESCUE

When Lupe returned to his house at eleven o'clock, Calle Obregon was dark and quiet except for the radio musica, a lonely trumpet, coming from the house of old Senor Velazquez up the street. He entered quietly. He looked into the living room to see for sure that his sister Magdalena had already gone to bed. Then, before going to his own room, he looked in to see that his mother was sleeping peacefully.

But she was not. Her breath came in little urgent whispers, so unlike her usual tranquil breathing that was so spare it seemed that she breathed not at all. He leaned his face to her face, searching for any other sign that might tell him she was in emergency. Or was she merely dreaming something of another world that her frail consciousness struggled to assimilate? But he saw no signs.

He went to Magdalena's room and called softly to her, and she woke, a light sleeper, and listened to her brother. She put on her robe and they went to their mother's room and stood over her several quiet minutes, listening and watching. Though not a nurse, Magdalena had experience in hospitals and crisis centers. She told him finally that she could be no more sure of anything than her brother. Should they call the doctor? Or wait and watch? And what could anyone do for this fragile life that had seemed already so long in flight to its maker?

They brought in to their mother's bedroom two chairs and sat for a half hour together, rarely speaking. Then they agreed to sit alone in shifts of two hours each, and Magdalena returned to her room and set her alarm clock. Lupe sat and watched, and remembered the old days. He and Magdalena and younger brother Polin on the beach with their mother in the mornings when they went to wash the family's clothes. Summer days walking the long shoreline trail to Chapala with Polin and the others for the mercado days. Papa dying in that very room one humid summer afternoon, after twelve straight hours of monsoon rains that same day had flooded and uncobbled the streets and washed away little fences and chickens and even pigs.

In two hours Magdalena relieved him and he went to bed weary and melancholic, but he fell asleep instantly. Instead of Magdalena or the alarm clock, however, the telephone woke him ringing at three thirty-five by the red light of the digital clock on his bed stand.

It was Tacho. Imagining the worst, Lupe sat up alertly and listened to the son. "Father, I have a little problem. We have a little problem."

Lupe waited for the rest of it, but apparently it required prompting. "Yes? Yes? Where are you?"

Even so Tacho hesitated; then said softly. "That's it, Father. Where. We're on the highway to Colima. We're parked way off the road, off the highway. We're stuck. I'm calling with Dahlia's cell phone."

"Are you harmed? Did you have an accident?"

"No, we're fine. And no accident. Except a little one a half hour ago. When I backed out of this parking place under a tree. My back tires went into a ditch and now I can't get them to drive out."

In the moment of silence that followed Lupe saw it all. As well did he comprehend the little terror in Tacho's voice. The young man spoke it. "I don't dare call the Romeros. And not Dahlia's family. Maybe her oldest cousin, but he doesn't have a car. Can you help us, father? I'm desperate."

Lupe wanted to laugh for these young thieves of love. He remembered a call of such desperation to his own father, so long ago he'd nearly forgotten it, but the memory suddenly and vibrantly alive in him now. His heart leaped.

"Tell me exactly where to find you and I will be there in no more than an hour."

He could hear his son's great sigh of relief. Then Tacho told him where, forty miles beyond Jocotepec. Three kilometers and a half past La Salinda, right at the first big coconut stand. Drive down that road one half kilometer, a little stand of coco palms on the left. They would shine their flashlight when they saw him coming.

Lupe could not resist one little wink. He said, "That will give you lots of time to think of a good excuse to tell Abuelito. And the Senor and Senora Davilo. A very good excuse."

84

Lupe told the story to Magdalena, who smiled, and said she would watch their mother till he returned.

Lupe put in the trunk of the Cadillac of all problems an extra can of motor oil, two gallons of water in plastic, jumper cables, a flashlight, tow rope, two meters of chain, and a bag of several glazed donuts unfinished from this morning. Fortunately, he had more than a half-tank of gasolina.

It was two hours before sunrise. Calle Obregon was dark and deserted. Lupe let the Cadillac warm itself a few moments curbside before his closed house door, number 13. He listened as the rattles and vibrations of his idling eventually harmonized into the background drone of his voyage. Then he rolled his old Cadillac slowly away from the curb, and eased downslope to the corner at Ocampo. He wheeled easily right, gliding silently down the sleeping street till he came to Estalia, where he turned right again and moved a little faster. He went upslope, coming to the highway, which was deserted on this moonless night. His two headlights alone shone in all that darkness. Sweeping a big left onto the careterra he drove away, red Cadillac finlights chasing into the night.

On the careterra he was the lone car among the flow of nighttime truck drivers, and he passed them all. Finallly he came to Salinda, and he watched his speedometer till he was three and one half kilometers beyond. He saw the coconut stand, boarded shut till morning, and he saw the road beside it, partially paved, that seemed to wander away to nowhere. He turned down it, craning forward to see their flashlight. Soon he saw it, waving, flinging light back and forth upon the lush, sleepy palm fronds high above them.

A little dirt road no bigger than a path led off this last paved road. Cautiously Lupe turned onto it, smiling as his headlights swept across the seablue ten year old Toyota that was Dahlia's gift from her parents, a reward for her teaching diploma and her first job six months ago. The sad Toyota severely slumped in the rear, its front bumper canted upward. It appeared though that the front tires both still touched ground.

Lupe halted his Cadillac, and saw that his car could easily approach the Toyota. But first he set himself in park, pulled the handbrake, and climbed out, enjoying this last little moment when he was yet unseen and they were in the full glare, these young thieves of love. Dahlia sat inside the car, shyly waving. Tacho stood nobly beside the door, holding onto it, ready to be rescued. Both lovers suffered equally to hold the rigid smiles that were the best they could do. Still hidden in shadow Lupe grinned; he could not hold it back. Then he forced himself to be sober, and he emerged into the light himself. He walked to Tacho, patted him on the shoulder, and Tacho said, "What do you think? Can you get us out of here?"

Lupe might enjoy it a little more. He said, "Who knows? First I'll have to see how it is behind. Come with me, bring your flashlight."

Lupe carried his own. Father and son with flashlights illuminated the embarrassment of the drive shaft highcentered mid-car, the rear wheels three inches above purchase. Their flashlights' peripheral light also illuminated father and son to each other.

The son's eyes pled for mercy, may it come tonight in many forms. This with the car was the first, the most immediate mercy required. "What do you think, Father? It looks to *me* like we can do it."

Lupe looked at his son, savoring a last moment of the suspense before he let his own private enjoyment gradually show itself in his smile. "I think we can do it too. I have a chain. We'll bolt it to your front bumper and to my front bumper. I can probably pull you forward just a meter or so and your wheels will take hold." Lupe took his keys from his pocket, selected the trunk key and handed it to Tacho. "Go take a look, see if there's anything else you need. Get out the chain. How is Dahlia?"

Feeling relief for the rescue, though it brought worse encounters nearer, Tacho could finally breathe deeply. He smiled a little of the old smile saying, "She's well. Ask her yourself." Tacho went to the Cadillac.

Lupe looked inside. He kept his flashlight toward the floor, that they both might be seen in the peripheral light. He smiled to her. She was sure of him and she smiled back, just a hint of worry in those green eyes. Dark long hair, beautiful, the pride of her family, everybody's darling and favorite teacher. Just before dawn. Far from home.

"Are you well?" Lupe asked, and he handed her a paper bag. "Two donuts."

She took the bag and smiled brighter. "Oh yes! I'm well. Just a little tired. And worried."

Lupe knew it was best simply to nod. To speak of this could be a long night's task. He was grateful to be merely the interested spectator in this comedia de amor.

But Dahlia seemed to need a moment of confession. She said, "I just don't know what to tell my parents. We never meant to be gone this long. I just don't know how it happened. We got tired, we needed to rest. And then *this* problem." Without looking, she reached her hand inside the bag, drew out a glazed donut and bit into it. Then she looked at it. She sighed. "Thanks, Lupe."

He reached to pat her on the shoulder. "You'll be out of here in just a few more minutes. It looks like no damage to your car. You'll be home in an hour."

She visibly shivered and closed her eyes that she might not imagine that homecoming more than she already had. "Oh Senor Lupe, I don't know what I'll say."

Tacho came to them with the chain. Lupe patted her once again and said, "No worry. You'll think of something."

Together father and son looped the thick chain through the upthrust bumper of the Toyota. Lupe drew the Cadillac close, within half a meter. They looped the chain again through the Cadillac bumper, then bolted the ends together. Tacho sat in the Toyota and reassured Dahlia. Lupe in the Cadillac eased back till the chain tightened, then signaled to Tacho that he was ready to haul. Tacho waved back a hand holding a donut. He held it in the grip of his teeth, that both hands might be free to hold the wheel as he braced for the pull.

The littlest effort drew the Toyota from its highcenter, the undercarriage sliding off and the rear wheels slapping back on the ground, wobbling the car a moment. Then it rolled forward on all four wheels, and Tacho gunned the engine and stopped and car and set the brake. He jumped out.

A wildness of joy and rising fear was in his face, but he was somehow able to smile through it and say, "Gracias a dios, Papa, you saved us." He looked into his father's face, where he saw a confusion of emotion in that face as well. Lupe saw it all, and grabbed his son's jacket forearm and shook him, for all that could not be expressed, and then said, "You better get going. You've got a lot still to think about, eh joven? Look, you *might* stop in Jocotepec on the way and get married."

Tacho's lip merely trembled at the joke, though he said. "You know I *would* marry her, Papa. And no doubt we will. But I never meant to have it be like this. What will her parents say?"

Lupe could see the boy's mind alive with terrible fantasies. He said, "Don't worry. You're a fine boy. Everyone knows that. Even the Davilos. I'm sure they want you for a son-in-law. Now get going." Lupe had spoken seriously, somberly, but now he allowed himself the amusement of the interested spectator. He smiled, remembering the excuse offered to him so many years ago, which he had used and which had saved him. "You can always tell them your car broke down at your father's house and you two spent the night there."

Tacho grimaced, wrestling with this that might be another joke, or might be something that just might work. But he could not reconcile it now. He could only shake his head, for all the confusion and fear, and go wearily to the car, where he and his soon-to-be-betrothed buckled themselves

87

into their seats. They gave him a last forlorn look.

As he watched these two thieves of love drive away, Lupe allowed himself the laugh that he had restrained, and he laughed until he watched them turn on to the main road and disappear, just as the first pearly light of morning began seeping into the eastern sky.

9 LUPE'S BARRIO VIGILANTES

Lupe arrived at his house once again preoccupied with the condition of his mother. Magdalena sat in the chair beside her bed in the early morning light. She told her brother that the breathing had become more or less normal in the last half hour and that they might for the time relax their watch. She smiled as Lupe related the events of his expedition.

There was no time for Lupe to shower. He filled a plastic travel cup with coffee Magdalena had made for him and he drove to the Penton house. The boveda of the roof had just been completed and the maestros were all throwing mezcla on the rough brick interior walls and smoothing it with long two-by-fours. Marcos and his crew of three were fitting the last of the orange electrical hose into the channels they had chipped with chisels into the brick walls.

The senor was at work in the far corner of the back yard with peons Chencha and Juan Rios, the heavyweights, moving and aligning the many great boulders they had gathered nearby to make the senor's miracle, a three meter high waterfall, which he had designed to cascade first into a pond, and then to overflow into a rock-framed river that would meander across the yard and empty into another pond beside the terraza. Nothing so extravagant had Lupe ever seen in even rich men's gardens, even those of the maestro of landscapers, Alejandro Trevino.

Marcos was equally impressed. "It will be as Juan Rios calls it, the fountain of all fountains."

But Lupe knew the deeper truth. "Yes," he said, "but the senor is paying for this, not Senor Penton, who pays only for the plumbing. Senor

Penton is allowing the senor his experiment, yes, and it will be fine, no doubt. But I worry that the senor will spend all his money. Then what?"

Marcos laughed. "You worry too much, maestro. I believe it is as Oscar Frances says of him and la senora, that they are the lucky rabbits. You see how they keep getting new clients, and new houses for us to build."

Lupe wished that he too could believe it could go on and on like that. That these extravagances of the senor would not bankrupt la compania.

While Chencha and Juan Rios cemented in place the two hundred pound boulder they had just maneuvered into position, the senor turned away from the waterfall and called to Lupe, wet cement and dirt smeared on his levis and tee shirt, smiling his satisfaction.

Lupe went to him, walking alongside the boundary wall that two maestros had bricked to a height of one meter. Nearing the end of it he peered for no reason through a gap in the wall, to the empty lot beside. To his surprise he saw a grown man laying in the weeds, his hat drawn over his face, sleeping. Lupe knew him. Rogelio Romero. And Lupe knew what the problem would be; why this maestro was not at work like the others plastering the interior of the house. As Lupe stood there staring, the senor came to him and Lupe hushed him with a finger to his lips. He motioned that the senor should look at this sad sleeper, whose empty medio-litro of tequila lay beside him.

Lupe shook his head, smiling for the foolishness of it. When he called to Rogelio, he assumed a mock severity. "Eh, borracho! Arriba!" Rogelio stirred, but did not waken. "Rogelio! Cabron! Wake up!" Lupe knelt beside him and shook his shoulder. Rogelio bolted awake, half raising himself while shading his eyes against the sudden light. He puzzled at the two faces staring at him. His face showed alarm when he saw not only the tolerant maestro but the senor as well.

Rogelio struggled to rise, blinking repeatedly. No doubt he was trying to retrieve something still missing, something that would reset this confusion into any kind of reasonable harmony, where he could pass unnoticed, and yet be counted on someone's payroll.

When Rogelio did finally stand, and hold his position against gravity's force, Lupe shook his head, frowning, as if he could not find the words, nor was there a need for them. But it must be spoken. "No mas, Rogelio. Three times. I told you."

Rogelio looked down, stricken, though this was the third time, he well knew it. He had no energy for appeal, only to stand. For only a brief moment he stared his maestro in the eye, and Lupe saw there bitterness simmering. But Rogelio had no energy for that now either. His shoulders

90

slumped and he reached down wearily and picked up his profession's tool, the trowel, off the ground. He then straightened himself, so he might set his feet solidly on the earth, ready for the homeward journey.

Max was shocked as this little comedy ended so suddenly tragic. He guided Lupe several paces back toward the house and said to his maestro, "Do you think it's really that bad, maestro, to fire him?"

Lupe showed in his face that this situation was not as it appeared to innocent eyes. "Rogelio I have found like this twice before, once as we finished the Frazier house, once already in this house. He is a lazy man, a sloppy worker, even when he is not drunk. I won't have the other men bear it. I have always tried to help Rogelio. I have known him for twenty years. I am still his friend. But he must be able to control himself at work. The truth is, I think he should get a job being a bank guard. He knows some people."

Then Lupe laughed as he told him, "There is one bad thing about this. Rogelio is a Romero, nephew of the abuelito grande of that family, who already hates me. This could make it very bad for me."

At lunchtime Lupe went directly to his mechanic Dino, who fixed cars in his backyard, for many in the barrio. Dino listened to the generator and shook his head that it might finally have to be replaced. As Lupe considered whether he would wait and continue to nurse the sad generator, or make the very inconvenient expense of fixing it now, a little red Volkswagen bug stopped behind him. Its exhaust sputtered and threatened death rattles, until the driver turned it off and stood out of the little red car.

Lupe remembered her at once. Constance. The follower of La Madre, the holy woman of India, for whom he and Carlos and maestro Felipe had repaired the roof in San Juan Cosala three years before. She still dressed as he'd always seen her then, in heavy grayblue skirt nearly to her ankles, a lighter blue plain longsleeve shirt, high collared, all buttoned up. Her graying hair she pulled back tight in a bun behind. Wire rimmed glasses. No makeup. A loyal foot soldier to her enlightened mistress.

Constance recognized him immediately, and said his name. "Hola, Lupe."

Lupe welcomed the encounter. He went pleasantly to her and spoke her name. She told him that she and La Madre had returned from India only two weeks ago.

"La Madre is writing books," said Constance proudly in Spanish. "But I'm happy I'm meeting you, Lupe. La Madre also wants to build a little casita next to our house. We're still out in San Juan Cosala. Maybe you could come talk to La Madre and tell us how much you would charge to build this casita."

This was certainly happier news than any he'd hoped to find in this reunion conversation. He spoke eagerly. "I and all my workers are now in a compania, and the owners are two very fine americanos, Max and Carlotta. I know you would like them, that La Madre would like them. Max is fair in his prices, and the work is the best, as you know."

Constance was sure there could be no problem. It was always nice to meet new good people. And fellow americanos too. From her little leather purse she drew a card and gave it to him. "Call and make an appointment with La Madre."

As Lupe drove his Cadillac back to the Penton house, having decided not to repair yet, the little whine that sometimes flared in the generator sounded a little louder than before. But he also fingered the little card, and that pleased him. Apparently it would become another job, just when they needed it. The lucky rabbits.

Two days later at the job site the senor arrived mid-morning in his Chevy pickup with bad news. "Rogelio came to our office this morning. He was very serious. He said that he was fired unfairly. That he deserves a compensation. He said he's talked to a lawyer. We must pay him immediately or there will be trouble."

Lupe frowned. He had only to think for a moment until he answered. "I will take care of this, senor. You need not worry about it. I will go see him this evening, maestro Felipe and I and my brother Polin. We will make him understand."

Max hesitated. Even so long in Mexico, he still had a foreigner's fear of the government and their unpredictable views of things. But he saw determination in his maestro's eyes. "Alright, Lupe. Do what you can, I'd appreciate it. Carlotta's very upset."

After the hour of comida Lupe and his two companeros walked two blocks down Ocampo to the small adobe that was the house of Rogelio and his sister Antonia. Both brother and sister had been once married but there had been neither happiness nor children for either. Antonia had walked away from a carousing husband, and Rogelio had been dismissed by his bride after a wretched four months for his love of tequila and his loathing of work. Their father had recently widowed and taken a job in Guadalajara and had given them use of the little house they had grown up in.

Antonia opened the door, mildly surprised to see these three, whom she had known all her life. She stepped back and asked them in, a short woman with grizzled, graying hair in a simple dress that went nearly to her ankles. To most she appeared perpetually stern, having little occasion to smile. She looked dubiously to her brother, who sat in a straight-backed chair in the middle of the room, pointed at a happy family scene unrolling on the television. Grimly defiant, he looked at his visitors as they entered and stood, all watching him, unsure if they should remain standing or sit side by side on the sofa, the little room's only other furniture.

Sullen but always courteous, Antonia spoke softly that they might sit. She asked if they would have a refreshment. Lupe thanked her, but said they were there to speak to Rogelio, and would not take too much of their evening. Rogelio muttered something unpleasant but undecipherable. He rose and went into the kitchen and returned with a little glass of his favorite. He sipped it, then sat again, glancing up at his visitors suspiciously.

Lupe cleared his throat and said, "You are trying to make trouble for the senor and the senora, Rogelio."

He glowered. "They make trouble for me." He stared hard at the floor a moment, gathering his spite. He looked to the maestro again and said, "Why don't you stand by your people, instead of these damned gringos?"

Antonia stood stiffly beside him. "It was not fair that these gringos fired him, maestro. I'm surprised you didn't speak for him."

Lupe smiled, but humor would be no use to him, and he let it fade. He said, "It is not the gringos that fired him, Antonia, it was I. He was drunk and he was sleeping, while all the others were working. It is the third time he has been drinking at the job."

Antonia winced; she had heard another version of this. She glanced briefly to her brother, who still frowned his defiance. She knew she would have to stand by him yet a little while longer nonetheless.

Rogelio sneered at them. "I already spoke with a lawyer. He's going after them. He says I have rights. He says all the gringos are using us."

Lupe said, "Yes, that is true of some gringos. But not these. And you know it. They have given us steady work now for a long time. And days off for the soccer championships. And fiestas. And they are generous with their money, they give us raises twice a year. And bonuses. When have you had an employer who did *any* of these things? These are good people, Rogelio."

Rogelio withdrew his eyes from these men, but his scowl remained. His words bespoke his bitterness. "My lawyer told me I deserve a compensation. They fired me unjustly. *You* say I was drunk, sleeping. Hah! I took a siesta at the break time, I slept too long, that's all. Anyone could make that mistake. I can't be fired for that. The lawyer told me."

Maestro Felipe, a Romero himself and older second cousin to Rogelio, though they had never been friends, spoke to him sternly. "We all know that is not true. When maestro Lupe found you, we had not even had our first break. You were drunk and sleeping before you had worked one hour."

Rogelio stomped one foot and screeched, "Liars! All liars! You love these gringos because they give you a little extra money and they say they're you're friends. They lie to you and you lie to me."

None of this surprised the three visitors. Lupe's brother Polin said, "You are the only one of all the workers who would say these terrible things, Rogelio. None of the men would stand with you."

Rogelio sipped again, then growled his words out, but their force had diminished. "I need none of you. My lawyer will stand by me."

Lupe stepped closer, in front of him, that Rogelio's eyes could not avoid him. The maestro said, "Lawyers are for scoundrels, Rogelio. Lawyers serve the rich and they serve themselves. This lawyer, whoever he is, does not work to help you, he works only to make money for himself. He will not care who is hurt, even if it is you. And it will be *you*, Rogelio. *You* will be the one that will be hurt the most."

Unable to follow this odd reasoning, and unsure if the fault was in the logic, or in his own clouded mind, Rogelio hesitated, that there might somehow be a truth in this that he need puzzle out. "How could this hurt *me?* I am already hurt."

Lupe saw the doubt in his eyes. He said, "Where is your survival, Rogelio? Where is your family? Here in the barrio is where. This is the best of what we all have, this little life by the lake. Don't muddy your waters, amigo. You know how many here have a good constant paycheck because of the senor and the senora. We've built many houses. They want to help us make a good future. If you make the great mistake of causing trouble for them in the way you plan, you will have many angry neighbors."

Maestro Felipe stepped to Lupe's side and looked down at his second cousin. Who eventually must look at this other stern face. His kinsman said, "You won't have to worry about the angry neighbors, cousin, because your family, even the ones who don't like to talk to you, will come first, and I will lead them. We will make your life so miserable you'll be hospitalized or you'll leave the village."

Lupe said, "I will be there too, Rogelio, if you make such a mistake. And all of us, family, friends and neighbors will be at your door. We will all be angrier even than you are right now. Try to imagine it, Rogelio."

Polin joined the others to let Rogelio feel the additional weight of it. He said, "But I hear there are good jobs in Guadalajara, or Puerta Vallarta."

The code of the barrio vigilantes spoke to him eloquently, suddenly shocking him back to primal realities. He blanched. All the fierce energy

94

that he'd been accumulating since his firing, drained all away from him in an instant. He slumped.

Seeing all this, having known certainly that it would end like this, Lupe lowered his voice and said, "I think your Uncle Enrique has a nice job for you. I spoke to him yesterday. He told me to tell you about it. They need a security guard at Banco Ultimo. Uncle Enrique would recommend you. He won't tell them all the truth."

Rogelio in his enervated condition still need not abase himself, and he stared at the floor with no passion, while he felt the heavy presence of these three others hovering so close to him. He knew it was all true. Still, he need not admit it. But the security guard job maybe wasn't a bad idea.

Lupe, Felipe and Polin each knew their unpleasant work had been accomplished. They needn't stay to drub it in. Each one in his turn went to Antonia, who stood nearby, who also by now understood full well the case against her brother, as well as the probable consequences. By her severe look at Rogelio she too now seemed ready to castigate her fool brother. But each one smiled warmly as he thanked her, and touched her hand, and as the three departed, she felt like she'd been cleansed.

10 TACHO CALLS ON ABUELO

A day later Tacho called Max and Carlotta to ask them if they would accompany him to a meeting both terrible and necessary. He must go ask his abuelito if he would be allowed to work for their company, with his father. A new necessity compelled him.

They went at twilight to the house two blocks up from the lake and a block behind the cathedral. A shy young woman let them in. Tacho introduced her to his companions as Estrella, the maid and an old friend from school. She took them to an unlit room with only one lace-curtained window. Fine old tapestried carpets overlaid a common cheap tile. A sofa and two chairs all red velvet and heavy hardwood, a glass covered black wrought iron coffee table, a large television, a small shelf of books. Three pictures were each featured on separate walls: a Crucified Christ, the Virgin in her constant pose with Juan Diego, and the Pope Praying.

Tacho indicated that Max and Carlotta should take the sofa. He sat in the chair nearest them and he waited in the tense silence without looking at them.

At last Senor Romero entered the room, a small, frail man wearing a rich, dark blue robe cinched at the waist in black. His dark slippers made soft shuffled steps crossing the carpets to his chair. The three others all stood but he showed by his hand sign that they should resume their seats. Nonetheless Tacho remained standing till his grandfather had seated himself and then the young man said in Spanish, "Good evening, Abuelo, thank you for inviting us to your house. I present to you my friends Max and Carlotta."

Both Max and Carlotta rose again and went to him and accepted the

97

small hand he extended. He made them a simple smile. It was a weary face, crossed and beset with more than seventy-five years of this life. He spoke soft words they must lean forward to hear, "Mucho gusto," and he bid them reseat themselves. "We have tea and limonada. Would you drink something?" Each spoke the limonada and the abuelo called out to Estrella their request, a papery thin voice that slipped away from him like leaves scuttling across a lawn. Then he settled back to listen to his guests.

"I have come to speak to you, Abuelito, about Max and Carlotta's company. They have asked me to work for them."

"I suspected so," he said without showing more. "My sons and my nephews have spoken to me of this also. It is your father's job–no?"

Tacho nodded, slowly, yes, wishing it were not so baldly stated. He glanced in need to his companions.

Max said, "Senor, excuse me, but may I say that it is my wife and I who are asking Tacho to work for us, not his father who asks it. Tacho would be a valuable worker for us. His English is very good, he drives, people easily like him. He would work for us administrating, not on the jobsite with the maestros and peons. And his father."

"Yes, yes," said the old man, obscured in the room's twilight, "but I know where all this leads. I know you all wish to make forgiveness for your father. Maybe not at once, but eventually." He hesitated, searching how to say it best. "But why should I forgive him? Why should your mother? I might even ask, why should *you*, Tacho?"

Tacho made a sound to speak, but his grandfather lifted his hand and stopped him. "Let me tell *you*, my son. First let me tell *you*." He paused again to see that he had them all. "I hear what everyone says, that your father does not drink now, since Marlena left him, that he works hard, that he helps people in the barrio, especially young ones. I hear all this. But, my son," and he paused to lean a little forward in his chair, "none of that will bring my daughter and my other grandchildren back to me. And none of that will ever make me forget the tears she cried to me, so many, many times, when your father was cruel to her. And I know you remember that as well as I. Or perhaps even better than I." He stared for the truth of this into his grandson's eyes, that indeed clouded and looked down away from his own sinister memories thus aroused.

The old man sat back and continued. "To escape that barbarity she moved to California. She is still there. The children are still there. Son, how can you ask forgiveness when the pain is still there for me, for her? She had to leave her village and her family. What we suffer, she and I, is that we must wake up to our separation every day. Perhaps till we both die."

This grandfather then turned his old eyes to Max and Carlotta. "Some things are difficult for others not truly of our village to see. We are a very old community. We all came from the barrio of Six Corners, even those of us who now have more money and live near the church and the plaza. My son Felipe still lives in the house I was born in. In the house my father was born in. And his father. You might well ask, how many of our generations have lived here, in the same houses? I would tell you that honestly, I do not know. Probably no one knows. Perhaps they have lived there to a time when our oldest ancestors, even before the Spanish came, had lived other centuries in little huts on the shore of this lake. But I do know that this is also true for most of those who live in the barrio. That these families there have lived in the adobe houses they were born in, and their parents and grandparents also lived there. Until no one can reckon the beginning of it. If there *was* a beginning. All our grandparents played together when they were children. And *their* grandparents played as children together on the same street as well. You see?"

He sighed and looked out the window at the last day's light lingering there. "My daughter no longer partakes of that community. She was driven out of it. It is well for her that she has come to be comfortable and safe in her new life. For me it is still a tragedy. All that is much to forgive."

The silence in that room lay upon them all more ponderously than the darkness that had finally settled into every remotest corner, mercifully obscuring all these palpable miseries.

Tacho leaned forward and seemed as if to speak; then looked down when he could not find any words. The old man spoke instead. "But I know your heart, Tacho. I know you want to believe well of your father and, perhaps, to have it be well between you again. Yes I know that." He sighed. "And that is not an evil wish."

Tacho merely listened, at his grandfather's mercy.

"And perhaps it is I who am making the mistake. I thought this before you came to me tonight. I have thought this often. Maybe God wants to help me, but I am blind to see it." He paused; he seemed reluctant to pursue this line. Finally he did. "You are such a good boy, Tacho, you have always been one of my favorites, your mother's too. Even as much as I stand against you in this matter with your father, I see your heart is good in all this. Who could not see it? And that has led me to think something more. What would be the result of your being here, working with your father? What would it be? I ask myself. You might become friends again, you might come to forgive him, as perhaps you are already doing. And then what? I ask. You would have more reason to remain here in the village where you belong. You might perhaps say to your brothers and sisters kind things about your father, and they might become curious and visit him. They also might become friends with him again. And they also might want to come back where they belong. You see? Yes, I have much anger in me but I am not stupid. I am seeing where all this might lead. I might at least have my grandchildren back, some of them, while I still have a little time to enjoy them."

Tacho now looked into this small old face, intent to recognize something there that he'd not dared believe possible.

The old weary voice went on. "So I have come to conclude, yes, even before you came here, that for my own selfish reasons I should permit this that you ask. Not for your reasons, or for your father's reasons, or for the reasons of these friends you brought with you. To your mother, God forgive me, I will disguise this a little and tell her that you are working with this senor and his senora, and apart from your father, as your friends have described it."

He seemed for several moments as if he were about to say more and the three others waited, tense, fearing he might unsay this.

But when at last he spoke it was in a lighter, though still tired voice, and the details of his face had become lost completely in the obscuring darkness of the room. "So let it be as I have just spoken it. But I have to excuse myself to bed, I have many old feelings that are stirring in me right now. I know they are angry for what I have agreed to. I had better lie down so I can make my peace with them." Out of the darkness that engulfed him emerged a whisper of his laughter.

Tacho rose and went to him. Max and Carlotta saw only in the room's deep obscurity that he knelt before the old man. They saw no movements of his hands or his head, but heard him speak almost as softly as his grandfather had been speaking. "I will never disappoint you, Abuelito. I thank you a thousand times for this." He rose again and went to Max and Carlotta who stood and together they walked to the door. Carlotta subdued her rampant emotion to say softly, "Thank you, senor, for having us in your house. We will take care of your wonderful grandson. Thank you for allowing him to work with us."

The abuelo turned to go, but then turned back and said, "Yes, before I forget. I do owe your father something, a thanks for firing that drunken nephew of mine, Rogelio. It's good someone finally showed him his barbarity."

Then the patriarch seemed to recall something of even greater importance, a matter severe, but which also caused his eyes to dance merrily.

This stopped his going; he said, "And I hear you're wanting to get married, grandson. To that fine girl Dahlia Davilo." Abuelito held him with his stare, insisting on confirmation.

Tacho went rigid. Yet he must go forward, through the eye of the needle. "Yes, Abuelito, this is true. We spoke together to her parents last night-"

"Last night?" the patriarch interrupted. "Very sudden, is it not?"

"Yes, Abuelito, very sudden. But as you know, we have dated only each other ever since I came back to the pueblo. It was always my intention, someday, for us to marry."

The senor grande allowed himself a wry smile. "Someday. Yes. Well, is your wife-to-be's car running alright? I heard you had a little breakdown."

"Only a little one, Abuelito. But her car is fine, thank you. Everything is fine."

The old man held his grandson's eyes for only a moment more, long enough that this young man might see in them some reflection of the glories and the narrow escapes he himself had known in the long years of his life. And then he bid them all go in peace.

Outside Tacho smiled his happiest. He said to them only this, "It's a miracle."

Carlotta still sniffled, but suddenly stopped and said, "But Tacho, you never told us you and Dahlia were getting married?"

Tacho blushed. "No. As I said, we decided very suddenly."

On a beautiful spring day services were held in the temple a block off the plaza and hundreds came. The cedar casket by the altar set high upon a cloth-covered dias. The priest stood behind it even higher with his arms outspread, speaking to all of them about the valley of the shadow of death and the confusion of trials to be encountered there and the certain rest and peace that awaited all his children. All these children at last he would take up in his arms, just as he had now taken up the ancient soul of this honored woman, Maria Antolin Gonzales.

When the service was over Lupe and Polin and Magdalena and many others of the family came down the aisle first and went outside and waited. Everyone else then passed back outside, offering their condolences to them. They shook hands and accepted all those embraces of compassion. Carlotta and Max were among these.

The casket the sons and grandsons carried outside and placed in the bed of a station wagon. That vehicle and its cargo began a slow drive away from the temple over the cobblestones, past the plaza where the police at the corner took off their hats in respect as it passed at a slow walking pace. And then all these hundreds of others followed behind in cortege. This same street Ocampo led in a straight line to the cemetery three-quarters of a mile away.

All these mourners and vehicles proceeded slowly. This pace also might accommodate all those so very old, some as old as the woman in the casket. Many of these elderly had played with her as children. Many had witnessed in the same temple her marriage sixty-five years before, and witnessed the baptism of all her children there. They had grown old with her, and knew they themselves would be one day soon carried in a casket similar to this to the same pantheon and be buried like their old friend in the earth of their ancient cemetery.

The procession filled the street curb to curb, and it moved ahead slowly, hardly seeming to notice the ones who stood watching them from doorways and windows along the way. Even these spectators watched solemnly, sensing no doubt the passing of the shadow of death.

A part of this procession, Carlotta and Max saw Lupe just ahead of them walking beside Magdalena and looking at the stones as he walked. They saw Polin and his family walking nearby. Carlotta with her handkerchief always ready moved to Lupe's side and they walked along together, as Max walked beside Carlotta.

Eventually all this crowd arrived at the cemetery. The sons carried the casket into the enclosure at the entrance to the cemetery that was roofed with a wide cupola but was otherwise open to whatever weather might be. They set the casket on a dias in the middle of the room and all stepped back and looked at the casket in silence. The priest came forward and said his prayers. Then a woman of the barrio, seated, began speaking little prayers as she moved her fingers from bead to bead of her rosary. After each bead she paused and all the mourners repeated the prayer.

Thereafter, Lupe and Polin and several others shouldered the coffin and began walking carefully through the graveyard as everyone began moving from under the cupola, following the two brothers. They maneuvered their way between headstones and around fenced plots with their burden until they came to a pile of fresh dirt and a squared cavity beside it that was perhaps a meter and a half wide by two meters long, two meters deep. They set the coffin near the cavity. A pile of bricks lay beside it, and a sack of cement and a smaller pile of sand and a mason's pan and trowel.

Many old friends and neighbors followed the coffin to its gravesite and all these sat themselves comfortably. Some had baskets with food, some had food in boxes or sacks. They greeted each other and talked of ordinary things, and often of the dead woman and her family.

Polin climbed first into the grave with a trowel in hand. Someone had already mixed the wet cement and had set the pan beside the hole and set there also fifteen or twenty bricks. Polin slowly and with the grace of eternity laid a little floor of bricks. Then he laid course upon course to create four walls upon the brick floor at the bottom of the grave. He worked slowly, stopping often, acknowledging the conversation of his friends sitting near and watching.

Finally Polin climbed out of the grave and Lupe stepped into it, taking the trowel from his brother. Brick by brick Lupe continued slowly raising the walls of this tiny house of the dead. When all four walls were their proper height, he climbed out and brushed his shirt and pants clean.

Polin and the others lifted the coffin off the ground and carried it to the grave and then with great care they lowered it into the brick resting place built so snugly into the grave's cavity. Lupe took up the trowel again and set his boveda form across the narrow span between the brick walls. He buttered his brick on both ends and fit it in place, sustained by the form. Then he buttered another brick's ends and placed this one beside the other; and so he continued until he'd made an arch of six bricks from one side to the other. Then he disengaged the form. A delicate brick arch remained in place. Immediately he reset the form a brick width ahead and began a second arch. He worked slowly, settling back on his haunches after finishing each arch. In that interval he spoke with those nearby and sometimes looked into the grave where the coffin was visible less and less with the conclusion of each new arch.

At the last Polin relieved his brother and himself spanned the last three arches of bricks, sealing forever the casket underneath this boveda roof and into this little last resting place her sons had built for her. Polin poured a mix of wet cement over the arch of roof. Lupe then began shoveling dirt. Sons and grandsons of the deceased one at a time took a turn, and all these shoveled dirt onto the little brick house of the dead within the grave. It soon filled and they continued shoveling until the fresh earth made a large mound and they patted this firm with the backs of the shovels.

More than an hour and a half had passed in all this. And even when it was finished no one went away. They ate food they had brought or food shared to them. They talked of the ordinary things of their lives. They talked of the woman they had all come to bid farewell and fair passage, even though the Sun passed low in the sky, and even though twilight soon would be upon them. Even so, it still lingered, the beautiful spring day.

PART TWO

11 CONSTANCE FINDS A STUDENT

Sunday in her little red Volkswagen bug Constance sped down the careterra toward San Antonio. Because of her devotion to La Madre, she prayed to Shiva that there would be at least one worthy student waiting to be picked up. Two had asked to be invited.

First, however, she must make the weekly little advertising stops. She had four primary, and a host of secondary. Today there was only time for the mainline, all of them on the careterra. She stopped in front of Dona's Donuts, where even on Sunday morning the inner circle of the wizened wise, very casually dressed retirees, sat sipping coffee and munching donuts on the front patio. They talked about the fortunes they knew how to make, about the pathetic bungling of Mexicans and Mexican bureaucracies, and about the various ways they knew to right the ship of state up north, the USS America, belittling and pitying those less enlightened.

Constance came out of her red bug with her folder of announcements and her scotch tape and her pushpins. These benighted of the patio round table watched her arrive, but only a moment. They'd seen her too often. She was nothing to their world; not even their lust would have her, so plain, so drab, so sexless the tight-buttoned blue and gray-blue shirt and skirt she always wore. So prim and humorless, an inflexible grandmother. Yet more than grandmother: she sported also the red dot in the middle of her forehead, her mark of devotion, emblem of another world, and estrangement from this. Constance knew they thought that of her. Most did, and it was just as well, for she would prefer to go forth on her holy missions unadmired and unnoticed. The rewards she sought were not of this earth.

Constance went past these who had already stopped regarding her, and she halted at the bulletin board. Her posting of the week before remained. She removed it. In its place she pinned La Madre's latest announcement, for her next Sunday's lecture on the transcendental teachings of the Bhagavad-Gita. Though, Constance realized, this more prized lecture would be wasted on anyone who had not listened to the preparatory lecture today. She looked at her wrist watch. Ten minutes till pickup time. She returned to the red bug and drove on.

She stopped also at the El Torito mercado and posted on their outside community board, then continued on the mile further to San Antonio and posted at the Mail Box Etcetera board. She also posted at the giant wall board of the SuperLake mercado next door, where most of the gringos shopped. This last board, the largest and the one most looked at, she posted in three places, so wide spread were the notices. She stepped back and looked at the mass of postings, and sighed, for it was a mishmash of announcements, a microcosm of the vulgar marketplace. How in heaven could her little postings of divine truth be recognized by anyone amidst this skelter, even by a troubled seeker?

At that moment she saw a modest and simple lady, thin in her Mexican dress, sitting intently upright on the first step leading down from the mercado. She might have been Mexican, but that her hair was contoured round her face in a style more cosmopolitan. As Constance stared at her, wondering if she might be the pickup, the woman looked at her and smiled. Then she stood. Constance walked toward her.

Constance said in Spanish, "Are you Patricia Arguello?"

A brighter smile showed that Constance was correct. The possible neophyte spoke yes in Spanish, but continued in English. "I thought you might be the one I talked to on the phone. You're with La Madre, am I right?"

Constance nodded, pleased, for this Patricia seemed both serious and intelligent, and had all the markings of a worthy student. "Yes," said Constance. "My car's parked over there. We might as well go, I don't see the other person who called. I told him I'd be precisely on time, and wouldn't wait. La Madre insists we start on time."

As Constance drove her pickuped person back to the ashram, she'd expected the novice to ask questions. They usually did; but this one was quiet. They passed Rancho del Oro and then the new place everyone was talking about, MexicoLimpio, and on through Tempisque, past the cluster of little beachside cantinas cooking everything grilled, and at last into the third world poverty and frill-free lifestyle of San Juan Cosala. Still the new one sat quiet and looked straight ahead, as if all the while she were meditating.

Despairing of information otherwise, and knowing she ought in some way to know a little about this person she was bringing to their inner sanctum, she finally said, "Have you studied any of the yogas before?"

This Patricia Arguello came out of her inner seclusion. She pondered this. She made a slightest smile and said, "Not really. But I've read the Gita a few times, and I value it very much." For an instant she seemed to consider if she should say more, but did not.

Constance inwardly smiled. This might indeed be the worthy student she had prayed for. She probed further. "Have you done any other spiritual work in the village?"

Patricia said, "Oh that depends on what you mean by work. I meditate. I have friends who are like me and we talk sometimes about practice. I've set in on some interesting groups. Some of them helped me a lot. But nothing longterm. Or recently."

The red Volkswagen at last passed beyond San Juan Cosala and it slowed nearing the roadside sign that showed a giant green lime, and the name of the barrio, El Limon. The red bug turned right and slowed till it very soon stopped at the ashram. Tall sheetiron gates and a tall wall surrounded the property. The tile roof of the simple house was visible above the wall, where everything had been painted the same invisible beige.

Constance climbed out, unlocked the gates and folded each side back. She re-entered the pickup-mobile and putted into the carpark pad, two parallel strips of concrete just wide enough for the tires. Constance bustled out again, relocked the sheetiron gates, and went to Patricia Arguello, who stood outside the car already, looking at the house. Constance led her forward and they entered the ashram.

The house was quiet and seemed empty. Constance hung up the cars keys on the peg by the door. She led Patricia into the small living room, where a couch set against a wall, with a low coffee table altar before it, whose centerpiece was a bronze Shiva dancing inside a ring of flames, his foot poised on the head of defeated Ignorance. Incense in a tiny holder burned on either side of the divinity. On the wall above the sofa a poster of blue Krishna playing flute. Facing the sofa was an easy chair that matched the sofa, both washed-out blue. A far doorway led to the kitchen, where some dishes in a cupboard were visible behind glass doors. Another doorway beside it was curtained in dark blue.

107

Constance asked Patricia to sit on the sofa and she did, primly, ready to absorb. Constance returned to the small foyer and into the walk-in closet that served her for a bedroom. There was space only for her thin cot and its foam mattress and her trunk of things at the foot of her bed. A small square mirror hung headhigh on a nail above it.

Looking in the mirror she was shocked to see she'd forgotten that morning in the delay leaving to paint the red dot on her forehead. Quickly she opened her unlocked trunk, drew out the toiletries kit and grabbed her red paint stick. Quickly she painted on her forehead the red dot, saying a quick prayer of thanks that La Madre had not seen her come home not wearing her dot of devotion.

Constance then removed her black laceup shoes, clunked them into their box in the trunk, and removed her delicate prayer slippers and put them on. She was ready. She returned to the living room and sat on the sofa beside Patricia, who'd watched her come in, pleased for the company amidst all this austerity and sanctity.

From a curtained room off the living room, usually unnoticed by first time visitors, La Madre emerged without a sound. Patricia was visibly startled, seeing this very tall and thin gray haired woman, wrapped from neck to ankles by a brilliant orange sari, moving to her chair like a much younger person. She showed no emotion; her face was sharp and angular, long like her body. She looked only a moment at the novice. She showed to Constance by the discretest sign imaginable that she had done well to bring at least this one. And a promising. La Madre settled slowly but gracefully into her chair, facing her acolytes.

La Madre looked at her sparse but adequate congregation and she made the slightest of smiles. Having assessed all she needed, she let her eyelids flutter till they closed. She seemed lost in trance. But only a moment, for she thereby seemed to gain strength and will in her spine, and she straightened and sat taller and then forward, till she was poised on her seat's edge, ready for all things psychic or mystic or metaphysical. She droned a slow rolling O that seemed finally to be vibrating intensely inside her. Then Constance took up the droning and it began to sound to Patricia Arguello like masses moaning, and it both startled and impressed her. Even so, she was unsure if she were invited to join or not, and she didn't.

The longly resonating drone of *Ooooooo* gradually elided into a ponderous hum of *Mmmmmmm*, and at that point Patricia understood it: the *Om* she might have expected. Patricia began under her breath to *Mmmmmm* with them, until abruptly the grand mistress and her first lieutenant stopped.

La Madre slowly opened her eyes. The Mona Lisa smile was upon her, though looking at no one. She let herself resettle into the comfort of her chair. When she spoke her voice glided confidently like a practiced melody, and both her spectators felt the force of it, and many times when she concluded a serious point, her voice fell several registers for emphasis.

She said, "I am La Madre. And even though you may have heard my name, I would like to give you the benefit of my credentials. So that you may see how seriously you might take what I am about to say."

Patricia nodded respectfully. And for Constance, this was the best moment of her week.

La Madre said, "I have been blessed with spontaneous enlightenment. At the time, I was a woman of thirty-five who had never studied the Vedas, nor did I have any teachers. I did not know who Krishna was. I was a real estate agent. Someone gave me a copy of the Bhagavad-Gita, and when I touched it, my spontaneous enlightenment occurred. I went into an ethereal state of divine bliss that lasted all afternoon. When I came out of that glorious state, I knew God had touched me and that I'd been called to serve him. I immediately moved to India. I began studying the Vedas and the yogas and I studied for several years with priests. I eventually returned to California and bought a piece of land in the foothills and opened an ashram. Many, many seekers came to me. The ashram continues. But I returned to India and lived there many more years. I have recently come back to Mexico to make some translations from the Sanskrit, a language I have mastered. We will be reading and studying from my own personal translation of the Bhagavad-Gita." She let her eyelids flutter closed again, a little withdrawl not appropriate but mandatory, while her novice assimilated the potent resume.

Patricia had known none of this information and was impressed. She nodded and smiled modestly, trying to express this to La Madre, who, however, appeared to be still away on an internal retreat. So Patricia smiled to Constance, who accepted her admiration with a knowing nod of her own, for she of course never ceased to admire.

La Madre's eyes reopened and she said, "So challenge me if you dare." She made a slightest smile again to indicate that she might be taken lightly in this. Or not. "To most students of spiritual work there are stereotypes of passive meditators who can sit for hours and hours, and who brag they are pacificists. There are saints who chant day and night in their cells. But I have come to tell you that this is a most incomplete picture of *true* spiritual work."

Patricia seemed keenly interested in this, for she in her brief career as a seeker had only encountered these stereotypes aforesaid.

La Madre knew all this would be true, and she went on. "Well it takes all types, doesn't it?" She rested back complacently, knowing it was so. "And what a beautiful image that scripture, the glorious Gita, opens with. Arjuna, a king's son but also a devotee of Krishna, as he looks upon the battlefield, contemplating a war upon enemies. But these are also men he admires, men he believes may be even greater in spirit than he is. The prospect sickens him. He loses heart. He ends with a line worthy of Shakespeare. 'Govinda, I shall not fight.'"

"Yes," Patricia couldn't help contributing. "I remember that line. It's just how I always feel."

This for Constance was a delightful surprise. There would be a little skirmish, perhaps a little enlightenment at the end, if the novice's spirit could but go that far.

"A-ha!" La Madre said, rising forward the very slightest to emphasize her indisputable point. "I can't tell you how many times I've heard that response in my life. And all from well meaning novices. But alas, novices who just don't see what's going on."

La Madre allowed her a moment to recant, but Patricia was still trying to comprehend the insinuation and her face was a blank. La Madre said, "You think all this poem is a metaphor, don't you? You think that when Krishna virtually orders Arjuna to join the battle, to kill or be killed, you think he's talking about life's little ups and downs and life's little crises. And these words of Krishna make you take heart and you go out and battle your crisis, and maybe you even win."

Patricia believed La Madre had pegged her exactly. She didn't even need to nod that it was so.

La Madre settled perceptibly back. "Now what you believe *is true*. I grant you that. But I am here to tell you on this bright Sunday afternoon, that it also means what it says *literally*." She leaned now forward to give her suddenly deepening voice even more authority, "You must sometimes in defense of your life, or in a just cause, go to war, attack and be attacked, and kill and be killed."

This startled Patricia. La Madre settled back again. She paused to let the raw truth worm its way in. Patricia squirmed on her seat cushion.

La Madre said, "And I am also here to tell you, my curious novice, that Krishna is also declaring the principles of a yoga that has not until my time become known. Warrior Yoga, my young seeker, Warrior Yoga. I may be its first pure exponent."

This was far beyond any of the esotericisms that Patricia had read or heard of. She tried to fit it into her spiritual schemata, but it resisted solution. "I guess I don't get it."

"Most people don't. I feel sorry for them. But the Gita makes it obvious. Krishna is directing us not only to take on the battles that come to us in life, that bloody us, though we may win our share. He also directs us who are ready for greater spiritual tasks to take upon ourselves this yoke, this yoga, *of fighting as a religious principle*." She hesitated an instant to see if her novice might be doubting, but she was not, and La Madre continued.

"What is the very line that finally convinces Arjuna of the militant wisdom of Krishna, and which is responsible for bringing Arjuna back to his senses so that he can go to war?" Constance smiled slightly, for the coup d'etat was coming. "It is your duty as a warrior-yoga, a kashastriya as the Gita calls it, which is nothing else but the more modern name I've given it, Soldier Yoga." She offered a little bauble from her small stock of humor. "Let's make it sound American—a marriage of east and west—Soldier Yoga."

But only a moment of that and she was serious again. "Krishha commands Arjuna to be a true kashastriya. He tells him 'there is no better engagement for you than fighting on religious principles.' And in the very next verse he tells our latent pacifist Arjuna, 'Happy are the kashatriyas to whom such fighting opportunities come.'"

Patricia, for all this education, shaking her head with disappointment at her own failure to rightly comprehend, said, "You mean we should be aggressive?"

"Oh my goodness no!" said La Madre with gusto, as if she'd hoped her novice would say just that. "No, no. We should not *be* anything, except enlightened. What I'm saying is that the Soldier Yogis merely have an *openness* to confrontation, whenever they find it in their path. They do not fear it, but they welcome it, always. Good reasons to go to war are all around you, my dear, every day, would we but look for them." Her face showed the happiness of the solution.

Even so, the novice was still perplexed, and finally said, "I guess I still don't get it. Exactly."

Constance knew this moment well and would like to have been the one to enlighten this live one, but she would in no way have been permitted. Instead La Madre proceeded on course. "I didn't really expect you would, not at the first anyway. Life's ugly situations confront us all the time and people usually back away from them and get trampled on. That's all I'm saying—let's not be trampled on anymore. It's good for your soul to hit back sometimes. You can feel the inflow of spiritual energy from this righteous lashing out. Don't take my word for it. Try it. Let your assailant know who's boss. See how good you feel afterward."

La Madre could see by the glimmer of a light in the novice's face that she perhaps had often experienced that. La Madre continued. "Yes, I can see what a big concept this is to take in all at one time, and I sympathize. So I won't burden you with anymore. We'll just let what I've said sink in. Hopefully we'll be able to talk about it if you can come join us for the discussion next time, when I can make all these ideas a little more clear."

Patricia did realize that La Madre saw into her mind truly, that she was on overload. She thought also that this mind-reading by La Madre *was* a sign of something worth trying, at least one more time, and she said, "Yeah, probably I will come next week. It's certainly a way of thinking about the Gita that had never occurred to me."

"It rarely occurs to anyone, I can tell you. I've talked to many people about my discoveries, experts, priests, saints, holymen, and I can tell you from experience–it's never occurred to *any* of them. But.... Electricity was around for thousands of years before Ben Franklin caught it in a bottle. You know what I mean?"

Patricia thought she did.

Seeming like she might be going to stand, La Madre said, "In the time left to us, I would like to invite you to meditate with Constance. Then if you feel the spirit moving you, you might want to make a little chanting, in the way that Constance and I performed it as we all sat down."

Patricia said she would. La Madre stood. She said, "Let me leave you with one last quotation from my favorite book. It is meant to save Arjuna's soul. Krishna warns him: 'If, however, you do not perform your religious duty of fighting, then you will certainly incur sins for neglecting your duties and thus lose your reputation as a fighter.' Terrible words."

She paused, that this novice might let this wisdom re-echo through her brain. Then she said, "So kind of you to visit our holy house. After you're finished with Constance, she might show you the grounds. Next door we're building a little casita that will be Constance's new bedroom, and also an office and kitchen and a little meditation room. You'll like to see it. We're a growing little community."

La Madre walked tall from her chair to the curtained doorway, and like sages of old she disappeared through the curtain, leaving the two others to their meager resources.

Constance looked to her captive audience and said, "Ready?"

Patricia was ready. She closed her eyes.

Before saying Go, Constance first said, "While you're meditating, if you want to use any images that arose for you when La Madre was speaking, we recommend that." Then she said, "Go." They meditated. Then they chanted. It was all very soothing to Patricia.

Afterward, Constance took her outside and through the back gate into the little lot next door where the casita was already half built. Constance showed her the bedroom that would be Constance's. It had a big window for the pretty view of the garden they would plant. They could have a little office there too, in the other half of the room. Patricia could see how wonderful all this would be. She introduced her to Maestro Lupe.

When Constance drove her back to the SuperLake, the chauffeur lieutenant said at the last, "I'll be back at this corner at the same time next Sunday. We hope you come. I do too."

12 LA MADRE INFLAMED

For the last two months Constance had awoken at her usual time, 6 AM, had given the next two hours to her devotions, and then prepared the tea and grain cereal that would sustain both herself and La Madre through the morning.

Which then brought her to her happiest moment of the day, when she would put on her heavy black laceups and go next door to see the new state of the construction. The eight Mexicans were all busy now plastering and preparing to paint, and they worked steadily. Maestro Lupe was estimating that the house would be finished in two or three more weeks. Constance from her daily visits had become astute at gauging the progress, and she was dubious of Bellacasa's timetable. Perhaps their maestro was forgetting the little extras La Madre was expecting, that she had been promised.

The workers were busy, and seemed not to notice her. Maestro Lupe greeted her as he always did, and let her wander through the little house that would be the first place of her own in many years that was bigger than a closet. The floors were now all tiled. The windows would be installed later in the week. She stood where she would place her bed, where she could see the orange tree outside, a brief glimpse of Sun each morning. Her room would not be closed, but would have a wide arch leading to the office where she could work or where La Madre could work. The shower and sink and toilet were in place in the tiny bathroom off the bedroom. All of it would be a bit of heaven, especially after the dismal habitations she had suffered all the years in India with La Madre.

After saying goodbye to the maestro Constance returned to the main house and greeted Raul, the gardener and sweet boy of all trades, whom La

Madre called her treasure. His sister Serafina was already in the kitchen preparing the mid-day meal. La Madre was in her office at her desk, computer on, her fat Sanskrit dictionary where she could reach it, two other books beside that. She finished speaking on the phone and hung it up.

She said, "That was Max, he's coming over. He thinks he's getting his last payment. I told him I want to show him what there is left to do."

Constance, standing beside a chair and little desk where she sometimes worked, beside the bookshelf of La Madre's self-published translations and explications, said, "I think he thinks there's less than there really is."

La Madre sat straight-backed and austere in her comfortable, swiveling tilt-back on wheels. She was wrapped head to toe in the orange sari. With a little foxy twinkle in her eye she said, "You have it exactly right, Connie. He is, as the good book says, bewildered."

But they spoke no more of it, wanting to conserve their energies for his arrival, the possible skirmish. La Madre returned to her rendering of Patinjali. Constance at her little desk answered correspondence and stopped to talk time to time with Serafina.

The buzzer to the front gates buzzed twice, and Raul let in the senor and led him to the front door and inside, calling to Constance. She came from the kitchen and simply nodded and said, "La Madre is expecting you." She led him into her mistress's office. La Madre looked up to see him and kept her eyes on him till he was shown the visitor's seat beside her desk. What lay behind that steady gaze no one could know. He sat, still watched by the deep-seeing eyes.

She said, "So you've come to talk business. Lucky for me. I've been wondering when you're going to get to those little extras we've talked about."

Nothing could have diffused his assertiveness more, and so La Madre's calculation and opening thrust had been precisely to the mark. Max knew of course what she talked about, but many of the details were obscure. She saw how he struggled for them.

"No need to worry, Max, let's go outside a minute. I'd rather show them to you anyway."

This delay and diversion Max had not counted on. He had an important appointment at the bank in an hour. But he must smile and accommodate. "OK, show me. We'll see what I can do."

She led him through the living room, past the kitchen and out the back door. They passed Smoky, the black spaniel who got into trouble and who lived mostly in a big cage there. They walked through the sheetiron gate that led to the casita. Lupe saw tall La Madre first, who always frightened

116

him a little, saint of some kind though she must be. Then he saw Max behind her, and Constance close behind him. To Lupe it looked like the senor was in a vise.

La Madre allowed Max the freedom to speak Spanish with his maestro; she knew the language as well. Lupe apprised the senor how the finishing went, and what were their immediate concerns, none of which was unexpected.

The senor then turned to La Madre. Immediately she pointed to the casita's front porch, whose last step maestro Felipe was smoothing. "We *must* have a nice wide walkway from here, around the side of the house, then through into my other yard, all the way to my back door. You know how messy it is in the rains."

This detail, of the sidewalk extension to the back door, he did not recall having heard before. Quickly he calculated it. A couple of days with a couple of maestros and a peon. Cement and gravel. To his guide he said, "Oh I suppose I could. What else?"

She walked him, and Constance followed after, to the far side of the casita, where it made the corner with the back wall. "Here," she said, pointing to the dirt, "a nice sized pad for an outdoor washer and dryer. You said the water lines were pretty close. You could run a little side extension of all the pipes and drains over here. It wouldn't have to be in copper, it could be galvanized. Then I want an electric line from the main box too. Not that much really. A 220 line would be nice."

He remembered her mentioning the pad. Nothing about the rest of it. Again he calculated. Not that much concrete. A morning's work for Marcos, a little pvc. *Maybe* he could afford it. He said, "What else?"

She said, "Inside," and turned to lead him there. Maestro Felipe moved to let them go up the front steps, La Madre surprisingly spry for her seventy years. Constance, a decade younger, but a pudge, more awkwardly followed. Halted inside the front door, La Madre pointed into the meditation room right. "I want that partitioned. I've changed my mind-I want *two* rooms there now. And the new one must have a closet. And a window."

It began to feel to him like a doomsday list. He started saying, "I don't know-" But she cut him off with, "Ah, that's not all! I see you've forgotten all your promises."

Promises? His mind floundered among its memories of their recent meetings, nowhere encountering such extravagant promises. But before he could protest, she motioned for him to follow her into the left rooms. Once inside she said, "For the kitchen, instead of the little cabinets you were going to put in over the sink, I want a tall wide set of cabinets that will be portable. I want them to be put on wheels, so I can leave them in the kitchen, or roll them into the study room and use them for cabinets there. It'll be quite handy. It can also be a room divider. A brilliant idea-no?"

This Max had never heard of, he was certain. Such a thing would cost more than a thousand dollars. Maybe much more. It made him laugh, though he apologized for the laugh. "And with all due respect, all those extras would push me *way* over the budget. I hope you remember I gave you the price for construction that you insisted you had to have, even though it was barely enough to cover all my costs. I only did it because I admire your spiritual work. And your scholarship. Patanjali is someone I read years ago."

"What?" she said, showing her astonishment. "What did you say? *Over* the budget? These are things you've *promised* me, Max. Promises don't have anything to do with a *budget*."

He wracked his mind for a polite way to be sarcastic, but he found none. So he said, "Senora, I'm sorry, I never *promised* you I'd do *any* of these things. You told me you wanted them, and I said I could *possibly* do them. I *might* do them. Depending on many things."

Her astonishment had grown till she would burst with it. Max nonetheless with a handsign bid her let him finish. "I distinctly told you that when we were finished with everything itemized in the contract, that I would do whatever extras you wanted-*if I could afford* it. I'll do the walkway from the front door around to the back of the casita. But all this rest of it would cost *way* too much money. You know you pushed me down on the price for this casita nearly to my cost. You know that."

He paused. She began. "Oh no no no *no*. You *promised* me."

Max, indeed bewildered, said, "No. That's *not* true. We have a contract. It says I must do certain things in this house. There's a list of them. None of these things you just showed me are on the list. I have the smallest budget with you I've ever worked with. I'll do what I can. I'll do the walkway, OK, let's say to as far as the back door of your house. OK. But that's it. All these other things are just way *way* more money than I can spend on this casita. With all due respect."

Cooly she let her fierce opposition relax. She could meet him calmly. She said, "You work that angle too much, Max—that you're doing this for cost. I've asked around. I found somebody who would have done it for less."

He shook his head, realizing then that he would probably never make his bank appointment. "There's *always* somebody will do it for less. Look, I don't want to argue with you. I'll perform every item on the contract. And the extra that I just said. But that's all I can do."

She remained severe. "You repeat yourself. And your deal's unacceptable. You *will* do me the extras." When she saw he would resist her command, she added, "Or you don't get your payment."

He tried to fluff it off. "Senora, you don't have a choice. The payment schedule is in the contract. Today you owe the last payment."

She scorned him. She almost laughed. "But you haven't finished."

Still he resisted. "We'll be done in two weeks. And the last payment has nothing to do with the house being finished. I showed you when we signed, that the last payment was due before we *would* actually finish. You made me a down payment before we started. You've always had to pay in advance."

She scorned him again. "I don't care what it says. You will finish my house and do *all* of my extras, and then I'll give you your money. When I'm completely satisfied."

Stunned, he stared at her: seeing only shangra-la's unassailable palace walls defying him.

Some bits of vagabond cunning from his former lifestyle filtered into his brain, a last maneuver. He said, "Look, with all due respect, I've been assuming this payment would be paid on time, as we signed it in the contract. The very real truth of it is, senora, that we may not be able to finish this job *without* that payment. We would certainly be delayed considerably, and I know how anxious you are for this to be finished. And Constance too. And believe me, I'm with you. We're all the *same* in this. We *all* want this casita finished. As fast as possible. I just need the payment, and whiff, in two weeks we'll be done."

Too clever for him, she said, "Ah but the extras, Mr. Max, *they* would not be done then would they? Not if you have the money first."

Caught in his own syllogism, he felt the slump of a great weight falling from his heart to his stomach. Just perceptibly this caused his shoulders in sympathy to slump too, the Mexican malaise. He tossed her his last little trick. "Look, I think I'm just going to leave right now and give you a little time to think over what I've said. Look—talk to a lawyer. He'll tell you I'm right."

"Good idea," she said, her voice suddenly deepening. "I mean, you going home. And *you* think about what *I've* said too, Mr. Max."

He spoke wearily. "Oh I will. But please—look at the contract, and then call a lawyer and see what he tells you. He'll tell you you're defaulting on the contract."

She sneered. "*That* contract. Oh I hold you to a *much* higher contract, Mr. Max. And woe to you if you break it."

Max flinched at her hard words. Still he said goodbye before turning away from her. He spoke to maestro Lupe only a moment more, told him the smallest of the unhappy news, then departed.

Constance had been frozen in a dreadful awed silence through all of this; awed before the powerful sweep of La Madre's will, as it had always been, bending weaker wills to her desire. But she also dreaded that her little bungalow would somehow go amiss.

Several days of a long bitter silence passed. The maestros and peons returned to work, but no new materials arrived. Saturday the workers worked their half day and went home. Constance dreamed that night that they never returned; but she didn't tell La Madre.

Sunday morning La Madre received an e-mail from Max saying that he would like to meet her again, early the next morning before the work would begin, and he would make a proposal. La Madre was confident.

Nonetheless, she did not like the proposal. He stood before her dressed in his most respectful clothes, and he spoke respectfully. He reiterated his former need of the payment so he could finish the job, but he would commit to only the one aforesaid extra.

He went on. "You've heard all that before, and from the look on your face you don't like it any better than you liked it last time. OK, I will also offer this. You must know of La Fraxa. It's a mediation service in Chapala. Sandra and Henry Thompson are on the committee. I think you know them, they're very well respected. What I propose is that you deposit the last payment with them, and give them the contract. Then I will fulfill the contract. To the letter. And the one extra I promised. When they verify that I have completed the work according to contract they will give me the payment. I think that's fair."

For all his novelist's insight into character, Max did not comprehend the divine mission of La Madre. She chuckled. "Very nice. And here's what I propose to *you*. Do all of it, and all the extras, then I'll give you the money. Just like I told you last time." Then she turned to Constance, who had feared it would come to this, and La Madre told her sad soldier, "Now show Mr. Max the door. And I'm sure he knows I expect all the work done in the next two weeks. Like he *promised.*"

Max left, and drove dazed all the way home.

The rest of the morning Constance pottered in the back yard, peeking through the fence boards every few minutes to see if the workers had arrived, however belatedly. But no one came. Constance held out the hope that Max would assemble his troops and talk it over, and then they would arrive after lunch. But they did not.

Mid-afternoon as she sat forlornly in the kitchen, La Madre suddenly yelled something unintelligible as she sat before her computer, what might have been a Sanskrit profanity. She came stomping out of her office, rage in her eyes and her face lines rigid with it. She saw Constance sagged in her straightback chair and screeched at her. *"He defied me! They're not coming back!"*

The fact did not stun Constance, for she had already come to believe the worst. Had not her dreams foretold this disaster? But La Madre's anger was a surprise, and a worry. Constance stood up and stepped back to allow her mistress more room for her fury, which Constance saw clearly had not yet come to full boil.

La Madre strode blindly past her to the front window, which was curtained fully, and threw back half of it, flooding the room with light. Into this light she screamed a fierce cry of betrayal that shook the panes, and was heard even on the careterra by the drivers passing, whose flesh quivered hearing it. She stood shaking, her fists clenched at her side, jerking and wrenching at the ends of her arms, wanting to take hold of something, wanting to squeeze tight.

He eyes stared horribly outside, but looked at nothing, looked only within: where she saw a terrible darkness, and a fire burning at the heart of that darkness. She let the darkness and the fire rise up and the fire burned her and filled her with flames. She growled. Growled until Constance began to feel faint, and she sat down again in the straightback. But still La Madre growled, and tremored in her hands, standing at the sunny window but seeing only darkness and the fire.

At last La Madre became silent and turned around, though she did not look at Constance, who was glad of it. La Madre's eyes seemed set deeper in their sockets, intensest blue centers that focused a flame. A dark deadly radiance shined out of them. Jaw set, her long face sharpened.

She moved away from the window, though she hardly seemed to move, as if she had become the slow, irresistible deliberation of planetary forces. In the center of the room she ceased moving. Her eyes slowly roved and at last came to rest on Constance, though Constance knew they saw her not. Constance knew also that something terrible was going to happen, and that whatever it was, it would not make the little house of her dreams be completed. She sobbed.

This sob called La Madre back to her earthly dwelling in El Limon, and her eyes flickered. She saw Constance in despair. She spoke, and her voice came now continuously from innermost caverns of herself, deep enough to drown, cold enough to freeze. "Ah poor Constance, nothing is lost, my pet. No matter what it looks like to you, he will come back, and he will do as I demand. Or I will destroy him."

Constance could hear in her voice that either of these results would equally gratify her mistress. Though Constance tried to restrain it this time, she sobbed again.

La Madre moved closer, a gesture of sympathy, but she would not be any more indulgent. She said, "You just want your little room of your own, don't you, dear?"

Constance looked hopefully at her. "Yes I do. Please. Couldn't we just do the arbitration and let them finish it?"

La Madre looked sternly and slowly shook her head. "I can't do that. I want what we were promised. I'll have it. And I won't be trampled on. And I won't let you be trampled on, even if you think you don't care about being trampled."

Constance tried a last plea. "To me, it wouldn't be trampling, it really wouldn't. And what if they *don't* come back and finish? Then what? So what if you destroy them if it never gets finished?"

For an instant La Madre closed her eyes and felt the fire inside her, felt it still enflaming her heart. She reopened her eyes, recharged, and stood taller. She said, "You have lost heart, haven't you, Arjuna? You stand on the plains with me, overlooking the battlefield. We know who the warriors will be. And you are afraid, aren't you? You don't want to fight."

Only gradually did Constance find her way to the meaning of her holy metaphor. She knew better than to disagree. Even so, she still could not agree. She sat mum, not daring to look at her Krishna.

La Madre continued. "You know what it is to be a warrior, Connie. We have had many battles, you and I, over the years. You have always stood with me. Do you waver now, just because you may lose a cherished comfort? Is that it, my dear? No, I won't believe it."

Constance was afraid. She would never be able to hold out.

La Madre pressed closer. "But we do not fight for comforts or for any material ends, Constance. We fight for honor. For justice. For the glory of fighting. You must take your disappointment—and I know how great that is. You must take it and make it into a sword of wrath and go strike the ones who are responsible for your disappointment. You are a warrior, Arjuna, O chastiser of the enemy. You are mourning for what is not worthy of grief."

Constance looked at her. There was much to admire. They had been truly betrayed.

La Madre continued, knowing now that she had righted her devotee's wrong perception. "O Arjuna, rise up and stand beside me. We will go into battle without hesitation and without fear."

Without willing it herself, Constance stood, absorbing the dark radiance from La Madre's eyes, and the heat and the faint flickers of its flames. She warmed inside. Her disappointment still wrenched her heart, but now she let the little flames flick over it and around it, and the sting passed away. She felt the desire to lash out, to let the flames dart away from her and sting the betrayers. It would do her good. She looked fondly in La Madre's eyes. She said, "Alright, I'm ready. I'll do whatever you say. What are you going to do to them?"

La Madre glowered. "We'll be like little sparrows, that no one would take seriously. But we'll peck at them. And peck and peck, until they beg for mercy. Or go down."

13 CARLOTTA AND THE SPARROWS

Driving the careterra from Ajijic to San Antonio Carlotta followed behind a twenty year old pickup of obscure color with an iron rack bolted to the bed, tall as the cab. Hanging from hooks on the top rail were two raw halves of beef, side by side, flopping and thumping against the rear wheel wells, accumulating road dust. Several horses and riders ambled at the edge of the careterra, ready to make a crossing, but hesitated as the meat delivery approached. This slowed the meat truck to a halt as these horses passed in front of it, while the squadron of flies that had been sniffing the horses drifted away to the more attractive hideless and defenseless carcasses. When the meat truck resumed its progress the flies valiantly tried to keep pace with the flesh of choice, but were soon blown away in the turbulence.

Rolling her windows shut, Carlotta followed, but let the meat truck move way ahead of her. Presently the truck turned down Calle Galinda to make its way into San Antonio and the meat market there. Carlotta went only a little further, to the SuperLake, which specialized in all things gringo and imported, and she parked. At the entrance she encounted Sandra Thompson, who had been on her mind.

"Sandra, hola. Max told me you've heard from La Madre, that she was considering the arbitration."

Sandra stopped and smiled, always well dressed, a southern lady married to a retired country lawyer gentleman, both of them avid in Democratic politics, now retired and basking. Though even in Mexico Sandra liked to express her politics and she dabbled in social services.

She laughed. "Oh yes, the mediation. La Madre called me yesterday. She cursed you I will say. She asked me some questions. I think she *might* do it. She wants me to come look at her construction."

Carlotta sighed. "Well I wish she would. Nothing like this has ever happened to us before."

Carlotta was about to ask concerning Henry Thompson' health when she noticed a fiery orange handbill on the community bulletin board that announced her company's name: BELLACASA. Puzzled, she looked closer. She read it with eyes agoggle.

To all those who have been abused and cheated by BELLACASA CONSTRUCTION. You are invited to join a pending Class Action lawsuit. Please contact us with your mistreatment. Bring all the facts and figures and pictures. E-mail: BellacasaClassAction@hotmail.com

Carlotta could hear herself shrieking though no sound came out of her. Stunned and reddening in the face with outrage, she marched to the board and ripped the handbill away.

She showed it to Sandra, who read it and shook her head.

"La Madre?"

"Who *else?*" snapped Carlotta.

"Well I don't imagine anybody's *ever* sued you, have they?" drawled Sandra, who had known Max and Carlotta the last year and a half, and knew well of their work and their reputation.

Silently Carlotta growled. "*Never!* We're good friends with *all* the people we've built houses for. Except Kriboom, who got the best deal of anybody. Isn't this slander?"

"Well it absolutely is, if there are actually no law suits pending. And Mexico's very tough on that. It's their pride you know. Nobody's allowed to besmirch your good name."

"My *God!*" bellered Carlotta, as the enormity of it sunk further into her being.

Sandra looked at the handbill again. "You know, in Mexico this is criminal. It's not civil like it sometimes is in the US. And that puts it out of our hands at Fraxa. We don't do mediation with criminal cases. You are going to sue her, aren't you?"

Carlotta stared, but still could hardly fathom it. "I don't know."

Sympathetic Sandra patted her on the shoulder. "Maybe you should call a lawyer. In the meantime I'm going to call La Madre. I owe her a call anyway. And I'm going to tell her that because of this postering, we can't take the case. I'll also tell her about the very nasty Mexican law concerning slander and advise her to stop immediately and to take down all the posters she's put up."

Carlotta slowly turned to look at her. "All the posters?" Then she imagined it well. "*Oh my God!* I'd better go to all the poster places and see if there are more."

"I would," said Sandra. "I'll call you as soon as I talk to her."

Thirty minutes later Carlotta came to the Bellacasa office with four more garish neon handbills. Max and Carlotta talked with alarm and anger about the handbills, until it tired them. Then they closed the office early and drove home and waited for Sandra's call.

When she did call, Sandra began, amused. "I think La Madre understands she made a mistake with the handbill. She didn't realize it was slander. She said she didn't want any police trouble. She said she'd take the others down."

"I've already done that," growled Carlotta.

"Ooo-O!" said Sandra. "Well, I'm sorry all this happened. I know how stressing it is. But, like I said, I think that'll be the end of it."

So she and Max also hoped.

By the end of a week they had stopped looking at the notorious billboards. On the ninth day, going for a donut at Dona's, Max spotted a new one glaring in neon red-orange at him from the bulletin board beside the front door. He stopped his pickup and ripped it down and cursed the maker.

The same day Max called a Chapala law firm, newly franchised from Guadalajara, Garamos and Associates. He met with a petite but very business-like young lawyer named Linda, but whom they everafter called La Petite. Her tiny and innocent appearance made her look no more than eighteen. She spoke softly but precisely, and she quickly made them confident of her capability. They showed her the contract and gave her all twelve neon handbills. La Petite said it was certainly slander, claiming the pending class action when in fact there was not even one lawsuit against them. She said she would call La Madre and explain the illegality of the postings and the severe consequences, and advise her to cease posting. Or La Petite would tell her that she had no choice but to file a criminal complaint against the slanderer and whoever was doing the posting. How could this not stop it?

Max and Carlotta saw no postings at any of the bulletin boards the next two days. The following sunny autumn day they went by invitation to the new and stylish Casa Grande a half block down from the careterra on

Colon, two blocks from the plaza straight ahead. Jim Penton had invited them. He asked Max to bring a copy of the book he'd finally finished, *The Golden Days of Maximiliano and Carlotta*. Jim wanted to introduce him to a friend and published novelist, who was also editor for years of the *Ojo del Lago*, the local gringo monthly newspaper, Alex Grattan, whom Max recognized, but had never spoken to.

Alex was half Mexican, but had lived most of his life in the United States, much of it in Hollywood as a screenwriter, editor and sometimes director. He looked all California, with a snappy wit and a broad intelligence. Most people liked him and were entertained by his thousand reminiscences and the glitter of his old acquaintances. He'd published two novels with a southwest university press, both stories of the clash of white and hispanic cultures in the mid-1900s.

Jim and Alex had already seated themselves and were drinking beer when Max and Carlotta arrived beneath the eighteen foot ceilings, in the ambience of the fiery modern Mexican paintings on all the walls. Jim waved and grinned at them. He and Alex were seated beside a little dessert cart topped with luscious samples.

Jim rose to greet them and introduced them both to Alex. The editor and author shook hands with both of them, Carlotta's the last, and she got the bigger smile. He seemed a simple man of the earth, with a twinkle in his eye, sandy hair stitched with gray, straight, over his ears. The observant waiter came and took their orders for one red and one white wine, and then went away. After they had all set, Jim said, looking to Alex, "Aside from the novel I see he's remembered to bring us, Max is the one who did the fancy fountain and river in my back garden. You saw it last month when you came for dinner."

Alex sat up a little, remembering. He said, "Oh yes, I do remember. Amazing. That little river that wanders all through the garden and goes into the pool next to the deck. The big splashy waterfall. Don't think I've ever seen anything like it around here. So you're an artist in construction too. Congratulations."

"Thank you, thank you," Max said, making a quick mock bow. "Carlotta picked out all the pretty rocks."

Carlotta laughed, removing her wide brimmed straw and setting it under her chair. "Not true at all. I picked out a few maybe. Max is the artist."

Max said, "Yes, it was a great experiment. Jim's lucky, I'd never done anything like this. The river could have flowed backwards."

Jim laughed. "Don't believe him, Alex. Max and his men are quite the craftsmen."

"You don't have to tell me," said Alex. "I've *seen* that fountain. And I've seen Smokey Stover's house up at the Raquet Club. That's really something too."

Max said, "Oh, you know Smokey. Then you saw the free standing cupola at their front door. That's one of my best creations. I designed it and directed the tile work, but my maestros did all the hard work. They made the fancy dome and the four thin pillars."

Carlotta perked. "Yes, that's my favorite thing we've done in Mexico. We saw pictures of the Biblioteque Nacional in Paris, where they have all these tall, free standing cupolas in the main reading room. We wanted to do one just like it. Max finally figured out how to do it. I just love it."

Alex said, "Smokey does too, now that I'm recalling it. He certainly enjoys showing it off."

The discrete waiter returned with the wines, set them before the new guests, and saw by their nods that the other two were yet satisfied, and he silently departed,

Jim Penton looked to Max and said, "Alex's just told me that a producer called from LA this morning to tell him they were interested in doing his first novel as a TV mini-series."

Such good fortune was the stuff of Max's dreams. Though he'd written enough words to constitute a considerable apprenticeship, and had finely-tuned query letters and synopses of several novels, and had solicited agents and publishers by the dozens of dozens, these hopeful novels were rarely read and always rejected.

Sipping his red wine, Max said, "Well I certainly envy that. And I'm really happy for you. I know what good fortune that is."

Alex wore a blue work shirt open at the throat, blue-tinted glasses. Basking in the compliments, he lit a cigarette. He sat back, taking his beer bottle again in his hand and sipping. He said, "It's only the first step of a long process. I don't get too excited yet. I've been this far before."

Max laid beside his plate a cardboard box that contained his own manuscript. He said to Alex, "After Jim told me last week that he wanted to introduce me to you, I read both your novels. I'm really impressed."

Alex nodded graciously. "I do appreciate that. I've been complimented before, but I appreciate it every time I hear it. Yes I do, probably just as much as the first time. What did you think of the books?"

Max considered only a moment. "Well I like the Mexican-American thing, like you. It's a lot of why I'm here. It's probably the same for you too, it must be." Alex nodded, savoring the writer's favorite moment, the happy review. "And one thing that I especially enjoyed, was that I never expected any of the plot turns. Normally when I read I can see it from a writer's point of view and I know what he's leading up to. But with *your* stories, I was always guessing it would go one place, and then you'd surprise me, and go another way. And I have to say that every time I liked where you took it more than where I thought it was going to go."

Alex laughed, delighted. "Well that's a fine compliment. Thank you indeed."

"Was it hard to find a publisher for it?" Max asked, coming to the burning point.

"Oh! Well, with the first novel, I'd given up on the publisher I'd sent it to, to tell you the truth. I'd sent them a summary and a couple of chapters, and they'd told me to send them the complete novel, which I did. And then I sat back and waited. So many, many months went by that I about gave up on them. After a year I had kissed it off. Then one day, I got a letter in the mail from them that said, Hey, we like it, we want to publish it."

Ah yes, Max, the stuff of dreams. Inwardly he sighed. Outwardly he spoke. "And then the next one they just took immediately I suppose."

"Yes they did," said Alex, enjoying the memory. "Can't say either one ever made me much money. But it's an ongoing marketing process really. The published novel gets me a few reviews, it gets me a little circulation. I can send out published novels to Hollywood instead of typed manuscripts. It's easier that way to get producers interested in my stories. I'm still waiting for the *big* contract."

Inside Max that last haunting line echoed and re-echoed over and over. As if Alex were reading the thoughts of his admirer, he said, "So Jim tells me you've written an unusual novel. About two of my favorites."

"Oh they're just about everybody's favorites who read Mexico's history," said Jim. "So much *not* like the usual stories of the reign of kings."

"Yes," said Alex. "A bit too much of the fairy tale."

"Yes," said Jim, a laugh ready to bubble up. "*They* probably saw it that way. Unfortunately, *nobody* else did."

They all could laugh at that, even Max, for whom Maximilian always beckoned in his innermost fancy.

Alex said, "But Jim tells me that your novel's a bit unusual. That it's not the actual story, *as it happened.*"

Max was energized. "No. I turned it into a fantasy, made it kind of a science fiction story of parallel worlds, which starts, on the night before his execution, when Maximilian loses consciousness and passes into a parallel universe. He wakes up and Carlotta is already waiting for him at the boat dock in Marseilles. They're boarding to go to Mexico and meet the contingent that has invited them to come be their king and queen. And in this parallel universe their story has a much different ending. Events similar to real historical events take unexpected twists and turns that eventually bring them to a very different conclusion."

Alex considered this a minute. "You mean, it has a happy ending?"

Max smiled simply. "Yes it does."

"Hmm," said the editor. "What do you do about conflict then? You gotta have a lot of conflict."

"Oh there's conflict," said Max, "but it's a little lowkey."

"Doesn't sound good," said Alex, speaking his mind. Then he brightened, for he knew as well to keep this fellow writer's courage up, and he added, "But you probably make up for it with the great characters, don't you?"

Max said, "I really don't know. That's why I'd love for you to take a look at it."

Alex smiled. "Well that's what I'm here for. Is that it?" He pointed to the box.

"That's it. Four hundred twenty pages of who knows what." Max passed it to Alex.

Alex said, "OK, gimme a couple weeks and I'll let you know what I think." Then he grinned. "How ruthless do you want me to be?"

Max laughed. "You be as ruthless as you want. I know I have a weird premise and I don't know if it works. It may just be political satire for all I know, and not really a novel at all."

Jim Penton laughed too. "Well from my point of view, there can never be enough satire." His good deed accomplished, Jim turned to his favorite, a sparkle in his eye, and said, "Carlotta, I haven't seen you around recently. Still working hard?"

She took her first sip of wine, then held it poised before her, and said, "I wouldn't mind more, if you want to know the truth. There is one new bright spot though. Our new secretary Virginia. After our disaster with that scoundrel Fonzo. You'll love this, Jim—our new secretary Virginia spent seven years recently in a convent in Spain."

Jim indeed brightened, his eyes intensifying, and said, "You don't say."

"Yes. Translating old Spanish church manuscripts into English. She came home to Mexico a year or so ago to take care of her very sick father. She lives with him in Chapala. And she's as darling as she can be."

Even more interested, he now smiled, and said, "You *don't* say. And how old is this special lady?"

"Actually, hard to tell. Probably somewhere in her thirties. Oh, and this too. She was born on December 12, the Virgin's day, which is why they named her Virginia. You can't imagine how maestro Guadalupe tiptoes around her. I swear whenever he sees her, he almost genuflects. He's completely starstruck."

Jim grinned, cavalier still after sixty years and more. "Well I'm ready to be starstruck too. When do we meet her." He laughed. "I'll bring Marilyn along to make sure I behave myself." He made his gentleman rogue's laugh from his belly, and all his listeners smiled irresistibly.

Max said, "It's worse than you think, Jim. She really *is* a beauty physically too."

"Oh goodness!" Jim threw back. "This does sound dangerous."

Alex reminisced. "I once knew someone like that in Hollywood. It was said of her, no matter how many guys were attracted to her, and all of them were, no one ever dared touch her or say *any* kind of suggestive *anything*—for fear of being struck instantly by lightning."

Max laughed. "I think you've hit it perfectly."

"So do I," said Jim with gusto.

Carlotta laughed loudest. "Oh you men! Such amazing ideas! Wait'll I tell Virginia!"

14 CARLOTTA AND MAX GO TO WAR

Carlotta was thinking of that pleasant afternoon even the next mid-morning as she went for the mail at Mail Box Etcetera. There were a few personal bills and a letter for Max from his daughter Jesse.

She looked up and saw the new neon handbill blaring BELLACASA. The anger surged and her face reddened with it. She ripped it down and hurried to the next door, the SuperLake community board. Two more emblazoned. She ripped those. She drove to the other likely boards and found one on each. She drove in a fury to the jobsite in Rancho del Oro, and yelled at Max from the van. When he trotted to her she showed him, and he too flushed and swore.

Lupe, who was cementing in a front window, saw their excitement and hurried over. Carlotta thrust it at him. Lupe had been shown the handbills from the first day's assault, and the slander had been explained to him. He too was outraged, at the disgrace upon his own craftsmanship, and upon the good name of la compania. He understood war between enemies, in the barrio. But this gringo way of war of paper was a bizarre new thing to him.

"What will you do, senor?" he asked.

Max himself wondered. "I suppose we'll have to go ahead with the lawsuit, like La Petite says."

Carlotta was confounded. "She's mad! She can go to jail for this! I can't believe she's keeping this up."

Brooding, Max imagined the days ahead. "Whenever she comes to town. We'll have to follow that goddamn little red Volkswagen around."

And follow it they did. Carlotta, lurking in the parking lot beside the SuperLake, first spotted the red Volkswagen gliding off the careterra and stopping in front of the market among fifteen others parked. Prim Constance emerged from the red bug, clad forever in the same blue-gray granny outfit, hair pulled back severely, the granny's bun behind, stern wire glasses. She held a file folder under her arm and a little gray bag suspended from her elbow. She marched to the community board and looked thoroughly till she saw her last posting was missing.

From her dark folder she drew another, brighter than sunshine. She held it in one hand while she extracted from her bag several pushpins. She stood back from the board again and gauged her best location. Head-high, in the space next to the lost doggy notice. One hand held it up, the other punched in a pin above and below the call to arms. She stood back, satisfied. She found another spot at the far end of the board and she drew from her folder another scarlet sunshine and punched the pins in. Again she stood back and was happy.

Peck. And. Peck.

As Carlotta sat silently witnessing this, a terrible anger and outrage boiled up in her. She had already, almost, imagined witnessing the crime in the midst of commission. But in her imagination she had not foreseen how scalded, scorched to the core she now suddenly felt. She also imagined other scenes, all of them the forceable destruction of the little grandmother and her mistress, no violence too much. And burning she remained, as she watched Constance re-enter her little red bug and drive off to Carlotta knew where.

Though Carlotta would follow her, she must first rip away the two posted slanders. When she went to the second one, where a man she had known casually at the agency had just stopped to read it. Carlotta reached in front of his eyes and ripped it away viciously, startling the man, who was trying to remember where he'd once seen this so-irate woman.

Carlotta hurried with a mad passion back to her white van and quickly drove onto the careterra, knowing the next stop would be a mile and a half away at the El Torito market. By the time she had raced halfway, beneath the glorious canopy of galeanas at La Floresta, she saw the red bug, showing braking lights, slowing and pulling in and parking. Carlotta drove to just beyond the parking lot and stopped.

She saw Constance at the bulletin board beside the front door put up another one, punching in the pins. Constance saluted this one and drove away.

Ready to kill, Carlotta ripped away this third one, stuffing it now in the bag she brought along, where she'd stuffed the other two, well crumpled. This one too she devasted depositing it.

Dona's Donuts would be next. Seize, capture and destroy. The wizened and wise at the outside tables merely looked and wondered at the sudden change of events, one posting, another immediately unposting.

Carlotta followed the red bug down the narrowness of Colon, creeping single file this busy morning. She turned off onto Ocampo where she could park and still see Constance go inside the little post office and set off her neon bomb. Carlotta soon saw her return and drive away. Carlotta scuttled across the cobblestones and onto the sidewalk and down to mid-block and stepped into the quiet post office, her heart beating wildly. She ripped away the bright poster while the postmaster watched her. He too only stared in silence.

Carlotta followed the red devil car down Constitucion to Galaraga, then up to the careterra, always more than a block behind her. Carlotta waited at the careterra after the red bug had turned left toward her home in El Limon, rather than right, where further mischief might be had.

Carlotta and Max both in the afternoon drove to Chapala and talked again with La Petite. She was still confident, dressed today masculinely in a suit and vest, though a frilly white collared shirt open full at the throat, beckoning, belied all the masculine regalia. She spoke English with a strong accent. "I know this is a terrible thing to see happening, but I'm sure we'll be able to stop it quickly. Andre my superior is himself calling La Madre, and will drive out to see her if necessary. It can only be that she is not understanding the severe consequences. It is not a thing like you can do something like this and then say you were crazy and the police let you go free, like in the United States. The Policia here don't listen to excuses like that. You know what I mean?"

They imagined it, and it helped pacify them.

La Petite continued. "Even so, I have prepared a full criminal complaint that we will file later today in any case. Just to give ourselves the teeth. When she complies, we'll withdraw the demanda."

The words for the moment soothed them both, though both remained at full alert, for the war would obviously go on, and who knew what might happen?

Nonetheless, the following day, they awoke apprehensive. They drank too much coffee at breakfast in their blessed isolation in La Canacinta, beside the cow pasture, behind the corn field. They left an hour earlier than usual.

135

Max went to join Lupe at his jobsite. Carlotta drove the careterra. She brought a camera, as La Petite had advised her, so they might make their most compelling and complete case to the policia. Carlotta followed Constance's mainline route, inspecting the boards carefully. But she was too early. Also she was too anxious to leave the trail. She cruised the careterra, studied the billboards without having to drive near them, for the neon bright signs were easily distinguished.

An hour and a half of this persistence was at last rewarded. Carlotta saw the red bug and its armed soldier going the opposite direction. Carlotta u-turned adroitly and followed her. Constance stopped first at the El Torito market, parked and went with her ammunition to the board. Carlotta could see the red dot centered in her forehead. Constance studied the board a moment, no doubt displeased that her efforts were being so quickly swatted away. But she was not daunted, for she had the patience of little feisty sparrows that would not be denied. She posted a replacement. She could create thousands. Or as many as there might be seeds in a mountain of birdseed.

Carlotta arrived too late to photograph, and realized she must be there already, stationed, hidden and prepared to record the crime and its perpetrator *in flagrante* with her camera. She drove in haste to SuperLake, which she knew would be Constance's next stop. She hid behind a windowless van parked twenty meters from the main billboard. She saw the little red bug approaching. She saw it park. Constance with her dark folder and her purse hanging from her elbow went to the board.

Carlotta peered out from her hiding place. She saw Constance studying the board again, and snapped a first picture. Constance pulled out a fiery handbill and Carlotta photographed that. Constance posted it, punching in the pins, and Carlotta photographed that. Constance posted the second one at the other end of the board and Carlotta photographed again. Constance remounted her red bug and drove on. Carlotta ripped away the handbills and discretely followed.

The following day Carlotta tracked her adversary again, but this time Virginia, the former nun now secretary, rode with her, that she might be a witness for the prosecution, for La Petite had advised this as well. Virginia witnessed every posting, witnessed as well her irate employer ripping and cursing.

For Virginia, already sympathetic and devoted to her employer, there was nonetheless amusement in this chase and parry. She tried to refrain her laughter when Carlotta returned to the car after ripping the last handbill from the post office wall; but small tittering escaped her nonetheless.

Carlotta looked at her, her own face grim with anger. But as she watched Virginia's unquenchable mirth, at last Carlotta saw it too. A little constrained laughter rumbled its way out of Carlotta, moving Virginia to more and better laughter. So that, despite herself, Carlotta also finally laughed with her friend, a blessed relief. A happy, momentary little release. But it was no solution. The war raged on. Carlotta squared her jaw again and drove after Constance.

Max spoke with La Petite nearly every day by telephone, and saw her every other day, bringing with him twelve to fifteen new neon handbills each time. As they sat in her outer office, next door to a sub-station of La Policia where complaints were filed and witnesses interrogated, Max said, "What can we do to stop this? I'm beginning to believe that she's not going to be stopped until they haul her off to jail."

La Petite that day wore a new hairstyle, shortened, arranged close about her tiny ears and her little pixy face. Max tried to imagine how this would play in court, in a fierce cross-examining. He couldn't decide.

La Petite said, "I am puzzled as well. Both times we've spoken to her, Arturo and I, she's said she wants no trouble and will stop posting. But she doesn't. We've explained both times what will happen to her."

Max handed her the photos Carlotta had taken. "Oh very good," said La Petite, looking closely at them. "So this is the little person that does the posting. Yes, I've seen her next door at the Policia a few times. She seems to have frequent business with them. Well, this proof is perfect. And you say you also have a good witness."

"Yes, a former Catholic nun."

She grinned at him. "This is a good trump card, as you americanos say. In Mexico the card of the eastern holy woman is always trumped by a Catholic holy woman. No matter their ages."

Max ignored the humor. "Is there any way we can make a restraining order against her? In the United States it's done when someone does something obviously illegal, and the court orders them to stop, until the case can be heard."

La Petite shook her head. "Unfortunately no. I've heard of this restraining order thing. But Mexican law has nothing like that. We *can* talk to the judge if you like, and we can tell him the urgency of this. Perhaps the court itself will advise her to cease her postering till the case is heard."

He looked at her hopefully. "Do you think the judge would do that?"

"Perhaps. I can say no more than that. He's in his office now, I believe, next door. Shall we go see?"

Max would have walked twenty miles for such an opportunity. He smiled as much as he could and said of course, for he only had to walk out the lawyer's office and to the sidewalk and twelve paces left and they were at the front door of La Policia, substation Zaragoza. Max followed his tiny guide through the outer office where witnesses gathered to give testimony to three clerks side by side at three desks, who all typed with great force on their twenty year old black upright Remingtons, for they must make enough impression for even the fifth carbon copy to record the sworn words of all these aggrieved Mexicans.

La Petite led him beyond all those, down a short hallway and she stopped at the open door at the end and leaned her head in. Just behind her, Max heard her greet someone unseen. She stepped into the room. La Petite went to the man seated behind a plain work table, a book upon it, a few sheets of paper, nothing more. The man himself looked like any of the other dark peasants in the witness room. He wore levis, workboots, and a plaid vest jacket that might be for hunting. Thirty five years old. Newly made judge in the PAN revolution.

Max stopped just inside the door and watched La Petite. The man rose to shake the hand she extended, saying, "Mucho gusto, licenciado." All properly formal. La Petite briefly explained their case. She showed him a handbill and translated it for him. She explained about Max's business, and the urgency for the good name of the compania. He nodded, he understood her perfectly.

He was indeed Judge Ernesto Guavarara. He reached to withdraw a small paperback book from a half-open drawer and placed it on the table. The unfurnished room was dimly lit and he leaned closer to read as he thumbed his way to the page he wanted. He found it. Right index finger follwed down the page as he scrutinized more closely.

"Yes," he said in Spanish, looking up at them. "It is as I remembered it. Certain steps must be followed. This book tells what each of them are. A demanda is made against a person for a criminal act. That you have done. Then the person named is served the demanda, and is ordered to come in at a certain date and give testimony. They may bring witnesses. You who make the demanda must also come in and give testimony, and then bring your witnesses. Then all this testimony, and all the evidence and reports will be typed up, and then all this goes to the judge, which is me, and the judge then decides."

As Max listened he seemed to be seeing the procession of the ages. "But that could take forever, senor. I hope you can understand—Carlotta and I are employing many, many Mexicans. We eventually hope to give our

138

company to our workers. How long do you *think* it will take the judge to make his decision?"

He seemed to weigh it lightly. "Really, it is impossible to say. Every case is different. Strange things can happen."

This last made Max feel a creepy tingle in the crown of his scalp. Mercifully, La Petite asked His Honor Guavarara, "Surely for so blatant an act of slander, the courts might do something. Even if only in an advisory way, I'm sure you know what I mean. To let the person know that it will certainly go worse for her if she keeps postering, even while the case goes to the inevitable judgment."

The judge had no need to ponder this. "No," he said. "I am afraid nothing like that can be done. The laws are very explicit. The steps must be followed. In order. All this takes time. Until the judgment is given, the police have no right to interfere for either party."

The creepy tingle in Max's scalp, a moment in suspension, suddenly revivified, making him shiver through his body. He drew a deep breath. There were plenty of questions left inside him, but Max knew that there would be no satisfactory answers forthcoming. The judge glanced to his watch for his next appointment, verifying that the interview had fully expressed itself.

La Petite led a slump-shouldered Max back through the witness room, where he would no doubt be coming on some future day to bear witness against his nemesis. They stepped into fresher air outside, and that helped, though little. She led him back inside her office and she took him to a seat and then sat before him. She patted him on the shoulder. She urged him not to despair. The law would bring him justice. Perhaps even La Madre would come to her senses and stop for her own good.

Max grasped at all these straws and left, however, still a slumped man.

He walked sullenly two blocks to Chapala's primary intersection, and thought to stop at the Paris Cafe, at a table curbside, for something to steady him. He realized it would do no good. He crossed the intersection and went past the municipal building and its armed guard. A half block further, as he passed the offices of Chapala Realty, wherein were the offices of *Ojo del Lago*, he saw Alejandro Grattan coming down the stairs.

The editor and book critic called out warmly, "Hey there, Max. Amigo. Donde vas?"

Max halted, deep in his daze still. He fumbled inside his brain remembering all the data that went with the happy Grattan face. Embarrassed by his remoteness from reality, he could only say, "Alex! I would've walked right past, no kidding. I didn't even see you. I'm in a fog right now."

Alejandro clapped him on the shoulder. "Say, you got a minute? I just finished your novel and I've been wanting to talk to you about it. I made some notations in the margin, and some notes in general, and we can go over those when we both have a half hour or so. But I can certainly give you my immediate impressions right now while they're fresh. I've been thinking about it all morning."

As Max let his mind reaffirm these, for him, ancient priorities and dreams, his breathing slowed and he felt the ground beneath his feet again. He smiled. "Blast away."

"Good," Alejandro said. "Now this is odd how I feel, thinking about it now, how good I think this book is, while at the same time I think it's completely wasted effort."

Max flinched, though he knew there was a compliment in there somewhere. Alejandro looked severely at him. "Don't get me wrong now. The last thing I want to do is crush a talent. And I believe you have an exceptional talent. Your scenes are so right for the story, every time, that I'm truly amazed. Perfectly pictorial. It's all ready for the movie. The pace is exhilarating, and you're deadly with the suspense. The characters are vivid and I enjoyed even the minor ones, the walk-ons. And you do descriptive writing as good as anyone I've read. But—" And he paused, that Max might know this next speech bore an equal importance to all the other. "This idea about Maxmillian and Carlotta is nuts, let me tell you. You were right about it being an interesting political satire. It could be, if you shortened it and didn't take these two characters so damn seriously. You obviously are mad about them. OK, *maybe* it's an interesting satire. But it's all wrong as a novel. Everything goes right for them, every possible little conflict that arises, they're able to brush it away, or someone else brushes it away. And having Benito Juarez marry their daughter to unite their two destinies and create the kingdom come in Mexico!—I did *not* believe for one minute. It's laughable. And as bad as anything that comes with your premise, is the plain fact that there's just no damn good conflict. I'm sorry, but that's important. If you want your novel published it is. And if you expect anybody to read all the way through it, it is."

Max's shoulders sagged severely. The critical acclaim that belongs to prize winners that had been ringing in his ears only moments ago, now faded from his memory as this new criticism roared through him like a little tornado. Yet deep within him he knew the truth of it. He had whispered it

140

to himself, in the deepest night many times. He had just wanted to make it all right for his heroes, no doubt about it.

Alex put a fatherly hand on his shoulder. "I know that's deadly, old boy. But I hope you take it like a man. And you should. You have gold in you I'm telling you. You're an absolute natural. You just need a good story. Say—why don't you write about Mexico? Mexico today. Hell, *your* life must be pretty interesting, yours and Carlotta's. You been down here long enough to know the place, the people. Hellfire, man, write that."

Max slumped still. This new enthusiasm of Alex's didn't much straighten him. He said his thanks, bid his buddy farewell, and trudged away.

15 LUPE PRAYS TO THE VIRGIN

Lupe had considered his strategy carefully, had assessed and cross-examined it for several days, until he was confident it was the right one. He would wait till the Virgin's birthday celebration, when, as everyone knew, the Virgin was most likely to answer special prayers, her little birthday gifts to the most faithful. Padre Morelia might think that Lupe was not among the faithful, but the Virgin knew his heart, wherein he spoke to her often, and she might perceive him otherwise.

Lupe's special offering to the Virgin's church was that he and la compania Bellacasa had contributed several thousand pesos to Padre Morelia, who supervised the celebration. Their gift had purchased a great and glorious fireworks display that would be shot off at midnight in the placita at Six Corners. This highlight of the happiest of all fiesta nights in the barrio was one block from the Church of the Virgin of Guadalupe, in the heart of the barrio, where Her church had always been.

He would wait until this gift of fireworks would be displayed to the Virgin and to all her celebrators at midnight. Then he would speak to her his prayer. He would ask her help. In whatever way it seemed fit to her to give it, so long as it strangled La Madre and Constance; by which he meant of course, not the persons themselves, but strangle their terrible tormenting of la compania.

However, if indeed he were truly as heathen as he sometimes thought he was, as heathen as the padre probably thought he was, then his prayer might not be answered. Then he would be forced to try other, more primitive methods, the last resort of heathens.

It was almost nine and the barrio was filled with people, sitting on steps, curbs or parked cars, or strolling the crowded cobblestone streets. Several called to him and waved before he had walked three steps. He could hear the musica coming from the placita a half block away and he went in that direction. To more of his neighbors he waved and nodded as they waved and called to him.

It would also be good for his strategy if he could find the senor and the senora. Virginia would be with them, the holy nun who had come, he had dreamed the night before, to save la compania. Then he might receive one of Virginia's good luck smiles. Even more luck would be a touch of her hand in welcome, another fortunate benediction. It was double luck that Virginia's birthday was also on this most special of days, for this was Lupe's own Saint's Name Day as well. He quickly crossed himself, and spoke silent blessings upon the Virgin of Guadalupe, and upon Virginia the nun and upon la compania and the senor and the senora.

As Lupe walked, hands in pockets, jacket collar turned up against the first chill of the December evening, he searched faces. He looked above the heads for the head that would be taller than most, the senora, and the gray-haired senor beside her, who would no doubt be drinking his Sol cerveza. Best of all, Virginia would be there with them.

As Lupe maneuvered himself toward the church, he saw the church band turn out of the gates and come blaring up the street, all horns and a passionate drummer who hammered it home. Even so, the trumpets and tubas kept their own beat, sometimes ahead, sometimes behind. Precision they had none, but passion and a big sound was possible for all these young musicians, who played to the crowds with all the gusto in them. Children and adults fell in behind the happy band and all marched along Ocampo, these followers grinning and laughing as they went away from the placita, carrying the celebration to those who could not come to it. Windows and doors opened as the booming, blaring band passed. Old ones and young ones looked out and laughed and waved to those playing, those following, none strangers here.

Lupe saw Marcos at a curbside half a block away, watching the band pass. Marcos lifted his right hand and held up two fingers in a V, something he'd brought back from California. In his other arm Marcos held his young daughter Teresa high, seated on his shoulder, a four year old and already a dark beauty with round black eyes darting everywhere, delighted with the crowds shifting around her. Marcos with his daughter walked toward Lupe.

Marcos smiled, looking for fun. But Lupe's preoccupation would allow him no fun tonight, even on this, his favorite fiesta. He said to his

144

compadre, "Did you see the senor or the senora today? After they went to their lawyer's?"

Marcos tossed it off. "Not me. And maybe, at least tonight, we all might forget about it and have a good time, amigo."

Lupe laughed. "I'm too nervous to have a good time. Ask Gloria. She's with Isabel. I can't help it. For many reasons this thing with La Madre disturbs me. I tell the senor he must not trust too much the law to protect him. But you have heard him. All the gringos trust the law. Maybe it is that way up north. But the senor should know better by now, how it is in Mexico."

Half listening, Marcos now only nodded, glancing here and there quickly, so much to see, letting the grim conversation fade away.

Yet it would not fade, because Lupe had recently resolved a plan. Should all else fail.

"Marcos, I want to know if I can count on you. If we should all have to go visit La Madre, at midnight, in El Limon."

Marcos stepped back in surprise, tottering so slightly his daughter on his shoulder, who clung tighter to his head, and so restabilized. Marcos said, "Visit La Madre? You think it's come to that?"

Lupe showed his impatience. "What are *you* waiting for?"

Marcos shrugged. "I don't know. The senor *sounds* so confident when he talks about his case, and the lawyer, and how the judge is on their side and all that. He *seems* OK. He really believes he's going to win. He *believes* it will all be made right in the end. So maybe I'm waiting for him to show me a little doubt, or to *ask* for our help."

"Pues, amigo, not this kind of help will he ever ask for. You know him. So I'm asking *you*, compadre, will you go with us if it becomes necessary. If all else fails."

Marcos smiled. "Who is *us*, amigo?"

"My brother, and Felipe Romero. Two others probably. One is Ruben the electricista from Jocotepec, who says La Madre won't pay him for a job he did for her a few months ago. We will go and give her a big scare. That is all. It will be enough."

Marcos still smiled. "Of course I would go. Will Tacho go?"

Lupe winced. "I have thought of it. It might be good. Or it might be bad. I don't know if I should ask him. Or even tell him."

Lupe heard the senor Max's voice calling his name and Lupe looked away from Marcos, imagining what the senor would say hearing their conversation. Lupe saw all the blessed three, the senor holding his Sol cerveza, Carlotta in a pretty hat, laughing, and then, bless us all, Virginia, the Virgin's emissary, beside Carlotta. Both ladies drank something steamy, probably a canela, both laughing to each other.

Lupe had never seen a nun so pretty. Tonight she held the furry collar of her coat close around her throat, such pretty hands. With utmost reverence Lupe went to her.

He offered his hand. She took it a moment, as always, and then he let it go, as she spoke her greeting to him. But he savored the brief, holy contact.

She spoke to him in Spanish. "Happy Saint's Name Day, Don Lupe."

She called him that every time recently, *Don* Lupe. Even Tacho had remarked it. He returned the compliment. "And felicidades on *your* birthday." There was no name or title for her in his mouth that seemed respectful enough. Simple Virginia was too ordinary; probably Santa Virginia would be too much; so he usually avoided calling her anything. He turned aside and crossed himself as quickly, as unobstrusively as possible.

"Yes," said Carlotta in Spanish. "Max and I are going to make sure Virginia gets drunk tonight."

Carlotta said this laughing, but still it jolted Lupe. He knew Virginia would not be drunk, hardly possible. He was surprised the senora felt free to joke so wildly about such a thing. But Virginia was laughing at their joke. And she *was* drinking a rum canela, he could smell it.

Max moved to Lupe's side, and he seemed very happy tonight, a good sign. Perhaps things had gone well today at the lawyer's. Immediately the senor was making jokes about Lupe's girlfriends meeting each other in this big party for all the barrio. Lupe could not get him to stop this foolish talk; no use then to ask him something serious.

All six of them walked side by side as if on a carnival midway. Max, Carlotta and Marcos bought chicken tacos for two pesos each and stood eating them beside the sidewalk grill where Vicente Candado and his wife Carmela and their six year old son Julio were heating the strips of chicken in a pan and warming the tortillas on a drumlid. Lupe and Marcos stopped briefly to make the recent gossip with them.

Carlotta and Virginia wandered further down the street to buy another canela in a paper cup from a card table in a doorway, from the young Rincon sisters. Polin and his daughter stood in a doorway nearby watching the crowds. Max and Carlotta with Lupe saw him and went to greet him and Anna, almost fifteen, talking about her quincianera. Polin questioned Lupe with his eyes, and Lupe showed him with his own eyes that he still didn't know anything from the senor.

Near the great acacia at the heart of the barrio they came upon four workmen busy assembling the last of the pinwheels on the castle of fireworks that lay on the ground, all twenty feet of it. The castle itself was made of castaway wood pieces and stout bamboo. Willowy branches served to make the circles for the pinwheels. These four masters of the pyrotechnics were on their knees tying with string the firecrackers and the flaring rockets to wheels and towers and all the junctions in ways only they understood. Small boys and girls of all ages too surrounded them in awe and watched every movement they made, every knot they tied, on this gigantic work of art.

Lupe watched Max and Carlotta's fascination with this and he asked the senor, "Are you staying to see this explode?"

The senor wore a short, zipped leather jacket and levis. He himself questioned, "What time do they shoot off, maestro?"

"Eleven, more or less. It will be fine, and since you are so much responsible, I hope you will stay and see our gift to the Virgin, and to the barrio."

Max laughed as if Lupe had been exaggerating his importance. "Of course we'll be there. The fireworks is Carlotta's favorite part."

"No, the band parading is my favorite part," said Carlotta, as she heard them the instant she'd spoken, and she laughed. "And here they come again!"

And so they did, returning down Lupe's street Obregon. All the merry crowd turned and saw the tuba and the drummer coming around the acacia and back toward the church, the biggest loudest horns trailing behind. Coming last were all the happy citizens who'd made the long parade through the barrio with the band. This time Max took Carlotta's hand and led her away from the sidewalk with Virginia following, and Lupe following her. They all merged into the crowd following the band, all of whom passed into the large courtyard in front of the church of the Virgin. All the horn players stood in the church doorways and pointed to the shrine of her painted presence and blared their loudest and most joyous to the dark queen. Carlotta grinned and clapped. Lupe watched Virginia cross herself and say a prayer, and he felt blessed merely watching her.

After the band ceased and the crowd in the church courtyard dispersed, they stood a while longer in the same spot a half a block away from the big acacia. The crowds moved back and forth past them. They saw Lupita walking by and waving at them, the wife of Carlos Romero. She held a baby, very recently born, held it out to show them, and grinned, so pleased. Carlotta could distinguish only the words in Spanish, "My new daughter," and Carlotta smiled and waved back, saying, "Yes, yes, how pretty. I have a present for her. I'll bring it tomorrow."

Moments later Virginia pointed out to Carlotta a young man standing in a doorway playing his guitar alone, and she and Virginia watched the coy pretty girls lingering to listen near him, to the sad, sweet musica he made.

Marcos had disappeared. The senor seemed well satisfied to watch all the crowd coming and going.

Lupe coughed, to be noticed, then said, "How was your meeting with the lawyer, Senor? May I ask?"

The senor stopped watching. He seemed for a moment to be listening to the tolling of a faraway bell. Then his face relaxed again. He said, "Nothing good, nothing bad. Like always. But she does expect we'll have our decision within two more weeks. Three at the most. The judge has just about completed all the steps." It all sounded so certain and positive.

Yet Lupe had listened to this identical answer several times in the last few months. Hearing it again, it was difficult for Lupe to comprehend why the senor did not hear himself repeating himself, this same *two weeks, three at the most, almost completed*. Worse, Lupe heard in the senor's voice that he believed what he was saying. The senor was too kind. Too trusting. A fatal combination. He needed help.

By his own kindness, on a night of peace and happiness like this one, Lupe would not force upon the senor the unpleasant opposite opinion. That all was *not* well, that it was time for men to take action themselves. Lupe stood before him, listening, nodding, silent, brooding.

Marcos returned with additional mischief. Tacho was with him, surprisingly without afianced Dahlia. Both went to Lupe.

Marcos the imp said, "I found Tacho for you. I told him you wanted to ask him something. About our plans." Marcos pushed Tacho gently toward his father, then turned to go, waving at them his goodbye, the V fingers of peace. Marcos the troublemaker.

Tacho leaned close to speak more privately. "Nothing serious I hope."

Angry that Marcos had thrown this little surprise at him, but happy that his son would sound this tender concern, Lupe could not make up his mind to speak or not to speak. He sputtered and let the nearby loud voices drown out his own feeble words.

Happily, Max and Carlotta and Virginia saw Tacho and intervened with their own slightly inebriated exuberance. Thereby, Lupe had time to regather his feelings and intentions, and assess his courage for the talk with his son.

It would have to be enough. Lupe leaned in front of Tacho to speak to

Max and Carlotta. "Please excuse us for a moment. I have some special business with Tacho. I'll see you again soon. At least when they shoot off the fireworks. The padre's going to bless the rockets before they shoot them. I want you to see that."

This father and son walked away from their patrons and into the milling, familiar crowd. Even so, Lupe would not hurry this delicate confrontation.

"No Dahlia tonight?" Lupe asked, as if this might be the object of his conversation.

Tacho smiled his largest, which was considerable. "She's here. She's off somewhere with her sister. I'll see her later."

"Has her family decided the day yet?"

Tacho still smiled; he would be a good husband. "Yes. Finally. A Sunday in June. The first day of summer."

Into this pretty picture, unfortunately, Lupe interjected a dark little cloud, possible rain for someone's parade. "Ojala, that we will all still be working then."

Tacho's perpetual smile drooped only slightly. He said, "What would make it not so?"

His father looked intently at his son, the slow learner. "You already know. If the senor and the senora and our compania lose all their business. That would make it not so."

Tacho pondered this, a quickly comprehended truth. "You think they will lose to La Madre?" He paused, to wonder that a moment, but dismissed it. "No one else thinks so." Tacho obviously among them.

Lupe looked at his son even more intently, affirming a different opinion, to him indisputable.

Tacho winced, perceiving completely his father's several, silent meanings. Seeing also where this might lead, the son said, "So you want to make her a midnight visit?" As Tacho said it, he still didn't quite believe it. When Lupe's jaw merely hardened at the question, Tacho did believe it.

Lupe also showed a gradual surprise. It was as the father had feared. "Perhaps you've been too long in the United States. You've forgotten, or perhaps you've learned new ideas. In the village we still do things the old ways. When necessary."

Tacho stood firmly, though he well knew that perhaps what his father said was true. He owed it to him to listen; even so, he would not be easily persuaded. Tacho said, "The lawyer has told the senor that he must not be aggressive against La Madre. That would look bad with the judge, who is already on their side. This visit to La Madre would make the judge turn against them. *She* is the one who is wrong, trying to force us to do that long list of extras without paying for them, and then claiming by her posters that there is a class action lawsuit against our company—when as everyone knows, *no one* has *ever* sued us."

Lupe sneered for the naivete. "Son, how you talk. Great damage has already been done. But you are in the office much of the day, so you tell me–how many new jobs since the postering started? How many? How many calls from possible new clients? From agents with clients? There used to be some every week."

Tacho sighed. No denying this. "But when La Madre is guilty, the law says she must make a public retraction. She will also be arrested and she will be sentenced to a time in jail. It's true she can pay the court so she will not have the jail time, but the lawyer says she will still be in jail at least one night. And her freedom after that will cost her thousands of dollars."

Lupe wanted to sneer again, but instead he only laughed. "You believe all this will happen? Truly?"

Tacho looked at his father as if to say, how could these authorities be doubted. "Yes, I suppose I do believe."

The bitterly-won knowledge of the ancient peon spoke in the father. This time he restrained the sarcasm he would like to have expressed. "And why do you think La Madre continues her postering? Does she not know what might happen to her? Do you think she is so blind with anger that she continues her revenge without considering that she might go to jail? And pay thousands of dollars? And be publically humiliated with this retraction?"

In the recent months Tacho had indeed wondered all these things himself. He had fathomed no satisfactory answers, though one or two hardly believable possibilities had leered ugly faces at him from dark corners of his imaginings.

But not enough to change his opinion. He greatly admired the senor. He wanted to believe that everything his patron said and wanted was true, was going to happen. That la compania would survive this attack of La Madre, and would grow, and that the prosperous compania would one day belong to them all.

Tacho said, "Alright, no one knows for certain, I'll admit that. But I have too much respect for the senor to do something that he would not want me to do. And I know he would *not* want me to make a midnight visit to La Madre. I am surprised you do not respect his wishes too."

Lupe uttered a growl that contorted his face like a cornered creature, though perhaps this was not from anger or disgust, but only from disappointment, that his son had grown stupid living the easy, naive life among the americanos.

Lupe restrained himself a moment, not wanting to show all the emotion he felt rising in him. He paused a moment to let it settle, then he spoke. "I respect who the senor is, and what he has done for us—*no one* more than I. But not *always* do I respect his ideas and opinions and his views of things, which are sometimes foolish, *and* harmful to him, *and* to us."

Tacho listened, but he showed no sympathy.

Lupe tried again. "If we all sit back and wait for the law, as you want to do, la compania will likely be destroyed. Then it will not matter in six months or so what the law does. But I see that matters to you not at all. "

Tacho's face burned with the challenge, with the heat of his father's words. His own anger rose, abetted by oldest memories. "So you will go threaten this woman? Or harm her?"

Lupe spoke savagely. "And you would let her destroy everything we have created? All our dreams for a better future?"

Tacho's own visible hostility now coldly opposed his father. "So I see you have not changed. You still like the violence."

As Lupe heard these words, the anger that had indeed fired his blood and had made the hot words tumble out of him suddenly choked in his throat, for he paled at the fierce and terrible glare in his son's eyes. The fight died in him. His own helpless eyes now looked away, and over the milling crowd, so near, so far. Yet he knew he was not wrong. He turned back to his son and spoke without passion, dragging along a heavy weight. "I wish only to make a good life for us, for you, for the family that you will have. It is not my way, or the way of the others, like your Uncle Polin, or your own Romero uncles, to let some thief take it from us. Yes, I will fight for that. Think of me what you will."

Lupe could bear this confrontation no more. He walked away into the crowd, seeing no one. But his luck would find him, in the person of Gloria, who immediately saw the trouble in his face. She glanced to the corner, saw Tacho looking sadly after them, and she knew not to ask Lupe anything. She walked beside him, close.

Marcos might have been watching all of this, for when he saw Lupe alone, he also approached him, but cautiously. Well he did, for Lupe saw him and frowned, calling to him. "You are a troublemaker, cabron."

Marcos smiled feebly. "I thought it was the right thing, maestro. Was I wrong?"

Lupe glared. "You *were* wrong. Disgracefully, my son thinks sometimes now like a gringo."

"So he's not coming with us?"

Lupe snorted. "No! I told you. Now that he's lived in America he thinks things should be all in order and everything goes by the rules. He thinks his own people are primitive, that we live in the jungle. We spoke bad words to each other."

Marcos sighed, disappointed. "Forgive me, maestro. I though it would be good that you would talk about it. Maybe bring you a little more together."

Gloria listened to all this quietly, her eyes all the while reading Lupe's worried face. She said to him, "Let it cool, Lupe. It's only the moment. I know how much Tacho cares for you."

Lupe refused her sympathy. "No. Still he doesn't forgive me for the old days. He said so."

Gloria first heard the mariachis as they rounded the corner of Calle Adolfo, and she said, "Oh Lupe, listen, isn't that the Mendeles brothers?"

Thus prompted, his ear quickly found the sound he most loved, and his blood altered its pace and its mood in his veins and arteries, perceptibly lightening his troubled and ponderous heart. Another ardent lover of mariachis from a nearby doorway cried out his own joy, and others called out too, and clapped for these barrio favorites.

Marcos liked better the Tejana style guitars and the American rock'n'roll, but he was grateful that Lupe's attention had turned to the mariachis. Marcos raised his arms and clapped above his head. His daughter, still on his shoulders, grasped his hands in hers, in front of her face, and she clapped them together to the beat of the mariachi's horns passing now nearby. The trumpeter Julio Mendeles saw her sitting so high and he winked at her as he passed, still playing. She squealed at him and clapped her father's hands together harder.

Despite his current grief, a cry of his own love for the mariachis welled up in Lupe, as it always did when the horns blared in sudden harmony as they did now. His cry of joy he yelled into the night and it tore away these bindings on his soul and made him forget for the moment everything else but the fabulous musica of the mariachis.

Yet a half hour later maestro Lupe was grieving again and remembering his argument with Tacho. Two hours later, most of which he had spent at home one block away, resting his aggravated heart, Lupe returned to the placita for the fireworks. Now it seemed even more of the barrio's citizens thronged the cobblestone streets, eating chicharonnes, taquitos, carne asada and chicken, and desserts in all their forms. They also drank cervezas and canelas and tequila. A trio of guitars played beneath the acacia, all standing, playing all the old canciones romanticas.

The crowd was especially dense near the great castle of fireworks, now erect, though leaning slightly left. This tower of bamboo was higher than the street light at the intersection, and roped securely to nearby poles and roofs. Three ropes tethered the tower to the ground. Its carefully fabricated little arms and assortments of pinwheels dangled precariously, very rustico, fragile and all liable to blow over in a gust of wind. Children were foremost around the base of the tower, playing chase and escape and screaming out the thrill of anticipation.

Lupe saw Virginia with the senor and the senora still, and he crossed himself quickly, for the good luck of the prayer. He slipped through the crowd going to them.

Carlotta was speaking to Marcos. "Is all your family out tonight?"

"Who knows," he said, dismissing that, "I guess you mean my wife, the mother of my children. I don't know where she goes. But you're out late, you two. I never see you much after dark." He saw Lupe arriving. He nodded.

"We're waiting for the fireworks," Carlotta said. "Lupe says we have to." She smiled at her maestro.

Marcos said, "Yeah, Teresa's waiting for that too." This little one kept her big doll's eyes on Carlotta.

Carlotta said, "Well, you can wait with us. Want a canela? Virginia and I just bought our last one. I hope it is anyway. We're both a little wobbly."

Marcos shook his head and looked around at the crowd. "No, I had one. And a beer. I've gotta be a good boy till I get Teresa home. And I gotta keep going, we're looking for mama. Be cool Max, Carlotta." He turned and smiled to Lupe, "You too, amigo. I hope you had a good rest." And Marcos and Teresa on his shoulders passed into the crowd.

Lupe saw Padre Morelia step from the margin of the crowd and stop beside the great fireworks. Now that the moment was here, Lupe wished that the padre would not be calling all this attention to him. It was really for the senor and the senora that he wished the acknowledgement. Then his little regret turned to dread as the large, festive, noisy crowd, wherein it is so easy to be anonymous, suddenly hushed, very reverently to hear their pastor. The guitars stopped playing. Only one radio in a window far down the block kept playing.

The padre said he would be brief. He said he was there to bless the pyrotechnics. And to make a quick speech. He turned to the well-trussed tower of explosives and made the sign of the cross three times in the air before it. He reached and touched the flimsy, disposable structure and muttered a brief prayer no one heard. Then he crossed himself and turned back to the crowd. He smiled to them all, to show them that the fiesta had been thoroughly blessed and might soon become merry again.

He said, "On behalf of the church, and from my own heart, I want to express a word of thanks to Guadalupe Gonzales, and his workers, for making this last exciting part of our celebration possible." Many of the large crowd clapped. The padre looked to find Lupe and beckon him. Lupe reluctantly went beside him; though he went quickly, for now he had something urgent he wanted the padre also to say to the crowd. Lupe spoke it softly. "It is also thanks to Bellacasa, Padre, our compania. Especially Bellacasa."

The padre realized his omission. He held up a quieting hand and spoke again. "And our thanks to Bellacasa too. Both our church and the barrio thank them." Lupe clapped and many others clapped again.

Then the crowd alternately hushed and buzzed as the maestro of the pyrotechnics came forward with his cigarette and checked a last time his handiwork. He wore simple clothes like all the others of his audience. Then suddenly without fanfare he set his cigarette to a fuse, and sparks flew away from it as the children screamed shrilly and thrilled. Parents also yelled.

Firecrackers began exploding at the base of the tower, chasing each other up to the first pinwheel. Ignited, the pinwheel sparked and flared and all six of its rockets sprayed firesparks. The pinwheel wobbled before picking up speed and then raced furiously round in a tremendous shower of sparks. The most daring of the boys and one girl darted through the falling sparks, screaming out when any caught in their hair or on their clothes.

More strings of firecrackers exploded, ascending to the next pinwheel, which ignited and whirred round blowing sparks. Suddenly a little rocket screamed away and down and into the crowd!-scattering thrilled parents and children alike as this wild thing struck the stones, bouncing, before suddenly spinning in one place and then dying out there.

All this continued five more minutes, firecrackers and rockets and pinwheels, and always too the most daring children racing beneath the showers of sparks.

At the last, four pinwheels simultaneously at the top began spinning and throwing sparks, until those, sputtering to a stop, set off a last chain of fireworks that exploded, ascending to the ultimate figure. This ignited at the top into a bouquet of roses for the Virgin, aglow in little rocket flames that flared brightly, held for several glorious seconds, and then as suddenly went out. And it was over.

The crowd cheered and clapped wildly. Though he only clapped a moment, and made no other noise, Lupe was the happiest of anyone.

He might then speak his earnest prayer: to the Virgin, from her humble, devoted servant Lupe. Please, strangle them.

16 LUPE AND
COMPANIA SURROUNDED

While he waited for his prayer to be answered, Lupe worked at the only house Bellacasa was building, in the new little development of San Juan de las Colinas. For Senor Sydney Huck, the very proper, slim Canadian who looked like he could enjoy policing the silence in a library. He wore his wire-rimmed glasses low on his nose, eyes looking over them, seeing you twice.

Mid-afternoon as Lupe spoke to the senor about the roof tiles on Senor Huck's house, the policeman of libraries came out of his house, where he had been measuring and calculating. "Max, we love what you're doing and it's all going very nicely, but we're disturbed by something. A couple of things." Senor Huck spoke in a voice that was accepting no nonsense. He tapped the tape measure on his pant leg. "Come look around back."

Lupe followed the senor, who followed Senor Huck into the yard and to the square steel door that allowed access to the underground water storage, a buried concrete box. "I've measured the aljibe, Max, and I'm afraid it's far short of the capacity you promised in the contract. It's nine cubic meters instead of twelve." He held his little notebook in one hand and tapped that now against his thigh.

The senor was not convinced. "That's hard to believe, Sydney. Lupe doesn't make those kind of mistakes."

Sydney stiffened. "Well it's true. I measured it myself." With his free hand he touched the little measuring tape he'd clipped to his belt, to show why he was so sure.

"Alright," Max said, turning to his maestro, who was understanding the discredit of his work. Max spoke in Spanish. "He thinks we're cheating him. I won't tell him what I think. I know you built this by the plans, but, just to make him happy, measure it and I'll see what we can do."

To encourage their discussion, Sydney Huck capped it in his precise English. "We *must* have that full capacity. We have a lot of lawn to water, and we have the pool. We won't be put off."

Lupe measured it and then stood with his hands on hips to say, "Senor, it is as I remember, it is just one meter less than twelve cubic meters. There were problems digging, some rocks very, very large that could not be moved. Big as a Volkswagen. But eleven meters and a little more is the capacity. Marco set the shut-off valve lower than it should be, and if Senor Huck measures to that, it is nine or ten. But the true capacity of the tank is eleven, with the shut-off valve put in the right place."

Max explained that to Sydney, who sneered at his explanation and demanded again. "I don't want the shut-off moved, it stays where it is. And I want more capacity, and I'll have it. Or I'll make a stink."

Lupe understood this well enough too. This man was like the diablo of Mina del Oro, even though this Huck was the opposite, a coward. He wrote down all the numbers and was pushy and nasty with his lists, in the safety of his yard. But he would never risk meeting his enemy after dark.

Huck continued, happier with himself than before. "And now I've found something else, come inside." Lupe and the senor followed him to the living room. He pointed to the floor. "See there? Where I've marked with pieces of tape? There's chips in the tile, lots and lots of them, I've counter nearly twenty-five in all. I expect all of those tiles to be replaced."

Max and Lupe both bent to look at thse alleged flaws. Some they could see, some they could not. Max said, "I don't know, Sydney."

"Oh no no," Huck said, snapping at him, "I'll show you." He pulled from his pants pocket a magnifying glass and went to the floor on his knees and hands to one of the spots they'd questioned. He put the glass to it and his eye to the glass. "Yes, look here, it's a chip. It's not a paint spot, or a piece of grit, it's a chip. And I want it replaced. I want all of them replaced that have these chips."

Max said, "You know, Sydney, this is the first time in all the houses we've ever built that an owner has found any chipped tiles. Ever. I don't see how my men could have done so many of them."

Sydney looked offended. "Well *I* didn't do it!"

"No, of course not. But maybe the furniture movers did it. They packed a lot of very heavy things in here last week."

Sydney was horrified. "Nonsense! It was your men. I want all of this replaced. And I'm going to check the bedroom floors too, and there'll probably be more." Seeing Max not immediately agreeable, Sydney frowned and added, "You know, Max, your reputation around here's not very good. We've heard it from several people."

Max had thought this might be coming. "You mean the notices about the Class Action Suit?"

Sydney nodded, that's exactly what he meant.

Max explained as briefly as possible his history with La Madre. Sydney listened.

Having listened to the end, he said, "Alright. I suppose that's a good explanation. We'd like to believe you." Then his eyebrows arched, and he spoke with all his authority. "But I believe *nothing* until you replace my tiles and enlarge my water storage. Whatever that takes."

In Spanish Max said to Lupe, "Lunatico, maestro, but it's not worth the arguing. It's all less than a thousand dollars. And it's not worth the bad talk he would make about us. Go ahead, replace all the tiles he asks for. And build a *new* little aljibe, only three meter capacity. Connect it to the other one. Minimum cost."

Then to Sydney he said, "Alright, we'll do it."

If Lupe had been allowed to, he would have set each new tile just a little off level. He would also have built a slowly disintegrating plug into the new aljibe wall.

Late the next afternoon, when Reynoso came to collect his extortion from the senor and the senora, they were all waiting for him. Jim Penton had come first, having heard the gossip and wanting to see the trap set.

Carlotta and Virginia arranged the little chrome dinette table with a fruit basket in the middle, on an oversized tablecloth that hung nearly to the chairs. No plug-ins were in that part of the casita, so Lupe had laid a long extension cord that went behind the equipale two-seater to the wall plug-in there. A tiny microphone Carlotta hid carefully beneath the oranges and bananas, its cord passing through a hole in the tablecloth, beneath the fruit basket. This hidden cord was connected to a small Sony tape recorder that Virginia would hold and manipulate discretely in her lap, also hidden. Carlotta would sit beside her and talk to Reynoso.

When Lupe entered the office, he saw Virginia, wearing black slacks and a lowcut blouse of flowery pastels, come in through the front door with a hatbox full of rolled house plans. She smiled as she always did and said, "Good morning, Don Lupe." He felt anointed.

Jim Penton had also heard her voice and came out of the inner office, where he had been talking to Carlotta. Virginia saw him and said, in fine English, "Oh hello Mr. Penton. They recruited you too?"

He smiled fondly at her. "Good heavens, Virginia, when will you stop calling me Mr. Penton? I already feel old enough. Call me Jim. Please. And no, they didn't recruit me, I just thought I'd drop in. You know how I like to do."

Carlotta came from her office and said, "Well, I know it's just to flirt with Virginia, Jim."

Virginia blushed, but Jim Penton laughed and said, "Oh why not? The old duffers like me-that's about all we're good for, a little flirting every once in a while." And then he laughed his deep rogue's laugh and Carlotta laughed with him, and even Virginia too-for who could resist Jim Penton?

Virginia turned still blushing to Carlotta and said, "I'll go bring in the rest of the file boxes from my car."

Carlotta said, "Better hurry back. No telling what these two will say about you." Virginia shook her head to cast off the embarrassment as she went back outside.

Lupe said to those remaining, in a voice subdued for gossip, "I think Virginia has a boyfriend. I saw her with a lawyer from Chapala, Rodriguez, at the tianguis last Monday."

"Oh well," Jim Penton said in Spanish, "she may go places with men, from time to time. But we all know it will never go *very* far."

Carlotta laughed. She said in Spanish also, "What do you mean by *that*, Jim?"

He looked at her most seriously. "Well, you know. I'm sure she's still a virgin."

Lupe, most serious himself, nodded his head agreeing. "Oh yes, senor, I am sure you are right. She will always be a holy woman. She's born on the Virgin's day you know."

A song of laughter burst from Carlotta. "Oh you *men!* Oh oh *oh!*"

Virginia re-entered, fortunate to have missed the previous conversation. She said, "Mr. Penton, when Reynoso gets here, you must remember not to be walking upstairs. Down here we can hear every footstep."

Jim laughed. "Oh I'll probably be right at the stairway door all the time, with my ear to the keyhole. Say, are you going to call in the police, if you get him to confess?"

To Max there was no mirth in any of this. It had kept him anxious since the moment Reynoso had come to the office eight days ago and demanded the five thousand US. Restless nights. Restless days, conferring with accountants and lawyers. Making a plan. Which could blow up.

"No," Max said, seriously, the only way he could be these days, "the lawyer counseled us against that. Though personally I'd love to. The lawyer says Reynoso is too well connected. He's had this job collecting money for seguro social for twenty-five years. He's got too many relatives who could help him. And come back at us."

Lupe knew Reynoso well. They had been a year apart in school, growing up. Reynoso had always been the clever one. Good at gambling, at cards, at pool. A few petty arrests, but no time in jail. His family saw how he might disgrace them and had arranged for him to have a job in the government. A fine fit. Reynoso made friends with all parties, and when PAN took over in Jalisco, Reynoso kept his job, which paid him well, and often. Lupe had always avoided any entanglement with this devious hombre.

Fortunately in this plan, Lupe would not have to encounter him, but would stay in the back office, the door only a pencil-width ajar, and listen. And he would watch outside, and if anyone should drive up, he would head them off and away.

Reynoso arrived exactly on time in his yellow Toyota Corolla ten years old, with a bad paint job. Reynoso, walking through the gate to the office, looked little better than his car, dressed in the drab pants he had worn all week and a store clerk's plaid short sleeve shirt. His hair he'd cut short the last five years to show a feeble kinship with the executives in upstairs offices who sent him on his wide-ranging missions of money-gathering. It was a good job for him. He didn't have to dress well, or even clean. They all had to give him the money no matter how he looked.

Reynoso knocked on the door. He carried his little black zipper folder with the worn logo of IMSS. Today there was nothing in it. It would be for the big impression. And for carrying away the large bundle of pesos.

The tall senora answered the door. Today she wore cowboy boots and looked taller than he remembered. In the ideal world of his fantasy, she would immediately hand him a sack of pesos, he would say thank you, and he would leave. But the senora did not give him any pesos, or anything else. She asked him to join her at the table. The new secretary was there, watching him constantly. He didn't like that.

He said in Spanish to Carlotta, "I said this must be private. She can't be here."

Carlotta and Virginia looked to each other for the resolution, but only a moment, lest he become suspicious.

Virginia adjusted her recorder to the chair as she rose, and convincingly said, "Oh I wasn't going to stay, I have to go to the bank anyway. Goodbye." Reynoso looked about him for other worries, and as he did so Virginia smoothed the tablecloth over the Sony, and mouthed to Carlotta that I

Turned It On. She went out the front door, got into her little gray Volkswagen, and drove away. Reynoso at the window watched her till she was gone.

He turned back to Carlotta, who still sat at the table. He said, "Do you have the money?"

She smiled pleasantly. "Please come sit down, Reynoso. Of course I have money. Everything will be just as you wish it. But first I want to go over the numbers you gave me. I want to be sure I have it all right."

Reynoso sat in the equipale opposite the senora. "Have a banana," she offered him. "That one on top is perfectly ripe." Reynoso took it. The senora seemed not to be opposing him with these questions. This would turn out well. The banana was indeed the best of the bunch. He peeled it, and waited for her to make her questions.

She began. "Senor, were you telling me the other day when you came here with all that terrible news, that Bellacasa is being penalized for making late payments three times, two years ago?"

It irritated Reynoso to have to explain all this again. The senora seemed to get the details tangled up so often. "Alright, senora, I will explain it as simply as I can. There is a new law, just in effect. For companies with thirty or more employees, who have been late in payments three times or more in the last two years, there is a penalty, of three times the amount paid in each of those late months. In your case, you made payments of nearly five thousand dollars US, so your penalty is assessed at fifteen thousand."

Reynoso slid his chair back, glancing briefly to the front door and to the door just ajar that went into the other office. He spoke again, but in a voice that Lupe now strained to hear the softer words of. "I am risking my job trying to help you. As I told you, if you give me only five thousand, now, I can have someone I know go into the records and alter the dates on your payments. Then it will appear that you have never been late with payments, and no one will come bother you again about that matter. The five thousand you give me will pay the file clerk who will make the alterations, and it will pay me a small amount for my efforts in your behalf. Believe me, senora, I want to help you. I have heard many good things about you in the barrio, where I live. I know your maestro Lupe from long ago, in school. Believe me, senora, almost none of this money will go to me. But it will surely save you from having to pay the fifteen thousand, which my chiefs will come after you for. And very soon."

A very convincing argument. When Carlotta had first heard it eight days ago, she and Max had been terrified. For where in heaven would they get even five thousand, let alone any fifteen thousand dollars. They knew

162

the IMSS footsoldiers to be relentless in their collections. They could confiscate goods, computers, cars until money was paid. They could put arch-delinquents in jail.

But today, having had eight days to investigate the charges oh so secretly, having discovered the hoax and the extortion, Carlotta was ready.

She reached into the bowl of fruit for what might have been a fat orange or the second best banana, but instead she withdrew the tiny microphone and she showed it to Reynoso. Carlotta grinned. "Say hello to everybody, Reynoso. We're all on record."

Before he fully comprehended what she had said, and what had happened to him, Carlotta stood, disconnected the cord from the small recorder hidden on Virginia's former chair, and carried the recorded to her office door, where Lupe now stepped forward, accepting the machine from his patrona, and then he sneered at Reynoso.

Seeing not only this unsuspected witness, but also his old school pal, Reynoso flushed scarlet, for all his already dark skin, and tried to stand, though he stumbled twice detaching himself from his chair. Lupe gave no sign that they had once been school friends, though he recognized well the fear in the face of the confessed extortionist.

Reynoso groaned, perceiving his doom. Carlotta said to him, "Didn't you think I could find someone to look into my IMSS files, Reynoso? Didn't you think I could find out that there were no fines against my company? That we owed seguro social *nothing?*"

These were significant questions, Reynoso knew, but it was certainly too late to be answering them now. He looked desperately to the recorder and its tapes that Lupe held tightly in his two hands. Lupe smiled the smile of happy revenge.

Reynoso heard Jim Penton come down the stairs from the roof, chuckling to himself devilishly. Reynoso thought this venerable old gentleman must represent some formidable death-dealing grandfatherly authority from the gringo community. Reynoso gripped the chair back tightly lest he wobble. Carlotta spoke coldly to him. "You know my accountant, you've seen him here, I introduced you. You should have known he would know people inside IMSS who could look into the files."

Reynoso's head bowed, not in acquiescence, but from the weight of accusation. Carlotta took it for submission. "I'm going to give you a little break, Reynoso. I'm going to keep this tape locked in a safe in the bank. And I don't want any bullshit from you, ever again, or I'll give this to your supervisors. I'll give it to *someone* who'll come after you."

Still he could not look up, but his heart made a little song for joy. Just the thing a gringa like this one would do, let him go. Still, he could not look up, but would wait for her to make the last words and dismiss him. Even so, he must make some gesture of agreeing.

He let his shoulders slump, a perfect imitation of submission, and he nodded several times with credible pathos, and his words were in accord. "I am very, very sorry, senora. I needed money for the children. Please forgive me."

He had not moved her; she remained severe. "I won't forgive you till you're out of my life for good, Reynoso. I won't embarrass you by demanding to have someone else come here to collect the money, so I'll still see you once a month. I'll pay every month what I owe, and you leave me alone. One little sign that you're trying to steal money from me, and I'm handing over the tape."

Lupe was most proud of the senora. This was good. The barrio vigilantes could not have done it better.

Reynoso continued watching the floor and nodding and saying yes, yes, thank you, thank you, yes, thank you, all the way to the front door, and outside and shuffling off and away.

Jim Penton stepped to the door and leaned his head out after him and said, "Shame on you, Reynoso," and this, worse than any of it, bit into Reynoso as he sped away in his jalopy.

Two days later Lupe drove the senora in his Cadillac of all problems to get her repaired van from the mechanic. They stopped at SuperLake on the way for sodas. Carlotta also checked the bulletin boards for one of La Madre's neon handbills, but saw none; most unusual, for she and Max took them down from all the six main sites at least once a day, even after all these many months of postering.

Carlotta turned to remark this to Lupe, but as she did she saw instead the terrible little red Volkswagen parked squarely in front of SuperLake, where everyone who came in or out would see it. It would have been as innocuous as any of the other parked cars there, except that the orange-red neon posters glared double-size from the inner side of every window of the vehicle. The company name, Bellacasa, and the words Class Action Lawsuit were underlined in black. There would be no tearing down of these notices.

"*That's it!*" Carlotta screamed. "Lemme out, I'm gonna go kick the goddamn windows in and set fire to the car." She jerked the Cadillac doorhandle open and went to the little red bug and stood over it in her rage. Yet how in the world could she squish the life out of this vermin?

Lupe parked as quickly as he could and hurried to the senora, for it was obvious she was having the trauma. He held firmly to her arm with his hand, that she would know he was by her. He looked quickly inside the red car to see if doors or windows were opened or unlocked. Not so.

Lupe said to her, "Easy, senora, we will do something. First, let me talk to Pancho."

Pancho, owner of SuperLake, middle aged and a wise and rich old owl, came to the red car with Lupe dressed in old levis and a shirt with the front half hanging over his belt. Lupe explained what was the case. Pancho knew Bellacasa not at all, nor did he know of their quarrel, but he did not like the car using up his few parking places. Pancho went back inside and a few moments later returned with his own sign on a huge cardboard that covered the front of the car and spoke his proclamation in English: No More Parking Here With Signs.

But this satisfied Carlotta little. Lupe saw that her blood still boiled. So perhaps this would have a good effect, in spite of its evil. Lupe said to her, "Something should be done to this woman. Do you not think so, senora?"

She looked helplessly at him. "I don't know what that would be, Lupe. Short of breaking her legs."

He saw she neared the truth. "Perhaps not a bad idea, senora. I know many people who would be happy to do such a thing."

Carlotta with a grim smile looked intently at him. "Sometimes I'm for frontier justice too, maestro, but this one would be just too hot to handle." She saw Lupe disapproving her logic. "Oh I see, Lupe. You really mean this, don't you?"

He nodded, and why not.

She laughed. "Think of it, maestro, what they'd be saying about us then. She's a seventy year old woman for Godsake! Attacked and mutilated by Bellacasa. How would *that* look on the bulletin boards?"

Lupe forced himself to nod and seem to agree. But he was thinking that not only was it time to make the move, but also that all of it must be kept from the senor *and* the senora. If the Virgin was ever going to answer his prayer, it seemed obvious that it would have been by now, before this terrible new deviltry of La Madre.

The poor senora. If she had been alone no doubt she would be crying out her anger. Instead she yelled at him. "I know she's going to keep this up! But I'll get photos! I'll take them to the judge, I'll take them to the mayor, to the chief of police! I'll make them all come see what that bitch is doing to us!" The poor senora.

17 LUPE'S MIDNIGHT VISIT

Lupe and his four companeros waited three more days till the new Moon, the Moon of late night visits.   January midnight.   The deepest darkness. They gathered first in Lupe's adobe on Obregon. Magdalena was long since sleeping in her bedroom. There was no need for much talking; they had talked it enough already. Lupe had only to be sure that each man was dressed right, and had come willingly and in secret. Polin, Marcos, Felipe Romero, and Ruben Gutierrez, the electricista, a handy man to have on dark nights out.

Lupe drove and brother Polin sat beside him. Marcos and Felipe Romero sat in back, Ruben the bear in between them. When they were at the careterra Lupe could smell tequila and he knew it would be from Felipe. He could smell no mota, but no doubt Marcos had smoked at home. To each his own courage. Lupe must find his own where he could, for on a night so dark and devious as this there could be no appeal to the Virgin. He could not, however, refrain from making a small prayer of thanks to her that Tacho was not with them–for what had he and Marcos been thinking?

Ruben Gutierrez, a jolly man, but stubborn, still hoped to get his money back. Two thousand pesos. Perhaps a little interest. It had been a constant theme in their discussions. He continued with it now. "I want your promise that you'll let me make her give me my money."

Polin, a size smaller than his stout brother, was nonetheless as intrepid when need be; yet he also was not ruthless. "That depends on what you mean by making her. Our purpose is to convince her that it is in her best interest to stop her defamation. If we succeed in that, all of us in la compania will throw in enough to pay you your two thousand pesos for helping us. But no stealing. We are not criminals. We are here to demand justice."

Lupe kept his eyes staring into the darkness of the careterra, but he spoke with hotter energy than his brother. "No, this idea of *making* her do something is *not* good. We are not going to beat up an old woman. No matter how much we *all* want to do that."

"We might make her drunk on tequila, maestro," said maestro Felipe, grinning. "Why not? La Madre Borracha."

They all smiled.

Marcos said, "Ruben and I could rewire the house very quickly, so that she'd get shocked every time she touched a door knob or a faucet."

"Rewire to the toilet, hombre," said Ruben with gusto.

Marcos capped him. "Or to the bathtub, oooooeeeeee!"

Suddenly they were at the outskirts of San Juan Cosala, and the proximity of their intended host set them each one imagining and preparing for the moment nearly at hand. The businesses and houses beside the careterra were darkened and lifeless. A little light and a little musica drifted up one lonely side street below the careterra to greet them as they heard it and passed it by. The outskirts leaving town were dark and quiet too, and in moments more their headlights lit up the tall sign of El Limon scribed across a giant green lime. A little paved road led away from it. Lupe turned and drove down it. A block further he slowed, turned right and saw the tall wall of La Madre's little compound. He stopped across from it, set the brake, and extinguished the headlights. The night was black and silent around them, excepting the arhythmical idling and chug of exhaust from the old Cadillac.

Each of the five men as they stepped from the car wore black pants and black jacket or black sweater, and all wore black gloves. They were part of the night. Marcos and Ruben each carried a small metal toolbox. Felipe and Polin carried flashlights in their gloved hands. When all had exited, Lupe backed his Cadillac of all problems carefully beside La Madre's wall, where he halted, and turned off the ignition.

Polin went to the corner to be watchman, though in this midwinter midnight countryside not a soul or machine seemed abroad. Both Marcos and Ruben, from prior working on the compound's electrical systems, knew the entire schema in their minds. From the street's tall electrical poles they knew the line that was hers, and where it tied to the wall, and passed over it and to what box it connected.

Felipe took a child's mattress from the car's trunk and climbed with it onto the Cadillac's hood. From that vantage he reached the mattress high enough so that its middle settled upon the hundred fragments of broken class embedded in the top of the wall to discourage unlawful entry. Then Felipe hopped off the car.

Marcos climbed onto the car hood on rubber sole shoes, then onto the car roof, where he could easily adjust the mattress so that it would bear his weight without slipping. He could feel the shards of the wall glass slicing into but anchoring the mattress in place. Marcos hoisted himself up and onto the mattress, his legs straddling both sides as if he were riding it. Felipe remounted the car hood carrying Marcos' tool box and handed it up to the midnight electricista. Marcos lifted his trailing leg over the mattress so he could sit there, both legs dangling toward the grass of the yard below. He saw only a weak light on a far wall near the carport entrance and one window within the big house lit. Marcos dropped to the ground, making a thud; but thereafter no other sound.

There seemed no life in the yard. The old caged dog had recently died, perhaps from long loneliness in that cage. Mercifully for him; mercifully too for these men of the night. Marcos saw both front and sliding rear doors of the house were closed and curtained. He crept silently without need of flashlight along the wall till he saw the junction box there: wires in, wires out. Still without need of flashlight, Marcos popped open the box and with his sharpest cutters he severed with a click one thick incoming line. Yard light and house lights extinguished.

Someone within the house gasped so loudly that Marcos heard the astonishment where he stood.

On the other side of the wall Felipe cried out a small, "Andale pues!" Ruben and Lupe beside him enjoyed the outburst, but kept the vowed silence.

Suddenly Polin the watchman was hurrying toward them, waving a flashlight, a light saber slicing the darkness, the swordsman unseen. He spoke an urgent whisper near them, the possible danger hissing in his voice. "A car comes! Out of sight!"

Prepared for emergencies, these four rapidly urged each other into the disaccommodating Cadillac, for two of its door were pinned to the wall, and these desperadoes had to get in one behind the other through the remaining two, unblocked doors. Both doors clicked shut behind them. Deep darkness was upon all the little street: four men inside a parked car, sitting still as statues, waiting to be left alone.

A fence of purple bougainvillea was illuminated behind them, visible to Lupe in his rearview mirror. A moment more he saw headlights, now slowing and turning down the little lane of their hiding. The big headlamps glared brightly upon them and illuminated horribly every rock and tree and bush and fencepost near them. It glared ferociously upon the conquered wall, the child's mattress flopped over it, the sleek old Cadillac lincoln green and cream, desperados seated like innocent stone statues inside.

When this intruder's. headlight dimmed and the ignition turned finally off, Lupe knew by the engine sound that it wasn't the police and it wasn't a worried neighbor. He'd heard that distinctive idling engine too many times. For the headlights still fully in his eyes he could not see the driver, but he heard one door click open, then another; then both closed. So the senor had brought someone. Or more likely, someone had brought the senor. Only one person that could be.

Lupe opened his door, ready for whatever would be. The intruders' headlamps extinguished, leaving them all in merciful darkness. Lupe's eyes had adjusted to the darkness, and he saw Tacho in a baseball hat with no insignia and a wool jacket, approach from the passenger side. Approaching from the other side, the senor wore a leather jacket zipped up, collar up, no hat, unhappy with his favorite maestro.

The senor's eyes were a little wild and he spoke anxiously. "Lupe, how much have you done? What have you done? This will not be good for us!" Despite his urgency and near panic, the senor spoke in the same passionate whispers that Polin had uttered moments ago, making himself by that whispering, Lupe amused himself thinking, part of their confederation and conspiracy of quiet.

Lupe answered openly. "We've done nothing yet. We're only here a few minutes. Marcos is over the wall. He cut out the power. Just now."

The senor groaned. He took a flashlight from his pocket and he climbed onto the hood, then onto the roof of the Cadillac. With much energy he mounted onto the mattress until his head hung over the wall. He called softly into the invaded yard, "Marcos. Marcos. It's me, Max. Please get over here!" He heard Marcos' steps approaching. The senor shined his light beam into Marcos' face. Marcos turned his own flashlight on the senor, lighting up the dangling and undignified arms and head atop the wall's mattress.

Marcos said in the senor's English, "Hey, what are you doing here? How did you find out?"

The senor said nothing, but Lupe from the other side, himself now on the car's hood, answered his electricista. "Tacho told him. To make trouble on his father."

Standing below but near his father, Tacho said, "I didn't do it to make trouble for you. What an idea! I did it because the senor has a right to know what you're doing. If something goes bad, he'll be in as much trouble as you will."

Lupe turned and looked at his son, and frowned. But when he spoke he turned again to say it to the senor's rear end and dangling legs, so he would hear it, for whom it was better spoken. "He will only get in trouble if the police come right now and find the senor hanging over La Madre's wall. He should have stayed home. Nothing bad would happen here. But La Madre needs to hear what we have to say."

The senor heard Lupe but had no mind to turn and reply. Instead he said to Marcos, "I'm really pissed off about this. I can see Lupe doing this, but not you."

"Why not?" Marcos said, not needing an answer, "he's my friend."

"So am I. You should have told me about this. This could have been very bad. What am I saying?–it *still* could be bad. Listen to me, you owe me this much. Get back to that junction box and splice those lines back together as fast as you can. Even if you can only do it half-assed."

Prior to this moment, in the throes of their secret conspiring, Marcos had readily believed they all might go in the dark and do something that would help the desperate situation of la compania. Now, with the senor there, it seemed a completely different thing. Not for fear, but for respect of the senor, he would of course acquiesce to this that the senor asked.

Marcos said, "OK. Put down a rope. It'll take a minute to splice, no more."

The senor now lowered himself backward till his feet again touched the car roof, which was beginning to sag from so many climbers. He quickly slid to the hood and then off onto the dirt of the callejon.

The senor said to Lupe, "Get a rope over the fence, so Marcos can get out of there."

Lupe had not much to say anyway. He had already made his arguments to the senor many times, about possible direct action against their enemy, and he knew what the senor believed. Lupe would never change him.

Felipe and Polin mounted the Cadillac hood with the rope that had already been tied to the Cadillac undercarriage. Polin tossed over an end that would reach the ground.

As they waited the senor said to Lupe, "I know you do this because you're my friend. So in a way, I have to say thank you for trying to help me. But also know, that this doesn't help me. We've talked about it. I thought you knew how much this would upset me."

Lupe understood upset. He himself was only now realizing that they would all now go home, and La Madre would continue on as before, destroying everything. The anger flashed through him, numbing his heart to any consolation. He growled, not exactly at the senor, or at Tacho, but at whomever might wish to know his heart and mind. "And *I* say-*this* is not right, that we let this terrible woman do this to us without striking back!"

The senor seemed almost to agree with him, seemed probably to be comprehending his anger and the rightness of it. But still he would not alter his opposition. "I *am* striking back, maestro. In the right way. She will pay for all her damage to us."

Lupe could only pity this innocence. Which would, even so, do nothing to bring peace to his own troubled soul. "The old ways may seem crude and barbaric to you, but they have worked for us, as much as anything has ever worked for us. You should step aside and let us do what should be done."

The senor looked at him intensely, without hostility. "Please, maestro. This time, do it my way. Please." The senor saw from the sadness in his maestro's face that he would not oppose him. The senor went to the car and watched above for Marcos' return.

Tacho stood by his father, though he too watched the top of the wall. Lupe, still bitter from the interruption, spoke to his son alone. "You betrayed us, hijo. You've become too much the gringo."

Tacho too bristled. "I don't believe in violence anymore, father. You taught me that lesson long ago. A lesson I now see you still have not learned."

Lupe spit on the ground. "I need to learn no lessons from gringos. You don't see that La Madre works with violence. She must be answered the same way. Even so, we would not have harmed her, I told you that."

Tacho smirked. "You think breaking into her house at midnight, five big unknown men, is not violent? She is old. You think only to scare her, but she might die of the fear. What then?"

Lupe laughed bitterly, for he liked that scenario. Of course now it would not be. "What then? We would go on with our lives, without her, that is what. La Madre deserves worse than what we were bringing her."

Tacho stared coldly into the dark night. "You are still a man who likes violence."

A small but terrible dagger to the heart of this humble, proud man. A turbulence of emotions swirled up in him, yes, many of them akin to violence, but he dared speak or express none of them. He swallowed them down hard.

Suddenly a subdued glow was visible above the wall: Marcos had reconnected the lines. The rope over the wall came taut as Marcos from the far side obviously began his climb. Polin and Felipe, still on the car roof, were ready to help him over the mattress. This last little effort of the aborted expedition suddenly was enlivened when a flaring spotlight illuminated Marcos from behind, as he struggled to gain balance atop the mattress. All of them knew the sudden danger. Incomprehensible shouts, women's voices, came from deep inside the yard.

All of them saw Marcos astride the mattress, ready to drop to freedom onto the Cadillac roof. But he could not resist one last defiance, and he lifted a hand displaying an erect middle finger to whomever might be guiding the spotlight.

A rifle shot exploded in the night. The brick wall upon which Marcos balanced so precariously crackled with the bullet ripping into it. Polin and Felipe leaped from the Cadillac to the ground. Lupe, the senor, Tacho and Ruben all ducked behind the car in unison. Though he was not hit, Marcos cried out and tumbled off the wall and fell backside first onto the Cadillac roof.

"Vamonos, everyone!" cried out Lupe, even as he scrambled onto the car hood to help Marcos regain his feet and slide off onto the ground. He was wobbly but not damaged. The senor and Tacho, their mission accomplished, ran to the senor's Ford pickup and were quickly inside, and the engine started.

Because his pickup was nearest their line of retreat, the senor moved away first. Still choked with contrary emotion, Lupe lingered there a moment, knowing where all that bad feeling should go. He honked the horn loudly, several times. Then again and again. From the back seat Ruben cried out his approval and leaned out the window holding a metal pan for mixing mezcla which he'd picked up from Lupe's floor. Ruben began banging the pan with a mason's trowel that he'd found beside the pan. This loud tinny drum shattered all the quiet of the darkness, a terrible cacophony with the blasting and screaming of Lupe's car horn. It was the devil's own nightmarish band. Ruben in joy screamed out his own cry as Lupe slowly moved the Cadillac away from the wall and onto the road; but slowly, slowly, that the drummer might a little longer hammer away as Lupe honked and yelled his curses out the window with Ruben. El Limon all resounded with it, until at last these desperados drove away into the dark night that had brought them forth.

PART THREE

18 LA MADRE VISITS MUNICIPIO

Constance in her grandmother grays and blues, hair drawn back to a tight bun behind, could have been an Amish chauffeurette as she manipulated La Madre's emerald black Chrysler Intrepid slowly toward the stately Municipio building in Chapala. It was late afternoon. The day had been clear and warm, and first spring flowers bloomed in the plaza across the street, though it was only February. However, the passengers in the emerald black car would see all this awakening life only obscurely, or not at all, through their darkly tinted windows.

Patricia Arguello sat beside Constance, fashion worlds' apart. Patricia wore sleek black rayon slacks and a fluffy, pale, pink blouse that opened full at the throat. La Madre in her go-everywhere orange sari sat behind them, in the sumptuous middle, where she could watch both the old and the new devotee.

Constance resented Patricia Arguello's presence at this important meeting with the Police Chief. She knew she was indulging an attachment, which was a sin, but she couldn't help it. Constance had seventeen years experience being La Madre's fearless and competent right hand in everything vital, in all the great battles. Patricia Arguello today was absolutely unnecessary. Patricia Arguello would also today likely find out certain things she shouldn't know, didn't need to know. Also, Patricia Arguello didn't convey the proper piety, either by her dress, which was far too racy, or by her demeanor, which was chatty and too often did not demonstrate the yogic virtues. Neither in India nor in the California ashram had Constance ever seen La Madre so indulge such a dubious neophyte.   This Patricia Arguello might know about business, but Constance could never imagine her succeeding at any of the spiritual disciplines which Constance had practiced for so many years.   This was a flitty, whim of the moment girl who would be in a few months saving the whales.

Constance the chauffeurette parked the emerald black car before the august entrance to the Municipio, allowing La Madre the briefest possible walk, the briefest possible exposure to the vast public's eyes. She shifted into park and let the car idle.

Patricia Arguello stood out from the car first and opened the rear door, and offered in a hand of assistance. La Madre spoke as she turned to Constance. "Find a parking spot as near as you can, then come join us in Carmelo's office. Patricia is coming with me." Constance, marked with the fierce red dot, grimly listened. La Madre then took Patricia's hand and drew herself forward and stepped out of the car and stood tall, gaunt and orange, a piercing red dot in her forehead also. Patricia wore no dot at all. The neophyte turned away from the Chrysler as La Madre turned, and the two of them strode quickly across the dirty sidewalk to the closed double doors. These were guarded on each side by a khaki-uniformed policeman, automatic weapons across each of their chests at the ready, a smile for no one.

La Madre came at them and passed them as if they were boys with toy guns. The policemen flinched in their pride and slumped a little in the shoulders as they bowed a humbled, brief recognition of her greater consequence. She accepted their deference without looking at them, and strode past and into the Municipio, svelte, fashionable Patricia Arguello stride for stride with her.

Constance remained at the curb in her chauffeur's seat, staring after them, unable not to, even as much as it hurt. The car still idled, the driver burning high octane resentment like a runaway diesel as she watched them disappear inside: together.

This wayward animosity so unusual in Constance would have tormented or consumed another person, without true spiritual discipline. Not Constance. Troubled and indulging unworthy thoughts as she was, she nonetheless had presence of mind to resort to her personal mantra that La Madre had given her so many years ago. *Kum By Ya.* Constance spoke it over and over to herself, and quickly the rhythm of it became a wave passing through her body, and she placed her attention fully on that. In a moment she felt that wave as a continuing presence in her body. This old familiar presence was her sanctuary. Her richest treasure. No one and nothing could take it from her. For a few quiet moments she rested in this old familiar place, where nothing could harm her.

Not even the great buildup of resentment she'd been generating, which now from her sanctuary she could feel dissipating its energy without renewal. Though there would not be time in this meditation to exhaust all of it, merely to remove the savage edges. A nasty taste of Patricia Arguello would linger for who knew how long.

Constance drew a deep breath. She gripped the steering wheel severely, that she might feel the bone and muscle of her body in her service. She believed herself ready to drive away, and reassert her rightful position.

Constance drove the Chrysler onto Avenida Principal. This late in the afternoon few people were on the streets. Half the shops were closed for siesta, and many parking places were available at the curb, all less than a block from the Municipio. Constance parked the car and could safely ignore the parking meters. She hurried the little distance to the corner, as much as decorum allowed for a devotee, carrying only her little black leather purse slung over her shoulder. She bustled past the armed guards, whose arrogance was still in abeyance, and she entered the building, not needing direction.

The front counter and several of the tables and offices were occupied with Mexican citizens and weary secretaries. Hardly anyone noticed Constance as she passed among them to the stairway. Thus it was for her almost always, for Constance cultivated an elusive, invisible style. She mounted stairs methodically, and quickly she was on the second floor. She took the corridor right, went three doors to the end, and saw the door to Police Chief Delavaca's office closed. She heard muffled voices, male and female. Bastardly Patricia Arguello laughed. Constance knocked lightly twice, then pushed open the door without waiting to be invited. The happy three paused in their conviviality to look to Constance, who presented to them all a gloomy prospect.

To Constance these three seemed captured in a timeless tableau. La Madre was settled into the one sumptuous chair in the office. She had turned away from the others, seeing Constance. The trace of a fleeting smile on La Madre's face Constance also knew displayed her amusement for the company of the other two, not for her own loyal devotee. Police Chief Delavaca in the tableau stood erect from his desk and leaned forward, resplendent in his immaculate uniform. Not a hair on his head or in his moustache was amiss. He was jovial, enjoying the afterglow of a well-delivered punchline. His revered hat sat like a visored, squat sultan on his desk corner. He had extended a hand, a generous welcome, to Patricia

Arguello. She also stood, looking like a match for him in her designer clothes, the big gaudy laughter for his marvelous joke still on her face, looking fabulous, as she accepted the gallant hand so warmly offered. Yet even amid the spotlight, Patricia Arguello also had turned to regard Constance, entering.

But all three regarded her only that one instant, the brief life of that tableau. The next instant all three looked away, back to each other again, resuming their mutual enjoyment. Patricia Arguello laughed a second time at the chief, if it weren't in fact a third or a fourth. Carmelo Delavaca finally let go her hand, and he spoke in English that she might repeat such a fine joke to her friends, for it had been told to him by the Governor himself. La Madre reclined in her chair nearest the Chief's desk and watched all of them. Her study included Constance, as her dutiful but drab lieutenant seated herself in the remaining chair, nearest the door, a straightback beside Patricia Arguello, who was once again between the mistress and the true devotee.

Police Chief Delavaca made the appropriate gentlemanly nod of welcome to Constance, but nothing more. He turned to La Madre and said, "As I was saying, I talk with the Governor often. The next time he visits me here, perhaps I may call you, that you may meet the great man."

Constance knew that for La Madre there was no such thing as a great man, unless he were also a yogi. Yet there would be no need today to be rigorous, and La Madre nodded a sweet yes, and said, "I would be honored. I hear good things about the Governor. Do you think he would be respectful of foreign religious leaders? Or is he too greatly devoted to the Catholic church?"

The gallant Police Chief nodded discretely, intimately, that the great man had no biases when it came to business, that there was no great need to worry about devotion at all. "He welcomes everyone. But since you will come as *my* guest, you will be *especially* welcomed." He made another large smile to Patricia Arguello, and said to her, "You *all* of course would be welcomed. To meet the Governor." Only at the last did he let his eyes again drift to Constance, and there his eyes hesitated only long enough so she too would feel included in the pluralization. Then his eyes drifted again to Patricia Arguello, a sight which warmed his smile; and then back to his primary guest, who had silently witnessed all of Carmelo's admiration.

La Madre remained reclined in the sumptuous chair, her gaunt gray head pillowed in the plump headrest. Extremely at her ease. She said, "I always said you're a smart man, Carmelo. You know what it takes to succeed. It's not money, is it? Its friends. Well connected friends."

He smiled his complete agreement. First to La Madre he spoke. "Yes, Senora, it is true. It is an old Mexican saying. Friends can do what money cannot do." For the joking end of the aphorism, his attention drifted to Patricia Arguello, and he added, his eyes for that instant asparkle. "But it is an old Mexican saying also, that it is money that brings you the best friends." He laughed; he had no doubt they would understand him completely.

He thought he saw amusement in the orange mistress, and he certainly saw amusement in young Miss Arguello, and he was pleased. He let his fingers flit to his moustache, smooth it quickly to its tips, then let those fastidious fingers settle to rest on the revered Chief's hat. Patricia Arguello's perfume reminded him of honeysuckle. Such a pleasant conversation this was.

However, he knew why these interesting people were here. He briefly cleared his throat to indicate that they might begin the business. He said, "Yes, as I told you on the telephone, all the delays in your case have been well done and worthwhile. Finally we have the judge we have been waiting for. My new good friend Anjel Contreras. He is important in the party of PAN. They gave him his job. Just as they gave me my job. May Moctezuma preserve our great party."

Patricia Arguello had seated herself and now she withdrew from her little paisley handpurse a spiral notebook and a Shaeffer pen. She crossed a smart leg across her other knee and poised herself to write in the opened notebook she held in her left hand. She looked up again to the Police Chief. "You said Contreras, Chief? Anjel?"

He nodded solemnly, confirming it. Patricia Arguello wrote this down. Constance knew how pleased this information had made La Madre. That austere woman, however, would only let him see a portion of that pleasure, allowing him but the smallest smile in gratitude. No matter to him, for there would be truer and better currency.

La Madre from her reclination said, "Has His Honor Contreras looked at the case? Does he know my point of view? And my wishes?"

Carmelo's smile was most reassuring, as he said, "Oh yes absolutely, he knows everything he needs to know. I even have a surprise for you. I didn't tell you on the telephone because I myself did not know then, but Anjel Contreras is in his office today, which is unusual. He's coming to my office in a few moments to make greetings with you."

Patricia Arguello half rose up in her seat with the good news and said, "Oh that's wonderful! La Madre even told us driving over here that we could always count on you. Told us what an honorable man you were. But anyone could see that—when they see that beautiful uniform. You're such a handsome man, I can't get over it."

Constance was aghast. She looked at La Madre, who continued her uncritical observation of all of them. Yet surely, Constance thought, she must see this hussy's inappropriate behavior.

Carmelo let his eyes linger longer on this vivacious young beauty than he should have, but he could hardly help himself. As quickly as he could he removed his eyes to see La Madre still looking at him and through him, though not obviously disapproving.

Instead La Madre showed herself to be a pure loyalist. She said, "PAN seems to be just the party for modern Mexico. A party of the people."

The Chief preened. "Oh yes, no one doubts it. The PRI are finished. They were all only for the morditas, the bites. Honor and justice were for sale. Criminals walked free. Now everything has changed. Honor and justice are once again in their true place. The people can trust their government again."

"Yes," Patricia Arguello spouted, and Constance instantly knew that whatever statement followed would gall her. "You can feel the change in the air. When I walk in the plaza even, it feels like a fresh breeze is blowing through our village. And I know it *must* be the PANistas." She glowed at the Police Chief, as if he were the incarnation of those politics she so admired.

Still, to Constance, La Madre seemed unperturbed by these ludicrous, high school efflorescences, which made Constance ashamed both to be a witness and to be thought a party to them.

However, this espirit invigorated Carmelo extremely. His hand, straying to touch the power of his visored hat, trembled a little with the excitement. What a recruit this one would make! But the stare of La Madre was on him when he looked at his imposing orange-clad primary guest, and he knew for the moment he must let go his thrilling perceptions about this ravishing politicalista.

At that moment the door opened and Carmelo's favorite spy, nephew Fonzo, entered but suddenly stopped. This young man with the long overcoat seemed startled to see the gray-haired woman, gaunt and old, but formidable, seated in a chair facing Carmelo on the other side of his desk.

Seeing his nephew, who was proving a very valuable confederate, Carmelo gave him the lawyer's smile and stood to receive him. But quickly Carmelo turned his attention back to his female guests, even though he still spoke to Fonzo. "Fonzo, I bring you here to meet friends of mine. Sometimes clients. Who deserve all our respect. This," he said, gesturing with his hand toward the orange sarong, "is La Madre. And this is her companion, Catherine. And this last is the very bonita Patricia Arguello." The Police Chief's eyes sparkled at his last introduction.

Fonzo stepped forward a little shyly, ignoring the grandmother and the bonita. The gaunt old woman nodded her regal head at him, acknowledging his presence and perhaps blessing him at the same time. She spoke in a strong voice. "Good to meet you Sergeant Fonzo. Carmelo has been complimenting you."

This statement was hardly believable to Fonzo. He was no sergeant and he could not imagine any reason Carmelo would compliment him to these strangers. Still, if it served Carmelo well as a lie, then Fonzo would corroborate. It would be good to be the sergeant, even temporarily. But for the moment he said only, "Yes, ma'am." The other one, Constance, merely looked at him, neither smiling nor frowning.

Carmelo seemed like he would amplify these last words of hers, but La Madre too had been waiting for Fonzo to arrive, and by a stern look at the police chief she silenced him. She wanted her own explanations. She shifted her chair so that she faced Fonzo more directly. After that, Fonzo didn't feel he dare move, lest her new alignment become false on his account.

She said to him, "I need protection, Sergeant Fonzo. I'm wondering if you're the man for the job."

It seemed doubtful to Fonzo, but he dared not be disagreeable, in case Carmelo needed corroborating lies. He imagined James Bond. He said with quiet confidence, "If that's what you need, I'm your agent."

Carmelo began to say, "Somebody's causing trouble for La Madre and we must...."

But La Madre stifled him. "I'll tell him, Carmelo. It's not *someone*, Sergeant Fonzo. It's the people who own Bellacasa, Max and Carlotta. They are going around town tearing down posters that I put up, warning the unwary about them. I want some police protection, and assistance. Some *special* protection, not just one of those idiots of yours, Carmelo, who drive around in those useless cars, who are no more policeman than I am. I want someone who will follow around Max and Carlotta, and stop them from tearing down my posters. I'm a famous religious person. Constance and I have a religious ashram, if you know what that means. We have innocent followers, like Miss Arguello, who come to us to mediate and to find God. I can't have a bunch of lunatics tearing down my posters."

In rapid Spanish Carmelo said to Fonzo, "There's a lawsuit, brought by your old employers, against this woman. Max and Carlotta say her posters are slander. Want the job, nephew?"

Fonzo could see that such a job might be devilish hard, working for this demanding woman. It might also take him away from more lucrative, private investigations. He thought to stall, awaiting an inspiration, and he said, "Why are these people bothering you?"

La Madre's face sharpened. "They have cheated me, and they are trying to make a case against me in the courts about slander. Thanks to friends in the right places, and thanks also to your good uncle, Carmelo, I am able to prevent them. For the time being. Till I am finished with them. And listen to me, Sergeant Fonzo-I am willing to pay well, as your Uncle Carmelo knows."

This would weigh heavily. Perhaps he could make time for this *and* private business. He looked at her again, this time confidentially. "Alright, I'm your agent."

La Madre stared hard and cold at Fonzo, binding him by the vow he had just made to her. "No more need be said then. You're the man. You track these people. Catch them in a criminal act. Anything. Take photos of their crime. Arrest them. Parade them through the streets. Put them in jail."

Fonzo said yes, he would do all these things.

"Excellent. Then Constance and I will leave you to do your job. Carmelo can tell you all about these Bellacasa people. Scoundrels. Carmelo will tell you."

Patricia Arguello half rose up in her seat with the good news and said, "Oh that's wonderful! La Madre even told us driving over here that we could always count on you. Told us what an honorable man you were. But anyone could see that-when they see that beautiful uniform. You're such a handsome man, I can't get over it."

Carmelo let his eyes linger on this vivacious young beauty longer than he should have, but he could hardly help himself. As quickly as he could, however, he removed his eyes to see La Madre still looking through him, though obviously not disapproving.

Instead La Madre showed herself to have a political conscience and to be a pure loyalist. She said, "PAN seems to be just the party for modern Mexico. A party of the people."

The Chief preened. "Oh yes, no one doubts it. The PRI are finished. They were all only for the morditas. Honor and justice were for sale. Criminals walked free. Now everything has changed. Honor and justice are once again in their true place. The people can trust their government again."

"Yes," Patricia Arguello spouted, "you can feel the change in the air. When I walk in the plaza even, it feels like a fresh breeze is blowing through our village. And I know it *must* be the PANistas." She glowed at the Police Chief, as if he were the incarnation of those politics she so admired.

This espirit envigorated Carmelo extremely. His hand, straying to touch the power visor of his hat, trembled a little with the excitement. What a recruit this young lady would make! But when he looked at his imposing orange guest of honor, the stare of La Madre was still on him and he knew for the moment he must let go his thrilling perceptions about this ravishing politicalista.

La Madre leaned forward and seemed about to speak the important thing, a familiar scene with the Chief, his favorite moment. However, all the recent revelations of that rascal Fonzo's, which had proved to Carmelo how easy it was to be caught indiscretely, talking into some unknown enemy's tape recording, had made the Police Chief extremely cautious. He held up an admonitory finger and with his other hand leaned toward his primary guest and handed her a card, which bore a message penned in ink that morning by the Chief himself. It said: *There will be no talk of Money or Dollars or Pesos. These things are to be called Tacos when we speak aloud. In case of bugs.*

La Madre nodded, she would accept the house rules. She passed the card to Patricia Arguello, who read it and passed it on to Constance, who read it but for whom it mattered nothing, since she doubted she'd be allowed to say anything anyway. Ah, but these would be the things Patricia Arguello shouldn't know.

La Madre resumed her intimate inclination toward the Police Chief. "I have very much respect for your PAN party, Carmelo, as you know. I have made some tacos that I would like to donate to your party's next banquet."

Carmelo had been reasonably sure that this was how it would be. But the extent of the generosity was everything, since these gringos sometimes had strange ideas about the value of influence. La Madre, as he closely, ardently watched, nodded once to Patricia Arguello. To Carmelo's pleasure this young woman stood once again, but this time she drew one fat envelope from each of her sleek black slacks' pockets, like a sultry slow draw gunslingerette. Instead of firing them off, however, she placed them very tenderly on the desk in front of the Police Chief. Even before he admired the size of these bundles, Carmelo admired the clever curvaceous body still standing in front of him, that could conceal such bundles and still not betray the voluptuous curves that were ever evident beneath the scandalous pagan clothes.

La Madre's words brought him back to the bundles. "I trust that you will make sure these tacos are distributed in the best way possible. So that everyone at the banquet has a fair share."

"Oh yes, yes," Carmelo assured her, hardly hearing a word she said, now that his senses had returned from their lurid examination of the giftbearer. He forced his attention completely on the gift, eager to know the denominations hidden by the manila wrap. That would have to wait. Like a prodigal son claiming his birthright, Carmelo opened his favorite side drawer of his desk, then reached with both hands and lifted the bundles from the desk and set them lovingly in the felt-lined drawer, empty, just dusted, waiting. Plunk, plunk. He shut the drawer. He looked up again with his most magnanimous smile.

He said, "You can indeed trust me to do the right thing with these tacos." He winked at La Madre—a bit of deviltry, why not? "And I know what a fine cook you are, senora. Always making those nice plump tacos."

Apparently Constance had been deceived about Patricia Arguello's innocence of their mission. More than that, Constance was offended that La Madre had not foretold her how much Patricia Arguello was in her mistress's confidence.

Patricia Arguello had reseated herself, reestablished her secretarial pose with notebook in hand, ready to inscribe all the precious words by whomever, whenever. She smiled happily to all the participants. Constance would like to have pummeled her where she sat.

Yet shamelessly she could not be stopped. She went on. She became effusive again. "Why, Police Chief, how exciting it must be to be on such familiar terms with judges and governors. You're just amazing."

The amazing man offered her an appropriate sly smile, as if none of this were amazing to him. Yet he was obviously happy she thought so. He said to his admirer, "Oh it is not so much, Miss Arguello. I was a lawyer before I was Police Chief, before I became well established in the PANistas, so of course I know everyone. Everyone knows me. But still, you must think of me as a public servant. As we say in Mexico, I am at your service, dear Miss Arguello." The warmth and solicitude of his smile could only be meant for her.

Constance looked for the dozenth time to La Madre, expecting to see at least a glimmer of the dissatisfaction she must be feeling, for these displays of Patricia Arguello must surely be an embarrassment to their religious order, surely. La Madre was acutely observing everything, as she always did, but she showed not the least sign of dissatisfaction or embarrassment. Constance locked her eyes on those of her mistress, waiting to be acknowledged, that she, Constance, might by a subtle sign express her own dismay, and perhaps by this, to unlock the floodgates of her mistress's accumulated but hitherto restrained disapproval.

At last La Madre perceived Constance's insistent stare. She made her the slightest little smile. Constance could not fathom it, and thought that La Madre must be adrift in her own meditation, that she had for the time disconnected herself from the embarrassments of the present. Seeing that Patricia Arguello and the Police Chief were yet lingering in their admiration of each other, Constance thought to make the unseemliness of this behavior a mutual concern between her and the devoted. She lolled her head side to side ever so subtly, and for her ultimate condemnation she let her horrified eyes roll in disgust away from the two offenders, as if nothing on Earth ever would surpass this vulgar scene. Her enactment finished, Constance looked back to La Madre, expecting complete complicity.

. Instead, La Madre ejaculated a hearty laugh from her core. Constance in all her years as devotee had never heard the devoted laugh like that at *her*, so the surprise and the force startled her.

Immediately La Madre turned her sudden hilarious attention on the Police Chief. She said, "Pardon me for the outburst, Carmelo. Odd things can make you laugh. I was suddenly reminded of an old joke, one about a farm boy and a city boy. It's a joke peculiar to my American culture. I don't believe the joke would translate."

Yet Carmelo laughed anyway; and so in happy resonance did Patricia Arguello. Carmelo confessed. "Oh we have some jokes in Mexico too, don't be fooled, about farm boys and city boys. And probably of the same kind, because these shouldn't be translated either." For Carmelo this was a spontaneous joke, a rarity with him, and he laughed hard and long when he recognized the perfection of it. And immediately La Madre laughed again, as loudly and heartily as Carmelo. Patricia Arguello laughed with them too, but could not match their gusto.

Constance sat alone and abandoned to her scowl. The anger burned in her face, as her universe blew its seams and became a thing unknown, unworkable.

As suddenly as she'd laughed, La Madre ceased laughing, and turned a consoling face to Constance. She said, "Now we haven't heard a word from Constance. And I certainly don't want her to be forgotten. Because she's the one I could never do without. The one I could never do without. Do without. Never do without. She's been with me fourteen years you know.

We have been through it all together, haven't we, Constance? Come back to me, dear."

As quickly as it had come apart, Constance's universe in an instant reformed itself: it instantly again became the sanctuary she knew so well, her refuge and purpose. Constance felt the anger and sorrow drain out of her. She was whole again, and ready.

Constance said, "I can't take any credit. La Madre inspires me, and I do in return whatever she asks me. Like you, senor, I am a servant."

Patricia Arguello smiled sincerely again and said, "How very fine."

La Madre knew at last that the mission was accomplished. She sat forward, preparing herself to rise, but seemed to teeter there, going neither up nor back. She said to the Police Chief, "Carmelo, I know how important all your business is, and I don't expect you to waste so much time with me and my poor flock of spiritual seekers, so I'll make my goodbyes and go on about my own humble business."

This was good news to Carmelo, for, while La Madre had been speaking to the old one, the police chief had again been thinking about the thick bundles of tacos.

But when he saw her ready to rise and leave, he rose himself and went to her graciously, extending his hand to his guest. La Madre accepted the hand extended, though still seated, though struggling to rise. When their hands touched, she stopped the effort to rise and stared into his eyes, obviously savoring the great common understanding she saw deep within them. She smiled and he smiled too.

Then she let his hand go and turned to Constance. "You may go on ahead and bring the car round to the front, Constance. Patricia, help me out of this damned chair."

19 CONSTANCE'S NEW ROOM

An hour later the guru and her devotees had returned to El Limon. Constance busied herself in the kitchen of the main house preparing a dal for the evening meal. She'd had to use yellow split peas from SuperLake instead of the chan dals they usually bought in Guadalajara. To the well simmered onions and peas she added the turmeric and chopped garlic and coriander powder. Immediately she smelled the rich, pungent spice perfume the spare kitchen. Rice in a pot on the back burner steamed. There would be enough for several at the meal. Or some left over for tomorrow if Patricia Arguello by the grace of Shiva chose not to stay for dinner.

Though she passionately wished it would not, her mind repeatedly attached itself to the imaginary goings-on next door, in the finally completed casita. Completed *not* by Bellacasa. La Madre and Patricia Arguello were of a certainty arranging La Madre's business affairs in the modern streamlined way that Patricia Arguello, with her degree in business from Heald's Business College, had so ardently recommended over the last two months. Though Constance had at all times expressed her doubts about these modern methods, La Madre had listened. At first she had seemed reluctant, but had indulged her persuader by listening even again and again, until at last she had been convinced.

The worst part of it all had not been foreseen by Constance. The reorganization of strategy to sell La Madre's many self-published translations of the sacred yoga texts involved setting up a website and a massive mail solicitation. There were also to be new plans for promotional speaking tours, as well as the augmentation of on-going plans to recruit new followers. All this had surprisingly required a reorganization of the office space in the casita. Both rooms must for the time being be employed for the business. Patricia Arguello required a desk and work space of her own. La Madre had insisted to Constance that this would only be temporary, and that soon they would be able to relinquish the primary bedroom space to Constance, who had in the meantime been so patiently understanding. While she continued to sleep in her little closet in the main house, on the uncomfortable cot.

Constance stirred the dal. She was alone in the house. All was silent, save only the bubbling of pungent peas and onions. Her drab dress hung heavily upon her body. She could feel the animosity wriggling in her blood. She spoke her mantra, but with small energy, and she knew it was not enough to lift her away from the poison inside.

She tried listening to the silence of the empty house. She became aware of the incense in the living room, on the altar. There was no incense in the new casita. Nor was there an altar. How preposterous. Only Lord Krishna could know by what delirious reasoning La Madre had allowed Patricia Arguello to convince her that there should be a strict separation of things spiritual and things business. She'd convinced her that in that casita office the spiritual might better be forgotten, and left to its proper sphere in the other house. So of course there was no need for incense. Too often anyway it confused whatever clients might come to the business office.

Constance was unable to resist imagining the scene next door. La Madre at the computer, learning some new stupid thing, while Patricia Arguello stood just behind her and gushed her admiration. How they must banter back and forth. Constance in all her life had never bantered. Or been so bitter.

At last Constance realized there would be no peace for her in these troublesome contemplations. She must instead face the reality squarely. She turned the flame on the dal to its lowest, and extinguished the flame beneath the rice pan. She rinsed her hands quickly beneath the sink spigot and dried them on the hand towel tucked in the refrigerator door handle. She scuttled out the back screen door, and along the new concrete path through the gate and to the doorstep of the casita. It was open. It had better be. Constance went inside.

La Madre was indeed sitting at her computer. But Patricia Arguello was not for the moment to be seen, for Constance could look into both rooms from the doorway.

La Madre looked up at her. "Oh, is dinner ready so soon, Constance?"

Despite her malaise, Constance strained to be loyal. "No, no, not yet. I just thought I'd come over and see how you're doing. Have you finished making up the website yet?"

La Madre sat back and swiveled to face Constance. "No, I've changed my mind several times. It's got to be just right. I want all the titles to be exhibited on the home page, and it would be ideal to have a little commentary about each one, and even get the selected quotes from my two reviews on the home page. But it just looks so cluttered with all that. But Patricia thinks she has a new arrangement that will satisfy me, but I haven't seen it yet."

Constance looked about again. The absence of the vile presence was very pleasing. Even though it risked a rising hope, Constance asked, noticeably timid, "Is she gone? Will she be at dinner? Did I miss saying goodbye?"

La Madre's smile was large. "Oh no, Constance, she is *not* gone, and she *will* be at dinner, and you did *not* miss saying goodbye."

Patricia Arguello's vile voice from behind Constance called to her. "Oh yodel-do, Constance. I'm so glad you're here. I had to drag this thing across the yard from the front gate."

Constance turned and saw fashionable Miss Arguello huffing and struggling with a carton as tall as she was, which she obviously could not lift. Constance went to her, showing no sign of her profound reluctance. Constance grabbed the near end with both hands. Gently she hefted a little, felt the weight inside, and knew they could carry it between them. Patricia Arguello took hold of the far end, and called out, "Yipee!—we did it!" These two contraries then marched forward to the front door of the casita, struggled only a little to get the carton inside. They laid it in the room that Constance had so long dreamed of sleeping in.

Constance stepped back and stared at the box. "What's in it?" she asked.

Constance had expected La Madre to answer. Instead it was irrepressible Patricia Arguello. "It's a fabulous shelf system, it's new on the market. It will handle scads of books and documents. And it can be converted into a computer desk, should we really get this business rolling and need another secretary."

Another secretary? Constance could barely fathom it. La Madre had intimated that this room would be dismantling soon. As soon as La Madre had learned how to run the two fancy computer programs Patricia Arguello had installed on the computers.

The fierce pride of the dispossessed possessed Constance and she must speak, though her fear of La Madre's disapproval made her words come out all mumbled. "Whatsa. Ithoughta. Whadya."

With no effort La Madre read Constance's state of being. La Madre had little use for tempering her words. Even so, seeing her oldest devotee so pathetic, La Madre let compassion rule her for the moment. She said, "Yes, it does look as though we're expanding, dear Constance. And so I must confess, we are. I was about to talk it over with you. I feel badly that you have to know before I can soften it a little for you. Because, you see, this is all in your best interest too, even though it may not *seem* so right now. These innovations we're making are going to make the kind of sales I've been hoping for—that we, Constance, you and I, have been hoping for all these years. And now I feel it's maybe in my grasp."

"Oh it is!" said the nasty cheerleader.

La Madre ignored her. "Constance, you know what it would mean to me to have sales up, and money flowing in here. Look at all the good we could do. I could build *three* new casitas. And of course big financial success would benefit you as much as me. We could upgrade your little Volkswagen. We could get you a wonderful apartment in town. You'd be so busy with my most important affairs, you'd have your own personal secretary. You'd be doing a *lot* of flying, seeing exciting new places, setting up in advance for promotions. New York. Chicago. London. New Delhi."

Constance could imagine herself in none of these happy, prosperous scenes. Constance wanted her room in the casita, and to have everything be just as it had always been. Before this terrible person came. Yet it was unthinkable to express any of this to La Madre. Through her mistress's eyes Constance already had perceived her own attachment and her disloyalty to her vow of service. Constance need not utter anything for her mistress to know all.

Constance slowly inclined her head till she had made a proper subservient bow. Also she saw it was the position readymade for the axe to fall. She humbly spoke a last desperate optimism. "So I suppose it will be a *little* while longer till I can move in."

La Madre hesitated, a rarity. She had hoped the question would not have been made. She said, "Well, no, Constance, *not* a little while longer. Probably not for a *while*, in fact."

Constance gulped; then she said, "I understand. I'll do whatever you think best. You know I always have."

"That's a good girl, Connie. But I'm not heartless, you know. I don't want you to have to continue sleeping in the little closet any longer. I've asked Patricia to help us find a little room for you somewhere near SuperLake. For the time being."

"Yes," said the always offending Patricia Arguello, "and I did find something this morning, on my way here, I forgot to mention it. It's furnished. Which is perfect, because we can sure use your cot in here some nights."

Struck again, Constance said feebly, "Some nights?"

"Oh yeah," enthused her nemesis, "the nights when there's just so much to do that I have to spend the night. You know. It saves a lot of time if I don't have to keep running back to my apartment in the village."

Kum By Ya was all Constance had to ward off the profane demons that beset her mind. As her stomach sickened with insult heaped on insult, she began her chant silently, only vaguely aware that to the two others she stood dumb and ossifying before their eyes. She had not one word at her command to speak.

A tear, or a modest whimper, these at least would have tumbled out of most who suffered this much affliction. Neither would tumble out of Constance, even though, sadly, the meek, enervated chant failed to bring her to her sanctuary. However, Constance had other resources, and among them the fortitude of a career footsoldier. She could hold her mud. She could let stomach sickness be there, let the demons scream and dare her. She could let them. And they would consume her. But she would not flinch.

Though at last she must say something. "Is there a shower? I mean, in the apartment you found for me. Is there a shower?"

"Oh heavens yes," exulted Patricia Arguello. "It's a studio with a little kitchenette. Just darling. You'll love it."

It would be loved when it would be host to the wake of this terrible person died with a dagger through her heart.

"I'm sure I will," said Constance, gliding ahead safely now in automatic, no need to smile, no need to be happy, no need to say anything more.

La Madre rocked just noticeably in her padded swivel chair, looking with the last of her compassion at Constance. She said to her, "There are strategic reasons for choosing that neighborhood, Cat. It's near SuperLake, MBE, and El Torito. You can be right on top of it. You can poster those places several times a day. They'll never be able to tear them down fast enough. And whenever you're home, you can park the car up near any one of those stores on the highway, with all the windows postered. You see how handy that will be, don't you?"

Constance told La Madre that it would be handier than anything. Constance told both of them that dinner would likely be ready in twenty more minutes. Constance went back to her quiet kitchen.

The next morning Constance was still groggy from her pummeling of the day before, and as she drove the red Volkswagen, postered fore and aft and starboard, through Ajijic, she stopped at Danny's for a quick coffee to go, something La Madre would not have approved. Too bad. Constance was in a rebellious mood.

She drove on, sipping the hot bitter bitch brew, refusing to flinch or grimace when little scalding drops flopped onto her fingers. She would not stop to poster today. The address of the darling studio was in her shirt pocket. Next to it was a check made out to the owner for the first month's rent, should Constance find it to her liking. And how could she not? What indeed *could* offend dear Constance anyway, who had proven herself so many years the adept of renunciation?

She drove beneath the splendid canopy of flowerless galeana trees at La Floresta, past the libramiento turnoff and slowed approaching San Antonio. She looked for Calle Cinturon. She saw it, a meager little street of cobblestones declining toward the lake a quarter mile away. She went slowly down it, seeing humble little cottages, most of them adobe, with gardens displayed in tin cans at the gate or near the front door. Life was lean in San Antonio, where only the poorest of the gringos lived among their peasant neighbors.

Fortunately number 126 was five blocks down from the careterra, which placed it only two blocks west from the plaza of San Antonio, where the modest goings-on would give at least an impression for Constance of life being lived around her. There would be lots of children in the streets. There would be no cars hurrying up and down. After the first days, no one would bother her, or even notice her. She would be again safely invisible.

She parked the red Volkswagen in front of number 126. She let herself in through the tin gate that shuddered as she opened it. It was a low roofed house, old gray stucco, with one small curtained window on each side of the green sheet metal door. She knocked.

A naked child of two or three answered the door. Quickly a plump young mother in a plain cotton dress came up behind the child and scooted him out of sight with her hand, and looked to Constance to say what she wanted. Constance spoke an understandable Spanish. "You have an apartment to rent? I believe someone came by to look at it this week, a young American lady. I'll be the one renting it."

The woman grinned, this was good news. "Oh si, si." The woman came outside, wiping her hands on her well soiled dress and she motioned for Constance to follow her past the lonely window and down a little hardpack narrow path that went between her house and her neighbor's. A gloomy little path. Constance followed. Toward the rear of the house was another sheet metal door and the woman quickly unlocked and opened it, allowing Constance the privilege of first entry.

Constance cautiously stepped inside. The odor of old wet newspaper was in the musty air. Perhaps too she smelled turpentine. As her eyes adjusted to the dimmest of light she saw a sofa in one corner, draped with what had once probably been a colorful blanket. A small never-varnished pine table sat beside it with nothing on it. In the corner opposite the sofa were a card table and an opened folding chair set into it. Beside that was a sink with drainboards on either side. On top of one drainboard was a two burner propane portable, plugged into the wall; a microwave beside that. A calendar above it nailed to the wall, presenting the merry month of February, each day a little flowery box. Paired beside the calendar, Jesus Christ himself hung from the cross memorialized forever in brass, to give comfort every day of the year. One window in the room looked straight onto an adobe wall five feet away.

The door at the rear of the room led into the bathroom. Constance went into it, bravely, prepared to be brave even if this too disappointed. She saw a bathtub, a plastic blue curtain that could be drawn for more privacy. A covered toilet in the small corner space beyond the bathtub. A cabinet sink and mirror too close to the toilet.

Constance turned to the woman who had been following her. "No shower? I was told there was a shower."

The woman till this moment had seemed indifferent to the fate of the apartment, but Constance's question roused her to a little exuberance. "Oh yes, senora, yes. Of course there is a shower. Let me show you."

The woman in her long sleeve sweater eased her way past Constance into the small bathroom and reached behind the bathtub's drawn back curtain. In a moment she turned back to Constance with a great smile, holding up a rubber hose attached to a plastic shower head. Enjoying it, the woman bent into the porcelain tub and adeptly fitted the hose coupling onto the spigot. She held the shower head down in the tub and she turned on the cold water full blast. In a moment the shower head burst with water spray, splatting into the tub. Cautiously the woman stood and held the shower head up above her own head, though the spray still splattered into the tub.

"See—a good shower. You hold this over your head. Easy to do."

It would have to do. All of it would have to do. "The sofa opens to a bed?"

The woman nodded solemnly that this was indeed its cleverness. "That is easy too." She eased past Constance again, bustling to the apartment's other principle attraction. She bent and jerked something and tugged a strap till a mattress catapulted forward on its own metal frame and displayed a bed one person might sleep on. The mattress revealed beneath it the contours of the frame's crossbars.

"Darling," Constance said in English. In Spanish she said, "I'll take it. I'll be moving in this afternoon. I can bring everything in one trip."

By late afternoon Constance had delivered her car load of possessions into the cave of her new apartment. She had made a little altar of the pine table beside the sofa with her bronze shiva in a circle of flames for the centerpiece. Her incense stand. Her favorite blanket that had been with her all the way through India now draped the sofa. Her hygiene items were in the cabinet behind the bathroom mirror. Her clothes were in the closet. She had a pot and a pan in the drawer beneath the burners. She had her own flatware and plates and cups on the shelf beneath the drainboard. Her teapot in the center of the card table. She was moved in.

Yet one last duty remained before she would be done for the day. She must park the slandering red Volkswagen as conspicuously and as near SuperLake as possible, and leave it there till late tomorrow morning. There would be a little satisfaction in this. A poke in the eye of Carlotta could so easily this evening seem like a poke in the eye of Patricia Arguello.

Constance drove the now-empty Volkswagen back toward the careterra, all its windows but the front filled by red-underlined recruiting posters for the on-going class action lawsuit against the enemy of the people. In a few blocks she was at her destination and saw the perfect spot halfway between Mail Boxes Etcetera and SuperLake, where Pancho the grocer magnate would not be able to make her move. She parked there, no more than twenty feet from the careterra. A shining red beacon to the passing and the parking.

Constance removed herself from the defamation mobile, and stood back and admired the genius of it. Peck. Peck. Proud of her part in the long war, she turned away and went into SuperLake for the essential items to stock her kitchen.

When she re-emerged she carried four full plastic bags in her hands and she wished she had not parked so far from the cashiers. She struggled a little with the load, and set the bags on the car roof so she could easily open the door. She put the bags on the rear seat, and settled herself into the driver's seat. Set to turn the key in the ignition, for the first time it came to her that she was going to her new dreary home. A tremor of sadness passed through her. But she knew she must not indulge that. Kum By Ya. Ya By Kum. More then renouncing for La Madre, she was renouncing for Shiva, for Vivekananda, the yogi warrior of renunciation she admired most. She felt the sadness gradually pass away. She felt strength come back into her. She was ready for the homeward journey.

Constance could see there were no cars or people beside her, even though her windows were mostly covered with slanderous handbills. Yet when she looked out the little oval rear window there was only a wedge of glass between handbills to peer through. She peered. She didn't notice anything, though it also might have been that her glasses were still misted from the recent sadness.

But something had just parked there, a white Dodge Caravan, though Constance could see it not.

Carlotta had recently come from Bing's Ice Cream in Chapala and had driven, chocolate milkshake in her right hand, sipping through the straw as she drove the few miles to SuperLake for her own groceries for the evening meal. Even though she had seen the red display mobile parked and blaring its obscenity many dozens of times the last few months, the shock of first seeing it was always the same. It aroused horror and anger. She saw it now and a hot breath sucked into her and she slowly let it exhale. With a wild madness in her eyes she seemed a bull snorting steam through its nostrils, zeroed in on its tormentor.

It was a special moment, for rarely had she ever seen Constance entering or leaving the slandering Volkswagen. Carlotta pulled her van behind Constance's red car, her bumper three feet from Constance's bumper. She set the brake, and climbed out and shut the door. Looking to gore.

It was at this moment that Constance thought she saw no one or nothing behind her, and she revved the motor and let off the clutch and the bug surged backward and smacked like a thunderclap into the white Caravan's front bumper. Constance, stunned and immobilized, fumbled with her door handle so she could go see what terrible thing had just fallen out of the sky upon her.

Constance jerked free of her car and was still dizzy enough with dismay that she staggered a little as she went to look behind her car, not yet seeing the tall terrible figure coming at her, a chocolate milkshake in her hand.

Carlotta screamed at her, "You bitch! Trying to kill me now, huh? You're not happy with just blasting your nasty lies everywhere, now you smash my car, trying to kill me!"

This additional shock attack staggered Constance further and she reached her hand to her car roof to steady herself. Constance could only mutter, "I didn't see you. I didn't know you were there."

"What a crock!" screamed Carlotta again. Then her fury turned from driver to vehicle. "Well, isn't this nice, all these lying little posters in this ugly little car." Then she bellowed even louder. "HEY! I can't see out of these damn windows *either! How about we give them a little wash!*"

Carlotta's hand dipped into the milkshake container and scooped out a handful of chocolate glug. Ferociously, she slung it on the red Volkswagen's rear windshield and in a happy frenzy rubbed it with her palm until it had gooped over all of it, the posters unreadable beneath. Her frenzy hurried her to the driver's side windows, where she slung and smeared chocolate milkshake again. Then to the front windshield, the only window unposted, but she splattered and smeared it anyway. A moment later she hurled the last of her milkshake onto the remaining side windows and smeared them muddy with the dark ice cream.

The expenditure of energy for Carlotta had been enormous, but she was releasing stores of old fury. As she stood back and admired what she had done, she felt extremely satisfied.

"There," said Carlotta. "All clean." She was dressed a little gauche for most tastes in her lime green capri pants and cowboy boots. She stood a head taller than prim Constance, and she seemed propelled by a dangerous wild energy.

Carlotta's surprise attack had utterly confounded Constance, but she was a yogi trained to battle, and very quickly her training asserted itself. She straightened her posture of defeat. Arjuna was ready for the battle.

Constance hissed at her. "Have your laugh, Carlotta. You think this matters at all what you did? Really? You think I won't be back tomorrow? The real joke is, La Madre doesn't even *need* to do this anymore, you're already finished. She's only still doing it because she wants to rub it in."

Carlotta's reckless smile became a scowl. She spoke her anger. "But we *will* win our case, Constance. She's lied and slandered us for eleven months, but in the end she *will* pay. You think we're ruined, but we'll bounce back from this. It's *her* reputation that will be ruined. It's already ruined with all the people in town who know us truly, and who know the truth of this. They all *know* what she is."

It might have annoyed Constance, for some of this was true. But she was invigorated by happier knowledge, from friends in higher places. She could even make a little mad laugh of her own. "*You* two are the fools. Say this crap all you want to, I don't care. I'll be there at the end laughing at you. You just took on the wrong person. You have no idea who and what you're up against. You don't even know what kind of war you're fighting. You don't even see what's coming."

Carlotta took all this as foolhardy bravado and Carlotta continued her own condemning scowl. "And this is what *I* say. In the end, no matter what LaMadre says or does, it will be known what she did, I swear. And you may take this carwash as a token down payment on that promise." Carlotta leered as she opened her van door and climbed in. She backed out and drove away, waving without looking back.

To Constance all this outburst of Carlotta's was swagger in front of a hurricane. It didn't matter a thing. Carlotta and her foolish husband were beyond pity. They'd be out of town before summer was over.

Constance turned away from the disastered car and began the long walk to number 126. Fortunately, she had a spatula and some rags there, which she could bring back with her and get all the chocolate mess off the windows. Then she would be able to see to drive the groceries home. Afterward she would drive the car back to the careterra, so she could leave it parked overnight in the most conspicuous place. That last obligation of a truly miserable day finally accomplished, she would then walk back to number 126 to heat herself a can of Chef Boyardee spaghetti, without meat, and make a little pot of Zhinsin tea before she had to try out that iron bed.

20 BELLACASA &
THE SPITZENBERGENS

Corrina called Carlotta and it was unimaginable good news. Corrina had just sold a lot to a newly arrived German couple, and she had shown them two Bellacasa beautiful houses and the couple had been thrilled. They said Bellacasa must be the builders.

"But don't they *know?*" Carlotta asked. "How long have they been in town?"

"Oh dear, I thought about that too. But I told them enough to give them an idea. I said you were involved in an old lawsuit with a whacko, that would obviously go your way, that everybody knew you were being unfairly harassed, and they said that didn't matter. They were so impressed with your houses that nothing would have mattered."

Carlotta held her breath. This could be wonderful or it could fall apart in the next phone call. "How soon are they ready to sign? How much are they spending on a house?"

Corrina was exuberant. "They'd sign tomorrow, I'm sure of it. They were talking about three bedrooms, a couple of bathrooms, about a hundred fifty thousand."

"Wow," said Carlotta, daring for the moment to believe. "That would pay off Lopez and get us out of debt. And give us a little breathing room, till we can weather this storm."

"I know it would, deary. I sure would be happy to see that. They want to meet you and Max first, of course. We could make it this evening, at the Posada, if you're available."

"The sooner the better," said Carlotta.

Just at twilight Carlotta and Max arrived. Coming together up the front stone steps they looked such a respectable couple. Max wore no Y-thonged huaraches, but shoes he'd polished; also a long sleeve white cotton shirt stitched in green, and tan slacks. Carlotta wore no cowgirl boots, but fine leather sandals; wore also a white cotton dress with fringed hem that showed off her tanned arms and throat and long auburn hair.

Corrina from the door of the bar saw them enter and went to them. She had dressed with restraint as well, in a simple blue dress with high collar and long sleeves. Her short frizzy nap of hair seemed to have grayed a little recently. But she was a cheery lady.

"Oh kids, I couldn't wait," she said, hoisting her gin rickey, clinking ice. "The Spitzenburgens—Lord I hope I'm pronouncing it right! They haven't shown up yet. I'm buying, what'll you have."

They all stopped a moment to greet Judith Eager at her table, where she was drinking wine with two old friends, before Corrina and her two friends took their own table. Max ordered Sol beer and Carlotta red wine. Yet before the waiter could bring them, and before the three could further discuss their German prospects, the prospects themselves stood framed by the bar's archway, peering into the restaurant, no doubt for Corrina.

"Yoo-hoo!" hollered Corrina a little theatrically, standing for emphasis, waving her many ringed fingers at them. "Yoo-hoo!"

Of course they heard her and turned, startled perhaps at seeing Corrina, or startled perhaps at seeing that they themselves were the people being yoo-hooed. Watching Corrina with her grin coming at them, they made their best smile, but it was feeble. More importantly for them, they must also step back, anticipating an unwelcomed, robust hugging and kissing. They both dreaded this style of manners among gringos in Mexico, which seemed so prevalent, and which was much too much for them.

Yet Corrina was perceptive enough to see their petite alarm, and she tempered her enthusiasm. "My, you have to talk loud around here to be heard! Well, so nice to see you again, Franz, Leonora. Max and Carlotta just got here a minute ago. We might as well go take a nice table outside. It's such a pleasant night."

The Spitzenburgens were appeased by this more proper greeting, but even so, they stood primly by. They were precisely dressed, in inoffensive colors, olive for him and mauve for her. A summer suit with tan open-collared shirt he wore, and her dress was straight on her thin rigid frame, her hair in a tight wrap at the back of her head. His dark hair was graying at the temples; he combed it all straight back, lightly moussed.

Franz expressed their hesitation, "Outdoors would not be good for us. Too much air. Could we take an inside table? It would be so much more civilized."

Corrina fortunately squealched an urge to tease them out of their timidity. Instead she humored them. "Oh why not. Let's stay inside. The garden and the evening breeze and the stars are way over-rated anyway."

Corrina brought forward her two builders of choice. Max and Carlotta were not dressed like the banker and his wife that the Spitzenburgens would ideally have liked to see greeting them, but Franz and Leonora had been in the village long enough to see that, sadly, no one ever seemed to dress rigorously. The Spitzenburgens were learning to be tolerant on that point. On others as well.

The two men shook hands and the two women also, only a little more warmly. Franz had prepared well his opening line. "My wife and I were very impressed with your houses. We especially liked that waterfall that overflowed into a river across the yard."

Max appreciated the compliment. "Yes, that came out very well. You know, so much water comes down the waterfall, and so loud, that you hear it everywhere in the cottage. You *could* make a house in hacienda style, with the three wings of the house all facing the waterfall and river in the middle courtyard."

Carlotta so admired the novelist in him. To toss off these pretty, seductive pictures. The Spitzenburgens seemed to be indeed enchanted, as they allowed themselves their first smile of the evening, likely contemplating their own three wings of hacienda and a waterfall and river in the midst of it.

As Armando, the impeccably dressed and irresistibly charming host, led these five collaborators across the lobby and toward a vacant table, Corrina chatted to Armando, and husband walked with builder, wife with nearly-wife. These two couples talked about what fine meals they were seeing on the tables they passed going to their own. It was a table near a window: early evening, the garden in shadowy shapes, but the great rubber tree strung with white lights over the wide patio where handsome black and white groomed waiters went by on their discrete missions. Most tables were occupied by English speakers, only one by Spanish.

Within the more climate-regulated dining room behind windows and doors, the tables on two tiers were mostly occupied. Here the suave waiters also passed and repassed.

Their waiter Edgardo was there immediately to help seat the women and to offer the two men a light, or to suggest the evening's especial aperitivos. Edgardo was short and a young grandfather, and after twelve years at this job he felt no need to be witty and dashing, a cavalier like the younger waiters. He could now be the elder statesman, to whom people wanted to give gratuities simply because he was so elegantly restrained. Having taken all their orders for drinks, he assured them he would be quickly returned, and he went away.

The Spitzenburgens knew what next direction they'd like to move the conversation, but first they studied the menu; wondering if perhaps it wouldn't be better to let these (no doubt California) builders say something first.

Carlotta did speak: "Have you lived most of your lives in Germany?" They nodded and said yes they had. "How lucky," continued Carlotta, "I've never been. Max and I both would love to go to Europe. You've probably been to Italy many times, haven't you? It is right next door, isn't it?"

Franz grimaced, but only a little, for he might have distastes, but he also wished to be thought a man who had seen much of life and was past being shocked by any of it. At times the effort strained him. "Yes, it is right next door. But we've been only once. Italy's just not for us. It's too messy, too dirty."

Corrina's exploded in laughter,"Oh Lord, that's a good one! What in the world made you come to Mexico then?"

Lean Leonora would not be embarrassed by it. "It's cheap, what else. Who can afford retiring in Europe?"

Carlotta blurted, "Or California, for that matter."

Franz said, "We probably *should* be in MexicoLimpio—it's so well protected and everything's so clean. Except that we don't like neighbors so close, even...light-skinned ones, especially without having a wall around your own property. So that's what we decided. That we'd get as big a lot as we could afford, and then build a very, very tall wall—oh three or four meters high—around the perimeter of the whole property. We're going to install automatic garage doors with high-powered remote control."

Leonora added, "And cameras. Just like MexicoLimpio has."

"Yes," said Franz. "Everything will be very high tech with us. That is what we like. Our television and our music system, Blaupunkt. Always. We drive a BMW."

"Yes," said Leonora. "We had it shipped over."

Waiter Edgardo returned carrying on the tips of his fingers a round bar tray bearing five drinks, and he set it on the aluminum stand beside their table. He smoothly handed round the drinks without asserting his own amusing, carefree personality as most of the younger waiters would have done. Edgardo had learned the less strenuous advantage of minding his business and bringing things before they were asked for. Edgardo the unobtrusive stood in silent attention, ready to take the first order, whenever it pleased them.

In turn they ordered salads and dinners. The Spitzenburgens were well surprised that here in Mexico they found veal in a recipe they knew from home, and they ordered it. Max asked for Scampi in garlic and almonds; Carlotta the baked salmon in poblano sauce; and Corrina the chicken breast parmesan. Edgardo assured them they would all be well gratified in their choices. The perfect servant then went silently away.

"You know," said Leonora, "the idea of the hacienda really appeals to me. Surrounding a courtyard. Everything looking away from the big wall, into the middle, where it's pretty and well kept. And that waterfall!"

"Yes," said Franz, able to warm to an idea, "I like that too. But I am most impressed by the way you do the tiles. All those pretty tiled shelves in the bathroom. I've never seen all the walls and every surface in the bathroom tiled."

Leonora's view of it varied. "Well some of those color combinations were too much for me, but I did love all the imitation stone tilework in the one house Corrina showed us."

Corrina had been waiting for a turn, uncharacteristically unobtrusive. She might now say, "The Lujack house, Carlotta, where you had the profit sharing party."

"Yes," said Leonora, as if she might have been moved, "Corrina told us that too. Profit-sharing. Well, that must mean you've been very successful here."

"We have been," said Max modestly, allowing for a misapprehension of time frames by his admirer. "It's because we have a very good relationship with our men. The same ones have built all the houses we've done—what? Nine, ten?" Carlotta nodded that it was so.

When Edgardo came with the salads and began assigning them to their consumers, a jaunty Morley Eager was not far behind, having come to pay respects to Corrina, and he then as well saw Max and Carlotta.

"Well, well," said the distinctive but, for the moment, subdued voice; though still in his eyes the mischief was ready. "So this is the little California band, is it? I see Corrina every week, but I don't see you two that often these days."

Max rose and shook his hand. "You know why you don't hear any gossip about us, Morley? Because we never leave the house after dark.

Except for special occasions. *You're* the one I don't see very often when I do come here."

Morley, eyeing as always the newcomers, said quickly, "Oh you know me, I only come out for the beautiful women. If you came more often with your wife, you'd see me."

As Morley leaned forward to Carlotta and Corrina, he might have appeared to Leonora and Franz to be some wanderer in off the street begging affection instead of coins, for both women smiled at his ruddy imp face, and they laughed at his sparkle, and let the little devil kiss them tenderly on the cheek. But the Spitzenburgens had before leaving Germany prepared themselves to be exclusive. Many little local customs, such as this, they would ignore; though they would still show that they could be pleasantly tolerant of the most eccentric of these customs.

They need not fear, for Morley was adept at reading his audience, and would never, for any of the fun, tax a fragile facade beyond its capacity to survive his humor. Corrina in the meantime introduced the pueblo's newest citizens, the Spitzenburgens, to this one she proclaimed the creator and owner of this illustrious hotel. She also explained to Morley that Max and Carlotta were building these newcomers a house on a half acre lot in Las Salvias.

The Spitzenburgens were, without sensing each other's reaction, equally amazed that such an apparent vagabond should be not only the owner of such a fine establishment, but also the man who'd dreamed it and had it built. The droopy moustache alone made him seem a man not capable of being taken seriously. Yet down here, so they'd heard, the women seemed to like the unusual men. Yes, more than ever Leonora and Franz realized how happy they would be with the big high wall.

Morley stood beside the table, cane in one hand, the other hand touching the table as he spoke, and yes, he might have been the mayor, in some last century wild west town. He said, "So the Spitzenburgens are *another* pair of discriminating buyers. Yes, I've been in a few of those Bellacasa places. Mighty fine. Lots and lots of tile and big windows and fancy ceilings. My friend Smokey Stover's got one. I hear tell for another fifty thousand dollars, after it's done, Max and Carlotta will sign their names in the cement sidewalk."

Franz and Leonora understood a joking exaggeration was meant, but they only clumsily comprehended the point of it. They tried to smile, but they were hoping the conversation would move on to something less subtle.

Leonora even so wished to be thought by her new gringo society as tolerant and humorous as the rest, and she said to Morley, "I've been looking at these beautiful pillars and arches in the dining room—and you say *you* built this restaurant and hotel, Mister Eager?"

"Not exactly," Morely said, stepping a little closer to Leonora, who sat in the chair nearest him and couldn't lean back any further. "I'm a voyeur, madam. Even in those days building the hotel I was harmless. The best I could do was to stand on the sidelines and watch. Old age would be hell if I hadn't had such a wild time when I was young."

The Spitzenburgens knew the vagabond hotel owner master builder had taken them unknowingly to the edge of the precipice, where in the next utterance they could be in the most dreaded conversation of all—about sexual behavior. Fortunately for these so endangered, Morley had his own code of honor and eased off, saving them any ultimate embarrassment.

He had a better subject. "Say, Leonora, maybe you should have second thoughts about Max and Carlotta. You know for you I might come out of retirement and come over to your lot and build you a nice little two person version of my hotel. Do you think you could stand me underfoot every day? Personally I think we'd get along dandy. Does your husband like to row? I like to row anyway. We have a nice little romantic lake out here." He pointed to it with his walking stick.

The faces of both the Spitzenburgen's soured in unison; she for the lemony romantic insinuations, he for the limey rowing on the lake However, all of it passed too swiftly for them to resolve before Morley took them round another abrupt turn. "Me? I'm too old for that kind of thing. It could be dangerous too. I mean not the romance, but the rowing on the lake. Why there was a watersnake, oh about ten years ago...."

"But let me explain. Watersnakes start out as cyclones, you know, those little whirlwinds. Anyway, about ten years ago one of these cyclones came out over the lake and then it touched down on the water, and it sucked up probably a million gallons of water, and a whole lot of fish too. Then when it came twisting off the lake, the watersnake started up a hillside. But then it couldn't hold onto its water and all those million gallons and hundreds of fishes fell out of the sky and washed half of a hillside of Rancho del Oro away. I kid you not. Took out two garages and a lot of boundary walls. Lots of animals and hundreds of chickens were washed away. Yep, it was quite a thing. I sure would hate to be out rowing on the lake, with a pretty gal like you, and have one of those watersnakes come get me." Morley laughed and had to stand back a moment for the gusto.

The Spitzenburgens were startled enough to turn to each other for consolation, or for further illumination, but there was none for either of them. Each turned to look again at Morley the storyteller. Obviously Franz could not just leave it at that. He said, "Really? I mean, is that true?"

Morley seemed horrified at the lack of credence. "True? Why watersnakes happen on a regular basis. Though it's not that often the watersnakes come to land and make such a mess. But watersnakes suddenly appear, when the weather conditions are just right. Then they're out there on the lake! Spinning really fast and moving in the air, like a snake, just the tip of it touching water. It's quite fabulous to see. In my life I've seen many of them, out this very window." He gestured lakeward with his walking stick, through the window, to far beyond the patio diners who all sat beneath the mammoth rubber tree.

As these two profoundly mystified Spitzenburgens looked off into the beyond which Morley had indicated, they seemed half expecting to see a watersnake even then take shape out there, though it was night.

Morley saw them staring way out there, entranced. "Yes, you can see them *even at night* I hear. On some very, *very* rare occasions, the lakewater has just the right kind of microbes in the water, so that when the watersnakes come flying in and sucks up all the water *and* the microbes, the watersnake in the air glows phosphorescent, kind of like neon. You see that same glowing phosphorescence in the ocean all the time. It's the most amazing thing I personally have ever seen—a watersnake way up in the sky out there glowing in the dark and gyrating back and forth over the top of the lake. Phosphorescent. Just imagine it! In the black of night! Glowing like neon, twisting up into the sky, like something completely magical. I bet you can almost see it."

And so it seemed they could, suspended as they were so precisely between truth and falsehood, still faithfully looking out across the water into the night, waiting for a miracle to rise up into the sky, all lit up, and whirl away.

Morley winked at Max and Carlotta and Corrina, and said, "That's a good note to leave on. Good luck with your project, kids. I'll always be one of your biggest fans. Thanks for the business."

Leonora and Franz soon enough drew back their attention from that glowing watersnake wonder that had so easily and deeply enthralled them. They saw that Morley was saying goodbye to them all. While they themselves spoke goodbye and watched Morley walk away, the couple had no idea at all what to make of that strange man.

Happily, Edgardo soon began arriving with their dinner plates, and everyone could be eating, and so be relieved of their social responsibilities long enough to get a breather, for the Spitzenburgens had a rule of not talking while they ate.

Over coffees of course there would be a few deft questions by Franz, seeking out the best possible prices for all the special items he wanted. Leonora must talk confidentially to Carlotta about tile colors she could and could not bear. But they were a happy little family and Corrina sat back, satisfied to let the four all become fast friends forever.

While all five finished their coffees, another couple, being guided by the pretty host Costanza to an outside table, passed nearby and recognized the Spitzenburgens. They were dressed elegantly, she in a long dress and a fur around her shoulders, he in a dark suit and red tie, holding a silver headed hickory walking stick, which he carried and fondled, but which did not touch to the floor.

These new friends, the Callisters from Wisconsin, said they were taxiing to Guadalajara after dinner, to a late music affair, which the Spitzenburgens visibly regretted not knowing about, so that they also could have gone, perhaps with their friends. Franz told them they had purchased a lot the day before and they would be pleased to introduce them to their builders, Max and Carlotta, who had quite the reputation. Bellacasa. The Callisters were very pleased to meet them. Nice to see that Americans could come to Mexico and prosper in a foreign business climate. Carlotta assured them that it was a daily challenge. Leonora could not resist telling Gretchen Callister that they had decided on a hacienda style house around a fabulous tall rock waterfall that flowed into a river that ran all across the yard. The Callisters said you don't say, and they could hardly wait to come see it.

As they all waited for the check, which Corrina insisted was hers to pay, Max went alone to the bar and ordered a quick last shot of tequila. A little flutter was in his stomach. The good flutter. He hadn't felt it in a long time. Would they really survive all this? Maybe so. He took the shot and drank it off. The buzz was there before he returned to the table; in time to say goodbyes to the Spitzenburgens, to Corrina, and to make the appointment for the contract signing at noon, at Franz and Leonora's.

Precisely on time Max and Carlotta arrived in the Caravan. It was a small gated community called Las Villitas that had been built eight years ago. At its entrance was a caged booth where a young Mexican without uniform asked them their names and whom they were visiting. He wrote their answers on a form on his clipboard and opened the iron gate.

They drove slowly a windy cobbled street bordered lushly with geraniums and hibiscus, past stuccoed cottages in every pastel shade with little manicured lawns, until they found number twelve. Corrina's old blue Mercedes was parked in front and Corrina came out of the car as Max and Carlotta parked behind her. She carried a manila file folder with all the necessary documents.

A subdued Leonora Spitzenburgen met them at the door in a simple brown house dress. She acknowledged their presence with a minimum of conversation and led them through the foyer and the living room into what she said was their music room. There atop the shelves of neatly arranged CDs were two white busts, Beethoven and Wagner. Franz stood up from his master's chair to greet them with a handshake and a serious nod. He wore a tailored jacket to match his creased, tailored slacks. On the mahogany shelves behind him were arrayed thousands of dollars of Blaupunkt technology, all with digital readouts.

Three chairs had been arranged facing the master chair, and the guests were invited to sit themselves. Leonora would bring coffee or tea, as they wished. She departed to fill their requests. Everyone sat.

Corrina laid her folder on her lap and opened it, extracting the contracts in triplicates, and handed one to the master, and one to Max and Carlotta, and kept one for herself. She tempered her enthusiasm, but still she was jolly. "Well, this is it, ladies and gentlemen. The happy moment. Oh I can just hear that waterfall now—can't you, Franz?"

Yes, everyone might delight in this pretty picture; but not Franz. His rigid face grimaced, as if he must relieve himself of something most unpleasant, yet still maintain the courtesy that was proper. "Ah, yes," he began tepidly. "I'm afraid there's a problem."

For Max and Carlotta the chill darted quickly through their blood, and they each felt the cold reach out and grip their hearts. Corrina let her own innocent grin petrify on her face as she awaited the further explanation.

The master of number twelve Las Villitas would not make them wait. "You see, our friends the Callisters called us last night, after we got home, and told us some terrible stories. About Bellacasa Construction. Which disturbed Leonora and I very, very much. To tell you the truth, Leonora was so disturbed that she can't bear being in the room with us right now, while I talk about it again."

Max, ever a believer in the truth at last vanquishing, leaned forward and spoke energetically, trying to make Franz's eyes look into the depths of his own. "Franz, all those stories are lies. Carlotta and I have filed criminal charges against the person who is slandering us, and very shortly the decision will be rendered in our favor, and the person who's been slandering us will be ordered to make a public retraction. She will also probably be put in jail. I can give you the names of ten very well respected members of this community, Morely Eager among them, the owner of that hotel we were in last night, and the names of *all* of our clients, who will testify to our character and to the truth of what I'm saying."

Franz had not heard this, and seemed to be considering it. However, the bad taste just wouldn't be so easily washed away. "It's just so messy, that's the thing. Even if I grant you what you say, we still have *our* own reputations to consider. This would just be so hard to explain to all our friends and neighbors. That Bellacasa is building our house, and then to have to see those terrible orange posters the Callisters told us about. I just don't know how we could bear it. And I'll tell you, for Leonora, she *couldn't* bear it. I'm afraid we just can't sign."

For a terrible moment these three guests breathed in the deadly silence, each one unsure what counterstroke to make. The Spitzenburg fortress, so simply and quickly fortified, seemed impregnable. Corrina forced a valiant smile and said, "But surely, if I could introduce you to Carioca, the president of the bank, and Jim Penton, vice-president of the Lake Chapala Society, and Alex Grattan, editor of the local newspaper, and if all these people tell you these slanders are malicious lies by a lunatic, surely that would convince you that Bellacasa is reputable."

Franz' face contorted with the worry of it all, but he could only shake his head in disagreement. "No. It still wouldn't do. It's the messiness, you see. It would be always having to explain away an embarrassing situation. We like things neat and clean. This just wouldn't do. No, I've absolutely decided against it, and I'm not going to change my mind." With that he settled back in his chair, though his feet remained squarely planted in front of him. He allowed into his face a little sign of expectation, perhaps wondering if his guests would now see there was really no need to wait for coffee and tea.

Corrina would not relinquish her sad little smile and seemed to be struggling for a more conclusive argument. But Max saw in Franz' eyes the unbendable iron teutonic will. He glanced a briefest most painful look at Carlotta, who tried to retain her determined look, but she seemed unable to speak. She could see it all too. Max reached to touch her hand, and said, "Ready to go, sweetheart? I'm dying for a little of that leftover lasagna out on the patio."

Her eyes blazed a fury that she would not speak, not in this house. She stood and Max also stood, beside her. Corrina could hardly believe that it could end so quickly and without some further appeal to higher sentiments.

Still, she must rise too, and shamble after her disgraced builders toward the door.

Greatly relieved that these disenfranchised would not make a fuss, Franz relaxed his severity and followed them to the front door, a tiniest pleasantry forming in his mind, with which he could make a little courteous farewell. His guests however did not wait for him to open the door, but opened it themselves and passed outside.

As they walked down the path to their cars, Leonora came to stand behind Franz and watch these others leave, so glad she had not had to hear Franz rebuke them. But she had a last desperate request, which she called after them. "Oh say! Would it be alright if we came by, whenever it was convenient, and took a picture of that nice waterfall and the river?"

That reminded Franz of something too. "Yes, that would be very helpful. And, if it is not *too* much trouble, I would also be willing to pay you for a set of plans for that hacienda house you were talking about last night. That is, if the plans weren't too expensive."

But perhaps their words did not carry well in the air of Las Villitas, for Max and Carlotta and Corrina all got in their cars without answering or looking back, and drove away.

Max and Carlotta rode home in raging silence. This had certainly been one of the possibilities they'd foreseen. They'd each prepared for that in their heads, but not in their hearts. But they suffered it now, inexpressible by words.

At home in Canacinta, going into the house, Carlotta said, "I feel like taking a little nap, Max. What about you?"

Max pulled her to him, still walking, and spoke grateful words into the auburn hair loose about her throat and ear, "Thank you. That's the one thing that does look good to me right now. You always have the best ideas. It's not the nap, it's the lying down next to you."

This relieved her too. "I'm too tired for ideas. I just want you to lay down beside me and take a little nap. Then maybe I'll be ready for the next round."

They closed the doors and didn't bother to undress, merely laid down on their big bed and gave their arms to each other, and drifted away. Like sparks in the night.

"Thanks for coming to Mexico with me."

"You didn't give me a choice, remember?"

21 CARLOTTA'S SUNDAY DRIVE

They slept late the next morning. He woke her. He was already showered and dressed and ready to go. "I'm leaving for a little while. I've got to take off for a couple days. I need to sit by myself for a while and think. Or not think, probably some of both. You probably would like to do the same."

She sat up in the bed, not happy. "No actually, I *wouldn't* like to go off by myself right now. I personally would rather try figuring it out with you in the same room. Whatever we do, it is still *together*, isn't it?" She dared him to hesitate.

This made him smile again. "Of course we do it together. I'm not going anywhere without you."

She mocked a laugh, "Hah—you're going off without me right now. You just said so."

"Yes, but that's just for a day or two. To tell you the truth, I've located a banker in Manzanillo who actually makes business loans. He's spent years in the US and he seems to be really receptive to new ideas, new companies. I've told him a little about our situation and he convinced me that he might be able to help us."

"Where did you hear about this guy?"

"From Jim Penton. Which gives him credibility. Jim knew him from some business in Ontario four or five years ago. They're still in contact. So I set up a meeting with him for Monday morning. I thought I'd go down to Barra a couple days early and see if I could get him to come over for a friendly weekend chat on the beach before our official meeting. You know—priming the pump."

She shrugged and looked away. "I guess it's worth a try. Not much left to lose, is there?"

He could not let himself look at what he knew was in her face. "I'm going to take the bus. One leaves Guadalajara in two hours. Why don't you drive down Sunday? I'll be at our hotel."

But now she looked at him; allowed herself a faint smile. "Alright. I'll take that, my dear."

By the following afternoon the bitterness of their failure with the Spitzenburgens no longer scalded her when she thought of it. They were merely again as before, riding it out, broke and bleakly in debt, looking for any break in the storm. And Barra de Navidad had always been good refuge for a sailor's distress.

Halfway along the three hour drive there, she saw the Colima volcano releasing its long coil of smoke into blue sky, a reminder of the smoky situation at home. In a twisting mountainous passage she navigated a series of new long steel bridges that allowed vehicles to cross deep rocky gorges that fell away hundreds of feet below them. Crossing that perilous chasm reminded her of home too.

But when Carlotta drove down out of the foothills, she smiled seeing her coconut palms suddenly everywhere as far as she could see: miles and miles of them: the thin dark ribbon of highway she drove threading through all of it going on to the sea. She smelled ocean in the wind blowing in the window of her white Dodge Caravan. She saw the dark and heavily laden sky moving toward land. She smiled again. Rain would be upon all of this by nightfall.

And she would be in Barra by nightfall. Max in the room at their hotel had been waiting for her these two days. She'd been playing Monk and Coltrane all the way from Lake Chapala, until finally, when the groves of cocopalms became all she could see, she at last felt the knot of anxiety inside her releasing. The problems were all resolvable with money. And the problems were no more important than money. Of course they would figure it out.

She came over the rise and she saw Manzanillo and the sea beyond, saw cargo ships anchored in the bay and docked at the piers, hard angles of steel and smoke-stacks, none of it pretty, all of that too only money and business. Today she could smile and drive past all that. She drove on for another half hour beyond the busy seaport until the countryside was nearly wilderness. The few houses she saw there, of old planks and rusted sheets of tin and dried palm fronds, had been assembled in some afternoon long ago, and a blast of good wind might blow any one of them away. Banana trees were everywhere; cocopalms now never in groves, only in occasional clusters. Sea salt and sea breeze in the air she breathed: the quiet beaches of Barra de Navidad then no more than ten minutes away.

There at last at the highway junction to Barra, a four way stop, she clicked on her turn signal, preparing to go left and onto the main thoroughfare into the village and its beaches and her man waiting for her. Yet as she began to swing the van that way, she saw it!—Itself turning left through the same intersection, but coming out of Barra as she was entering: Itself passing not ten feet from her going the opposite direction, a thin-faced, white-haired Mexican at the wheel, eyes a little droopy, driving what she believed she would never see again—*the miracle!*—her own—*glory be!*—two years ago *stolen* '80 Chevy pickup! Blue, identical dent on the rear fender, and—*no goddamned lie!*—the *same* California license plate she had put there herself thirteen years ago the day she bought the truck from the man in Petaluma out of an ad in the SF Chronicle.

Her baby. Not dead and gone forever, but passing there right beside her, so close she could have tossed her empty Coke can into the pickup bed as it passed by alongside her going the opposite way.

So even though she was halfway through her turn and full in the midst of her still-erupting joy and amazement, without hesitation she countered every safe-driving instinct she had cherished all her adult life, and she jerked the wheel back the other way, right, even as she had to crane her head the opposite left, to keep her eyes on the blue Chevy pickup, finishing its own left turn onto the highway she'd been only that moment exiting. Her van lurched right, just missing a little Volkswagen passing through the intersection, which she'd barely seen while she kept glancing back the other way at the blue Chevy, panicked that her pickup might suddenly fade and disappear, just as it had so suddenly reappeared again after two lost years. Then again she bolted forward and nearly hit an old flat bed truck that she also didn't see coming on into the intersection right behind the Volkswagen. Barely in time she braked: cars ahead and behind also braking and skidding, horns honking all around her. She now half-blocked the entire intersection.

Her acutely vigilant eyes nonetheless watching up ahead saw her '80 Chevy move away and into second gear, oblivious and free of the intersection jam: her Chevy pickup heading south on the main highway, toward the mountains, Puerto Vallarta eighty miles beyond them. Even though she felt adrenalin racing in her blood, she was not impatient. She saw the jam she'd made already disentangling itself. She'd be after him in moments.

While she watched after her blue Chevy, she maneuvered her van beside two halted cars next to her, and suddenly a lane between those two opened: she accelerated into it, then turned sharply back left and around another halted motorist, who shook a fist at her passing. She spun just a little in the gravel as she straightened it out and moved onto the highway, behind four or five cars and trucks that had already interposed between her and her risen-from-the-dead baby.

She thrilled: felt how flushed her face, how the blood raced inside her everywhere, and how she gloated!

After two years my baby's found me. Been looking for me all this time and now she's found me. And I'm going to have my baby back, because that sleepy-eyed old Mexican driving her will never get away from me, never.

Except that now, in single file behind so many others, she couldn't see the blue Chevy up ahead, though she knew it had to be there, since she hadn't seen it pull off either side of the highway. She felt the irritation welling; so she must remember patience: the inevitable: *he will not get away.* Soon she and the file ahead of her were going fifty miles an hour up the one lane each way highway. At the first curve she spotted her blue pickup still there up ahead, and she could count the vehicles intervening, four of them. When oncoming traffic passed and allowed her the clear lane she accelerated around the Ford Taurus ahead of her and easily resettled in the file. Then a few minutes later she passed the next car in front of her, and then the next. There was now only one car, an old Buick with an improvised iron rack on the roof filled with crates stacked haphazardly and tied down with yellow rope. She settled back, maybe relaxing. Better to keep this one car, or any car, between her and her blue pickup, that he not get suspicious.

Since already she'd come to realize: it would not do to stop the driver and confront him there on the highway. She had no proof in hand, and who knew what his attitude might be. She would have to follow him till he stopped, and then hope she had time to call or find police and make her claim. Wherever, whenever that might be.

Rain had already begun spotting her windshield. Darker clouds moved steadily toward her from the sea coast only a few miles away. It would be dark in less than an hour. She turned on her headlights.

Then the need that had haunted her all the last minutes of her sudden excitement burst through these preoccupations and expressed itself: *call Max.* Yet knowing even as she thought this how nearly impossible it would be, not knowing the hotel number, not knowing how to dial up information in Barra. The need still there nonetheless: to hear the comfort of his voice, the support he would be, the two of them doing this, as they always did everything: not just her alone.

But also knowing maybe this time it would be just her.

Soon a road sign alerted her that Highway 80 began its course in three more kilometers, diverging from Highway 200. Blue Chevy pickup and over-burdened Buick both slowed nearing the junction and she too slowed. She watched her blue pickup turn north onto Highway 80, watched the Buick continue on straight, and then she too made the slow turn herself onto the lesser Highway 80.

Thereafter she must drive just behind and directly in the rearview of the hopefully still-unsuspecting driver. He seemed in no hurry, content to keep it between 40 and 45; but even at that speed she let him gain a little distance on her, keeping back a hundred or two hundred yards. The dark overcast had already moved ahead of her into the mountains and she saw tiny flashes of lightning far out there, but heard no thunder. Rain began splattering; she switched on the wipers.

As she looked now steadily at the tailgate of her blue Chevy pickup, she smiled and the smiling relaxed her from the tension of the chase and its unknown conclusion. The smiling also awakened a fleet of memories of that blue Chevy pickup that seemed to rise out of lost canyons of her heart and drift through her consciousness.

A gift she'd given herself on her 28th birthday, and it now seemed to her that from that day and because of that truck she had grown into her womanhood. Had allowed her to quit her daily housekeeping bondage to Isabel, her invalid landlady. Had made herself the Marin County flower lady, driving each morning at 4am into Brannan Street in San Francisco to the flower market, in time to contend with the earliest of the vendors for the best flowers to be found in those gigantic open warehouses every a.m. Distributed all of it in her blue Chevy truck every morning to hotels and restaurants and shops. Loving that, even the early hours.

Other opportunities came to her when she'd met John and Larry in the Castro. Those two decorator brilliants had recognized her own fledgling brilliance, though she also knew that it had been the blue Chevy pickup and its big payload that first had made her valuable. So then for five or maybe six years even she'd driven every imaginable material and prop to big account stores like Levi-Straus and the Emporium and helped John and Larry do the windows and the floor displays, and they taught her well. Even more fun had been creating the fabulous environments and vignettes for the celebrity parties in San Francisco or Burlingame or the Sonoma County Club, always in the blue Chevy pickup.

Till John died, and then a year later Larry died, both victims of AIDS. Then both she and her truck went into mourning. She'd worked long and tedious hours at the wharf for Meatball Bait Company, her truck merely getting her back and forth from work to her little house a mile up the canyon from downtown Mill Valley as she mourned.

But everything changed when she'd met Max and had eventually come to believe in his extravagant dreams and his ability sometimes to accomplish them. And so she had gone with him in the Dodge Caravan. It was only later that she had flown back to the US and then driven the blue Chevy alone the 2100 miles back to Lake Chapala.

And how bringing that truck to the village had thrilled her, as if for the first time the truck was doing exactly what it had been born to do, hauling cement and rock and brick and steel I-beams, and also maestros and peons, back and forth from barrio and supplier to job site.

Until that miserable, fateful day when Max parked it in front of Malcolm's apartment in Ajijic mid-afternoon while he sat there drinking wine with his buddy until dark; and finally going outside to drive home, and then seeing the truck: vanished.

In the two years since then they had both stopped believing they would ever see it again; had thereafter only nurtured the fond memories. Though her heart had never allowed her to remove the Chevy pickup key from her key ring.

She smiled that moment as she thought of that. She glanced down at the key ring, dangling from the van's ignition switch, and saw the worn old pickup key still hanging there. She reached a hand to it and felt it fondly between thumb and forefinger.

Rain now fell steadily and in the last of the twilight she could see the road running straight ahead but always ascending toward the mountain ridges far ahead of her; how far she couldn't tell. She could see how dense already were the forests of the foothills either side of the road, though it was not green she saw now, but only the dark shadows of all of it, lush and impenetrable.

Yet quicker than she'd expected the road became steep and winding and she was among peaks and cliffs falling away from her narrow road off the left embankment. Her headlights through the rain illuminated cracks in the asphalt and sometimes whole pieces broken out of it. The speed of her Dodge Caravan she gradually diminished to 30 miles an hour, and then to 25, as had the pickup and the sleepy Mexican she pursued. She still allowed him a hundred yards or so of distance ahead of her. She saw no road signs to tell what pueblo or junction might lie ahead. Fortunately for them both, a car or truck going the other way passed them only rarely.

In utter darkness and the steady, steady rainfall, time seemed not to be. Still the decayed road wound miles and miles up the mountain side and never straightened, going always higher. Eventually she traversed a long safer passage where she could see lush meadows on either side of the road, without cliffs; but then suddenly again the cliffs were falling away beside the road on her right, with only the flimsiest of metal guard rails to guide her and to protect her from sliding off the road and over the cliff, a dropoff that she would neither imagine how far down, nor look that way to make any truer estimate.

Then, as if there had never been danger anywhere in the black of this night, the road came around a bend and flattened out and, without knowing how, she could sense they were driving through mountain meadows with no cliffs anywhere near. She could feel the knot release in her stomach, not having realized till that moment the knot had been there at all. Her headlights illuminated a sign that signified Ayala 1 km.

Would this be her companion's destination?

Even through the rain she was able to see small lights of the pueblo in the distance. Their road led straight toward these. Her blue pickup slowed as they passed among these few lights. It was still early evening and she could see at the lone stop sign there in Ayala a plastered one room building of several mottled colors with a neon Tecate beer sign in the window and a solitary gas pump in front of it, which had no customers on this wet night. Nor did her Chevy pickup stop there, nor at any of the four or five streets that diverged off the highway and would have led to the houses of that poor village where her pickup might stop for the night. The truck continued on, soon increasing speed as it passed beyond the village and on again into the black, rainy night of these mountains.

It had now become the time when she knew her Maestro Lupe would have returned from his Sunday in Guadalajara, to his only phone, at home. She followed once again her blue pickup back onto Highway 80, but the road gratefully was straight through a mountain valley and level and so she could use one hand to hold the cell phone and then poke the numbers with one finger.

Eventually the Maestro answered. They spoke in Spanish. He was astonished at hearing of the blue pickup, which many years ago he had himself subtly coveted. For the danger in which he imagined her, he was instantly anxious to go to her, half a day's drive from where he was. But she must delay him. She needed documents. Her old title for the miraculously found '80 Chevy pickup. The two year old police report of Stolen Vehicle made in Chapala.

"Also, as soon as possible let Max know where I am and to call me. Though I doubt I'll be in range much longer, and I might be out of range for the next couple days. As soon as the driver stops I'll call you again and tell you where I am. In the meantime, call Virginia, she can find it. She's got a key to the office. She'll know where to look for those documents."

"Senora, I will be there in a few hours. It will have to be me, no matter. Max may be hard to find in Barra de Navidad. Perhaps till morning. Or even tomorrow afternoon, after his meeting. That's too long to wait. And listen, Senora, muy importante. Do not confront that man who has your truck unless the sheriff or the police are with you. And don't trust either side of them." He made her promise that. "So I'll wait for your call. But all this makes me very, very nervous what you're doing. Muy peligroso."

Thus he waited for her call; while she drove onward through the dense growth she saw all around her wherever her headlights illuminated. Even sometimes she saw vines and liana in trees and hanging almost to the ground. So much rain coming down, and though it was October, summer's heat rose out of the earth still, and the air was sultry.

Yet after her recent strenuous drive through the mountains, this going was so easy that she could stretch out her feet and relax. Thus might she allow that other tension to command her: looking without flinching at the two red tail lights disappearing continually into the black, rainy night ahead of her.

The road continued boring straight ahead through the lush overgrowth and within what must have been no more than ten minutes the lights of another small pueblo loomed to the right and it looked to be a mile or more off the straight highway she drove. Nearing the village lights they crossed a very old iron bridge over a convergence of two streams, full and running, as she and he, pursuer and pursued, crossed the old creaking iron.

She saw the next sign: Hemenegilda Galeana 4 km. And another below that: Villa Purificacion 9 km. Both names made her smile. The Mexican at the helm of her Chevy indeed slowed and then turned toward onto the lesser road toward these two pueblos aforesigned. She turned the same way behind him, as distant as she dared, perhaps an eighth of a mile later, and maintained a speed always thereafter less than 30 as she followed him again.

And for the first time, she perceived that she might now have become noticeable.

So she must go modestly on, as her companion did not take either of the two entrances to Hemenegilda Galeana, where this narrower road discretely passed just outside the pueblo. Even though she could still see this pueblo's lights out her rearview mirror, she at the same time saw ahead of her but a few kilometers across the mountain valley the other lights, which would be Purificacion. Would that it would be purification, she thought.

Villa Purificacion indeed was the end of this lateral off Highway 80, beyond which, for all the mountain and jungle surrounding it, there was no need to go, or pathway to do it by. However, she knew none of this at that moment; she thought it equal chance he might keep driving all night past Purificacion to who knew where.

Her blue pickup turned onto a cobbled street, dimly lit, and she followed at the best distance she dared until she saw him turn a block or so ahead of her down another equally dimly lit. As her excitement grew, she waited at the top of the last street, just out of sight. Another car came down the street behind her, and then another toward her, both passing in opposite directions. Quickly she stopped in park, climbed out and made four or five hurried steps to the corner, graceful despite running in slacks and cowboy boots.

She saw him pulling into a driveway on the left. A large magnolia tree without blossoms loomed over the street from beside the driveway. Driver still in the cab, the garage door on automatic rolled itself upward, clanging open. The blue pickup entered and immediately the steel door clanged and rolled back into position. Immediately the garage light and the porch light, the only lights on in that humble street, both extinguished at the same time: and all the street was suddenly black. In eight or ten quick strides she was back in the truck, reading as she passed it the key words on the sign post at that corner: Peidras Pesadas. Palma. At the driveway of the Big Magnolia.

Before she put her van in gear she took out her cell phone and called her maestro again. "He finally stopped, Lupe. I'm in a place called Villa Purificacion. He parked my pickup in a garage. It looks like it's there for the night anyway. I'm going to find the police station. Then I'll wait for you. So you wait till Virginia gets there in the morning and get those documents from the files and call me when you're on the way. I'll probably spend the night in a hotel. Or maybe not. I don't know."

Afterward, she turned her van till it pointed the opposite way, turned it around without turning on the lights; and then very slowly eased her way up the street, thinking how she might find her way to the police station. The rain still fell and fell.

Her dashboard clock read 9:48. She thought perhaps the police in this small village on a Sunday night would not be open. But after driving randomly for only three or four blocks through a neighborhood with no street lights she saw lights and moving cars two or three blocks down a sidestreet and she turned that way. Soon she was certain that was the center of town, where the plaza would of course be, and, no doubt, the church and a municipal building.

When she was there she could see all about her a half dozen street lamps, all casting light on the slashing downpour of rain. She was amazed how this little pueblo so far into the wilderness of this mountain rain forest resembled her own little pueblo of Ajijic on Lake Chapala. All the buildings seemed newly painted in pretty pastels; the plaza in particular was swept and raked, planted with tall palm trees and overlarge banana trees and little plots of flowers everywhere. The elevated bandstand in the center of the plaza was peach and cream and a tall seagreen iron sculpture which looked like nothing at all stood beside the bandstand and nearly as tall. A perfectly cobbled stone walk in rectangle surrounded the bandstand; old, richly ornate wrought iron benches were arranged all along the four sides.

Yet with the rain and the late Sunday hour only three figures she could see walking, each in their own pace across the plaza: one with an umbrella hiding its scurrier's face, one holding a newspaper over his head, the last uncovered, sauntering, allowing hair and clothing to be saturated.

Two tall spires of the church across the street were taller than any other building she could see, crowned with cupolas. On the opposite side of the plaza she saw a grim ochre building, long overdue for repainting, too big to be anything but something bureaucratic. She drove toward it.

Many large rectangular windows faced the street, though only one revealed a light on within; though one was enough, if it were the right one. An iron balcony overhung the entrance at the center of the building, whose double doors were closed. She parked in front of it. She drew a deep breath, made sure of her cell phone in her coat pocket, and locked her van as she left it; then hurried through the rain to the big doors.

Contrary to her premonition, the left one of the double doors pushed open easily. She entered, then went left, where would be the lit room. Its door stood wide opened. The lettering on its glass door she could read, though it was reversed to her eyes: Policia de Villa Purificacion. She smiled. She went to it and entered. Hope was in her heart.

Seeing her, a uniformed man stood immediately, vacating in his hurry a chair behind a desk in an otherwise bare and simply furnished room. Standing, poised, he still held a cell phone to his ear but he was not speaking, and probably not listening either, since he seemed so surprised to see his late Sunday visitor that he stared at her flagrantly, full of her, who stood there at the counter.

Then he seemed to comprehend the situation, for he smiled, his lips exposing all the pretty white teeth, and all his face came bright; so well pleased. For only the necessary instant he bethought the phone still next to his ear, and he spoke two words quietly and firmly into it, and then flicked it off. Quickly again he reasserted his attention on his tall, unexpected gringa visitor.

He surprised her speaking English. "At your service, my lady."

She smiled to hear that, and answered him, "I've come a long way, I need someone to talk to. I hope you can help me."

Apparently bewildered by her outburst of English, he spoke with less confidence. "Sorry, my lady. English so so. Espanol better. You speak?"

In Spanish she answered him. "I speak it mas o menos well. I'm here to report a stolen vehicle."

His eyes widened, hearing her declaration, such was the surprise. In Spanish he said, "Your vehicle *stolen*, senora? But, you have not been in our village one day, or I would have seen you."

That amused her. So now she could feel a pleasure unrolling the story, a release after all evening on the road recycling the story over and over in her own head. "No, it was not stolen today. It was stolen two years ago. In Ajijic, on Lake Chapala. I made a police report. They never found it. But today I saw my truck near Barra de Navidad and I followed it all the way here to your village. I have written down the address where the truck was parked. Inside a garage. I want to go see my truck. I have the ignition key to it in my pocket. I'll show you that it's mine. My maestro will be here tomorrow with all my ownership papers and the police report from Chapala. The man driving my truck still has my California plates on. So he's probably not too smart." That pretty much covered it and it had her adrenalin running. Now she wanted to go see her truck. Sit in it. Turn it on. Rev it up just a little. Kiss the wheel.

For a moment the policeman seemed speechless, lips still open and smile gleaming; now all motion suspended. Then his great resources returned to him; he reanimated his smile and showed all the white teeth. He effused his maximum vision of compassion. "How terrible, senora. But where..." and his voice faltered slightly, before reaffirming to continue, "...where is this address?"

"It is on Piedras Pesadas, near the corner of Palma. It is in the middle of the block."

"Ah." he sighed, "Yes, Piedras Pesadas, of course I know where that is. And there is a great and old magnolia tree there."

She was more and more enjoying this. "Yes, the magnolia tree. It is exactly in the front yard of the man who has my pickup."

"Ah," he said again, again somber and thoughtful, hesitating between radiant smiles. But then as quickly resuming that original smile as he walked away from his desk and came toward her, extending his hand, speaking again in the English he employed, at minimum wage: "Good evening, my lady. My name is Estimo Muraga. I am at your service. My desk there. We make papers."

Agreeably, she did as he'd asked and went past the counter and sat in the one old wooden chair beside it. A black, antique Royal Corona typewriter sat upon his desk; a desk otherwise impeccably cleaned and neat. She watched him and waited.

Suddenly bureaucratic, he sat thoughtfully in his own chair and opened the top drawer and drew out a folder with papers inside and set it beside the typewriter. Then he turned to her and the great smile and the white teeth were gleaming at her again as he spoke. "You say this blue Chevy pickup still has your own California license plates on it?"

"Yes, it most certainly does, officer."

"Ah," he said, "I thought you said that."

She suddenly challenged him. "Do you know who lives in that house? Do you know the man who drives that truck around your village? Surely you must know him, at least must have seen him often."

Throughout her urgent questioning he shifted in his chair, even while he maintained the perfect smile looking at her. Before she had finished speaking, he was even nodding, so agreeable, to let her know that he was with her, that he would refuse her nothing, that he was indeed as vigilant as she'd assumed, that he would be eager to disclose to her everything he knew.

When she did finish speaking, he replied quickly, speaking only in Spanish now. "Yes, yes, of course I know who lives in that house. Everyone knows everyone here. But..." and he adjusted his smile so she could see that at least for one moment he could be just slightly more serious, "...but, knowing him does not mean necessarily that we are friends. I know many people, but I have only a few good friends."

She heard the agreement and that was enough: she stopped listening to him. She was already imagining herself in the blue pickup, driving back to Ajijic. Lupe right behind her in the Cadillac of all problems.

Seeing her fortunate lack of interest in these details, Estimo turned back to the folder of papers and opened it and fingered his way through most of the pages until he finally selected a set of five forms, and withdrew them from the folder and set the five on top of the folder. As he did so he spoke to her, as gaily as he could while he made himself a clerk. "We should begin the paperwork, senora. I must warn you, there will be much of it. Perhaps you would rather wait and come back and do all this in the morning."

Surprised, she said, "What do you mean wait till morning? I want to go over there right now and get my truck. You can confiscate it until my own documents arrive tomorrow."

Estimo ceased feeding the sheets of paper and their carbons into the typewriter and sat back in his chair. "Oh senora, you move too fast. All the americanos are like that. Too fast. As I said, there is much paperwork to do. Then we must request permissions of other departments. We must have authority to reclaim a vehicle from one person to another. My chief must sign everything. And he will not be here till morning. Nine o'clock. But the papers must be filled out. Nothing can be done without the papers."

Her shoulders slumped as she let her disappointment glide out of her along with the air she exhaled. Ah yes, the Mexican bureaucracy. She knew it well.

As he asked her for information, Estimo seemed to be reading the fine print off his forms now rolled into and ready to type on his frail Royal Corona. He seemed to have to look closely to see the fine print, or instead recalling the boxes and lines to be filled from his memory, since he lived most of his police life at that very desk, punching the keys of this old typewriter with a zesty, effective hunt-and-peck, with the constant stopping to make all the little corrections for every mis-stroke on each one of the five carbon copies he must provide.

As he droned on with little question after question, she spoke back answers in monotone, and soon, as she did so, she shifted her eyes to the expanse of light cast into the night beyond the big window. She watched the steady, steady fall of rain splotching and washing the window; until her eyes were drawn into the night far beyond windows and she watched the rain slanting diagonally through that cast of pale light across the plaza. That constant rain becoming itself a symbol of the eternal constant that was certainly the drone of questions Estimo presented to her: while she wearied of it by the minute, by the quarter-hour, by the half hour, until she felt that he must be drawing all her life's blood's history out of her and arranging it in black ink there on a page, which then might be scrutinized and judged by whatever bureaucratic gods now looked down upon her. And all this steady, constant rain might have been the weeping of the gods; but not for any sorrow, rather for the comedy which so provoked these torrential tears of their laughter.

This first page of forms recounted the myriad details of the original vehicle theft. Estimo stopped his peppy hunt-and-peck typing, at which he was adept, and stopped his questioning only when he must stop, to make the five-fold corrections one at a time with his correcting tape. He must also stop when he filled the entire page of the form, removed that page and then reinserted another five sheets of the next form before placing a carbon precisely between each sheet.

After completing the second set of forms, documenting her education and her complete work history, he stopped and turned abruptly toward her and spoke. "Senora. I must have the little rest. Only a moment. You understand, so many papers. We have a little refrigerator in the other room. Something for you? Fanta, three flavors. Cold coffee, I warm it. Cerveza even."

"*Orange* Fanta?"

He nodded, delighted she had chosen so well.

"OK, yes. Cold or not."

Estimo rose and went into the back room, but halted at the open doorway and turned back to say, "I have a little job to do back here—allow me a minute or two. But there is a very fine view from the porch of our very fine building here, where you might stand for a moment and look out, taking a little rest yourself. The view of the plaza and the iglesia behind it alone are truly worth the trip into these mountains." Then he slipped into the room and away from her view.

It sounded like a good idea. She stood up from the chair stiffly; it felt like she had been sitting there for hours. She went up on her tiptoes stretching. She walked toward the counter and past it and out the still open door. She walked down the hall whence she'd come and out the door of the main entrance. The rain still fell and fell. Only a small light in each corner of the plaza now glowed, casting a delicate light, constantly pierced with rain, over the bandstand, the plants and the walk and the furniture of the plaza in all its pretty pastels. All of it pretty. Rain pretty.

Then a fierce shudder passed through her that seemed to come from far away and it came without warning. She shivered in her own skin as the shudder passed beyond her and away. As if it had been a warning, she turned and came quickly back down the hallway and into the room and stopped at the counter.

224

Estimo stood in the doorway to the further room, where he leaned comfortably against the open door jamb, cell phone to his ear, apparently stopped in mid-thought and mid-speech, looking at her sudden appearance. In silence he made his smile irresistible, but instantly withdrew out of sight behind the door jamb.

Then she had made only two more steps around the counter and toward her former seat when Estimo reappeared, smile gleaming, the cell phone in neither of his visible hands, for each of them held a bottle of orange Fanta. She sat down. He set her Fanta before her and said, "You seem to be quickly rested, senora, and ready to continue our paperwork. Enough break for me too."

She looked at him well, seeking deeper levels but not finding them. She spoke. "Yes, let's do keep going. I don't feel good about not keeping an eye on that garage. What time did you say your boss gets here in the morning."

"His name is Julian. He comes at 9."

Estimo rolled form number three and its five copies and five carbons into his machine. This one compiled her complete employment history and most of her financial doings for ten years. Again he asked his question and typed in her responses. All of it seemed to please him. He commented about most of it. Wearier and wearier, she finally only answered the necessary and merely nodded at his comments, but Estimo seemed not to notice or lament her lack of comment as he chattered on.

The first half of the fourth form recorded all known friends and family, both in Mexico and in foreign countries, who could be listed as friends and references. The second half of the form allowed her to confess any and all misdemeanors or felonies.

The final fifth form, required only for non-citizens, transcribed all her activities and movements for the last thirty-six months living in Mexico. She and Estimo completed the last form five minutes after midnight. She had drunk a cup of cold, bitter coffee a half hour previously, but she felt no benefit from it at midnight.

She rose to go and said to him. "I'll be back before nine in the morning."

"My lady, if you wish I am at your service to find you a hotel room."

But she had already decided. "No," she said. "I'm not going to a hotel right now. I'm going to go back and park just around the corner from him, where I can keep my eye on that garage door."

Estimo frowned and tried to discourage her. She didn't care his opinion, she was going there. She had a cell phone, she'd call if there was trouble.

It still rained as she walked back across the plaza after midnight and then drove her van slowly back into the night, down the street called Palma, that she knew would take her to her corner. She drove there and she was the only vehicle on those streets. She parked just around a corner so that through her windshield she could see the big magnolia, could also see through its branches the house and the still closed garage door.

In the rain that would not cease she kept her vigil, talking to herself about her life to keep herself awake, singing little parts of her favorite songs, imagining every house they had built, how much they had sold them for, how it calculated that so often recently they had needed one new contract to stay afloat and finish off the last one. But all these reveries were not enough, and she drowsed asleep for moments at a time before reawakening again. Realizing finally and vaguely that at this late hour the pickup would probably not be leaving.

Even so, she struggled to keep awake and watching. The hours drudged by. She drowsed longer and longer between reawakenings. The rain fell and fell. She slept heavily the last hour before dawn and she dreamed pleasantly of being asleep inside a little boat, floating and bobbing on the undulating water. When she woke up at last the Sun was just risen and the rain had stopped. The air and all about her was cleaned and silent and of another world; perhaps purified.

She opened the door to climb out and stretch into the pretty, rarified morning. When she'd finished stretching, she looked down at her front tire and saw it flat. She gasped. Then thought how thankful that Lupe had fixed and given her the spare before she'd left Ajijic. She turned to get it from the rear hatch, but as she did so she looked down and saw that the rear tire on that side was flat as well. This gasp was deeper and louder than the first one.

Quickly she went to the far side of the van and saw what she was a long, stunned moment contemplating and comprehending. Two more flat tires. Astonished, she kneeled down to inspect the right rear tire. She had to run her eyes over the face of the tire a second time before she saw the knife cut, more than an inch wide, midway between rim and tread, precisely placed. She looked as closely at the other three, and they all showed the same one inch knife cut, each one in the same place in the middle of the tire wall.

Son of a bitch. Son. Of. A. Bitch.

226

22 CARLOTTA IN PURIFICATION

As she walked along Calle Palma toward the center of the village, she turned the puzzle over in her mind and studied it from every angle, but she could not unlock it. This failure allowed a grim mixture of irritation and apprehension to accumulate in her and increase the pace of her walking. When she came to the end of Palma she turned left toward the plaza, ignoring the early morning pedestrians who passed her, themselves enjoying the brilliant freshness of the morning after the long, hard rainfall; though she hardly noticed anyone and she could enjoy none of the beauty of the morning. She went into the municipal building and down the corridor to the police office and entered the still open door.

Estimo was not to be seen. In his place was a large, mostly bald man wearing a wrinkled white shirt with long sleeves, unbuttoned at the collar. He looked up at her from behind the same desk Estimo had manned last night. In Spanish and with neither a smile nor any other sign of interest, he posed a question, "Yes?"

"I was here last night with Senor Estimo. I reported a stolen vehicle. I am to meet with your chief, I believe Estimo called him, Senor Julian, this morning. Is Julian here?"

The man answered her with sudden interest, but still no smile. "Oh, so you are the one. Julian, yes, he is the one to talk to."

From the back room another man emerged. She estimated him to be in his mid-40s, thin and somewhat handsome. His black hair fell across his forehead and he wore levis and a red and black plaid flannel shirt not tucked into his belt, seeming not to care if he cultivated the handsome image he'd been born with or not. No badge or aspect of uniform declared him either police or chief. He smiled at her pleasantly and she saw in his face nothing to worry her. He spoke as pleasantly as he smiled, and in good English. "I'm Julian. I've been expecting you. Please come sit at my desk."

As she followed him into the back room she remarked to him his good English, and he told her that he had lived eight years in Pittsburg, had even gone to school there. He had found the good money not worth the Americanization, and he had returned two years ago and been rewarded with the job of Chief of Police in this village in which his family had lived for more than a hundred fifty years.

"So you know everybody of course?"

"Oh yes. And even all their friends and family who visit them from other parts of Mexico."

"So you know this man who has my pickup. On Calle Piedras Pesadas. Where the big magnolia is."

The way he sighed as he said "Ah," reminded her of the same sigh she'd heard from Estimo when she'd mentioned the magnolia to him. Yet as he answered her she sensed no deception in his words. "Well, yes, I do know the man. His name is Emiliano. A man busy in many businesses. Though I don't know if any of them have any address. But he is probably not a criminal—I mean not a car thief. That is not his style. If this pickup is proven to be yours, and stolen, then I think it likely that Emiliano is a victim as well; though a foolish victim, for he probably bought this from a man who claimed to own it, and who probably gave him some bill of sale that anyone should have known was false. That is my belief from what I've heard of this man. Though I have only had two or three dealings with him in my life, so that I cannot say I know him personally. He has some family living in the pueblo as well however." Then he became thoughtful to himself for a brief, hesitant moment; before speaking again. "But who knows what the story will turn out to be. We will see."

Then he turned to her and for the first time he seemed to see her, physically, in the moment; and as she in turn looked at him, his face and the way he stood there seemed true to her. He said, "All that is lacking are your titles to the vehicle. With that I can make petition for authorization to confiscate and deliver to the true owner."

She shuddered hearing the words. The always menacing and always looming bureaucracy was again rising up in front of her. She quickly forged a small courage to ask the dread question: "How long do you think this *authorization* will take? Till I get my pickup in my hands?"

"My chief is in Manzanillo, so I will notify him as soon as you show me the titles. Then it should not be so long. He should be able to decide the case the same day. Or by the next day."

She shuddered. She spoke with little hope. "And you can't confiscate the truck till you get this man's approval, in a day or two? But he'll run away with the truck by then. Surely, if I show you my titles, and still have my key, you will take hold of my pickup and keep him from taking it away again."

Julian smiled at her naivete. But he listened and heard. He considered within himself for another silent moment, and then said, as if between confidants, "If you have the true papers, and you have the key with you, *perhaps* I can find a way to do something. *Perhaps.* While we wait for the authorization."

She looked hard into his eyes. Would this be one to trust? She'd been wrong quite a few times in Mexico.

She said, "My husband and I do construction on Lake Chapala. Our maestro will be here in the early afternoon with the documents. Do you have enough to go speak to this man, this Emiliano? Surely he will be reasonable, if he is also a victim."

Julian hesitated only briefly, then said, "Yes, I have already looked up the Stolen Vehicle report and see that you have, as you said, reported your truck stolen. And you have the key. So yes, we can go talk to Emiliano and see if he will cooperate in helping me get this truck to its rightful owner. We'll see."

All of it was what she wanted to hear. She heard no nuances in his words; heard not the hesitations, not the least uncertainty; though uncertainty for her lurked there nonetheless.

Julian led her into the adjoining room, where she had spent most of last night with Estimo, and he went to take a ring of keys from a nail on the wall. It was only then that she thought to tell him the latest. "Oh, I should tell you. While I was parked last night, watching that garage door, and when I fell asleep, someone put a knife in all four of my tires. My van is still parked there. The tires can't be repaired. I need to buy four new tires."

Julian still held the key ring in his hand exactly where he had taken it from the nail, suspended in motion, as he absorbed this new information. A moment later his hand swung free of the nail and he deposited the key ring in his levis pocket before he spoke. "Then someone already knows that you're here. That smells bad. I guess I'd better take my pistol."

He went to a wall safe and opened it without dialing any code. He withdrew from it a holster and belt, a gleaming black pistol straped into the holster. Deftly he belted it around his waist, and let his hand touch and gauge the pistol grip where it rested against his hip.

Next he went to his bald deputy and spoke in Spanish to him. "As soon as Estimo comes in, have him call his friend and get me four new tires, as fast as possible. Size?" Puzzled, he looked at her.

She said, "235, 70 by 16." He repeated those numbers and had his deputy write them down. The man said he would do all his chief had asked him.

With growing confidence she followed Julian down the big corridor and out the back entrance. Near that door he bid her enter his police car, a new Chevy Nova, white, at a cost of half the local police budget for the year. That all the public might dread the vehicle's authority, a red plastic cone had been mounted on the roof, electrified to light up of course. She got in; he sat in the driver's seat and started up and pulled slowly away from the ugly ochre walls and moved on down the street toward Palma.

In a moment they were there, passing by her crippled, slumped van, not quite hidden by the trees at the corner. The police car parked at the curb, beneath the great magnolia that seemed to stand like a great guardian over the yard and the house and the garage. *Pass beneath this who dare.*

She glanced instinctively to the garage door, and saw sitting there in a green webbed aluminum lawn chair a large young man, barely twenty, wearing a tank top and displaying well toned muscles in arms and chest. His hair was cropped short. Several tattoos were scribed into his arms, which were folded but relaxed against his abdomen. He seemed to smile, but it was not smiling.

She turned and saw another young man, a few years younger than the other, saying something she didn't understand where he stood beneath the magnolia, a rake in his hand. He wore a slouch hat that greatly shaded and greatly concealed his face. This tall teenager said the same words a second time, and this time she understood him. "Looks like a gringa's come to visit." She couldn't tell if he was looking at her or not. Then this one turned and called to someone she now noticed squatting on the roof. "Tell me Caballo—a gringa or no?"

The one squatting on the roof called back. "Good eyes, brother. Keep watching her." She saw this Caballo was older that the other two. More muscles too, it seemed, though he wore a light jacket. He had long, black, sleek hair that hung nearly to his shoulders, and he was unshaven, though his black beard was cropped closely to his face. The hard, determined lines of the face, even of the skull bones beneath it, showed through the beard.

She stopped walking forward when Julian beside her stopped walking, at the innocent waist-high white picket fence, beside its unlocked white picket gate. She studied this group, formidable indeed. And none of these were the little old sleepy-eyed Mexican she had trailed for hours through the mountains last night.

Julian looked toward the husky young man seated next to the garage door. "Rasca, I need to speak to your father. Is he home?"

Rasca shook his head doubtfully. "He had a long drive yesterday. He got home a little late. He's still sleeping. What do you need, sheriff?"

"It's a personal matter, Rasca. I can only speak about it to him."

That moment the front door swung open and the little Mexican walked outside even as he was lifting the two straps of his gray suspenders onto his shoulders. Underneath he wore only a long sleeve gray cotton undershirt, sweat stained in the armpits. Tiny white stubble covered his jaw; white hair cut short, uncombed and awry on his forehead. He brushed that hair away and looked at Julian coldly, perhaps fiercely, and said to him, "OK, I'm here. What do you want?"

She felt the tension in the air warp and turn in on itself, folding and refolding until it had doubled or tripled: the air become brittle with it.

Julian tried to smile at his host, but it seemed to be of no use, and Julian let go the smile and merely said, "It seems that this woman has a title to this Chevy pickup you drive. It seems that perhaps you have been sold a stolen vehicle. You see I make no question of your having been involved in the original theft of the pickup. Of course not. I hope you understand that."

Emiliano sneered at him. He said, "That is my truck, senor. I bought it fairly from a man in Manzanillo. He gave me a written receipt for the pickup and he signed his name. I gave him good money. It has been two years that I have owned this pickup."

Julian spoke as if in sympathy. "I believe everything you've told me. I am hoping you will see that you and this senora have much in common. You have both been victims. Now the law is here to see that justice is done. To both of you. That the senora may have her stolen truck returned to her, if her papers prove true, and that you may be given back your money after the police have investigated this false sale and arrested the true villain and forced him to pay back all your money.

Listening from the roof, Caballo yelled down to them all a defiant, "HA!" and added to it a ruthless laugh that was meant to scorn Julian's words. Caballo then said, "That will be good for the senora, but it will be NOTHING for us. Those are lies, policeman, because you could do nothing to find that man *or* get our money. You know it. Leave our truck alone I say!"

Both Rasca seated in the lawn chair and the third brother Miguel beneath the slouch hat called out to them, "Go away and leave us alone!"

Even when that ridicule had quieted, she continued watching the hostility in all their faces, and she began to believe that one policeman and one gun was perhaps not enough for the situation. In that momentary quiet Emiliano added his own further defiance, "This woman and I have nothing in common. I own something she wants. Yet she stands here and has no proof. You've already admitted that, Julian."

"But I have seen the stolen vehicle report. I am here to see if your license plate matches the one on the stolen vehicle report. Her papers are being delivered this afternoon. And she has on her person, this moment, her old key to the ignition of the pickup. Are you afraid even to let her try her key in the ignition, and see if it starts the engine? What harm in that? I am not here to confiscate this vehicle. I will *not* confiscate it. I swear. I'm here merely to talk to you about it. So surely you can't be afraid to let her try the key? Surely. I will see that she does not drive away with it. I must check the license plate anyway."

Emiliano smirked as he considered all that. Then he turned back to Julian with the sneer declaring his scorn of them both. "Afraid? You can't do anything to me. I haven't done anything wrong. Alright. I'll give you that much. Go ahead." He turned toward Rasca and said, "Go ahead, son, open the garage door. Let the senora have her little bit of fun." He turned back to Julian and to her, saying, "And then I want you both to leave. Go back and do your business where you come from, whatever business that is."

Rasca unlocked, then lifted the rollup door. There it was! Her baby. Just waking up from a good night's sleep. Been dreaming that mommy was near.

As emotion welled into her throat she pulled her key ring from her pocket and walked inside the garage, on the driver's side. Her hand caressed the fender and its fondly-remembered dent there. Her other hand reached to take hold of the chrome door handle. It opened to her touch, so friendly. Inside she saw new seat covers, shiny new floor mats. A new CD player in the dash where her old tape player had been! How thoughtful. She sighed and sat herself beneath the wheel her hands knew so well. She lolled the wheel back and forth a little. She sighed again. She put the key in the ignition. She turned it: fluidly: the engine instantly roared up as her foot depressed the accelerator.

But outside Emiliano was already yelling at her and at Julian. The chief stood at the open entrance to the garage and watched with intense interest. Emiliano called out, "That's enough, senora! Enough! Damn you both! *Stop it!*" He started into the garage, coming at her in the cab, and she saw the fire in his eyes. She shut off the ignition and put the key back in her pocket even before she slid off the seat and began to work her way around the open door and around Emiliano blocking her way. Seeing her leaving, Emiliano stood back and let her pass him and leave his garage. He himself then came outside, nodding curtly to Rasca as he did so, so that Rasca immediately closed and locked the door.

"Go away, both of you!" he yelled at them. He was waving them away with his hands as he spoke, shooing them away.

Guiding her with his hand on her elbow Julian helped to turn her out of the yard and away from the great outreaching arms of the magnolia and the turmoil beneath the tree.

As they passed through the gate she looked back and saw in the front window, where the full curtains had been drawn back, the face of an old but pretty woman, a shawl about her gray hair, staring at her. Suddenly it seemed that the old woman saw the gringa looking at her, and the old woman smiled in recognition.

As they drove back, as they both settled their breathing and their pulsing blood till they were both reasonably placid, she said to him: "I guess I don't have to wonder anymore who slashed my tires." She laughed; then she did wonder and finally spoke it: "But just how did they know about *me*? Last night. That I was here for the truck?"

Julian shook his head, funny and sad, then said, "I am sorry to say that Estimo is their cousin. No doubt he called them to warn them."

Shocked, she asked, "Isn't that illegal, even for a policeman? even for Mexico?"

"No, senora, not technically illegal. Because he warned his cousin when he was off duty. During his break last night probably." Then he tried to console her. "Emiliano will have to listen when you have the papers here. I see he likes to make a big scene, frighten people away. But he cannot do that with the police. But I still must have authorization to proceed with actual confiscation and delivery to you. It will be a day or two."

This last was no consolation, and she pleaded. "He will get away in a day or two. He could be gone an hour from now. Please, Julian—can't you just impound the car for a couple of days, holding it for nobody, just holding it. Till a judge or something can give me permission to get my truck back."

233

Julian, as they drove back to the police station, worried the idea in his head and said to her finally when they'd stopped in front of the station, "I will do what I can. There may be a way I could justify such a brief impounding. But I hope you realize this—I would have to call for reinforcements to carry out this confiscation at Emiliano's house."

"So be it then. My own reinforcements will be here soon. Till then, I'll need a room. What hotel in town would you recommend? It doesn't have to be the best."

"The best is the Rudolfo."

"It doesn't have to be the best. I'd rather have something not too obvious."

"Then you mean Pluto and Jardinia. Callejon Buffon. Two blocks from the plaza."

"What is the name of the hotel?"

"It has no name. It is their big house. They live downstairs. They have six rooms upstairs they rent. Shared bathrooms. It's discrete, if that's what you want."

"That's what I want."

"Before you go there, let me speak to Estimo about your tires, so we will know when it will be ready." He went quickly inside while she waited; and when he returned he told her. "By one o'clock they will be installed, senora, and the van can be delivered to your hotel. The cost of tires will be four and a half thousand pesos."

She had expected that much. "Do you have any banks here?"

"Oh yes," he said. "We have one little Banamex on this street, which we will pass going to meet.Pluto and Jardinia. I'll stop there for you."

While she was inside the Banamex, small indeed, she answered a call from her maestro to say that still he had not been able to contact Max, whom they knew would be at a meeting with loan officers at a bank that morning, a meeting a week ago prearranged, their future riding on it. Good news was that Virginia had given him all the documents she'd asked for, and that he was already the other side of Guadalajara going the speed limit in his Cadillac of all problems, many extra litros of oil in the trunk, along with his rolls of duct tape. He had a map. Maestro Felipe was with him. They should arrive one hour after noon.

It was music to her, melodic, with all the probabilities of a happy ending.

Julian drove her then around the corner to a two story barnlike house with spears of Lombardy poplars in a long row like sentinels all along the long side of the house. It was all yellow stucco and red tile roof, ample windows upstairs and downstairs. Julian parked and opened the door for her, and then walked with her to the front door of the house and himself rang the buzzer.

Moments later the door opened to reveal a skinny middle aged Mexican, his face wrinkled like a man much older. His brown eyes were deep set and seemed to be wondering as he opened the door, wondering about no known thing, to no end, but wondering as if they were wondering always, wondering long before he'd opened the door and looked out on his callers.

Julian greeted him in Spanish. "Salud, Senor Pluto. I have brought you a houseguest. She will be in our town a few days perhaps. I hope you have an empty room."

Pluto smiled, wrinkles widening and deepening. "All my rooms are empty. She may have her choice. Buenos dias to you, senora." And the thinnest and frailest of men bowed, slowly, gracefully, to her. She smiled at her host and thanked him. She turned to Julian and said, "This is perfect." Then to Pluto, "How much for a room?"

He said, "Today I would accept a hundred pesos for a room."

She smiled and said, "Such a bargain. I want to rent all six of them. I'm expecting friends."

Julian departed, letting her know he would be in his office all day to receive her documents when they arrived. She followed Pluto into the house, into a large living room tiled in shiny white squares. A fat blue sofa and two stuffed chairs, old but looking comfortable, were set around a wrought iron and glass coffee table. Several large framed photos hung on the walls, showing no doubt family and ancestors. From an adjacent room, smelling like the kitchen, a short woman emerged, probably the same age as Pluto and nearly as thin, dressed in a simple green cotton dress that clung to her shapeless body. She stopped walking to look over their tall guest in her slacks and cowboy boots.

Pluto bowed as graciously as before, first to his wife and then again to Carlotta. To his guest he said, "My wife, Jardinia." To the wife he said, "Our new guest. She's renting all the upstairs, all six rooms. She has friends coming this afternoon."

Without smiling, Jardinia sharpened her look at this woman. In a high-pitched, brittle voice, yet one full of authority, she said, "No parties in this house, senora. If that's what you're thinking."

Carlotta laughed. "No, no parties. This is all business. These friends who are coming all work for me. I have a truck here in your village that I've come to bring back home. There won't be any partying, I promise."

Jardinia seemed persuaded, but not disposed to linger and socialize; she turned and went back into the kitchen. Carlotta counted out and handed twelve hundred peso bills to Pluto. She said, "For two days." He put them in his pocket without counting them again and indicated the stairway beside the kitchen door, that he would show her the rooms upstairs. She went ahead and he followed.

Each room was like the other: one double bed with frayed quilt that had covered many sleepers; a small wooden desk against the wall beyond the foot of the bed; a mirror above it; a straight wooden chair beside the desk; a closet (she supposed) behind a thin floral curtain where a door might once have been; the worn, scratched linoleum two shades of gray. Each room had a window. The three on the west side of the house all looked out through the tall sentinels of the Lombardy poplars at the street below, where Julian's police car even now was just pulling away from the curb.

Having been assured that the senora was well contented with the rooms, Pluto bowed and backed his way out of the room and disappeared downstairs. Relieved, she closed the door to the middle room on that west side of the house and laid down in the bed, feeling the regrettable sag of the mattress. Yet bed had never felt better. She closed her eyes. She felt sleep rolling towards her from the furthest carverns of her psyche: how she welcomed it. Yet she resisted, perceiving it a sin against her vigilance. Resistance, however, was not long effective, for, like someone falling into water, she passed rapidly into sleep, then drowned in it.

Some unknown time later a rapping at her closed door awakened her. Quickly she sat and recalled to herself the life that was hers in this village. She went to the door. It was Julian, smiling and holding her van keys. "I have your van, senora. With new tires. It's parked right in front of your window here."

That happy news woke her fully. She took the keys from Julian and then turned and went to the window and looked outside. Looking sweet: the pretty Dodge Caravan, washed by the rain, not even any mud in the wheel wells from the long drive last night. Two shiny and new tires visible. Ready to hit the road.

Behind her, Julian spoke. "It looks like you have been able to sleep. I'll let you get back to it. I'll be at the station."

She went to him and made him shake her hand. She smiled excessively how pleased she was. "You've been very kind to me, Julian. You've stood by me. I've needed that. Yes, I'll see you at your office. Soon."

He closed the door behind him and she lay back on the bed, surrendering to the sag of mattress and soon again freefalling into sleep without dreams.

What woke her this time was not rapping at the door, but a sudden, shocking, shattering of glass. She jerked awake and looked in time to see a rock big as a fist bouncing off the tile floor and ricocheting off the wall and bouncing to rest against the desk on the adjacent wall. She looked then at the window, not many sharp angled shards left hanging in the frame, but large shards lay now on the floor, broken further, splintered; shards even upon the corners of the green bedcover near her feet.

She came quickly off the bed and stood in her stocking feet, leaning across her bed, one hand braced on the head board, straining to see out that ruined window who her rock-thrower might be. She saw no one on the lawn that extended the full length of the house, alongside all the tall poplars. No one on the sidewalks or in the streets. No cars. Although now she did hear, perhaps just around the far corner, the sound of a vehicle shifting gears and speeding away.

She went to the door and opened it, then hesitated whether she should first tell this to Pluto and Jardinia, or call Lupe and see how close he was. In that moment of hesitation she heard car wheels screeching; then outside, below, a sudden single-noted crash again of glass that had no reverberations. Then a second identical crashing of glass. Wheels screeched again, and, before she could get back to the window to look out, the reckless car was gone.

She spun and ran out the door and down the stairs and outside to see the far side of the van, invisible to her room's window. As she already knew, two windows bashed in, not by rocks this time, but likely by some crowbar wielded from the backseat of a driveby. The passenger side window and the big window next to it, one big smashed hole now in the middle of both, and the remnant buckled and shattered in ten thousand pieces, though still all those tiny fragments clinging together.

Angry and apprehensive, she slumped her shoulders and walked wearily back toward the front door of her hostel. She walked upstairs with both Pluto and Jardinia, who'd heard only the shattering glass upstairs and were anxious to see that disaster. Pluto seemed able to abide all calamities and said very little, standing at the broken window and looking out, gently nodding his head for the wonder of it all. But Jardinia was horrified and voluble. She excused Carlotta the victim from her vilification, but no one else. Hoodlums and criminals and juveniles who didn't go to school and the parents who raised them and the employers who wouldn't hire them and the governments who permitted anything and the police who couldn't catch anyone. Her wrath scorched all of them.

In a lull of this upset, Carlotta took from her purse five hundred more pesos and gave it to Jardinia, patting her little hand that held it, making the wish that these pesos would help pay for the damage and the worry. Jardinia was gradually calmed, but would not be pacified; she did, however, thank Carlotta for the compensation. Carlotta assured her also that she would herself clean up the broken glass, but Jardinia was adamant against that. Instead she ordered Pluto to the work, and wife and husband both went downstairs to get him the broom and a scoop and a can. Carlotta decided to save Jardinia the second grief: would tell her nothing about the van's disaster. Julian she must call immediately, however, right after calling Lupe. She looked at the watch in her purse. It was 12:33. She took out her cell phone and called her maestro.

"Where are you, Lupe?"

Cheerily he answered, "Right in front of your window, senora, finding a parking place. Senor Julian told us where you were. Ay caray! What happened to the windows of your van?"

She stood and looked out the window: saw them her boys at the curb, getting out of the Cadillac and waving up at her. Instantly the sight lifted her spirit out of the misery of foreboding that had engulfed her. She waved energetically out the window and yelled in Spanish, "Oh am I glad to see you! Get up here both of you!"

Both men smiled as they came up the walk and into the house. She was midway downstairs to meet them and hugged them both. Maestro Lupe, squared and stocky, a face that was the perfect image of the ancient Olmec headstones, save that those old stones are all somber and stern, but this face bright with good will and hints of laughter sparkling in his eye. Maestro Felipe Romero, stood beside him, taller, streaks of gray in his long hair, handsome as if he might have been brother to that Hollywood Romero, Caesar; but Felipe looked severely all about him, seeing no mirth in any of it.

Lupe carried the big envelope of documents proudly in his hand and gave them over to her. Then he too looked back toward her unseen van parked outside and said, "What happened, senora? It looks like big trouble."

Big trouble indeed. She led them upstairs and into her room. Pluto was there already with the broom and bucket, daintily lifting the shards of glass off the floor and the bed and dropping them in the bucket. Otherwise he ignored the senora and his two new guests.

She told them everything—the flat tires, the rock in the window, the smashed car windows, the scene at Emiliano's. Even after all that she surprised herself with the optimism in her voice. "But now that we have these papers, Julian can go and confiscate the pickup and at least put it away in storage until we get the final authorization from his chief to drive it back home."

"Authorization?" Lupe asked, evoking his own dread of bureaucratic involvement. "But it is your truck. And here is the proof."

Smirking, Felipe said, "And this is also Mexico, maestro. So there is always authorization, and more documents. And eventually mordita. Never forget the mordita."

Yet she must defend her knight Julian. "No, I don't think Julian's after mordita. He's not said one word about that. I think he may be an honest man."

Both Lupe and Felipe glanced at each other and registered eye to eye their suspicion of the senora's likely naivete; but said nothing.

Even so, she knew their thinking; knew also they might be right; still said, "I'll take my chances. He's been very good to me so far."

As she spoke those words her eyes drifted out the broken window to the back windowless wall of a building across the street, whose unseen front faced onto the street a block away. She had noticed the building wall a few times, a vague backdrop to her street, pale yellow paint badly faded and streaked with a darker yellow in several places. But what she particularly, suddenly now noticed, she had certainly not seen there earlier that morning; or even ten minutes ago. In black someone had hastily painted in large very legible letters: *Vate Gringa*. It translated easily: *Go away Gringa*

She stared astonished at the warning. The other two beside her at last saw her preoccupation and also turned to look. Lupe said to her, "That isn't for you, is it, senora?" And in response, but half to herself, she said, "That happened in the last ten minutes and I didn't even see them do that." Reminding her of the ghost that had knifed her tires.

The three of them went back down stairs and toward the van and the Cadillac parked next to each other. While they agreed to take both cars to see Julian, they each began to hear a man's voice, muffled, calling out something, likely from beyond the corner of the windowless building whereupon the warning had been written: words strident but drawn out and at first unintelligible. Yet soon they each one could distinguish it, a chant, repeated over and over: *Vate, Gringa, vate, vate.*

Lupe trotted quickly to that corner of the building and disappeared around the corner. The chant faded and then ceased. Lupe soon reappeared and walked briskly back to their parked cars, shaking his head. "I couldn't see anyone." When he again stood beside them the chanting started up again and seemed to come from the other corner of the building, to the left. Lupe trotted that way and around the corner of the building. Again the chanting faded and ceased. This time he returned to them from the opposite corner, having searched completely around the building. But again shaking his head, well puzzled. "I don't see where they could be hiding. There's no bushes or anything there, I should have been able to see someone."

They drove to Julian and she told him about the assaults and the warnings. He seemed not surprised. "And I think this also means you are right about our taking possession of your pickup as quickly as possible. I will first call my chief in Manzanillo and tell him I have the proof and that I need his authorization as quickly as possible. But before we go see Emiliano again, I must have all the forces I can muster."

The forces, when mustered, included Bernardo, the bald, lethargic policeman she'd already met, and Jeronimo, a deputy not imposing at all, tall but frail and probably still a teenager, in levis and t-shirt, with only the police cap Julian gave him as they all went forth to mark him as someone official and to be respected; though no one would fear him. Estimo would not be of the party, for the conflict of interest. Julian also gave a police cap to the janitor, Enrique, and asked him to ride with him in the police car and then stand beside him when they spoke to Emiliano; though he assured Enrique that nothing more would be expected of him. Julian was pleased that Lupe and Felipe would also be going with them and standing beside him.

The police car and the Cadillac of all problems caravaned down Palma and turned onto Piedras Pesadas and both parked at the curb beneath the magnolia. The four officers of the law emerged from the police car, but waited for the tall senora and her two amigos to come alongside them on the sidewalk and stand before the innocent waist-high white picket fence before entering. Julian then led his troops to the front door and knocked.

The formidable Caballo opened it and glared out at them, his black, sleek, lank hair hanging and framing the scowl on his face. He would not even ask them what they wanted; he would force them to ask, to beg.

So Julian must first speak: "Good morning, senor Caballo. Again I would speak to your father. Personally. It is about the pickup of course."

Caballo, however, was rudely and suddenly jerked aside by a hand unseen. Immediately Emiliano stepped into the doorway. He too glared at them all. As if to make the barrier of his presence of double thickness and triple density, he folded his arms defiantly across a chest that showed more muscle in his t-shirt today than anyone of them would have believed of this old man yesterday.

And neither would he abase himself to speak a greeting or make any sign of accommodation. He merely waited; ready to slam the door and go back inside. So again Julian must speak first. "Senor, with respect, I have in possession the true and authenticated title of ownership to this '80 Chevy pickup you have in your garage. I have reported this to my Chief in Manzanillo and he is now as we speak looking over the senora's claim. Of course I have also presented him with your unfortunate situation and your claim. Even so, it will probably be one day or two, or perhaps even three, before he directs me what to do. Therefore..." and he paused, that he might draw up whatever unsummoned reserve still lay within him, before resuming: "Therefore, I have been ordered to place the pickup into storage, for safekeeping—perhaps for your own safekeeping, senor Emiliano—until I have the final orders to release the vehicle. Please hear that I am not confiscating the pickup, senor. I am merely placing it in my own police storage yard, for safekeeping, for a day or two. Or three."

As the sheriff's posse stood there waiting for the dread response, Carlotta noticed Miguel, the unknowable son who lurked beneath the dark slouch hat, sauntering across the yard toward the posse. He stopped halfway to the gate and waited, watching. Behind Emiliano she could see both Caballo and Rasca craning to look over and around their forceful father.

He sneered. "Papers? Anyone can have papers." He thrust a hand forward, holding an old envelope that had been folded in half. Julian took it and read the sloppy handwriting. Read it twice.

"I see," he said, handing back the paper to its owner. "This is a receipt for the sale of this pickup to you, I grant that. Unfortunately, such a receipt for the money spent is not sufficient for the law. A sale of vehicle requires a signature of the owner on the very title itself, which in this case is in the possession of the senora; and there is no signature on it to show she has sold it to anyone. This man in Manzanillo, Senor Hermoso Reynoso, most likely stole this pickup and falsely sold it to you. I hope you understand that the senora is not your adversary. She is a victim. As you are. Both victims of Senor Hermoso Reynoso. If that be truly his name. But in any case we will investigate this thoroughly. We have an address here on your receipt. The entire Manzanillo Stolen Vehicle Division will be working on this case night and day until your money is restored to you. If that is what the Chief decides. But who knows?—perhaps he will believe that you still have the rights to this vehicle and will give it back to you. Yes, who knows. I am certainly no one to make those big judgments."

From behind Emiliano, Caballo growled out loudly, "Go to hell all of you." Beside him Rasca snarled also. "Take our truck? You? You'll have to throw all of us out of the way first. There's not one man out there brave enough to try it." Miguel the unknowable on the lawn moved one step, then another, closer to them.

Carlotta saw Julian fidget and let his fingers brush the pistol grip as if to gauge its place and readiness. Till that moment she could hardly have believed it would come to force; but now a little rush of adrenalin into her blood, noticeably intensifying everything, made her believe it might be otherwise.

However it was Emiliano who suddenly redirected and diffused all those energies. He turned to the sons behind him and spoke to them something brief and unintelligible to the others. He turned back, but raised a palm in warning to his numerous adversaries: that however appeasing he might seem in his words, he was still unvanquished. He spoke his words to Julian: "Alright, take it. Put it in the storage yard. For now. You don't have to promise that no one will take it, because one of my sons will be watching it at all times."

From beneath the slouch hat Miguel said, "And watching the gringa too." He laughed at her; it was part of the message.

Greatly relieved at this unexpected and easy resolution, Julian exhaled considerably before speaking again. "I greatly appreciate your cooperation, Senor Emiliano. I have always heard you are a fair and honorable man. Your whole family." Then he gestured toward the garage. "Could you please open the door so that we may start up the vehicle and drive it. We already have a key, you won't have to surrender yours."

Emiliano glared again and said, "I insist the senora not be allowed to drive or to sit in the vehicle."

Julian glanced to Carlotta, but knew he couldn't consider her wishes, and simply spoke, "Yes, of course, she must not be driving it."

Julian himself took the key from the senora and went into the garage and climbed aboard and started it up. He manipulated the stick shift on the column till he'd figured it. Then he put it in reverse and backed it very carefully from the tight confines of the garage. He backed it out onto the street and then stopped it there in park, idling, and stepped outside. He directed Bernardo to drive the police car with Jeronimo and the janitor back to the police station. The senora and her men should go back to the police station in the Cadillac and he would meet them there.

After all three vehicles had caravaned back down Piedras Pesadas and turned onto Palma going back to the village center, Emiliano still stood at his open front door, arms crossed and defiant, glaring down the road after them. Caballo and Rasca were still within the house, still concealed behind him, and they began laughing and laughing, sounding like hyenas on the hunt. Their laughter was infectious and soon Miguel on the lawn heard them and sat down and began laughing as loudly, himself become another amused hyena, also ready to prowl.

23 CARLOTTA'S ESCAPE

Carlotta and Lupe and Felipe went back to their rooms. Suddenly she was more tired than she'd been in days. Lupe and Felipe each chose a room on either side of the senora. All three seemed well ready for a nap. She believed the worst of it was over.

However, she slept not long: for apparently no reason she awoke again less than an hour after she'd lain down. She sat up. There was someone out there. Nearby. Someone for her. She looked out the window, from which every shard of broken glass had been removed from the frame; though no new glass had been yet installed.

At first she saw no one and nothing unusual. Her van still there, where it had been assaulted, with no new assault visible. The loud Vate Gringa written on the wall still glared; and would no doubt for long after she had departed from that village. Then she saw the old woman. Standing near the corner of the building across the street. She clutched a shawl that draped her gray hair. A tiny thing she was. When Carlotta leaned out the window and looked intensely toward the face of this lady, the lady herself smiled recognition and lifted a frail hand to wave at her, to beckon her. *The same woman who had looked at her out the window of Emiliano's house yesterday.*

Seeing no need to bother Lupe or Felipe in their rooms, she went downstairs and outside. The old woman still waited. Carlotta crossed to her and stood before her, more than a head taller than this old dainty one. Who still smiled at her, even as she had smiled the day before.

Carlotta began with formalities of greeting, but the old woman by a wave of her finger let her know those formalities were unnecessary.

Or there was no time for them. She didn't smile now and she spoke urgently, though her voice came in whispers, which caused Carlotta to lean her head closer to hear the Spanish words. They were simple and few. "Beware, senora. My husband and sons are hard men. And dangerous. Beware. Better you leave here now. Before." These grim words spoken, she resumed the smile and turned to walk away. But halfway through her turn she turned back and said, again whispering, "My name is Guadalupe. Called Lupe. I hope for you. Que le vaya bien."

Stunned, Carlotta felt the ever ready apprehension rising again, the more potent for being so vague, so mysterious. She returned upstairs where the others still slept, and she let them. An hour later, however, when the two men wakened, she told them about Guadalupe called Lupe. They persuaded her to go with them to visit Julian.

But this time Lupe himself would discuss the matter with Julian. "The senora must have protection, Julian. You've seen the windows. And this now—Emiliano's wife warning us. It's only justice that you have someone there tonight, guarding her van. And if you have the men, someone else to watch the house."

To Julian it all seemed reasonable. Added to the other reasons only he knew, and which had already made him secretly concerned. He would place Bernardo in Bernardo's own old Ford station wagon, parked just behind the senora's van. Jeronimo could sleep on a palate on the front porch of the house; though he would not sleep, he would watch all night vigilantly.

And so it was done. They waited with little hope all the rest of the afternoon for Julian to come by and say he'd received the authorization, but he never did. At dinner time they left their police guards and went to a café near the plaza and ate a platter full of tacos made of juicy shredded pork and cilantro, wrapped in hot tortillas that had been patted out and grilled only moments before. Coca-cola for each of them.

They had set on the front porch talking and enjoying the twilight and the quiet and waiting for sleep to beckon. Sooner than it did, all three went upstairs, leaving Bernardo parked in his Ford at the curb, Jeronimo with a little blanket roll sitting on the porch with his back against the wall. Carlotta went to her room alone, and Lupe and Felipe went together into Lupe's room.

She lay on her bed and tried to sense how ready she was for sleep. It was slow coming, and before it did she heard a horn nearby honk twice quickly, urgently, and less than ten seconds later another rock, or something very like it in size and weight, sailed like a homing pigeon through her open window and banged on the floor and off the wall and rolled to a deadly stop two feet from her bed. In shock and horror she realized it was no rock, but a round canister, perhaps even some kind of bomb.

She screamed and came off the bed and across the room toward the door, all the time watching the canister that suddenly popped open a cavity and began pouring out roils and billows of black, dense smoke. So quickly it filled the room that she had to grope blindly for the doorknob, turn it, and stumble into the hallway, coughing, coughing, the black billowing smoke slipping out into the hall right behind her.

She ran to the room next door and pounded a fist on it. Lupe instantly opened it and stepped out and saw the black smoke drifting out into the hall and toward other rooms. From the front porch, Jeronimo had heard the commotion and hurried up the stairs. Bernardo in his car saw the smoke billowing out the senora's window and he hurried out of his car and up the walk into the house and across the foyer to the stairs, where the four others now scurried down, the black smoke swirling and spreading right behind them.

Pluto and Jardina together bolted through a closed living room door and saw the bustle and the terrible smoke. Jardinia cried out and cried out for the fire that she thought it was. Lupe already knew it was only a smoke bomb, that there would be no explosion, and so he was not worried about the fire and told her so; but she couldn't listen. Jardinia ran back into the living room and began gathering up pictures in frames that were all over her walls. Pluto flopped his hands helplessly at his side and shook his head in amazement and asked what they should do. As all seven of them stood there in the foyer of the house, bewildered and bedeviled, they all heard a wild shriek of joy from outside, and then a revving engine out front, heard it spin out laying rubber and screech and slide around the corner and away.

Carlotta, the quickest to comprehend it, raced outside and saw with more stunned amazement than anything before had provoked: all four tires of her pretty white Dodge Caravan in flames, flames convulsing the whole round of the tire, as if, perhaps, gasoline had first been poured over each of the four tires before someone had set the match.

Pluto with unexpected quick thinking came running down the walk to the car with a fire extinguisher half as big as he was and would have begun squirting the tires, except that Lupe, much stronger and more adept, took the red canister from his frail, clumsy hand. Lupe then sprayed down the flames of each tire, covering each one with white gooey foam, until all the tires had stopped flaming; though all four smoldered and smoked for at least another half hour.

Inside the house and despite her hysteria, Jardinia provided two cooling fans with long extension cords, and they were able in forty minutes to drive most of the smoke out of the upstairs; though Carlotta's room would be smelly and unuseable for at least a day.

All the van's tires were ruined. The paint above the fenders had burned until it had melted, and grease stains of smoke streaked upward from the wells, even onto the hood. But the engine started. She could engage the transmission and let the van move slightly forward and back, despite the fried tires; and the breaks pumped and took hold and stopped movement. It seemed likely that only the tires were destroyed, and the drums and brakes and brake lines undamaged.

Sending Bernardo and Jeronimo back to the police station to call Julian at home and tell him the bad news, Carlotta, Lupe and Felipe went to confer into Lupe's room. That window was opened, and the air there was now breathable.

Yet it was also obvious to all three what they must do, and how quickly. They had only Julian to convince. A half hour later Julian himself arrived in the police car, having risen from bed to come see the new disaster and speak with the victims.

Julian told them the hard truth, that he could arrest no one immediately for all this violence without witnesses. And there was no time for any investigation.

"So there's only one choice, Julian," she urged him, "We've got to get that pickup out of town, and me and my van and my men too, as fast as possible. We can't wait days for that authorization. Surely you see that, Julian."

He did and he didn't. The urgency was obvious. The bureaucracy was another thing, which customarily ignored both urgency and the obvious.

But Lupe spoke persuasively. His mother and his aunts had worked many years in the bureaucracy; there were always the loopholes. "Can it not be, Julian, that the pickup can be delivered, not to its owner, the senora, but to another municipal police, who can guard it until this authorization can happen? We can leave tonight, Julian, take the pickup to another pueblo. Perhaps even Chapala, which would be the greatest service to the senora. Who has suffered much here."

Julian shook his head. "First—I should speak to my chief—that should always be my first step—and I cannot speak to my chief until morning and perhaps not until the afternoon."

Still urgent, Lupe spoke. "Surely, Julian, your chief, when you explain these assaults against the senora, indeed against the Municipal Police, would believe these drastic measures are necessary. It is a special case, Julian. If we stay, what will be next?"

Julian paced several intense moments between the door and the opened window, always looking down at his shoes, balancing many factors, some doubtful, some uncertain, most of them dangerous. At last he stopped pacing and looked at Carlotta and sighed. "Alright, I suppose I can't let this get any worse. But you wish to take the van too, don't you?" She nodded of course. "Then we need four new tires again. Tonight. Right now."

"Estimo?" she questioned, doubtfully.

"No," Julian said. "That would be a big mistake. He must not even *know* what we do. It must be someone else."

"It could be me," grinned Lupe. "Tell me who sells tires in the village. Even if I have to wake them. Even if I have to buy tires not matching. Or not new."

Julian smiled. "Very well, maestro. If you can bring me four tires, I will bring a tire iron and tire hammer and we will mount the tires here on the sidewalk in front of the house. Then we can carry the tires one at a time if we need to, and have them pumped up with air at Don Jose's shop. Then, when all four tires are put back on, I will get the pickup from the storage yard and we will drive straight out of here."

"To where?" asked the senora.

"We'll decide that after I make a call or two from the station."

Bernardo and Jeronimo remained behind, seated in the van, ordered not to leave it this time. Julian drove off for the station. Lupe and Felipe drove away in the Cadillac looking for tires just before midnight. Carlotta would remain at Pluto and Jardinia's. She'd moved now into Felipe's room so that she could still keep a watch on the street and on her endangered van; Felipe had moved into one of the rooms across the hall.

Lupe and Felipe returned to the van in slightly less than an hour with one well used tire that would indeed fit the rim, though wider than the burned and melted originals. Julian came to meet them with the tire tools he'd promised, and he helped Felipe jack up the van and remove a front tire. Felipe then took the desecrated tire to the sidewalk, removed the carcass and then scraped with a hunting knife the charred remains off the rim. Next he muscled with the tire iron until he had the new tire on the rim, and Julian drove away with it to have the air pumped into it.

In another half hour Lupe returned with another tire, this one new and exactly the correct size, and he left it with Felipe to replace the second tire. Lupe was gone a little more than an hour the last time but finally returned with the two last needed tires, one nearly bald, and the other with very little tread remaining, neither one an exact match either to the originals or to the other two; but all four fit on the rims. In less than another hour all four tires had been filled with air, attached to the still blackened wheel mounts and secured tightly by the lug nuts.

The rest of the escape plan was brief and desperate. Julian alone must go to the police storage yard a block from the police station to retrieve the blue Chevy pickup. No doubt one of Emiliano's sons would be nearby, watching it to prevent the very abduction they were planning. Julian must confront the son and tell him that the violence of the day forced him to move the pickup to another police jurisdiction and that he would duly inform Emiliano where he had deposited the pickup, as soon as Julian returned to Purificacion. No doubt also this would not be agreeable to the sons or to the father. But no matter. Julian still represented the police and the will of the law. He carried a pistol. He also carefully calculated that he would have five to ten minutes head start before the son could report the abduction to the father, and that would be enough for the three vehicles of their caravan to make their getaway.

As Julian drove away to go for the pickup, he asked that his compadres have both the van and the Cadillac of all problems idling and ready to move out the instant Julian returned with the pickup. There was only one road leading out of town. They would try to go straight and without stopping all of the hundred ten miles through the mountains to Guadalajara and then to Chapala.

After Julian drove away she went upstairs and gathered everything from her room and took it downstairs and stowed it into the van. Lupe and Felipe did the same. Then as directed she got into her van and started it up and let it idle. She glanced only once back at the shattered windows and sighed; but that was all fixable. Felipe rode in the Cadillac as passenger and Lupe drove; he turned his car round and parked it just behind the senora and he too left it to idle. And they waited.

As they waited they heard gentle thunder crackling far away, from what direction they could not tell. Soon tiny drops of rain began to dot their windshields. While they waited.

Until suddenly headlights shone brightly upon both cars as a vehicle squealed turning the corner onto their street, and quickly they saw that it was the '80 Chevy pickup. When it pulled alongside them they saw Julian, grinning, leaning across the seat to speak out the passenger side window, saying, "Time to go. Fortunately my pistol convinced Caballo that he could not stop me. But he went straight to get the father and brothers and I am sure they will be after us soon. Vamonos!"

And with that grito he shifted into first gear and let out the clutch and they watched the blue pickup dart away down the street. With emotion and adrenalin choking in her throat, Carlotta put the van into gear and pulled quickly away from the curb and after her pickup. Lupe in the Cadillac of all problems was quickly after her and she could hear one of her maestros calling out "Hijo-LEY!" as they sped off into the night.

All drove at the maximum speed that the roads and their vehicles would permit. Only a kilometer or two on the way first Carlotta and then Julian realized that Lupe's Cadillac must be their standard of speed, since going faster than sixty miles an hour the Cadillac's lights slowly diminished in their rear view mirrors even though it tried to keep up. A risky accommodation, though they must make it.

It would of course be a fourth car coming up on them that would rouse all their apprehension. The rain fell faster and she increased the speed of her wipers. As she drove she kept a continual glancing into her rearview mirror, first to spot the Cadillac's headlights, note the distance; then, with just a flash of apprehension each time, glanced past the Cadillac and into the utter darkness beyond it: seeing if other lights might suddenly be coming into view, perhaps gaining on the Cadillac. The first ten minutes all behind the Cadillac remained only darkness. In ten more minutes they had made their way back to Highway 80 and were preparing to turn left onto the highway, apparently the only three vehicles out driving these roads on this inhospitable night. It was then she saw the far, far headlights, so small she could barely distinguish two separate beams. Her stomach turned and she knew her stomach told her truly: it was them.

Julian would see the faraway lights, and be studying it soon enough. Lupe probably already had seen them. It was physically discomforting for her to have to make the slowdown and stop at the junction, but they must do it, though not for long. As all three moved in caravan onto the highway 80 they all three quickly accelerated to regain maximum speed. The road went straight ahead, but in the subtle dark shadows of the night, against the sky, she could see tall sharp peaks close up ahead, and the road was going straight into all of it.

The road began suddenly and intensely to wind and turn back on itself going always higher and they must reduce their escape speed to a miserable 25 mph: imagining the onrush of their pursuers; now, but surely only for the moment, unseen. One narrow asphalt lane in each direction; ditch and cliff face were on one side of her car; the dropoff on the other, a fragile, metal, two foot high guard rail for protection.

She had hardly slept the last two days and felt the heaviness in her body, craving sleep; yet every cell in that body tingled and her blood raced and she could not possibly have slept. Always with half an eye on the rearview mirror, they drove on as fast as they dared. When the curves became more gradual and drawn out, they were able to increase to 30 and sometimes even 35; but not often. As the rain fell faster, she could see on the illuminated road just ahead a film of water washing down the rock faces and across the road, underneath the guard rail and over the embankment and into the far, far below.

The next time she looked in the mirror she saw the dread pair of headlights only a few car lengths behind the Cadillac. Without making a sound she gasped. But she only saw the headlights; not the vehicle itself; of course not the driver; nor riders.

She knew for certain it was them with the sudden *Honk! Honk! Honk!*— on and on honking as they crowded so close behind the Cadillac that she couldn't see their headlights, only the glare of light where the pursuing car rode the Cadillac's bumper. In a few more alarming moments their road came straight across the middle of a meadow and cars, for the moment without drop-offs beside them, could safely accelerate speed, and all did. The honking continued but the fourth car, seeing how far ahead the other lane was free of headlights, swerved out around the Cadillac and tried to pass him. Nonetheless the maestro swerved his own front wheels partially into the oncoming lane and blocked the other car, which was forced for the moment to fall back; but still honking. Then again trying to pass, but again the Cadillac cut it off and harassed it into retreat.

Suddenly the road again became dangerous twists and curves and the perilous dropoffs. It seemed that the angry pursuer could only honk and keep menacing the Cadillac's rear bumper. She was terrified for them. For this winding section of the road the cliffs fell away again a thousand feet alongside her passenger door.

In all this time they had only passed one other vehicle going the other way, coming down out of the mountains. This must have made their pursuers bold, for suddenly they stopped honking and bolted around the Cadillac into the oncoming lane, though any oncoming car would have killed all of them. Lupe reacted quickly and again swerved toward the other car, but he had little room for error and must be cautious, so near the cliff edge; and the rock face and the rocky ditch so near on the opposite roadside.

Even so these two pairs of headlights in her rearview mirror seemed locked in combat, swerving back and forth against each other in the little roadway there was, screeching audibly, no doubt wheels somewhat slippery in the rain. Death could come for anyone in any of the next seconds.

She felt a scream mounting into her throat, with all the energy there to explode it; yet the same strangulation of terror restrained that scream: and she could only sit there frozen into silence by her terror as she drove on, her wild eyes flitting back and forth between the mirror and the dangerous road ahead. Meanwhile, both cars continued side by side in her mirror careening and still somehow miraculously navigating the perilous turns at the same time. Then a further last terror: *Gunshots! Many!*

Shrieking when a bullet shattered her mounted side mirror and blasted it off the car body, wires ripped loose and remnants alone sticking out to show where the side mirror had been. Shrieking again to see that the tailgate on her pickup now distinctly showed two bullet holes in it. Shrieking. But still driving for her life, and praying for the lives ahead and behind that she could not see.

She looked back again into her rearview mirror and saw the four headlights still locked together, but several car lengths back from her suddenly. Looked just in time to see suddenly Lupe's headlights, the right pair in her mirror, jerk violently to the left and saw the other car's headlights jerk also that way, hard left: and then she heard the *crash!*—all four headlights thrown far left, seemingly into the ditch and the rock face of the cliff: halted: neither vehicle moving further.

In the fear of death she felt herself move like an automaton. She took her foot off the accelerator and slowly depressed the brake. She was dimly aware that ahead of her Julian had slowed and was also stopping. Still she could not take her eyes off the rearview mirror. Still the four headlights in the ditch seemed forever locked together there: probably less than one hundred yards back. Dreading, dreading what she might find there, she nonetheless shifted into reverse and began gradually to move backward.

When suddenly one pair of lights far back there in the crash site drew away from the other. With a leap of joy in her heart she saw that it seemed to be the one on the outside, which should be the Cadillac. Lupe. Felipe. She stopped going backward; stared back into the night, breathless. By smallest increments the faraway pair of headlights eased away from the other, and then by the same small increments it began to move forward, toward her, though the second pair of headlights remained far back there in the ditch, unmoving. She watched in desperate hope. Until at last out of the darkness the headlights and the car drew alongside her: the Cadillac and her maestro, and the other maestro.

Before she could scream out the joy breaking loose in her, Lupe leaned across his compadre, grinning, a happy Olmec, saying, "Ay caray, senora! What beasts these men are! What barbarians! But their car is finished. Their front axle broke against the rocks. And both of them inside are still sleeping. I believe they are sleeping. I didn't dare try waking them. Julian can call in and report their accident. Now andale pues, senora! Let's get this old pickup of yours out of here fast and get it to Chapala."

Through the rest of the night and all the way to Chapala Julian was true to his word and would not allow her to drive her pickup. An hour after sunrise he himself, with the senora at his side, delivered it to the Chapala police, saw that it was registered there and watched it be parked in the fenced-in storage facility.

Afterward Carlotta drove Julian in her van to the Nueva Posada, and she bought him the combination grande breakfast and offered to pay for his room there in the hotel for a few days if he wanted to see the village. The room and sightseeing he declined. She wanted to buy him wine or tequila or a present for his wife, but he would accept none of that. He said her good opinion was all he wished for.

Just before noon she drove him in the van to Guadalajara to Transito Central and she paid for his return ticket on the deluxe bus. Before he boarded she kissed him on both cheeks and on the forehead and said he was one of the two best men she'd met in Mexico; her maestro Lupe the other.

The Chapala officer in charge of Stolen Vehicles, Pilio Gomez, assured the senora that everything would be done in proper procedure, and that then she would be able to take possession. She asked how long that might take. He was not sure. They must first make the paperwork. Perhaps tomorrow he could give her a firm answer.

The following day Pilio told her that his own chief told him that the bigger chief from Guadalajara had to be the one to come make a personal inspection of the pickup, and then he could deliver it to the senora. He thought that should take no more than a week. Although the bigger chief was a very busy man.

A week later the bigger chief had not come and she began making phone calls to offices in Guadalajara to speak to him personally. She left messages and she waited for return calls. None ever came. She drove to Guadalajara and sat in two different offices more than an hour each one, but she could only make an appointment to see her man eight days from then. She went home and rattled on to Max about the injustice and they drank wine on the back patio and turned the grim stories into the black jokes they reserved for the greatest horrors. There was no other remedy for it.

Three weeks to the day of her return with the pickup Pilio confided to her that some if not all of this delay and red tape might be more easily managed if a payment were made to someone he knew in Guadalajara, who was unnaturally influential and who could probably resolve her knot of problems in one day.

This angered her worse than any of it; the inevitable mordita, which she knew, they all knew, was always lurking. Pilio's suggestion put her in an instant huff and she glared at him and screeched, "Never! I've paid plenty for that truck! Give it to me, damnit!"

She knew these were not the passwords that moved the wheels of mordita, but Mexico had harvested her enough—no more!

So she screeched and defied him and that felt good and it was even some consolation. But she still did not have her truck, though she went to the yard twice a week for the first month to go look at it and sigh.

Eventually business intervened, more loans to scare up, a hunt for new clients, and she began to relax her vigilance and forgot about the pickup for days at a time. Once Max in the middle of dinner said, "I talked to Pilio today. He said the offer is still on the table. They want five thousand pesos. Think about it. It might be worth it."

She screeched again. "No! Never! Just make them give me my damn truck!"

But they didn't. Pilio explained to her that of course it was through no fault of anyone. It was simply that work at the bureau was so excessive that the bigger chief had simply not had the time to get out to Chapala to inspect the pickup. Nonetheless, this bigger chief's secretary was authorized to assure everyone concerned that he would be there as soon as he could.

Another month passed, and then another. Pilio at that juncture told her that he was optimistic because he had been informed that a *new* bigger chief had replaced the old, and that this new man himself told Pilio it would be a first piece of his agenda to come to Chapala and resolve all the stolen vehicle situations, of which there were now many; foremost of these of course was the senora's.

A week later on a next visit Pilio expressed regrets that the new bigger chief had suddenly been unaccountably delayed. It might be a week or so more. Feeling especially sympathetic with the senora, Pilio said she might be glad after all these regrettable delays, that there was still the man in Guadalajara who could make all things happen, and that he was still willing to accept these few, paltry thousand pesos to do this favor for the senora.

Again she yelled at him: *"Never! And damn you all! That's my truck! Give it to me!"*

After that outburst, which she knew would not change the stalemate, she had not the courage to return again to see Pilio for nearly three weeks.

Then one evening, as she and Max sat on the back patio at their little house in Canacinta, Pilio came to their front gate and rang the bell. He was smiling. He had the best of possible news for the senora. The bigger chief from Guadalajara had indeed finally come to inspect her pickup. He had examined all her documents and they were all in perfect order. Pilio was there that moment to tell her that tomorrow morning she might come to his office as early as she wished, and that he would deliver the key and the pickup to her, once and finally and forever.

She was thrilled. She even kissed the sweaty forehead of the rat. She looked back at Max and bounced on her toes. Then she turned back to Pilio and said, "Wait—why can't I drive back with you right now and you give it to me?"

Pilio frowned. Even so, he would not allow his irritation to show, that the senora seemed ignorant of basic etiquette. So he spoke solemnly. "Oh but senora—of course you will need to go to the bank first. You can't be forgetting the storage fees for your pickup. Senora, we have stored this vehicle for you longer than five months now. Five months. The storage fees have come to five thousand five hundred pesos. And of course there are the thousand pesos for me to do all the paperwork for the release. Nothing can be done without the paperwork."

24 LUPE AND THE WARRIOR'S BOAT

The last house they finished was for Steven Remington, and Lupe thought this one was the handsomest and showed off the fine skill of the maestros better than any of the Bellacasa houses. Steven Remington the owner was a bachelor, a friendly retired lawyer from San Francisco who dressed carelessly, like someone who never left home. He had lived in Ajijic ten years, and had come to know the senor first, and then his houses. When Steven inherited from his mother, he commissioned the senor to build him a house that would reflect his cowboy tastes but would also benefit from the beautiful interior embellishments Bellacasa had become known for.

A showplace. Yet for the first time since they'd finished the senor and senora's first house in Chula Vista, they were finishing a house without another one ready to go somewhere else. It seemed long ago, but once they had been doing three houses at the same time; hardly credible as Lupe remembered it now, the frenzy of work, so much hiring, such dreams for the future.

Thursday and Friday last week peons and maestros alike had undertaken to remove all the last traces of construction, and to do a last thorough cleaning, inside and outside. Steven Remington Saturday claimed the house he had with so much pleasure watched them build day by day for half a year. Sunday he had discovered a water leak in his upstairs shower, and he had also decided that he needed in his bedroom switches for his garden lights. And would Lupe please construct a little barrier by the outdoor faucet that would force Alma, Steven's old chihuahua dog, to locate another favorite pissing spot, not so much in the way.

So this morning, Tuesday, Lupe had arrived to meet Marcos, coming from another job, and Tacho, who had been doing errands in the senora's blue Chevy pickup, so recently and so miraculously returned from the dead, coming with materials from Lopez. Lupe let himself in the front gate with the senor's key, and went across the quiet courtyard, every brick of which he knew. Senor Max would be in town all morning. Lupe went to the spigot by the patio where the garden hose lay. Standing, he could smell the ammonia. He saw there was room to build a little barrier three bricks high that would enclose the spigot area in a half meter of space, enough to coil the hose and keep the dog away. He would need forty bricks. A half bag of cement. A half bag of river sand. His bag of mason's tools was in his car.

Lupe heard the front gate click open and someone coming. Tacho, carrying river sand and cement in the amounts Lupe had foreseen. The son called to the father, "I have the bricks in the pickup." Tacho set down the two partial bags near the spigot. "Hey, something else. Did you know the senora put a new transmission in the pickup? I told you the old one was going bad. But she had Lorenzo put in an automatic. What about that? Now you could drive it."

A minor embarrassment, this thing about not driving a stick shift. Made worse when it was mentioned by the know-it-all son. "Oh I've driven the stick shift, Tacho, it's not so hard. But the automatic is much better. Stick shifts are too much work, having to bother with the clutch all the time."

Lupe would not let it be known how much this news about the new transmission pleased him. The '80 Chevy pickup was a great worker. He had tried to keep his admiration of the pickup a secret, though he had hinted a few times, without being able to help himself, to both the senor and the senora how one day he would like one similar sitting in front of his own house. He envied Tacho driving it. He could imagine how good he himself would feel driving it with the automatic. Never would he admit it, but he believed that the senora had been thinking especially of him when she had made this change of transmissions.

Yet would the blue pickup be servicing any more new constructions? The nostalgia for those exciting, busy days returned to sadden him. "How is the senora affording this transmission, Tacho? I know they had barely able to make our last payroll. I know they have debts they cannot pay."

These things worried Tacho too, but he did not like to admit it. "Maybe I'm stupid too, but I think they will come out alright. We'll build more houses. They'll pay all these debts. "

Lupe doubted it. "I worry most about Lopez. The senor owes him many thousand pesos."

Tacho knew precisely. "Fifty two thousand, three hundred eighty. Luis Lopez told me when I picked up the bricks. He said to ask the senor if he'd be able to make a payment soon."   Lupe frowned. "To do it I believe they would have to borrow money. From the US. I am ready to accept that our company has built its last house. We were doomed when we did not strike back at La Madre. You have some of the blame for that, Tacho. For letting the senor stop us."

For Tacho this argument had worn itself out long ago. He also did not relish it because he had in secret, a time or two, in the darker and darker days since, thought his father might have been right about the midnight visit. Against this miserable thought he opposed another view of the long one-sided war, from a more rarified vantage: a determined optimism, based on the hopeful disposition he innately possessed, and which had been augmented and made blindingly radiant by the senor's own blind optimism.

He said to his father, "I still believe they will be vindicated in the end, that the courts will say that La Madre is guilty and must apologize publically for her lies. Then all will be well. You will see. Their lawyer has looked at all the testimony. All the evidence and the laws are in their favor. How can Max and Carlotta not win?"

Lupe shook his head in pity, though it must also be himself he should pity, for the great fall would come down on all of them. "Tacho, you are still young and much of your time has been in the United States. So you can be excused for not knowing your sad country better. Unfortunately, it will be no good consolation to me that your education will come because of this tragedy. Much as I love the senor and the senora, they are sometimes fools. You are one too sometimes."

These words roused Tacho. "You think so, eh? A fool with foolish ideas, eh? You did not think the senor was a fool when he talked of sharing the company with us. Nor when he said we would work only eight hours in our work day, not the usual nine, and still get a full week's pay. That there would be special paid holidays. Those were *all* crazy ideas to us. But finally we did believe all those crazy ideas. I *still* believe him, even when he says don't attack La Madre. Even when he says the company will build again, and our old plans will go on again."

These dreams were even more important to the father than to the son, for the father had dreamed them so much longer. The father's grief was also greater, believing they would fail for not having acted, when the dreams more than anything were worth fighting for. "I tell you that was our only

259

chance. But you didn't see that. Someday you will know what a big mistake that was."

Tacho fiercely defended himself, even as he also tried to resist the icy fingers of fear that chilled him to the heart, hearing his father's terrible prophecy. "No! He's right and you're wrong. He's a man of peace. You think war is the answer."

Lupe as fiercely leered at his angry son. "In rich men's cities, maybe you negotiate. Here in the jungle you *are* at war, like it or not. You will see. We live in peace when we can, but we go to war if we must."

Tacho growled primitive angers. "Those all could be excuses, papa. Maybe you don't see yourself so well. Maybe you just need this excuse to shove all your anger at someone. Maybe *that's* it."

Lupe had not been to college as his son had, but he well understood the nasty implications of these fancy ideas. "Go to hell! I have had my days being out of control, and I have paid for it worse than anyone knows. And now I am *not* a man of violence. But that doesn't mean I have *forgotten* how to be angry when that is necessary. And I am no coward. And it may be that *you* are only talking all this peace because you *cannot* fight back when someone slaps you in the face. Maybe that's all you *can* do, show off that big smile that everyone thinks is so great. Maybe *that's* it."

This was a difficult blow even for an irate, resentful son to deflect, and indeed Tacho did not deflect it. The blow was devastating as any could be to him, and Tacho's ire and resentment coiled together like two snakes and lashed out at his angry father. "You *are* a violent man! You were back then! You still are now! You don't deserve to be the senor's maestro!"

These slaps in the face by his son stung him bitterly, but Lupe possessed no more energy for a counter stroke, for the great sickness had come over him again. It was called: the father and son at war. A perverse war that no one could win, and both sides must lose everything. Though his face still burned with anger, Lupe turned away from his son and said, "No! That is all I have to say. No. I refuse any more of this terrible talk. I'm doing my work and you may leave the bricks by the front gate."

In heaven's mercy Marcos and his younger brother Julio at that moment came round to the front of the house and Marcos called to them. "Hey, I would have rung the bell, but you two were screaming so loud you wouldn't have heard me. What the hell is going on?"

Neither father nor son wanted to respond. Tacho finally said, "I'm getting the bricks," and he went past them and back around the house and disappeared.

260

Marcos turned to Lupe. "So, amigo, more bad words with the son. You two are stubborn. Somebody needs to talk to you both."

Ten years younger than his brother, but already a journeyman plumber/electrician, Julio carried the tool box. He said, "Are you two going to be going on like this at the wedding dinner tomorrow?"

When Lupe spoke, sickness of the war of fathers and sons gripped him again, but he couldn't help it, for the anger still simmering. "I am not *going* to any wedding dinner! The Romeros don't really want me anyway. They're just inviting me because Tacho asks them. And I don't *want* him to ask them. I don't want him to do *any* favors for me."

Tacho reappeared bearing a cardboard box of bricks, only his head and baseball cap exposed above the topmost bricks. He had heard all their loud conversation. He was still explosive himself. He barked out: "Yes, that is maybe a good idea. That you *not* come. I don't want Abuelo to see what a wild man you can become!" Tacho dropped the bricks on the grass still ten meters from the spigot and hurried away, so many emotions swirling inside him that he comprehended none of them, though he was lashed to misery by every one of them.

These last words of Tacho's were the worst and most grievous to Lupe. He turned away from Marcos and Julio, though it was not necessary, for both brothers in sympathy had also turned away from him, that Lupe might have a moment of privacy to recover himself.

Eventually, Lupe spoke, though he did not turn around again. "There is never forgiveness in these things. A terrible lesson to be learning at my age. So many years I wanted my family back, my son. Now he's here, and it is still not over, all the old troubles. Still here. So what is the good?"

Marcos and Julio certainly could not explain to him these philosophical things. They could only catch him when he fell. They stood ready. Marcos said, "Tacho doesn't want to fight either, maestro. That's why he left. Neither one of you wants to fight. Just lay off it a while, it'll go away. You've got to go to the dinner."

Lupe seemed less angry, but he was still firm. "I *won't* go, I tell you. Who needs the Romeros?"

"Whatever you say, maestro. But let's change the subject. Get your mind on something else. OK? Tell me about this. What time do we leave in the morning to go pick up the boat?"

Lupe's face relaxed as he struggled to recall this information from worlds far away. "Oh yes, eight in the morning. At the pier in Chapala. The man says its sixteen kilometers to Scorpion Island. He said it will probably take an hour to get there, another hour to tow the boat back. You and I and Julian should be back before noon. I hope no one has said anything to the senora."

Even by the next morning he was sure no one had. He arrived at the pier in Chapala twenty minutes till eight in the Cadillac of all problems, even though the fuel filter had clogged and halted him a few hundred meters onto the careterra above Six Corners. Lupe had stopped and crawled beneath the beast and disconnected the fuel filter. He had cleaned it somewhat with the tip of his ignition key, and then he could drive on. Soon Marcos would be coming with Julio, the third man necessary for the short portage of the boat.

At the pier Lupe waited, still edgy from the ugly morning before. He kept the radio on, enjoying a few last moments with the musica on the car radio; but soon he was restless and turned off the radio and he walked out on the pier. No vendors had set up so early, and the peace was like in the old days on the pier, when the water came all the way into the streets sometimes. Lupe walked further, till he could see Scorpion Island, a small bump way out in the lake. Four or five lived there, a family who owned a little food stand that rarely had customers. And the boat maker, Juan del Lago, who sometimes would come to Chapala, but never with his boats.

By a Huichol Indian tradition that was old before the first Spanish came five hundred years ago, these boats had been originally made on this island only by a few master builders. When each warrior of the tribe came to claim his own boat, he must receive it by hand from the maestro builder and carry it with one companion down to the water and row the boat to shore alone, to prove his worthiness to own such a beautiful craft.

The warriors had come and gone, but the master builders still lived, though now only two, Juan del Lago and his cousin Stefano, knew the old skill. These cousins, abiding in the old tradition, lived on Scorpion Island when building a boat. Otherwise they lived as one large family with twelve others in a farm near San Gregorio.

These stories of the boat makers had been known to Lupe and all his cousins and uncles and neighbors all their lives, unto all their generations. Though in experience Lupe had only known these boats as a fisherman's business venture, in which rowing a boat from Scorpion Island to Chapala or Ajijic was a thing the fisherman who bought the boat did every day, and so there was no glory in it nowadays. Lupe had never known anyone but a fisherman to buy one of these handcrafted boats, which were twice as expensive as the light aluminum boats that were most often used by ordinary people who rowed for pleasure. However, to many young ones of the barrio, these boats of Scorpion Island *were* notorious for pleasure, as everyone knew who had ever listened to the girls in the barrio bragging about taking a ride in these beautiful boats with a fisherman on moonlit nights.

It gave Lupe a great pleasure to imagine the senor and the senora rowing in this boat, out on the lake. The senora would be smiling her greatest smile, which would be a thing to behold. The senor would be rowing hard and trying to make jokes to her.

A horn honked and Lupe turned to see Marcos in his red Ford pickup stopping in a parking place half a block away. With Julio-but it wasn't Julio. It was Tacho. Lupe cursed and turned to look back at the lake, at far distances. It was not Tacho he was angry with, it was Marcos for having the cajones to bring Tacho, when he knew how much that would upset Lupe. Today Lupe only wanted to forget all these bad feelings and memories.

Lupe walked toward them, trying to make the smile. Marcos' smile was large though it was restrained, for he wanted to laugh at all the effort he could see it caused the maestro to be cordial. Tacho stood quietly and solemnly beside Marcos in a levi jacket and brown denims and work boots.

Tacho said to his father, "I didn't come because of anything to do with you and me. I came because I want to do this for the senora, to be one of the three. That's all. I don't want any arguing."

This was all good news to the father, though he knew there was still much time together for something explosive to happen. He vowed to sit in the rear of the boat and say as little as possible.

Tacho accepted his father's nod as agreement, then added, "On the way back, I'll ride in the boat while Gonzalo tows it. I want to see what it's like riding in one of those. I don't have to be back until three o'clock to start getting ready for the dinner. That still gives us plenty of time."

Two golf carts from the fleet at the pier drove these three across the great sand beach toward the distant lake, whose waves on shore could not be heard from the pier. Gonzalo from the barrio was the boatman. His skill was not in guiding his motorized boat, which anyone could do, but in knowing the whims of the lake and its dangerous shallows, where a boat could ground, though the boat were far from land.

The Sun had been up for only an hour and there was still a chill on the lake. Each of the three wore their jackets buttoned. As they climbed aboard Gonzalo's aluminum traveler built for six, he acknowledged each man by his name. He told them how he had moved from Six Corners to Chapala to be closer to his work. Lupe told him they were going to Scorpion Island to purchase a fishing boat from Juan del Lago. With pride Gonzalo told them that Juan del Lago had been a passenger many times in Gonzalo's own ugly commercial aluminio, and they had often talked of the beautiful boats and the secrets of making them.

Lupe sat on the seat nearest Gonzalo's tiller. Marcos sat forward of Lupe, Tacho forward of Marcos. Gonzalo needed only a gentle shove to move his boat over the sand and into water. He pushed until Lupe could feel the boat float free. Gonzalo climbed aboard and took his cushioned seat by the tiller. He was lean and he loved the water like a sailor. He wore a gray baseball cap and set his well-pleased face into the wind and let out on the throttle. The boat moved into the small waves and their frothy little whitecaps.

Quickly they went beyond these waves into water nearly placid and more recognizably blue, but which would everywhere be murky and its bottom unseen. Tacho had put on his baseball hat, and Marcos wore a hat woven from soyate from San Luis Soyatlan, which Lupe had never seen him wear. Then it was Lupe realized that he had forgotten his own very essential hat. Hopefully, they would all be home by noon and hats would not be necessary.

For a long time no one spoke. The motor was loud, but so constant that in a short while it had become a drone that they all disregarded. For more than a kilometer their motor boat stayed within a few hundred meters of the shore. Rounding the point away from Chapala, Lupe saw the shoreline extend far far beyond, but only one little mote of civilization along all that shore.

Lupe felt the peace of the water. He watched the waves moving always away from the boat as the craft churned steadily forward. Scorpion Island, though still small against the immensity of the lake, revealed the stumpy trees and manzanita at its shorelines. Two fishermen far out in the lake seemed hardly moving as they trolled out their nets in the perfect peace of the morning. Cormorants in the distance hovered and then suddenly dove straight down, piercing water; but immediately up and in flight again with the little silvery charales squirming in their beaks. This was how it was in the old days, before the gringos came, before there were boats with motors, before motorcars made their noise and their smoke in the village. Lupe could remember those days well. In that world forever gone there was not even money to trouble them, for they traded everything.

Gonzalo spoke several times to Lupe, little questions about friends in the barrio he had not seen since moving to Chapala. He spoke also about the perfection of the morning; all the previous week fog had lain upon the water in the first hours of day, and hindered the boatmen. Then the two of them grew quiet, and became merely voyagers, regarding the splendor of this sea.

In the front of the boat Marcos and Tacho leaned forward in their seats, staring intently and pleasantly ahead like seaman coming to port. Occasionally they spoke and laughed, but all of it drifted away in the slipstream before Lupe could grasp it. He thanked the Virgin for that blessing. The quiet lake and the birds and the faraway fishermen were the only companions he wanted today.

The boat at last arrived, coming onto the sand at the beach where most of the island's visitor's docked. Two sheds of improvised tin sheets were fifty meters from the water, each without a wall facing the shore. Inside were barrels and boxes and in one of them a cot and a rumpled blanket upon it. Manzanita grew everywhere up the slope, so that the dry earth and these sparse trees gave little hope of life beyond.

The three boat bearers climbed out of the boat, trod only a little in water, then stood upon the beach, looking back at Gonzalo, father and son awkward on either side of Marcos. Gonzalo said, "I'll lie down in my boat, take a little rest. You take your time."

A little trail that had been walked upon for centuries led away from the beach and wound its way through the manzanita and up the slope and away until they could see no more of it. All of them had many times in their lives walked this path to its end, to the Caracola for tacos and beer after the boat ride. Most always Sunday. Most always with a girl.

Today, however, they would take the path rarely taken, which diverged from the main trail about halfway to the Caracola. This narrower trail passed through equally barren ground before coming to a knoll near the center of the island. The narrow trail had almost disappeared when these three climbed the last slope and came to the top. They could see the lake in every direction.

Juan del Lago stood watching them come toward him. Juan wore sailor's denims but no shirt and no shoes. He was thin and his body was firm, though much gray had been in his thick black hair for years. He stood beside the wooden trestles he and his cousin had twenty-seven years ago erected on this spot, replacing another such structure that had stood there for more than fifty years it was said, until it had collapsed from age and decay. Upon the trestle sat a curve prowed boat, seeming to rest on its keel, still uncaulked and unpainted. Juan del Lago stood beside it holding a carpenter's plane. Curled shavings lay at his feet.

All three showed surprise that the boat was not finished. Juan del Lago smiled. "Oh no, senores. This is not your boat. Your boat is there." He pointed to a spot behind the trestles which they could not see. They walked to where he'd pointed and they all saw the beautiful boat. Painted the soft yellow that was the senora's favorite color. It set upon the ground, blocked in place, erect and proud as any of its sister boats gliding the lake. The sheen of the waterproofing was all over it. Two wooden oars lay inside the boat, the paddles at rest on the gunwales. But as they all saw, and everyone had known for centuries, the majesty of this boat was in the long sweep of the prow: onward: upward: away.

Juan saw the reverence in their eyes. He said, "Which one of you is rowing this back? Or are two of you rowing? You're not fishermen, are you?"

Tacho alone of the three was embarrassed to answer. Marcos hesitated, for this talk of warriors was unexpected and for him too were aroused memories and mythologies, for a long while forgotten. Lupe experienced none of these complications and he said, "No one is rowing. We came in a motor launch from Chapala. The launch is going to tow the boat behind us."

Juan del Lago nodded. "If you are not fishermen, that is probably the best way."

Tacho for his sudden little heartache could not let it pass so easily. "How long does it take to row back to Chapala? Or Ajijic?"

Juan del Lago smiled; he recognized the flame igniting. "For who? For you? Or for a fisherman."

"Or a warrior," Tacho said, out of a dim past suddenly recalling the old stories his father had told him, when they would go to the lake and swim and watch the fishermen. These recollections made him smile.

"A fisherman *or* a warrior," spoke Juan del Lago deliberately, "could row to Chapala in two hours from here. Perhaps less. Anyone else it would take a long time, maybe all day."

"But two men could do it faster, I suppose," said Marcos, suddenly becoming cleverer than either of his two compadres, who themselves rarely made mischief.

"Of course," said Juan del Lago. "But even two ordinary men could not go nearly as fast as one fisherman or a warrior. And for two men not used to rowing, this journey to Chapala would be a very hard afternoon's work, if all went *well*."

Tacho eyes returned again and again to the yellow boat they had purchased for Carlotta. In profile the boat's prow came to a rising point that made it seem that the boat was already leaping forward, even where it sat before him on the ground. A foot wide plank fore and aft and in the middle could accommodate three riders. Tacho stood beside the boat. He had been this close to many of these boats, where they had been moored on the beach near the barrio. Yet this one seemed special. Likewise it was a special gift. Yet unborn, since it had not yet been carried to the beach and launched. The sheen of waterproofing seemed like armor. This one, unlike all others Juan del Lago made these days, was not for a fisherman. It was a warrior's boat.

Tacho turned back to the others and said, "I think it's stupid that you're going to tow this boat back. This boat should be rowed back. By someone. By me."

Lupe could have snorted his laughter at this ridiculous enthusiasm, but it would only cause all the bad feelings again, so he kept quiet. Let Juan del Lago do the laughing.

Yet Juan del Lago did not laugh, though he did smile as walked around his trestled boat and went to stand before Tacho. This young warrior in the making looked away from the new yellow boat and to the tanned and lined face of the boat maker. Juan del Lago looked at Tacho and saw the flame flickering in his eyes. The boat maker said, "You may think you're strong enough, but it is a long way. You're not prepared for that. I don't recommend it."

Lupe moved toward Marcos, who was admiring the jointure of the hull. He and Marcos could laugh a little if they turned their backs to the foolish son and the boatmaker, who was putting him in his place. Lupe began to make the joke, until he realized that Marcos was preoccupied with something that might not relate to any of this, and certainly not to Lupe's joke.

Lupe said, "What is it, Marcos?"

Marcos seemed to have lost something. His eyes were faraway, as if recollecting. Then he came back to himself and said to Lupe, "Maestro, I think I've dropped my wallet on the trail. I'm going to hurry back and look and find it. It will just take me a minute. Wait right here till I get back." He was already moving away.

Lupe called after him. "Of course we won't go away. We need you to help carry the boat."

Though he would rather be well separated from the boatmaker and the foolish son, it seemed discourteous, and so Lupe wandered near them, as if with a curious eye to see all the fine details of the boat's craftsmanship.

Tacho thought for a moment about Juan del Lago's recommendation. Something inside the young man could not accept this. He said, "What could go wrong? I could take forever to get there. I might have to sleep all night in the boat. Or I would have to wear both arms in a sling for my wedding."

Lupe was dismayed at the boy's persistence. The father might be permitted to add one other consequence of stupidity. "Or you might fall in the water and drown."

"Yes, that is possible," said Juan del Lago. "If an inexperienced man rows too hard and too long, his body will ache so badly that he will lay down for the sleep, and perhaps sleep into the night. Then he wakes up from an amazing dream in the dark and in his forgetfulness and confusion he walks out of the boat and into the water and that is the end of him. Yes, such things have happened."

Lupe shivered. This was much more horrifying than any of the scenarios he himself had imagined.

Tacho smiled at them both. "Nothing like that would happen to me. I want to do it. I want to."

Juan del Lago laid a hand on his shoulder and smiled. "Then do it, son. Do it. I will stand here and watch you go. If you get a few hundred meters away from shore without turning over the boat, I will burn a little fire for you and you will see the smoke of the old boat maker saluting you."

Lupe watched in further dismay as he saw that Juan del Lago was not making fun of Tacho, but was in fact encouraging him. This was irresponsible. Lupe stepped forward and shook his head. "This is enough. No one is going to row this boat back to Chapala. You're inexperienced, just like he says. Anything could happen. It's far too dangerous. I say absolutely not."

Tacho seemed not to hear him. He looked away from the yellow boat in the direction of Chapala. From this knoll in the middle of the island he could see the smudge of gray far away over the water that he knew was Chapala. Another smudge ten kilometers further up the coast was Ajijic.

Lupe was waiting for some statement of surrendering this stupid idea. He wasn't sure if Tacho's sudden quiet and his staring off across the lake was surrender or not. Life seemed suspended in the silence.

A distant motor started up, then throttled down. A moment later Tacho was the first to see Gonzalo's boat coming out of the landing cove they could not see from the knoll, and onto the lake, making a straight line with full power toward Chapala. Tacho saw Marcos sitting in the middle seat waving at them with his hat. Marcos also yelled words, but these were lost in Gonzalo's revving of the motor and the distances.

Tacho laughed. "That is Marcos and Gonzalo leaving. They're going back to Chapala without us."

Lupe whirled to look that way, for he had heard the distant motor but had thought it merely another innocent sound of the day. Lupe screamed after the boat. "Son of the *devil*, Marcos! What are you doing? You're leaving us here! How do you expect us to get back?"

"How indeed," said a smiling Juan del Lago. "How else but as a passenger in the boat your son is rowing to Chapala? Perhaps he will teach you how to row and you two will get there before nightfall."

To Lupe this was so preposterous that he merely stood with his hands on his hips looking from the stupid smile on his son's face to the boatmaker, who seemed to want to resume his planing, as if this situation were already resolved and were a thing that should cause him no further concern.

But rowing home was out of the question. "No more jokes," demanded Lupe. "Someone else must tow us back then. I'll pay for it. Or we must call to Chapala and have another boatman come for us. And when I get back I'm going to make Marcos regret he did this to me."

Juan del Lago had indeed begun a few soft strokes with the plane, deepening the curve of the prow, but Lupe's exasperation made the boat maker chuckle and he stopped planing. "We are far from civilization, senor. There are no phones on the island. There is only the brothers who cook in the restaurant, and they are still sleeping, I am sure. And even if you could rouse them, they have no motor boat to tow you. So I believe you have only three choices. Swim. Wait for another motor boat to come here, though I see only one or two a week come out here this time of year. The third choice is to let your son row you home, as he has offered."

Lupe could feel the fates aligned against him. He scowled. He kicked a stone that skittered off into dry, bent grasses. He turned away from these two whose silence and calm mocked him. He wandered away from them, wandered around the trestled boat to allow his desperate mind to call up some overlooked something that would solve this unsolvable mess. He cursed and kicked another stone. Yet it slowly settled over him that he was trapped and must submit. He growled. Someone, sometime, somehow would pay for this.

He returned to face his mockers, a beaten man, but his scowl remained. He let it for a moment become a smirk as he said to Tacho, "You're eager now, but I say you will be late for your wedding dinner, and then what a disgrace. Your bride will blame you. Abuelo will say you have shown disrespect to his granddaughter and to his family. All this because you must row a boat."

To Lupe's extreme annoyance, Tacho the irresponsible merely smiled, as if none of these disasters mattered to him. "We still have most of the day. The dinner itself is not until six o'clock. We can make it. Even if you cannot help with the rowing."

Lupe would not say any one of the ten thousand ridicules and profanities that yelped inside him to be uttered. It would be a long day. No doubt a hundred moments would arise that would allow him to laugh and torment his son for this foolishness.

There would even be this little smirk for the boatman himself, who had encouraged the foolishness. "But Juan, since Marcos has run, now *you* will have to help us carry the boat down to the beach."

But the boat maker was immune. "Oh no," he said, with a hint of arrogance, "that is never done. It is bad luck for the boat maker to be one of the bearers. In the spirit world, the bearers are carrying the boat away from the father who made it, that they may give it newborn to the lake, who will be its mother and nurturer. It would profane the spirit of the lake for the boat maker himself to be part of this bringing of the boat to the lake. It would be arrogance, a barbarity."

Lupe would like to spit on the spirit of the lake. His anger surged again. "So what can be done? You say we must row, but there are not even enough of us even to carry the boat."

Juan del Lago smiled again, he who seemed to know everything. "It is possible for two men to carry the boat. In the old days, it was *always* two who carried it. It is only in the weak present days, when no one honors the tradition, that the boats are carried by three."

Tacho with two hands lifted the prow of the yellow boat off the ground, let it carefully down and up in his hands, sensing the heft of it. "It's much lighter than it seems. We could do it, father. It can't be that far to the beach."

"Only two hundred meters," said the smug boat maker. "In the old days it was said that these warriors were so excited to have their new boats in the water, that they would *run* the two hundred meters, even while carrying the boat."

Lupe again could not speak his mind: which was that all these legendary, exuberant warriors could be damned. This damning would be added to the curses that would mutely continue tumbling about inside him for the next long while.

Tacho still held the curved prow in his hands, as if waiting for his father to come for the back end, that their ordeal might begin. Lupe sighed a bitter, bitter acquiescence; yet he vowed to speak no word of it all the day, though it killed him. He walked to the boat's stern. He felt old and achey in his back and hips as he bent to take hold beneath the stern. He lifted and he groaned. It was just as heavy as he'd thought it would be. Tacho held his own end level with his waist, and seemed not so taxed as the father.

"You couldn't get twenty meters like that," said Juan del Lago. "There is only one way to carry it. I show you."

The boat maker went first to Lupe. With ease and grace he lifted the boat away from him and raised the stern over his head. The oars rattled but remained in the boat. He turned Lupe so he faced forward, then placed the boat on his right shoulder. "That's right. You carry on the shoulder, but with the legs." Juan del Lago went to Tacho and took the prow end from him and when Tacho had turned also forward, Juan del Lago placed the keel on Tacho's right shoulder. "Make slow even paces. The foremost bearer must call out to the one behind if there is an obstacle, for the one behind sees trouble too late. I will be watching you when you leave the island. Que les vaya bien, amigos."

Lupe groaned with each of the first twelve steps, though it shamed him. As his legs that bore him up every day carrying cement and bricks now shamed him, for they quivered with every step. He knew if he even stumbled slightly, he would fall and the boat would crush him. His head was so bent and bowed from the weight of the boat on his neck and shoulder that he could not see ahead of him, past Tacho, to see where they were going, or how far away was the shore.

Soon the trail began to decline and immediately the boat felt lighter. Lupe heard some barnyard business behind him and thought to slow, but he feared it would be dangerous to try such a synchronized maneuver involving Tacho. Two goats scampered around them and away down the trail.

The trail leveled and the narrow ridge of the keel bit sharper into his shoulder. Each step seemed to aggravate the pressure. A small boy and girl, each dressed in dirty shorts and tee shirts came running alongside, laughing and asking silly questions. Sweat was soaking into Lupe's shirt. Like a beacon from heaven Tacho said, "We're almost there. The water's just ahead." Lupe's legs held firm. He stared down, always staring down, but in that servant's pose he did see the dirt blessedly become sand and then the sand become wet with water from the blessed lake.

In unison they slowed and stopped. Slowly they lowered the boat to the sand. Lethargic waves hobbled up the beach to within a meter of the elegant prow. Lupe sat heavily on the sand beside the boat and massaged the severely afflicted shoulder and neck. This would pain him for a week. Not yet to speak of what the damned rowing would do to him.

271

Tacho sat on the sand too, and leaned his back against the boat. He could see his father was in no mood for a celebration, but he could not restrain his smile. And must claim the victory. "We did it. Two of us. Like the warriors."

Pain and exhaustion Lupe had ways of combating. This sentimental crap was for boys, and it was not dignified that a grown man even talk about this foolishness. Even to ridicule it. "Well it nearly broke my back, I'll tell you that much. I wonder if forcing someone to work until their health is broken is a crime. I see that in Mexico no one cares about these things."

Tacho bounced to his feet, mocking the old man. "That's enough of sitting around here. We've got to get going. You just get in back and I'll row for a while, until we're way out there and going well."

Lupe would accept that offer. He was suddenly hungry, and at not yet ten in the morning was already tired enough for a long siesta.

Together they glided the boat across the wet sand into water. Tacho pulled the oars free and set the oars into the metal oar locks, paddles to the rear. They walked the boat forward until the water was halfway to their knees. Lupe, as he held on to the gunwale and set himself to climb in, could feel how easily the boat could slip from side to side. A little terror shivered up his spine. It would be so easy to fall out of this boat, easier than he'd imagined.

He took a deep breath and climbed in one leg at a time and fell like a sack of corn into the seat as the boat rocked side to side. Tacho came on with more grace and sat erect on the front plank, facing his father. He took hold of an oar in each hand, gripping them like a fisherman, and he made a few awkward strokes in the water. The boat turned and drifted, till a wave caught it and moved it back toward shore. Lupe restrained his laugh.

But Lupe was fooled, for in a few more moments Tacho seemed to be stroking his oars more assertively, as if suddenly he had figured it out. Prow foremost, the boat moved into the lake. The smudge on the far horizon that was Chapala now reflected whites and yellows from the Sun risen well up into the sky.

Lupe could find no comfortable way to sit on the plank seat without a backrest. He felt the Sun too hot on his neck. He folded up the collar of his jacket, which would be too hot to wear in another hour. A taco would be good. Or eggs and bacon, like Gloria made them. How fabuloso a strong black coffee. "I'm hungry," he said aloud, before he realized he had spoken.

Tacho as he rowed glanced at his father and made a snort of laughter that was unkind. He said, "Warriors fast all the day of their trial. I will eat at the wedding feast."

To Lupe Tacho sounded like he was in a movie, using ridiculous words. Lupe answered him. "I didn't say I *would* eat. I only said I'm hungry. I can't eat when I'm in a boat anyway, it bothers me. I could use a hat though. I left mine at home. But I suppose warriors do not bother about sunstroke."

Tacho slowed in his stroking and shipped the oars paddles forward. He leaned his elbows upon his knees and breathed heavily, but soon he had recovered. Then he saw something far behind his father, and that held his attention. "Look," he said. "The boat maker is sending us a smoke signal. He's saluting us, like he said. That means we are on our way."

Lupe looked back: he saw the smoke twisting up from the center of the island. "That means nothing. He is congratulating us that we have not so far drowned. Ninety-nine percent of the trip is still ahead of us."

Tacho looked severely at his father. "You might be happy to have an adventure, father, at your age. Most of you old guys never leave the house, except to go play pool or drive a car to the market."

Lupe shook his head at the audacity of the young pup. "I have had many adventures, son, and I have survived them all. Trials that are real trials. Not this, rowing a little boat across a lake. That is no trial."

"That may be. But I speak to another thing. I have heard it said that when the man stops having adventures, he grows old and cannot act in emergency, but must then have others act for him."

Lupe would not be fooled by fancy talking. "There are adventures that are not like those in the movies. Adventures that happen inside a man, which no one sees, which are the hardest adventures. These you know nothing about, because you are still too young."

Tacho's edge had returned and he was ready to snap back; but instead he returned to working the oars. He set them in the water and began pulling again, and the boat moved forward again.

In the little silence Lupe let his eyes wander away to the hazy drift of clouds crossing their path. A covey of more than a dozen pelicans flew near but passed on toward the barren shoreline north. With each modest surge of the boat forward Lupe watched the furrows of water slide away from the boat. All in all, a serene morning. The possibility of danger seemed remote, though he still could feel the tiny buzz of anxiety deep down whenever he saw how far they still were from their goal.

Something that was not a furrow rippled in the water. "Dios mio!" called out the father. "It's a snake! Look!" The son looked and smiled. "What a terrible thing," said Lupe, the note of fear audible in his voice. "There are probably hundreds of them in the water. And all poisonous."

"I don't think so, they're harmless," said the son. He continued his methodical rowing, ignoring the snake, as if it were not worth his attention. "We might stop in a while and go swimming, when it gets a little warmer."

Lupe perceived that he was being ridiculed, but he could not help shivering as he imagined himself out of the boat, in the water. Though it fueled the ridicule, he spoke his repugnance. "What a barbarity! Who knows what's in that water, *besides* the snakes? I would *never* go into water that I can't see into. Never. Though I know you're going to tell me that warriors do that all the time. Because they are never afraid of anything."

Tacho turned to look back at his father, unruffled. He would not be baited. "This rowing is hard work. I would like to stand up and stretch and walk around a little."

"Nobody expects you to do all of it yourself. You're lucky I'm the one that came along, and not Marcos. Of course I will row my share. We can switch places whenever you are ready. But please be careful. It would be too easy for one of us to fall in the water."

Shipping the oars forward into the boat, Tacho slowly removed his jacket. He removed his shoes. He set his cap in the angle of the bow. He seemed to be preparing to move aside, that his father might take his place to row.

But suddenly the son jumped from the boat into the placid water, setting the boat to rocking sideways so energetically that Lupe grabbed hold of the sides with each hand and became instantly terrified.

"Tacho! Don't you dare do that! Get back in here! Immediately!" But Tacho had sunk from sight. In the next instant Lupe saw himself alone in the boat, adrift, far far from shore, and nothing to do but hold on for his life and yell. *"Tacho! Tacho! Get back here this minute!"*

Tacho heard nothing because he swam beneath the boat where he'd seen a fleet of silvery charales fleeing. He came up for air and gripped the gunwale near the upswept bow with his hand. "There's charales down there! Hundreds of them!"

Lupe sat back greatly relieved; but not less disturbed. "Tacho, get in this boat right now. Who cares about charales?"

Tacho reached into the bow and took his baseball cap and without explanation sank back into the water again. Lupe groaned. Showing off. Endangering both of them. This time, however, he was less doubtful of

274

Tacho's return. He was right, for soon Tacho burst head and shoulders out of water, holding up his baseball cap, shut into a bag by both hands. He shook the water from his shining black hair that whipped around his face. Then he hurled the cap and its contents into the boat toward his father.

Many, many silver charales flopped and squirmed at Lupe's feet. This so shocked him that he tumbled back on his plank seat and would have fallen on his back, had he not grabbed hold with both hands to the gunwale. The boat rocked back and forth severely. As Tacho hoisted himself aboard, it rocked even more, and Lupe closed his eyes so he would not see himself falling into water and drowning.

But soon the boat steadied again and Lupe opened his eyes. Tacho sat on the plank seat facing him, all of him soaked and dripping water so much that now there were puddles of water on the boat's bottom. Lupe's shoes were in it.

Tacho was grasping on the floor to capture one of the elusive charales. At last he did. Smiling and dripping water from his hair, Tacho offered the fish in his fist to his father.

"No!" cried out Lupe. "Of course not! What would I want with one of those things?"

"You said you were hungry. This is good food."

"Of course not! I'm a grown man, I can wait until dinnertime. I can even wait until tomorrow if I have to. You eat the thing."

Tacho was so soaked that he looked like a creature of the water anyway. His smile brightened. He said, "Yes I will." He held the desperate charale by the head between two fingers. He set the wild tail of the thing in his mouth and bit down, teeth severing the body from the head, which he then tossed over his shoulder into the water. He chewed methodically, enjoying the meal, or so it seemed.

Lupe was horrified. Then the horror lessened rapidly as he realized that no doubt Tacho had done this stunt to shock him. He shook his head to give his son at least that measure of his disgust.

Tacho said, "That was good. A little salty too. But one isn't much of a meal." He reached down and grasped another one and put it as before in his mouth and chewed off the body, and flipped away the head. Then the same with several more till there was only one uneaten. He smiled seeing his father's disapproval. "We have to do this. We're warriors. We eat what is provided. We go to the end of the path. The smoke on the island is watching over us." The smoke still seemed not far away; Chapala so very, very far away.

Lupe showed him all his disbelief. "Where did you hear all this warrior stuff, anyway? Or is that what they put in comic books these days-warrior stuff? It's not on TV, is it? Or maybe it's only on the American channels."

Tacho would not be baited, nor need he be, for the son was now a mystery to his father, which put him beyond the need of confrontation. With a sly smile Tacho said, "I don't know where I get it. Maybe it comes out of the air from the Indians. They are the ones who spread all those stories, aren't they? But hey-the *first* time I heard about warriors was from *you*. You *must* remember that. Or maybe you have forgotten. Maybe you have. We would go to the beach, you and I, we did that almost everyday. I remember those afternoons well. I always loved the boats. Loved seeing them out there with the fisherman, pulling on their nets. So I asked you a lot of questions. And you told me how they made the boats, and you told me about the fishermen, and about the warriors, who had not existed for a long time. You were the one that told me something I've never forgotten. That the spirit in the lake goes inside a man and that is what makes him a warrior, the spirit of the lake going into him. Those were great stories. I think I must have forgotten about all those conversations we had while I was in California. But today, coming out here for the boat, is bringing it all back to me so much that it's amazing me, to tell you the truth. Also, remember, today is my last day as a single man. So, who knows what's making me do things?"

Lupe blushed to be reminded of all those long ago days together on the beach. Wonderful moments. But horribly inappropriate now. "Back then I was only telling good stories. I was never meaning that someone should go off pretending to be a warrior. You don't think warriors just rowed boats all around the lake every day, do you?"

Lupe was unsure how much of this thing of warriors might be contrived to get the father off the track, or to shock the father, the favorite pastime of older children. He changed the subject. "I don't care what you do, as long as you don't get in the water again. That scared the shit out of me. And you almost tipped the boat over getting back in. You let me row for a while. What would you know about rowing? When I was younger, Marcos' father Jorge had a little aluminum rowboat, and we rowed every day. You weren't even born then."

Tacho leaned away so that Lupe could slip forward past him. Tacho then eased himself back to the rear seat plank and sat on the bottom as his father had done, his back against the seat. Water from his clothes puddled around him. He pulled off his wet shirt and laid it across the stern to dry. He leaned his head back to the Sun; he closed his eyes.

Lupe gripped the oar handles, and felt how they pivoted in the oar locks. He was letting it come back to him. In truth it had been fifteen years since he had rowed a boat. The times rowing with Marcos' father were ten years before that. He had also been watching Tacho, and he saw and could remember how important was the rhythm of the stroking. Slow and easy. It was a long way to go. He set the paddles deep in the water. He leaned back and pulled, pulled, and came to the rest. It was all coming back to him.

Tacho seemed dozing. Well it was; then the father might have time to recall his skills without the comments of the son. Lupe could see the thin smoke still rising from the island. The island was exactly behind the stern; no doubt Tacho had used it for a guide. Lupe looked over his shoulder, to see that the bow pointed to Chapala, still so small on the horizon. He turned back, better he not have to look at that great distance. He dipped the paddles and pulled back hard. Rest a count of one, two. Then dip and pull hard again. Over and over. They must do it all day long, if they wanted to get home.

After ten or twelve pulls, Lupe had to rest a little extra, a count of twenty or twenty-five. As little wearinesses became soreness, which would become aches and then worse, Lupe more and more profoundly realized how brutalized his body would be going so far. Soon a worse worry troubled him, that both their bodies would become so brutalized they would *not* make it that far. From where he still lay in the Sun with eyes closed Tacho said, "It's a great day for rowing. Not too hot. I feel a little breeze coming up too."

"Yes, these are good things to be thinking while you rest. Make a *good* rest. Because we have much, much work to do. Aren't you now ashamed of yourself, bragging how you were going to row all this way alone? Now you can see how impossible that was."

"I could have done it. It would have taken me a longer time, but still I would do it."

"And you would be a cripple the rest of your life. Admit it."

"A warrior admits nothing. He acts, and that speaks for him."

"Donkey shit, my son. This is making an old man of me. All in one day. All because you forced this stupidity upon me."

Tacho had placed the baseball cap over his face, and so he spoke without being seen. "Not I who forced you to come. It was Marcos. I was doing this alone, for myself, no matter what."

Lupe could only speak after finishing a pull, at the brief rest. "You can say all these things, but you made all this happen, and you are the one I will talk to about it as the one responsible."

277

"Alright then, talk. Even if it was only by accident, you're lucky you're on this journey with me. It's the day of the warrior's journey, and here you are."

Lupe snorted. "It's the day of the sufferer, and here I am."

Both father and son each sensed they best retreat from this skirmish and they relaxed into a mutual silence. As Lupe labored in his pulls with the oars, he came to his rest each time with an "Oooff" that seemed more the groan of his entire body than of his voice works.

Tacho for a while passed into sleep, lulled by the repetitive forward surge of the boat. In that time Lupe rowed and rowed until the aches in his arms and shoulders throbbed, and then gradually grew numb. Still he rowed, for there could be no stopping. Eventually the numbing made him not feel the aches; it seemed a strange immunity to receive from pain.

He tried not to look at the smoke still rising from the island, which rose very thinly now, farther and farther away. He rested a moment looking, trying to comprehend how far they had come. He really could not. He drew in a deep breath and he forced his fingers to release the oar handles, and it seemed like flexing bone. His right hand was especially pained as he extended its fingers. Suddenly a violent spasm in his forearm spread like a steel claw through his wrist and seized his hand till the hand clenched like a cripple's. He screamed like he'd been bitten by a snake.

Tacho jerked himself awake, and saw his father with one hand trying to shake the other hand, a hand that looked to be broken by torture. Lupe cried out, "Aieee! It's a cramp! A terrible cramp!" Tacho raised up and sat on the plank seat nearer his father and leaned closer. "Maybe I could massage it."

"No! That would be worse. This shaking is helping it. It's starting to relax now. Oowee- this is a bad one."

"You move back here and rest for a while." Tacho looked back at the smaller island, and forward to the slightly bigger Chapala. "Hey, you did well, father, we're way out here now. I'll take it all the rest of the way."

"Hah! You'll be worn out in fifteen minutes." Tacho smiled and let that pass. His father reseated himself in the stern, careful with the limp, still aching hand.

Tacho resumed the rowing. He hummed a little song Lupe recognized from the radio. Tacho seemed happy, though he said, "I don't know if I am ready to be married. There is so much responsibility."

Lupe snorted. "Till you are married you have the carefree life of a child. After marrying, you are buried under responsibilities that never end. You are right to have a dread."

"It's not Dahlia. She's perfect for me. It's having to provide all the things that will be necessary. And then when there are children, there will be even more things necessary. I wish we could have waited a little longer."

"Hah!" Lupe blurted, recalling his middle of the night rescue adventure. "I could say that these things have a way of sneaking up on the young and foolish. But I am an old man who has failed at marriage, so what do I know? And who would listen to me if I did know something anyway?"

"Do you really believe you failed at marriage?"

"Of course I believe that. It is the truth. You of all should know that. Sad to say, I was even more irresponsible when I was married than you are. As I see it now, I was doomed to fail." Lupe had plunged into these introspections without considering where they would inevitably lead. Now as he regarded the ugly landscapes of that past, he became sullen and waited for the subject to die of inattention. Tacho seemed to sense the dangerous possibilities here too, and for the moment said no more.

In that pregnant silence Lupe felt a fat blob of remorse struggle free of the muck it had been buried in for more than a decade. He felt the remorse as a dormant, blind creature which had briefly awoken and sensed that there might be air to breathe, a spot of light somewhere. Though the words nearly strangled themselves in his throat, Lupe spoke them, though timidly. "I am truly sorry for all the suffering I caused your mother. And you children. I would give anything that it had never been that way."

Lupe knew he had no right, and he did not expect it, but nonetheless he hoped that Tacho would say something, even the smallest kindness. Yet Tacho seemed to be deeply engrossed in the rowing, bending to it and pulling back with such energy that his eyes stayed closed, his mouth set firm. Lupe's timid words drifted away as if no one had wanted them or needed them.

Then so be it, spoke the maestro to himself. No one owes anyone anything. A moment later, however, a few other shaky words escaped him, brothers to the others. "How is your mother? You never say. I hope she is well. I truly do."

Tacho still rowed. Yet now he opened his eyes and looked at his father, allowing himself the smallest smile. "Yes, she's well. She has many friends. She likes the life in California. She has a good job."

Lupe waited for more, like a thirsty wanderer who'd been given a thimble of water after twelve long years crawling in the desert. But Tacho offered no more, and Lupe felt shy of coaxing him. So the two relapsed again into silence. Lupe laid back and let his hand dangle over the side into the slipstream of water that cooled it, soothed it, as nothing else would. He closed his eyes.

The Earth's turning had positioned the Sun at its zenith. The end of February. A clear warm day. In the afternoon in the middle of the lake it would be hot . Tacho allowed the morning excitement of the adventure to fill him again, and that gave him strength to row. He hummed a peppy song that reminded him of daring and victory. Happily, the song's rhythm was in perfect accord with the rhythm of his rowing. The boat moved ahead at good speed. His bride waited to greet him at his wedding dinner. This day, the last day of his freedom. Aieeee.

As he rowed he watched the blue sky and the random drift of low clouds. He watched the thin line of shore where life was too small to be seen. He watched the water to see the carp jumping for flies, though he rarely saw more than a tail splash as the carp submerged. He would count the fish jumping, to ten, and then start over from one.

However, his eyes returned most constantly to the thinner and thinner spire of smoke that still rose from the island. They were still watched. While he hummed his happy song, and kept his rhythm, and drew energy from the rising smoke, the boat moved steadily on. It seemed to Tacho that now his strength and skill and endurance were greater than before, and he believed that he could row them all the way to Chapala by himself.

But soon he saw how wrong he was, for his shoulders and arms rapidly grew weary, then achey, with fatigue. His body seemed to row automatically, with its own momentum, and even when he thought of stopping to rest, his body seemed unable to stop, seemed only able to go on, and on, and on. But eventually the aches became sharp pains first in his forearms, then in his biceps. There was indeed a limit. He stopped rowing.

Lupe expected it. "That's enough for you, son. You get back here. I'm good enough to row for a while. I was just fooling you with that cramped hand. So I could sneak a little breather. But I'm ready to go now."

Tacho gave a silent blessing, for he had believed his father unable to row anymore that day. Tacho lay back, eyes closed, his mind drifting to images of Dahlia. For all the day he had forced himself to focus on his rowing, on the rising smoke, on bringing the boat home. He had warded off all thoughts of the woman he would marry the next day. Now he imagined the boat at last coming onto the beach of Chapala. He had all day imagined Marcos and Felipe there, and many of the others too, laughing at them and making jokes. But now as he lay back, he imagined the scene and he also saw Dahlia there. In her wedding dress, fussing, urging him to hurry back to

Abuelo's house, where it was safe. That pleased him as well, to see his little darling so worried.

He spoke aloud before he knew it, and when he heard the words he was unsure to whom he had spoken them. "Getting married scares me a little. It's so serious."

Lupe had made several pulls on the oars and was feeling the rhythm of the routine again. "The responsibility of marriage is exactly as we are doing today, Tacho. Marriage is exactly like this rowing. You must do it over and over and over again until it hurts. You cannot stop, ever, or the boat and its passengers will stop. Then they will all be in danger, and you and the crew who depend on you will not survive. The rowing will be your job and yours alone. You must row. Every day. All day. Yes, there is a lot about marriage to be scared of."

"I'm afraid that when I'm married I will never have time to do something crazy like this. I'm also afraid that if I am married long enough, I will never *want* to do something crazy like this."

Lupe enjoyed this conversation. "Yes, and I am a living example of exactly that. You see how much I didn't want to do this rowing. Even though I am not still married, I had so many years of it before your mother left me, that I grew to think like a married man, even though I was not. You see how routine my life is with sister Magdalena. So even though I can see how excited you are to be doing these warrior things, and even though I am here with you, doing the same things you are doing, I still wish I was home, in my best chair, watching television."

Tacho's soul trembled and he closed his eyes again, that he might more intensely feel the Sun upon his face, feel the water gliding by, feel the breeze in his hair. Eyes shaded by his cap, he said to his father, "We're over half way you know. Isn't it great?"

Lupe rowed no more than a few more minutes until he felt the pain returning to his afflicted hand. His arms and shoulders and back were sore, but he was sure they could do their part in the rowing for a good while. But the hand was soon throbbing, and he began to feel his grip on the oar handle slipping. He tried to ignore it, to keep rowing and hope the pain would numb itself, or pass up his arm. He ground his teeth.

Despite everything, a terrible spasm of pain stabbed into his hand, causing him to cry out. At the same time his hand, with a mind of its own flailed out, and in doing so dislodged the oar and the oarlock from its mooring in the right gunwale. In horror Lupe watched the oarlock and the oar fall away into the water and slip out of sight forever. Lupe shrieked.

The horrible cry made Tacho's skin crawl. He jumped up and thought at first it was only his father's hand again in torment. But he also saw that his father was craning madly over the side. Something had been lost. Tacho then saw that the oarlock and the oar were gone.

For a moment he was certain they were doomed as he felt a great sob of terror swell up into his throat, choking him. He too leaned to look over the side, even though it tipped the boat severely. The boat still moved ahead, though it had slowed, and it was no doubt the oar was irretrievable. Tacho sat back and drew his father back in as well. They sat there a moment in the midst of their misery to decide what might be done to rectify this apparent disaster. Neither mind was capable. Both mumbled words that the other did not hear, words which were without meaning or value anyway.

Lupe had lost the use of his hand, and therefore of his arm, so it was a certainty that he would row no more.

Yet out of their darkness Tacho suddenly saw what might be done. The only thing that might be done. He climbed into the foremost seat in the bow of the boat, and he pulled the lone remaining oar free of its oarlock. He held the oar in both hands, his one hand near the paddle, his other hand high up, so that he might sweep it to one side, then the other, like an Indian paddling a canoe. It was awkward, at first, not only passing the oar back to the other side, but also lifting it so it cleared both the gunwales. He also must quickly get used to changing his hand position from right side to the left. Yes, he must and he did, and after several unproductive moments Tacho was able to turn the prow toward Chapala and the boat was moving ahead again. Not with the surge of before, when they'd used two oars, but at least they were moving.

Lupe wanted to cry for the happiness of this miracle of grace. "Tacho, this is amazing! I would never have thought of that!"

Tacho's back was to his father now as he rowed, and so he could smile without revealing the satisfaction that other's confession gave him. This Indian rowing was inefficient and it would tire him out just as badly as the other, but for the moment the novelty of it and the thrill of escaping what had seemed a disaster filled him with a heady energy.

Lupe lay back in the stern and closed his eyes to rest. He knew his hand would not be well enough for him to row again, barring some miraculous recovery. He knew it must be the son who brought them in.

Though there was a soreness in his body that seemed as if it would be permanent, Tacho felt an exhilaration he had not known all day. His back must now be turned to the rising smoke from the island, and he could not look at it anymore for encouragement. However, he did not need it. He faced home.

The lineaments of Chapala were large enough for him to make out the biggest buildings and he could name them. The spires of the cathedral were prominent. Tacho breathed in deeply as he rowed. It seemed to him more than air that he breathed, for something rarer still seemed to hover in the air around him. With each breathing in of that rarified something he felt the power fill him: power to dig the oar deep in the water, swing the oar to the other side and dig deep again, and then deep again.

Tacho rowed on rejuvenated. His new position and the new way he swung the oars seemed to use new muscles; or used the tired muscles in new ways, so that he felt himself rowing with fresh energy. Also sadly unmistakable to him was that for all the effort of the rowing, the boat moved ahead much slower than in the old way of rowing. So be it. Endurance would be all.

Tacho rowed on for longer than Lupe thought his son could possibly row, and still he rowed. And what would they do if he should fail? He wouldn't think of it. The Earth's turn had moved the Sun ahead of them now and they rowed nearly into it. Lupe had removed his own shirt and laid it partially over his face for shade. It was a winter Sun, now low in the sky. There would only be two hours till the earth's turning moved it below the horizon and the night began.

Lupe rested in the stern, still coddling his strangled right hand in the palm of his left hand. He could see on the faraway shoreline of Chapala more landmarks he recognized.

Lupe spoke to encourage rather than to converse. "Do you think those cabrones will be on the beach waiting for us to come in?"

When Tacho had come to his periodic rest, he turned, twisting his body above the waist, that he might stretch as well as he could. When he did he looked to his father. "Of course they will be there. But I hope Dahlia will not be. I hope she doesn't know anything about this. She thinks we towed the boat back. She probably thinks I'm home now getting dressed. If she is at the beach, it would be bad. I hope she doesn't know anything."

Neither man spoke the dark thought that was mutual to them both, another alternative, that they would not make it at all.

"Tacho, you are already beginning to think and talk like a married man. You are already doomed. You notice I live as a bachelor with my sister. A good arrangement. I am a free man again, and that is something to be proud of. But it comes too late, because now I only want to sit home and take it easy. But for you! This being a free man is something worth having."

Tacho smiled. "Pues, I'm trying to make the most of it. I've got a few hours left. But I'm so tired I may fall asleep at the wedding."

"I already see how it will be. Abuelo will blame me for causing you to row this boat today. As if he doesn't already dislike me enough."

Tacho turned forward, ready to resume rowing. But he spoke over his shoulder. "Abuelo doesn't hate you. His grandsons and nephews always speak well of you. He knows what you have become. And the truth is, he is a kind man, even if he does remember old grievances. Which he still does."

The rest seemed not to have recovered Tacho's energies as the other rests had recently done. As Lupe watched his son row on again, he could tell both by the slower rhythm of the strokes and the perceptible slowing of the boat, that Tacho must have little energy left to him. Still several kilometers to go.

Lupe called to him, "What will be for the dinner? I suppose everything. Does Abuelo still cook up the venison for these banquets?"

"Oh yes," Tacho called back, without turning around, though he did hesitate in his rowing to answer, to give himself a little pause. "Venison and all of it. He'll probably have ten kinds of meat."

"Does he still bring in the mariachis? Or do the young ones make him have marimbas? Or worse, the electric guitars."

Tacho enjoyed a reflection, and shared it. "It will probably be mariachis. But Dahlia and her friends almost persuaded him to have a rock 'n' roll band." But now he must turn back and row on again, while these several pleasant images thus aroused lingered in his imagination. He rowed on.

Lupe continued with questions and opinions about the great banquet. Both father and son knew that the rower must give all that was in him to the rowing, and that he could not respond, except at rare resting intervals, and perhaps not even then. Lupe also talked about the songs on the radio at the job site, and the arguments between the maestros and the peons over what radio station would be listened to. No doubt Tacho had come to prefer the American songs more than the musica mexicana.

When Tacho looked toward Chapala he could no longer judge the distance, for his eyes were blurry with sweat. And still Tacho rowed on, though the boat now progressed slowly.

Watching his son struggling so valiantly, Lupe was moved to be humble and generous. "I was wrong in my opinions about warriors, Tacho. I must admit it. You have proven me wrong. You did just what you said you could do."

Tacho's rowing was slowing down rapidly. The Sun was near the horizon beyond Jocotepec and late winter twilight had begun to soften the lines and dull the colors everywhere. Chapala's landscape was now in shadow. Lupe could see the shapes of houses, windows. He could see specks on the beach that must be people. Who knew how far away?

Lupe laid his head near the gunwale, so he might for a while see the water passing beside the boat as the furrows went away. It was very soothing to watch.

But *something* darted up at him out of the water: the head of a snake rising only centimeters away and Lupe screamed. *"Aieeeee!"*

As weak as Tacho was now manipulating his oar, his father's cry of terror chilled the son's blood and crippled for one instant his body, recoiling in shock terror of its own. His arms and hands spasmed. The oar slipped from his grip and floated quickly away sternward.

The same instant Lupe leaped forward after the oar, but he grasped only air and water as the swift oar drifted quickly past him astern and away.

Terrified of the water though he was, and as futile as the effort would be, Lupe jumped overboard after the oar and disappeared underwater for several seconds, a poor swimmer at best. Quickly he came up gasping for air and flailing his arms as if he were terrified of drowning, which indeed he was. Beneath water, his legs thrashed for their lives, until suddenly his toe touched mud: firm mud that his other foot too could stand upon.

In astonishment Lupe stood erect, water lapping on his chest. He lifted his head out of water, then reached for the boat that still floated freely beside him. He realized their amazing new situation and he yelled for joy, *"Aieee!"*

This sad fact of Lake Chapala would be their salvation: that in some of her shallower embarrassments she was only a few feet deep, and that even sometimes a mile or more from the shorelines.

Tacho leaned his head out to see what his father had done. He expected disaster.

But he saw the miracle of his father standing up, head out of water, and he too realized that they were closer to shore than he'd dared to hope.

"Aieee!" Lupe cried out again, for he felt as if he had been delivered from hell. "No more rowing! That is the beauty of this. It is only my hand that is ruined. My legs are still good. I will *tow* us home!"

In prayerful expectation Tacho watched Lupe unwind the docking rope from its stanchions and wrap the end several times around his fist. The maestro walked three strides through heavy water toward Chapala as the line grew taut, stopping him. Then he moved forward with more effort of his big thighs and calves, and reluctantly the boat followed after him.

"*Aieee!*" cried out Tacho, shaking his own aching fist into the air in celebration. Their speed was slower than any rowing, but the boat moved ahead. Even so, with every step Lupe took, the disgusting mud sucked up over his shoes with every stride. To Tacho watching, his father looked like a plodding, mythical creature. Yet behind him, the boat moved forward, itself an obedient, though unhurried servant.

Even so it was the pace of earthworms. The wretchedness of the mud with every step also was a psychological burden, for Lupe constantly must fend off images of ghastly creatures who lived in the mud crawling up his pants leg. The colder water of the lake too he had underestimated. Especially now as the evening came on, a late winter evening. He forged ahead. Little lights from the shoreline began to twinkle on as the darkness settled over him.

Suddenly Tacho heard a gasp from his father and then saw him fall forward and disappear in the water. A mighty surge of adrenalin rushed through Tacho's body and without knowing how Tacho leaped over the gunwale and into the chilly water of the lake.

Arms ached but he would not notice it. He swam like a desperate beginner to the spot where his father had gone down, and he dove and immediately found a flailing arm and grabbed it and jerked it toward him. Both father and son now could stand on the firm but muddy bottom again and they rose out of water gasping for air. Tacho pulled on the rope that was still in his father's hand and drew the boat to them. Both grabbed for the gunwale and held on until their breaths were recovered.

"Ay caray!" spoke Lupe at last. "I thought I was drowned! I don't know if I fell in a hole, or if my feet just slipped from under me." The water lapped to the middle of their bellies.

Tacho said, "I think I can do the towing now. My legs feel strong enough. You get in the boat, it's my turn."

"Oh no," said the father. "We both tow. Then one can catch the other if he falls. Or we both drown together." He held the rope up in his fist. Tacho unwound the second docking rope from its stanchion and unfurled it.

He said, "I'm going to tie this around my waist. It will be easier to pull that way, I won't have to use my hands."

"Good idea," said his father, happy to hear all this agreement.

They plodded on, slowly. It was dark now, and no Moon in the sky, and they could barely see the surface of the water in front of them. For both, this created the illusion that they were plodding on through a dark infinite space where, despite the great effort of each muddy step, they were making no headway.

Lupe fixed his eyes on the only sight there was in the weary darkness, the lights of Chapala. He knew which came from the beer garden, which from the upper floors of the Nido Hotel, which from the Azteca restaurant near the cathedral. He marched toward these lights like a burdened sloth, and prayed to them. As the ache in his legs increased he remembered a peppy mariachi tune from the morning radio, and he began singing the innocent words. Each chorus ended with the call of the desperate lover to his girlfriend waiting at the window.

He said to Tacho, "I know you don't like those mariachi songs, but they are the only ones I know."

Though he was nearly too tired to speak, Tacho nonetheless answered. "It sounds great right now. Just great." And when Lupe took up the verses and chorus again, Tacho sang it with him. Though he fumbled through some of the phrases, those last notes of the chorus were contagious and he sang it with all the gusto that remained to him. "Ay, ay, ay, cara mia, mia!"

They hardly noticed the water becoming shallower, only that their steps were having less resistance, until eventually they felt the water only up to their waists. Flutters of new energy roused them to walk faster, though it seemed they were then more prone to stumbling. The lights just beyond the shore were brighter and beckoning. They spoke not a word of it to each other, but both felt certain now that they would make it. Though they might pass out on the beach and sleep till the next morning.

The water lowered to mid-thigh, and then to their knees. Each step was easier and easier, and the father and son sang out ever more loudly the mariachi song of the anguished lover. Neither looked back to see the boat, for it was no use in the darkness; yet it followed faithfully. Nothing now could stop them as these two side by side struggled forward, slipping occasionally, but always again forward, forward, the happy lights waiting for them. Cara mia, mia.

Like two shipwrecked sailors coming at last to shore in a new world, the father and son stumbled out of the water at last. The boat by then dragged in the sand, so that with the last effort that was left in their bodies they must haul the boat forward out of the water until it settled serenely on the beach, which seemed as dark and desolate as the night before the dawn of time.

Home at last, the agonizing muscles of their legs refused to support them any longer, and both men fell onto the beach and groaned with the first recognition of the great pain throughout their bodies that would plague them for several days to come.

As they both lay there side by side, the water draining from their clothes and bodies into the sand, and the sand clotting their clothes, they panted still and waited, though it be forever, for their breathing to become normal. They waited also for a long, well-earned sleep that was all that mattered now.

But that was not to be, for soon each one heard noises from further up the beach, excited voices scattering this way and that in the night. Lupe looked that way, though it mattered little to him whatever it might be. He saw sabers of light slicing the darkness, that way and this. Flashlights. Someone hurrying, not caring where the light shone. Several wavering lights, several hurrying in their direction. He heard distinctly words, perhaps familiar voices.

When one of these lights swiped across them, Tacho also looked up and watched what seemed to be coming at them with so much hurry. Someone called out, "Yes, it's them! There's the boat! It's them!" Both father and son knew it was Marcos who had spoken.

In a minute more the flashlights were all pointed at them, illuminating their two sad bodies that seemed to have been flung upon the beach, perhaps mangled and broken: for even though so many flashlights shone upon them and jubilant friends called out to them, still the two bodies hardly moved in response.

Marcos was the first to reach them and he kneeled and shook the shoulder of each one, until both father and son had nodded to acknowledge that they were indeed alive. Weak as he was, Lupe would not be deprived of the curse he had all day been nursing, so that Marcos would have the full menace of it. "I will get you for this one day, Marcos. One day. I will leave you someday in the middle of the desert without water and let you walk alone a thousand kilometers."

Marcos laughed, relieved that his compadre had so much spunk left in him. "You may do it, maestro. I will deserve it. But what took you so long? I've been waiting with the boys since the middle of the afternoon."

Several of the Romero brothers and cousins stood beside them also, joking and taunting them. Felipe Romero especially was enjoyed the spectacle. "Maestro, I thought you hated the water! What a day this must have been for you. I suppose you'll tell us you're going to become a fisherman, now that you've learned so well how to handle these boats."

288

Slower than these most eager ones, other figures approached, also with flashlights. To Lupe's chagrin, he saw that one of them was Abuelo, dressed in a fine suit and fine shoes, hardly fit for the beach, but no doubt perfect for a wedding dinner. Lupe tried to lift at least his upper body from the sand so that he might address the formidable old man, but it was a feeble effort. He spoke anyway. "It was my fault, Abuelo. I dared Tacho to row the boat from Scorpion Island. I confess it."

Abuelo stood over him, partially illuminated. He laughed. "You are a terrible liar, maestro. I already know the truth from my sons and nephews. It is Tacho who thought he was big enough to become a warrior."

Arriving the last, but the most apprehensive, was Dahlia, who hurried with her own flashlight pointed at the fallen body of her husband to be. "Oh Tacho! Are you alright? Is he alright, Abuelo?" Though she wore a fine dress, she sank to her knees beside him and brushed the hair away from his face, forever handsome in spite of all the grime upon him.

He smiled at her as he said, "I'm sorry we're late for the dinner."

She sat back, allowing the displeasure she had rehearsed all afternoon to fly out of her. "Oh you had everyone so worried! What a terrible thing to do, frightening everyone like that, especially me. I hope you will apologize. And you must promise never to do anything so crazy again in all the time that we will be married."

Tacho smiled at all her loveliness, but he also turned to look at his father, and he said to him, "Didn't I tell you? It is just as I knew it would be. This was my last adventure."

The father smiled in return. "Oh you never know. Look at me, old enough to be a grandfather. And what did I get trapped into today?"

Then Abuelo spoke again. "Alright, we have all had our fun. But, as the groom has so rightly spoken, we are all late for the dinner. So boys, help get these sad cases onto their feet, and bring them to the house, even if we have to drag them. We'll have to clean them up a little, and perhaps prop them in the chairs through all the evening, but we will do it."

Then he leaned down to take Lupe's arm and begin helping him to stand. "Come, Don Lupe, the night is not yet over. You must come to dinner and sit in the chair beside me and tell me everything that happened today that made you two pitiful boatmen take all the day to row from Scorpion Island. Why in my day, we knew all about the warriors, and one of us could make that journey in the time between breakfast and lunch."

25 MAX GOES DOWN

Winter in the Mexican highlands, when lives are lived intensely, may seem only the briefest of seasons. All winter flowers could be seen to bloom on the lakeshore and upon the hillsides as well, for the chill of the highlands could not entirely subdue them. As the Sun rove higher in the sky each day, the deep earth warmed, and quickened to life seeds and bulbs and roots, and the brilliant profusion that is Mexico, so briefly dormant, came forth again. Little gusts in the afternoons whipped and spun over the lake, and along the cobblestone streets of the village; it tossed skirt hems, it blew off sombreros.

It had also been half a year since the last rain, and the lake was reduced and withdrawn again from the shores and the life of the community; and still two more months till the blessed rains would come again. Before they did, dust from the hills and the beaches would be in the streets and sidewalks and in the air. Days would be hot. Cicadas would be heard all day winding up the engine of their cry, at first like a ratcheting that might be mistaken for something truly mechanical by one who'd never heard it; until it became at last a siren, some alien creature desperate, wailing in and out of frequency with power enough to broadcast its cry for rain for miles and miles.

But not yet, for it was spring, and to everyone who breathed in these airs of rebirth, it seemed that it had always been spring. The cicadas still had long to sleep. And everything once again might yet be renewed. Or at least lives might be dismantled and reconsidered, if that was all their geniis could contrive.

And so it was that spring morning that Max and Carlotta carried boxes and furniture from the little house that had been the Bellacasa offices these nearly three years. They had packed all this inside the Dodge Caravan and in the bed of the blue Chevy, and still they returned to carry out more. Virginia wandered back and forth with them, sometimes carrying and loading, sometimes merely talking. In a black rayon jumpsuit with white blouse she seemed misdressed for the work.

Carlotta had just settled a last box of files into the corner of the van, when Max arrived with another last one, and settled his. Carlotta wore gray-green pants and sleeveless blouse of minute yellow roses, and her boots. Max wore a dark green tee shirt and beige denims without belt, and his Y-thong huaraches. He sat beside Carlotta in the cargo doorway for a moment's rest. She told him what was on her mind. "Virginia wants to keep it a secret, so don't say anything please, but she's about to be engaged."

Virginia the bespoken came that moment out the front door, carrying two mops and two buckets. Carlotta said to her, "I told Max about your gentleman, Virginia. When's the big day going to be?"

Virginia blushed as she neared them, but she spoke as if anyone might know. "Oh that. Well yes, but it hasn't happened yet. We've gone out, oh, and we've gone to Mexico City. Yes, I like him very much. But, oh! His children, Max! For nothing in the world do they want their papa marrying again. And you know, they are all grown and married themselves, but they are still all making such scenes! Yes, I like him, but I'm beginning to wonder if it will not be too much trouble I'm marrying."

Max grinned for other reasons. "This is going to be a blow to maestro Lupe, Virginia. Maybe we shouldn't tell him till you've moved away."

Carlotta laughed. "Lupe? What about Jim Penton? No—they won't like it at all."

Virginia tried to smile around her embarrassment at these old jokes, but she couldn't for a moment look at them. Then she could and she said, "But I suppose it still may happen. I do like the man. He would want us to live in Guadalajara. I would miss seeing you two."

Carlotta would miss it too. But it was spring, after all. And young ladies' fancies were taken. "I hope you do get married. You've been living alone too long."

Virgina could smile, well knowing the lonely truth. Too long. "I hope it happens too, to tell you the truth. It's nice to have somebody to stay up late with."

Carlotta was reminded of another romance. "You remember Rebecca Allen, Virginia? Polly Allen's daughter? She's getting married too. I just got the invitation. She's going to have the wedding in Ajijic. She wants to invite half the town it sounds like. She says her mother won't speak to her and says she won't attend. The wedding's next week. Her father's paying for a big reception at the Nueva Posada. We're all invited."

Virginia laughed. "Oh yes! I remember Rebecca's friend. The chubby little lady that looked like Polly. Oh won't *that* be the talk of the town."

Carlotta saw Lupe's Cadillac of all problems round the corner at the end of their street and rattle and sputter coming toward them. Soon she could see the cheery face of maestro Lupe through the dusty windshield.

She shook her head and turned to Max. "That poor car is about ready to die, just listen to it. I've made up my mind to give him the Chevy pickup. Somehow that seems like its true destiny."

He said, "I'm all for it." He snorted: a morbid amusement. "I can't see that *we* will be needing it much from now on."

Carlotta ignored the sad note and said, "I'm glad you feel that way. I want him to have it."

Instead of parking Lupe drew alongside of them. He left the engine idling and spoke to them through the open window. "Ay caray, you are still moving. And I am still building the wall for Senor Stover, and I am only on my lunch time. But I came to say that we have something to bring you. A little present from everyone. But we must bring it to your house in Canacinta. Tell me a good time, or a good day."

Carlotta shrugged, such a question; they hadn't been so available in years. "Whenever you like, maestro. I think Max may go see La Petite in the afternoon today, about our case, but that is all we're doing."

Lupe shook his head. "Not today then. After you are free of the lawyer business. The lawyers would spoil it. We'll come tomorrow late afternoon. Six o'clock. A little before twilight." He turned to Virginia, and smiled for the mischief as he spoke, though it cost him a special effort for the tiny tiny jealousy it aroused. "There's is gossip in the barrio, Virginia. I am hearing that you might be marrying."

"Oh horrors!" Virginia squealed, blushing profoundly. "How is that possible? How does anyone know? I've only told Carlotta and Consuelo, my old old girlfriend. Who told you?"

Lupe thought himself a sly fox. She had not only readily admitted it, she would insist on his revealing his great cleverness. "No one told me. In Chapala at the tianguis my sister Magdalena saw you with Senor Roberto. Your hand was in his arm. Magdalena's cousin Carmena lives in Chapala, and she knows that he is a widower. Then I thought very much about all this—I hope you will forgive me—and then I finally decided it must be that you're getting married." He smirked. He had not been certain; she could have denied it all.

She smiled as she looked wickedly at him. "Lupe you scoundrel. You keep all that to yourself, will you please?"

"Oh, yes, yes, of course. I only mean to tease you. Whenever did I have a chance to tease you before this? Santas de dios! Besides, none of the others would believe me. Anyway, I'm too busy building this wall for Senor Stover to be gossiping." Lupe eased the Cadillac into motion. He again reminded Max and Carlotta of the next evening's appointment. He sputtered and rumbled into a U-turn and drove away.

It was early afternoon and children of all ages after school were coming up the street. These three soon finished emptying the house that had been an office, and then locked the gate, both van and pickup loaded to their limits. Virginia had blessed them and driven home.

Round the same corner where Virginia's old car had gone from sight, another old nameless, colorless, featureless car appeared. It slowed and halted behind the van. Two men inside. Slowly both emerged, one either side. A rancid distaste congealed in the mouths of Max and Carlotta when they recognized the lean droopy posture of Reynoso, the IMSS extortionist, letting his eyes go everywhere but on them. Black hair all combed back, a slinky look, a slinky guy.

Max and Carlotta saw Reynoso's reticence to come forward, to be any part of this moment. He was likely a reluctant accomplice of this other, shorter and stouter man, who hadn't bothered combing his twined and twisted hair, but had only pushed it flopping behind his ears. He wore brown pants, rarely washed and never pressed, with a favorite dark shirt with two pockets, where he arrayed three pens and a pocket calculator in the one, and his receipt book and his excuse book in the other. In this shirt he was the man in charge. The man to reckon with.

Senor Navarro introduced himself as Reynoso's superior. The chief's favorite, most comfortable shirt would not remain tucked in his belt, and the two buttoned front shirt panels could only hang over his superior belly, and it was useless after lunch for Senor Navarro to make any effort to tuck it back in. But he knew the secret. It was not in the clothes the man was successful in this job, but in his ability to resist all the excuses; and many were brilliant and almost irresistible

He interested himself much in their tidy packing of the vehicles. He could afford to be amused and making jokes, for there was no appeal from his authority. He spoke a modest English. "Lucky I came today, Senor

Max, Senora Carlotta, or I would not know where to find you, would I? How lucky for me then. Are you leaving town?"

"No," Max said, bracing himself for something unimaginable but inevitable, "we're not building houses these days. We're closing down the office. Reynoso must have told you we're not registering any new jobs." Thus he might appear unfleeceable, and these men might go away.

Senor Navarro's face was as pudgy as the rest of him; he perpetually seemed pleased with everything, even the bad news. Cordially he replied, "Yes, he did tell me. It was then I realized I had never checked your back payments. It is a thing we do to everyone all the time. I was amazed I had never done this for your Bellacasa, in all the years you've been paying us."

Carlotta had also braced herself, but she heard the sound of doom in his sophistry, for she had heard it so many times before, from many other bureaucratic quarters. She took in a large breath. Which tried to set her feet more firmly on the earth. She would surely need it.

Max too saw it coming. "OK—get to the bottom line, Senor Navarro. It's mistakes and penalties and payments, isn't it?"

Senor Navarro looked squarely, coldly at his man and gauged him. This Max seemed like a much more reasonable man than Reynosa had pretended. "You must not be so pessimistic, senor. Even so—there *is* possibly a problem. Of the kind you mentioned " Then he tried to laugh, as he said, "Or it may *not* be a problem. Maybe nothing at all. But this is what I have found. We have gone back over the last several years of all your payments on all your jobs, and we are finding that *perhaps* you have not paid for certain months. Oh not *so* many. There are five months that we will say *may* not have been paid."

Carlotta intently followed him, the raptor plunging to its target. "*Not paid?* Are you crazy? Reynosa comes here to collect every single month. We *always* pay him. We *have* to. When I'm late with a payment even a week or two, the creep makes me sign a document that says if I don't make the full payment in the next ten days, IMSS will confiscate and sell my goddamn truck, or my computer, or whatever else he puts a lien on."

Max was astonished at the audacity of the grab. He said, "Wait a minute, Navarro, what do you mean the records of some of the months are missing? You mean you *lost* them? Or mis*placed* them?" Max seemed to expect an answer.

Senor Navarro suddenly found himself beset from both sides, and he thought it best to answer the easier questions. To Max he said, "Not lost exactly. I can't really say what's happened to these receipts, it's a puzzling question. Also it's not in my department. But if you have receipts for those months, since you say you've paid them, you can show them to me and you'll be free of any penalties and I won't trouble you anymore. About those months."

Max wanted better answers. He aggressively said, "And if I don't have the receipts? What? A ten thousand dollar fine US?"

Senor Navarro rolled his eyes, for the senor was way short of the mark. "Oh no, Senor Max, not it you could not find *all* five months. Those months were three years ago. The principle and the penalties would be compounding every month. It would be a much more serious amount than ten thousand. Perhaps double that."

"WHOA!" yelled Max, "this is fucking crazy, and both of you know it. Reynoso has already come here a few months ago to steal money because of late payments. Did he tell you that? Did he tell you we made a tape of him asking for the mordita?"

Max didn't care if either bureaucrat answered him or not, for he was raging, and would continue. However, Senor Navarro had not heard this story of Reynoso's unsuccessful extortion. He turned to his assistant and in Spanish he said, "So you've been freelancing here, cabron. And you made a mess of it, that's much worse. Rats like you make it hard for the seguro social to do its own official collecting. I may report this."

Senor Navarro glanced to Carlotta, who was still seemed ready to come after him. He turned back to Max. "It is good you tell me this about Reynoso. The collectors have great temptations. He is a clumsy man. He embarrasses me, if you want to know the truth." He made it sound like he and Max were comrades against a common enemy.

Carlotta barked at him. "No goddamn wonder he's a thief. He's working with goddamn masters, isn't he?"

The tricky metphor was lost to Senor Navarro, yet he kept a shrewd eye on her, for he could see how volatile she was. The chief collector merely said, "Reynoso is the reason people speak badly of the seguro social." He saw that she didn't believe him, so he turned to the less angry husband. "No—I see you think I am being false, Senor Max, but the truth is I speak in a very official capacity." He withdrew from his hidden back pants pocket a folded green computer printout. He snapped the printout open and stood erect, with effort, and reviewed the document, and he and his document were as official as any two such could be, despite his deshabile.

The deceitful logic of it began to unravel Max's brain. "So you mean *you* lose the records? Months and months of records? Or just Bellacasa's records?"

Senor Navarro was glad to explain that they had not been singled out for special investigation. "Oh no, not just you, senor. We go around checking most everyone like this. There's always a few questionable months it seems. Always. But most of those people, fortunately for them, have good records of their payments, so for them it is no problem. When we see that, we don't bother them anymore. However, it has come to our attention that you are, shall we say, sloppy in your bookkeeping. So who knows what we'll find—eh, Reynoso?—you clumsy fool."

Reynoso said nothing, looked at no one. He had hoped they would all forget him. Though he knew that these present moments would be the best part of his day. After they left, there would be ranting and shaming from Navarro on and on. As well, if this bold action of the department was spoiled, Navarro would say Reynoso was the blame for having freelanced them first.

Max reddened with the effort both to comprehend the comedy and the madness of the irresistible extortion, and also with the effort to harness the energies unleashed by this comprehension, now romping wildly through him. "My god man, the gringos can eventually give up trying to do business in this godforsaken country, but the poor Mexicans! Christ!—what do *they* do? Do these scams come down from the top guys, or do the guys in your office come up with these?"

"Oh no," said Senor Navarro, for it was crucial to him that it be understood, to how old a tradition he belonged. "No, senor, this checking back payments has been policy in IMSS since long before I started. You are lucky. You should have been checked long ago. They are usually quite aggressive. Like cucarachas on a sugar cube." He laughed, a clever little joke he'd made up long ago, that everyone seemed to think amusing.

Carlotta hardly dared to imagine where these receipts of three years ago might be found. In the packed boxes? In the cupboards at home? Or who knew where. She said, "So I show you these receipts and you leave me alone?" He nodded officially that it was so. "And if I don't, we owe you all that money. Or you put us in jail."

It was pleasant to feel himself above such ruthlessness. "Oh no, senora, not jail. That would be cruel. No, it is better you are out, where you can make money, and make payments too. No, we wouldn't put you in jail if you could not pay. We *would* confiscate all your property. And you could not register another job until we were paid in full. Now I must ask you to sign this. Then I will leave you a copy. For your files."

"I'm not signing anything," spoke Max, louder than he need do.

Senor Navarro heard this not often. When he did, always it came from the most arrogant. It pleased him to answer. "It matters nothing, senor. Reynoso is my witness that I gave it to you, and that is enough. For you the clock is already ticking. I will be back in one week for a copy of the five receipts. Or a first payment on your principle and penalty."

Senor Navarro knew that for the victims this was the most excruciating moment of all, for the irresistible brand had been burned into their psyches and they could protest however loud and long they would. They were marked and the pounds of flesh would eventually be claimed and carved, and even killing both these IMSS collectors on the spot would not prevent more armies of bureaucrats coming after their marked corporate bodies.

Senor Navarro knew they despised him and in a lawless world they would probably beat or even kill him. But that was the greater, unappreciated aspect of their good government. It was a good parent, it nurtured you, it gave you tools to make money with, it protected you from rebellious bad losers like these two. Senor Navarro need not apologize and he need not smile, and he certainly would render no sympathy. After refolding the green documents, tucking one in his official shirt pocket and handing the copy to the frazzled senor, Senor Navarro could even safely turn his back on them both and walk away. He'd see them again soon. He'd bet ten to one they didn't still have any of these old receipts.

Still riled and numbed at the same time, Max left Carlotta home to nap, and he drove to Chapala to La Petite's office, that she might have finally the little legal consolation that would be left to them. Though it was still late afternoon, the day was yet warm. Flowers bloomed in window boxes and in the little gardens of the plaza, where a young guitarist stood and played beside a cigar box, that anyone might reward him with coins or pesos. Max dropped in a few, for his own good luck, in his time of greatest need of it.

When he came to the front gate of Garamos and Associates, he saw the door open and Azucena the secretary talking with someone. At the police substation next door a half dozen local citizens stood and squatted by the door waiting their turn to make their complaints, give their testimony; weary all.

Max ambled inside the lawyer's offices, sick with a great bureaucratic malaise. He smiled at Azucena, who stood beside her desk, amused at something La Petite was saying to her. Both stopped talking and looked at him. La Petite wore another of her little girl frocks, a navy blue jumpsuit with a white blouse and lace collar. Max noticed that she seemed to be pregnant; he couldn't recall her being married. He began to tell his new problems, but La Petite spoke over his words. "Oh, so good you are here, Mister Max. I have news. I had just tried to call you. Sit down." She motioned toward the loveseat before Azucena's desk and Max sat, still only troubled by Navarro.

La Petite sat beside him and he saw in her manner the consoling friend. Yet suddenly he sensed it was the wrong kind of consolation as a cold steely hand seemed to grip the back of his neck. "Not good news, Max. I'm sorry. The judge has denied your suit. He says in his opinion La Madre did not slander you. Though he did also order her to stop putting up her posters. If that is any consolation."

It was so little consolation that Max bolted to his feet and glared down at La Petite with disbelief, even as he braced himself for the outrage he felt boiling up in his stomach and ripping his chest as it vomited out of him with a scream that made Azucena drop the telephone she had just picked up. *"He WHAT?"* Max in horror hesitated, seeming to allow La Petite one last chance to unsay the impossibility that she had spoken. The Impossibility. Of course, she could not, but merely mumbled the same words again, though it was hardly necessary. Max had heard her well enough. Another cruel wave of emotion made him also realize that deep down in that unsuspected cavern from whence that cruel emotion had just arisen, it had always been known that the end would be this, exactly this.

He covered his eyes and shook his head, that some of the horror might be shed. But none of it was. His legs weakened rapidly and he had to reseat himself. As the rage rattled and boomed inside him, he looked at La Petite again and said, "How can that happen? The judge said it was the worst case of slander he had ever seen. You said we were certain to have the verdict."

She looked sad and defeated. She must share this with him, at least these first terrible moments. "All that is true, Max. But a new judge took over the case, just recently. Apparently he did not see the case as the other judge saw it. It should not be possible, but it is. I'm very sorry. It's also possible something happened behind the scenes that we are not aware of."

"Behind the scenes? What the hell does that mean?" He waited a moment for her to answer, but she was reluctant. In the next moment Max knew her meaning anyway. "And that's it? There's nothing else I can do? That goddamn woman just gets to wreck our lives, and the lives of my workers, and that's it? It's OK?"

She continued to look sad and sympathetic. "You might appeal, Senor Max, but it would be another two years, and probably the other court would not change the decision."

For nearly a year Max had restrained his avenging impulses. Nothing now restrained them and he bellowed a curse that truly frightened both La Petite and Azucena. Filling with a madness to avenge his wrong, Max was on his feet again. His eyes roved wildly about him, seeking a target. "Where's the judge now?" he hissed. "Where is he? In the same office, where I saw the other one?"

La Petite had risen and moved several steps away from him. "I don't know, Max. Probably he is. But I don't think—"

There would be no more listening to her, no more need for her. Fists clenched tightly, Max bolted to the door and outside and almost ran to the front gate and out of it. A few more dazed steps and he pushed his way past the weary mexicanos and came inside the outside office of the police station with so much hostile energy that everyone there stopped what they were doing to stare at him. No one made a move to stop him. Max charged past all of them and down the corridor he so well remembered and came to the end of it where the judge's office should be. It was closed, locked. He pounded his fist on the door.

Someone who seemed to be someone's secretary stepped timidly into the hall far behind him and called to him in Spanish. "Senor. The judge is not there. He has gone away on vacation with his family. To Acapulco. He will be gone for another week."

This fueled his rage the more. He screamed for all of them to hear, "You son of a bitch judge! I'll get you for this!" More rage erupted. He kicked the base of the door, but it merely shuddered against the lock. He stepped back and raised his foot higher and kicked ferociously beside the door knob. It crashed and swung inward, slamming the wall and bounding back at him. He shoved it open again and stomped inside. Back up the corridor someone screamed and voices called out, loud and urgent.

Max saw the same desk he had seen before, the same simple chair. New was the tall dresser against the wall with many drawers. Personal photographs were displayed upon it, and upon the desk. Two framed certifications of competence hung beside each other above the drawers. It grieved him that there was no body to assault, but in his blind rage he would make due with what he'd found.

Each happy framed photograph he grabbed and hurled against the wall, shattering glass in each one. With energy enough for two he seized the desk and threw it savagely against the wall, and two legs of it shattered as it collapsed in the far corner. The joy of his madness filled him, and he ripped open each draw and flung it at a wall and savored the shattering of the thin wood. Papers and documents flew in the air all around him.

When he had destroyed the last drawer, and toppled the drawer-less dresser, he turned about quickly, looking to wreak more mayhem. But he saw everything solid was broken. All the papers and booklets were haphazardly everywhere, as if flung by a sudden cyclone.

Max was ready to carry on his destruction to other rooms, but three policeman burst through the doorway and jumped him from behind and threw him to the floor. One of them smacked him on the head with a mallet. That was the last thing he remembered.

He awoke laying on a concrete floor. He saw a rusty floor drain a foot away. It reeked of piss. The crown of his head ached like it was broken. In tiniest bits, and very slowly, he recalled the memories of his madness. He had a great desire to close his eyes again and retreat back into the vast unconsciousness. He closed his eyes and asked for the darkness. But it did not come, and he knew it would not. He opened his eyes again.

He raised his head and saw the bars of the cell. He turned a little and saw two shabbily dressed Mexicans sitting on the only bench there, against the wall opposite the bars. They stared at him, and grinned. One of them got up and came forward and said in Spanish, "I help you." With great difficulty Max sat up, aching everywhere. The second Mexican came to join the other, and these two lifted Max by the arms until he could stand, supported under each arm by one of them. They walked him to the bench and let him sit down. One offered him a cigarette. Max nodded no. The other man offered him a taco wrapped in a small foil; unbitten. He said, "The guard brought these this morning. You have it." Max couldn't eat; no thanks. They stood in front of him and grinned again.

Max had much still to reassemble mentally, so he might secure himself back into the present moment. Their amusement confused him. "Why laughing?" he asked them.

The taller, younger one said, "That was a good one. You made a lot of people happy."

"What could you possibly mean?"

"Smashing up the judge's office, man. That was good! The policemen who brought you in here told us all about it. Ay-*caray!*"

"Yes," said the other, "a lot of the compadres in the hallways were cheering you when they carried you outside. You were knocked out. We'll take care of you in here till you get out."

Get out. A grim idea. How get out? And get out to what? Does Carlotta know? Max said, "How do I get out?"

"Who knows?" said the older. "We been here two weeks. They said we could call somebody but we don't know anybody. You probably know somebody."

An outer door opened and closed. Footsteps echoed in the hallway, coming nearer. A man in a uniform stopped at the cell door, looking through the bars. It was a long moment before Max realized that the man in the uniform was Fonzo Suarez. His fat bronze badge said Police Chief. It had to be a Halloween costume. Suddenly Max heard a resounding cosmic laughter from dimensions only he could hear that moment. "Unbelievable! But now I get it. If you've become the fucking police chief, that explains everything that's happened to me since I came to Mexico. Good God! Wait till I tell Carlotta!"

The Chief made a cagey little smile. He spoke in impeccable English. "Senor Max. I never thought to see *you* in this place. Well, you have made a big mess in the judge's office. This is very very bad. I think it is lucky for you *and* for the judge that he was not there. They tell me this is all because he gave you an unfavorable decision in your court case."

So his court of last resort was to be Fonzo Suarez, rascal of rascals. He would have to make his pitch to this one? He couldn't do it; he had to leave clean at least some little corner of his battered corpus where dignity might lie down in peace. "I'm sure whatever they said is true, Fonzo. I don't remember much of it. Could I call Carlotta?"

"You know what the judge will do, don't you? When he comes back and sees what you have done? Wrecking his office is bad enough. But even worse he will say that you have insulted the honor of his high position. He is a proud man. He will punish you. Severely."

"Fonzo, I have a lot worse things to think about right now. Let him punish."

Fonzo frowned. "Senor, you don't understand. He could make you stay in this cell for *years* if he was angry enough. None of your problems are worse than that."

As Max mulled Fonzo's opinion, he saw how true it was. "OK. So why don't you just let me go home?"

Fonzo chortled. "That would not be so easy. I might do it if I could. But it would not be easy."

"What would be the hard part of it, Fonzo?"

"Well, I would be taking a risk. I would have to lie and make false excuses."

"Don't tell me that would be the hard part."

"No. It wouldn't. But I should be compensated. Freeing you should be worth a lot."

Max screamed at him. "*Goddamn you, Fonzo Suarez!* Cut that shit out! I don't have any goddamn money cause *you stole it from me*, you little punk! *You* stole it! What you didn't steal, the rest of your fucking politico buddies stole from me!"

The unexpected blast was so harsh and so true that it diminished Fonzo instantly to his more usual and menial self. He slumped his shoulders, though he still held the poor man's fate in his hands. And Senor Max certainly seemed a beaten and impoverished man. Fonzo also remembered that once, slightly, Fonzo had liked the senor and the senora.

"Alright," he said, "I'll let you out. But you'll have to hurry out the back door. And I warn you—you and Carlotta better get out of town as fast as you can. When the judge comes back, he'll be after, your, head. *Ay-yi-yi!*"

26 CARLOTTA'S BEAUTIFUL BOAT

Max went home to Canacinta in a taxi, his head still throbbing. There Carlotta nursed him and fed him. As he told her what had happened at La Petite's and at the judge's office and in jail, she was not surprised, but she vented her anger nonetheless. He was then again prompted to spew more of his own anger; but energy for this expired quickly, for both of them, and soon they merely sat quietly on the floor in front of the fire she had made in their fireplace.

The evening had turned suddenly cold, no doubt from the north, a last little icy farewell from winter. They sat together watching the flames consuming the manzanita logs. They had much to think about and consider, but neither spoke anything of that to the other. The flames alive and moving constantly were enough for them. There was peace for now in that.

But not forgetfulness. Eventually Max said, "Do you think we have those receipts from three years ago? That thing with Navarro this afternoon seems like a joke now. I mean, it was such a horror then."

"Perhaps we have them. Somewhere," she said, "But what does it matter now?" But then she brightened, and for the first time that evening her sullen, gloomy face smiled. "Well, I have just the entertainment for a wintery evening in early spring. A prettier fire. More warmth. More light. More fuel. I have just the thing."

Her cheery face and voice roused him from his own despondency, and he smiled back at her. "A sus ordenes."

"Then come with me, Sir Max." Carlotta rose and led him by the hand to the closet where they had piled so many boxes late that afternoon. She opened the door. Box upon box. "This is our life on paper for four plus years. How comical that it's just in the last few months that Virginia got it all in order."

He delighted in her idea. He lifted two boxes off the top of the pile and carried them to the brick fireplace. Carlotta brought two more. Another trip accounted for the remaining five boxes of file folders, filled with bills and receipts and contracts and bundles of legal documents. All of it flammable.

They sat together on the cool tiles, watching the fire burning meagerly on charred and charcoaled limbs of manzanita. Melancholy smoke wavered and curled before rising out the flue.

Carlotta pulled a folder from the midst of many in the box nearest her, and laid the paper contents on the fiery coals, laid the empty folder on top of that. Eager flames leaped to life and ignited paper into fire, flames curling and consuming in a roar all this readily combustible. The sudden flaring and roaring excited Max and Carlotta both, and both smiled brighter for the heat and light. Max took a fat folder from another box and disembowled the contents and flung them on the hungry flames that had already entirely consumed Carlotta's first offering. Then he flung the folder in after. These voracious flames shot up so suddenly and blew out so much heat upon them that they both scooted back instantly, Carlotta with a little gasp. The thrill was intoxicating!

It must be from then on at a safer distance they would by turns toss into the fire the sacred documents of their Bellacasa lives: phone bills and electric bills, receipts for tools and cement and sand and tile and paint and kerosene and every other imaginable thing. Copies of afffidavits and testimony made on their behalf by witnesses and lawyers. Contracts with clients for houses. Special orders for handmade tiles, for custom cabinets, for sod grass and palm trees and nasturtiums. Water bills from many locales. Bank deposits and withdrawal slips. A thousand pay stub duplicates. Sheaves of IMSS payments. Perhaps the months in question.

But all these sacred documents were heaped and turned instantly to brilliant exhilarating fire, heat and light. The great fire blazed into the darkest hours of the night, and still the devotees made their sacrifices to the gods: who in their haughty, faraway kingdoms looked on, and were perhaps pacified, or perhaps they were not. But the fires blazed loudly and the smoke rose through the chimney to the heights of heaven as these two gave all the paper they had to give. Till the boxes were empty, and the fire had extinguished, and only the cold faraway stars looked down upon them beside their sacrificial hearth.

They slept the sleep of the dead, but they awoke the next morning, these two weary pilgrims, to the same end of their dreams. They came again to the fireplace and looked at the heap of moon gray ash that filled it. Into the largest of the now empty boxes, Max and Carlotta scooped all this ash in shovels till the fireplace was clean and ash filled the box to the brim. Max folded it closed and applied a crosswork of duct tape to the box until it was sealed. Together they placed it on the center of the dining room table. It must wait there a little while longer for delivery. Carlotta topped it with a bow of black crepe paper.

It was a long day packing, which offered them a thousand moments of letting go. Carlotta played Monk and Coltrane and Stevie Wonder on the portable player she kept by the front door, connecting her to timeless realms that were before Mexico and would be after. The sudden late spring chill still lingered, and they wore light jackets whenever they carried loads to the van. Already the kaleidoscope of these Mexican years began jumbling into odd and unsuspected perspectives as they disassembled the life they had lived there. They sighed, they laughed, and box by box, they let go of it.

Early afternoon Max called Lupe and told him the outragious news he'd had of La Petite the day before. The maestro of course was not surprised, but he spoke a heart full of consolation. Lupe heard the story of the smashing of the judge's office and of Max's brief stay in jail and his banishment, and Lupe was shocked and sympathetic, though he had to confess at the end that the story made him laugh and he wished he'd been there to see it, and that the men would all come congratulate him when they heard. For that great destruction Max could have free dinners everywhere in the barrio. As for the disaster with La Madre, Lupe would not need to remind the senor that he had told him it would end so. He had always also known that outcome would make them leave Mexico, so Lupe and the men had had several months to prepare themselves for this inevitable day. But Lupe would hear no more talk of these problems; they were still coming to Canacinta that late afternoon with a little happy surprise.

When they did come they were in two cars following Tacho's wedding present pickup, a ten year old GMC, red and white and chrome: bearing in its bed a long handcrafted wooden boat, yellow for the lady's favorite color, the long sleek upswing of the prow canted even higher as it rode the cab of the pickup like a viking's helmet. The little caravan turned off the careterra and down the country road between cow pastures and soon turned onto the road that led them to the house. The two cars driven by Lupe, his Cadillac of all problems, and Marcos, his own Toyota mini pickup, parked in the open field beyond the front gates. Tacho parked his pickup in front of the already opened gates, behind the senora's blue Chevy pickup, whose bed was empty; curious to these visitors, for the van was obviously filled to its limits.

Marcos and Julio emerged from the Toyota. Lupe, and Polin and Rafael, and Felipe Romero came out of the Cadillac. Tacho and Carlos Arguello joined them at the open front gate and all stood and saw their long foreboding now a reality as they saw the packed white Caravan.

Max and Carlotta had come to a halt in their loading. They sat on the rear terraza eating tuna fish sandwiches and drinking the long-saved bottle of Carlotta's Blanc du Noirs champagne to its dregs. The front door had been open all day, and still was. They heard the several car doors slam, and voices, Mexican, beyond their gate and fence. They were expecting them.

Though Carlotta of course was in no way expecting what she saw when she walked out her front door and into the yard: the sleek prow of a beautiful yellow boat pointed to the sky. It looked ready to be launched skyward and into some unfathomable realm of blue water sky far up and away. Her first view of the boat, knowing that it was to be hers, and this illusion that accompanied it of the heavenward launching would remain in her mind forever with the oldest, most cherished of her memories.

She choked with the sudden intense swelling of a most perfect emotion. Her hand flew to her mouth, lest the tumult inside all come blubbering out of her at once and embarrass them all. Nonetheless it overwhelmed her, and she sobbed once, for the happiness she saw in all their faces, for the love she bore them all, and for the sight of the beautiful boat. Max smiled, nearly as happy as she, and then hugged her, that he might a little help bring her back to Earth.

To help glide them all over the awkwardness of these intense public emotions Lupe spoke loudly to the senora. "But I see you must have expected our gift. You left the blue pickup empty, so you could put the boat in it and take it back to California with you." His sly grin dared her to say it was not so.

Carlotta laughed, another momentarily forgotten little joy rising inside her. "Oh no, Lupe, you're wrong about that." She hurried to the van and out of her purse there she withdrew an envelope and returned with it to her maestro. "This is for you, Lupe. My little gift. It's the title to the truck. I've already signed it over to you. The keys are in the ignition. It's yours."

For the shock Lupe could not restrain himself. "Ee-ho-lay! Senora! I cannot believe it!" He accepted the envelope, but stuffed it in his pocket in his hurry to go to the truck and climb into the cab and feel the true possession. His smile was as big as it could be. But in a moment more it came back to him, the true and happy purpose of their visit. He came out of the truck and returned to the senora.

"May the Virgin bless you, senora. And you too, senor. For the truck. And for everything else."

All could see in his face that this unusual effusion was becoming too much for the maestro. Maestro Felipe called out to him. "Now you'll be in Guadalajara every weekend, to see that one you take to the Folklorico." Lupe looked down so they would not see him struggling with these multiple embarrassments. With a hand he waved away Felipe's impudence, not otherwise worthy of an answer. All the men smiled, grinned or laughed, seeing their maestro squirm.

Lupe ignored his detractors and, though the technique of it bothered him to awkwardness, he went to the senora and hugged her and kissed her on the cheek. She whispered in his ear something he would never tell or ever forget.

But he could have no more of this. "No, this is not what we came for." And he turned to the senora, as happy as he had ever seen her. "We want to take you down to the lake and help you launch the boat. You and the senor must take a little ride on the lake."

Carlotta had not imagined that obvious next step; and was she prepared for it? She looked to Max who seemed almost ready to laugh, seeing her confused, but caught by the requisite courtesy she must show her beloved benefactors. She said in Spanish, "Oh I suppose we have to, don't we, Max?"

"Well, easy for you. Who do you think they expect to see rowing? I'm the one who's liable to embarrass myself."

In any case, there was no refusing, or delaying. Tacho and Carlos and Rafael got in Tacho's pickup. Carlotta said the rest should ride in Lupe's new blue truck, she and Max in front with the maestro, and the other four in the bed. The two pickups turned, and slowly drove to the dirt road that diverted from the cobblestones of Calle Linda Vista and inclined toward the broad open beaches of the lake. Slowly they drove across the sands till they came to the quiet little waves.

They untied and they lifted out the long beautiful yellow boat and brought it down to the wet sand and pointed it toward the lake, where winter would make a little last farewell of its own, before the brilliant spring truly might begin again. Chilly gusts of wind flitted and flurried everywhere over the water. A billowy mist seemed to be forming way out on the lake. Low gray clouds seemed borne by contrary winds, moving and shape-shifting even as these men and the woman watched all this scuttering overhead.

Max and Carlotta followed along as the men pushed the upturned prow into the water, and then let go of it when they felt the water lift if free of sand, and float it. Even so, as all stood beside it, they were little more than ankle deep in water. Two long wooden oars lay inside the boat.

Lupe officiated. "This is it, senor! You are the one! You first. Then the senora."

These two did as they were bidden, and settled themselves, Max in the bow, seeing how the oars fit into the oarlocks, while Carlotta sat in the rear on a cushioned seat that had been constructed only the night before, facing her oarsman, her sometimes prince, and facing also the wide glittering lake that seemed to be all the world before her, muted austerely in wintery gray and silver tones. As Max began rowing, awkwardly and to little effect, Carlotta sat back and felt the breeze in her face and smelled the rich respiration of the lake. She could feel them moving on the water, and she felt as happy as she could ever remember.

Seen only by Max, who faced shoreward as he rowed, Lupe and Polin held up their metal mason's pans and beat them with their trowels loudly and fiercely, and Tacho and Marcos each blared the truck horns, and when Carlotta heard and comprehended all this cacophony, she turned back to see them and laughed.

Above the racket, Max spoke to her. "They're cheering because I'm actually rowing this thing. But don't worry, my dear, I've done this before. On that little pond in Golden Gate Park. You remember the one."

She did. But nothing could worry her today. Max kept rowing. They made easy headway. Little gusts of wind spurred the waves and the boat away from shore.

The silver gray shine of the sky was mirrored in the water and they seemed to be gliding upon and into another dimension that was all silvery and unsubstantial. She was enchanted by all of it. "Oh how wonderful! Is that a little fog I see out there on the water? Yes it is—let's go way out there. Keep rowing."

As he rowed he looked at her seated facing him, bundled in her warmest jacket, a scarf around her neck, a wool hat tight on her head and over her ears. Her face radiated her happiness. He could say nothing less than: "You look like a fairytale princess sitting there. Your highness, will you marry me?"

She laughed at him. But suddenly she saw he was asking in truth, not jest. She laughed again. "Well what a time to bring up a thing like that! Just when we're getting run out of town."

His eyes looked deeply into her: he saw the love he always found there. "Does it feel strange that we're suddenly leaving all this?"

"Well yes, it does feel strange. But maybe my emotion should depend on what's next. What *is* next, Max?"

He watched the shoreline recede further and further into the distance. "For me, it will be writing a book. About Mexico. A real book this time. But hey—that's beside the point. I asked *you* a question, about marrying me. Was that flip answer of yours a yes?"

She was absolutely happy. "That's a yes. A definite yes. Just keep rowing, I'll go with you anywhere, as long as it's in this wonderful boat. Oh my!" she suddenly cried. "That wind is really picking up. And is it just me, or is it getting colder all of a sudden?"

And so it was. Warm spring air lay upon the coast, but cold sudden winds were down out of the north, creating a little unexpected turbulence over Lake Chapala. Feeling confident, however, that these gusts and chills were but a thing of the passing moment, Max rowed steadily onward toward the heart of the lake and the lovely mists of fog way out there. Carlotta settled back and watched her beautiful yellow boat surge on as the waves swept under and past them, going, going, the wind now surely at their backs.

A few miles north of them and high in the sky, turbulent contrary winds collided and whirled furiously around each other, until finally they resolved equilibrium, and then spun in the air with a finer focus, narrowing gradually to a funnel. As it spun faster the funnel elongated until finally it reached down to the lake. As its dervish energy attached itself to the fluid element, this whirlwind drew water skyward into itself. The spinning winds that had been invisible now became visible as a snake of water gyrating high into the sky, even as it still skipped across the surface of the lake, drawing upward more vast quantities of water into its insatiable watersnake body. As its mass and velocity increased, the snake of air and water swerved rapidly and erratically west, twisting higher still into the sky. Above the watersnake, a dense, dark cloud followed it, the sinister matrix which had spawned the lethal whirlwind.

No doubt as this husband and wife to be rowed they noticed the sudden darkening of the sky; but they did not see the writhing watersnake sweeping and swaying ever closer. Whatever they saw or did not see, they seemed to be doomed, for the creature moved relentlessly upon them.

However, by the grace of God and the Virgin, Max at last heard the howling that shattered his sleepy innocence, a howling that seemed the terrible voice of the watersnake. Max turned and saw the creature of wind and water whirling its delicate and dangerous mouth across the water toward them, so close that both of them in sudden maximal alarm cried out at the destroying beast. They were close enough to see streams of water spiraling upward off the lake, centrifuged inside the beast's serpentine body, while water spray flew many many meters off the surface of the lake in a whirl all around the insatiable, whirling serpent.

Panic like electricity roused Max to full alert, desperate to row away; but he hesitated that he might see the true escape path: he saw the watersnake swerve and dart so swiftly and unpredictably wherever it swept over the water, that he could not for the moment know which way was out of its path, or which way was shore.

Fortunately, the shifting momentum of the water had turned their curved prow shoreward, so perhaps luck also was with them. Max leaned into his oars and pulled with more strength and vigor than should have been possible for his wearying arms. He rowed as hard and fast as he could, the terror of it rattling in his throat, for he must as he rowed stare straight at the spiraling, gyrating creature, so unstable and irreconcilable that every new instant it twisted away and back and onward, always seeming to chase after their frail little craft, rowed by a tired, terror-stricken man whose first great voyage on the lake might be his last, and hers as well.

So with his horrified eye on the cyclone, he rowed and rowed, as their doom pursued them. Carlotta too strained her own courage as she also turned to look behind, and tremble, and stare down the fury pursuing them. Yet indeed luck was with them, and the wind came at them from their behind. At the same time Max began to hear behind him a clattering of pans and a honking of horns. He also saw the gyrating watersnake suddenly bend midstream and begin to whirl away from them west. The howling diminished too, even as the horns and the pans rattled louder than before.

Though their hearts still beat wildly and their eyes glowed wide with so close a passage into the heart of the terror, their frail yellow craft came near the shore, and then finally upon it. Lupe and all the others had waded out to meet them and pull them finally to safety. Their hearts too still beat wildly, even though the devouring watersnake by now spiraled smaller and farther and farther away.

It was a merry but still shaken band that drove boat and passengers back to the house in La Canacinta. The men tied the yellow boat to the roof of the Dodge Caravan, its sleek prow forward, resting on the cab. Amphibious action was now possible. They were certified by witnesses for all dangers and disasters. Bon voyage.

Their last act the next morning before locking down the house for once and all was to carry the large taped box of ashes, careful of the black crepe ribbon on top, to a spot in the van they had saved for it. They drove the last time up the cobbled road to the careterra, and turned toward Ajijic. They did not slow or stop but passed through, perhaps with little silent farewells, who could say? They drove in silence the kilometers into Chapala, were they turned left and went two blocks and stopped, double parked at the curb. The beautiful yellow boat riding the waves atop the white Caravan.

As he got out, he asked her, "You want to come in with me? Say hello?"

She grinned. "I don't think so. But give everyone there my love."

Max opened the side door and removed the carton of ashes, careful of the black crepe ribbon on top. He walked across the islanded street and went to the open doorway numbered 226, and he entered. Three young Mexicans with hats in hands stood at a counter, listening to unfortunate news from the disinterested man in a suit behind it. Max saw the sign beside a nearby doorway: IMSS Collecciones, Guillermo Navarro. Max went to it, saw it open slightly, and eased the door open with his hip, careful of the precious box. Senor Navarro sat behind a desk, reading a memo. He looked up. He smiled. This was indeed the man of all he'd hoped to see today. With something large.

Max set the fattened box on Senor Navarro's uncluttered desk; the box obscured more than half of it. The black bow still looked festive, though darkly so. Senor Navarro gave to his favored guest a friendly smile, though it bespoke as well a great perplexity at the package.

Max smiled his own friendly smile, and said, "It's all in there, senor." Not waiting for receipt, gratitude or farewell, Max turned and walked back out the door and out the building. No traffic was upon these early morning streets as he crossed to the van, smiling his brightest to Carlotta, who kissed him, and he her, and they drove away, the beautiful yellow boat riding the waves atop the Dodge Caravan.

ABOUT THE AUTHOR

These novels of John Hoopes are available at either
Amazon.com
or Createspace.com:

The Dolphins of Oceanus
Ralph and Bobbie On the Road
The Spy in Love
Lake Chapala Serenade, I & II:
MexicoLimpio
Max and Carlotta Go to Mexico
Lady of the Sorrows, I & II:
San Francisco
Panama City

Fall 2011 these books will also become available:
Escape to Mexico (narrative non-fiction)
Pictures and Stories (collected poems and plays)

John Hoopes currently lives in Sacramento, California, with
his wife and his four grandchildren. You may visit him at
his web site at www.bellamagicbooks.com